ROCKEN
Edge

WENDY K HARRIS

COPYRIGHT WENDY K HARRIS © 2008

BRITISH L   ION DATA
A ca   rary

ISBN: 978-1-899392-52-0

Published By

COACH HOUSE PUBLICATIONS LIMITED.

ISLE OF WIGHT, ENGLAND
THE BEACON BUILDING, DAISH WAY, NEWPORT,
ISLE OF WIGHT, PO30 5XJ
+44 (0)1983 533625

www.coachhousepublications.co.uk

Book & Cover Design by

DAVID BOWLES

COVER DESIGN FROM AN ORIGINAL PHOTOGRAPH BY TERRY HARRIS

PRINTED ON THE ISLE OF WIGHT BY CROSSPRINT LIMITED

A Note To The Reader

If you should visit the Isle of Wight, you can find many of the places mentioned in the story. But some of them belong in the realms of the imagination, or may have been washed away by the sea.

WKH

Isle of Wight, 2008

For

David and Lizzie

Sweet granddaughter,
Clementine.

CHAPTER

One

Where was the lighthouse? Clare imagined it would burst into view, dazzling her eyes, as she walked round the final bend of the steep winding road to the shore. But there was no lighthouse. It was difficult for her to bear – this absence. The vision of a massive white tower, with its circling beam, had acted like a homing beacon, urging her on. And Rose would be waiting beneath it, illuminated, smiling, beckoning.

Clare trudged along the esplanade and stopped to gaze wearily out at the heaving grey sea which merged into a steely sky. Vigorous waves swept the clinking shingle over the yellow sand. Black and white oystercatchers skittered on pink legs, jabbing strong orange bills into the rocky shallows. At the end of the deserted beach, to her left, there was an empty bandstand, like a pagoda. To her right was an inn called *The Spyglass*. A giant pirate wearing a blue coat stood outside. Round his head was tied a scarlet bandanna with white spots. A green parrot clung to his shoulder. The pirate's wooden face looked lined and scoured, but sort of wistful, as if he longed to be back on his ship, terrorising the seas. Rugged cliffs reared up beyond both these buildings. But there was definitely no lighthouse. She was certain Rose had said to head for Ventnor. Clare's knees threatened to buckle under this heavy burden of disappointment, and the weight of her backpack. The baby – zipped inside her black puffa jacket – seemed to have turned into a sack of potatoes.

A lonely coil of wind whined up the esplanade and snaked itself inside her clothes, as if it had been looking for her. She turned to face the row of shuttered buildings. How strange it felt to be shut out, after being locked inside the old abbey for all those months. She pictured the bunch of iron keys that hung – along with a rosary and crucifix – from a grubby rope tied round Mother's fat middle. A shudder convulsed Clare's body. She gulped the sharp fresh air. Better to be outside, even though her legs ached with cold in the thin jogging pants Father Ryan had given her last summer.

The tracksuits were cast-offs from the boys' hurling team. She sometimes caught a whiff of their sweat. The suits were charcoal grey with big shoulders and a black stripe running down the side of the legs and sleeves. Clare could see the stitch marks where the badges had been unpicked. The fleece linings were worn into little hard balls that felt rough against her skin. *I've bought you some new things to be going away with*, Father Ryan had said, leading her into the vestry. Clare imagined denim jeans and bright cotton tee-shirts. He dumped the pile of clothes into her arms. *These will be suitable . . . for nearer your time*, he muttered. Clare inhaled the stale smell of the school's second hand shop. Disappointment closed her throat so she couldn't say, thank you. And Father Ryan looked so embarrassed; beads of sweat broke out on his pink forehead. His brow was normally as pale as Our Lord's beneath the crown of thorns. Clare had backed away, mortified.

Last summer, Clare thought. And now it was the end of January – she hadn't realised, until she'd seen the date on her rail ticket. She wished it was summer now. Standing in the road, she shook uncontrollably. She couldn't put her hands in her pockets because her arms were supporting the baby. How could anything so small feel so heavy? At least she could feel the child's warmth. With one hand she reached over her shoulder for her thick plait of hair. Ginger. That's what the kids at school called her. It made her mammy cross. *She* said it was red. Poor Mam. Clare always tried not to upset her. But Clare liked the word, ginger. It was warm and spicy, like ginger cake, and ginger bread men, and ginger beer. She tucked her plait inside her collar, winding it around her throat like a scarf.

She shifted the weight of the baby, and felt in her pocket for her precious piece of paper. She knew the directions by heart, but the faded words gave her comfort. They conjured a bright picture of Rose scribbling them down, pushing back her messy pink-streaked hair, with its tangled plaits and rainbow beads. The comfort was a small deep throb, as if a fragment of the old Clare might still be alive somewhere, beneath the squash and squirm of the ball of worms that lived inside her. Father Ryan told her it was a vipers' nest – there because of her sins – and it wouldn't leave her in peace until she'd atoned. But Clare couldn't envisage snakes. She could only imagine fat pink worms that somehow got into her when she was very young. They'd slid into her dreams, and then – to her horror – she felt them inside her. She hoped they might slither out with the baby, and all that other stuff, but after the birth she could still feel the slippery knot in there.

She tucked the note back into her pocket and her hand touched the glass beads of her rosary. Maybe there was a church nearby. But how would she dare go in? How could she dip her fingers into the holy water? She noticed she was standing in front of a café, *Rachel's Café*. The sign on the door said CLOSED. But someone was moving about in there. She stepped closer to the misted window and rubbed it with her cold hand, but the moisture was on the inside. She could just make out the blurred shape of a woman sitting at a table, drinking something. Clare's stomach rumbled. If only she could be in there, clasping a mug of hot soup, unfreezing her fingers. She licked her chapped salty lips. Perhaps, if she knocked and asked nicely, the woman might take pity on her. After all, she wasn't a scrounger – she just needed to warm herself, and recover for a while. But wouldn't the woman be sure to ask questions about the baby and all? Anyway, the thought of food was making her feel sick again. And she ought to be moving along before it started to get dark. She'd managed to find her way from Worcester right down to the southern shore of the Isle of Wight. Rose wouldn't have given her the wrong directions. The lighthouse must be a bit further on – in another part of Ventnor. She started to walk. She would have to drag herself back up the hill to the bus station and ask the way.

*   *   *

Inside *Rachel's Café,* the aroma of fresh coffee was masking the paint fumes, its bitter steam condensing on the misty panes. Rachel wiped her eyes and noticed a hand rubbing at the window. A pale face topped by a

3

red hat, or hair, was trying to peer in. What was the matter with people – couldn't they understand the word *closed*? The face disappeared. She got up and pulled down the new Mediterranean-blue blinds to shut out the sight of the lurker.

Sinking back heavily onto her chair, she felt shocked at her own indifference. Not like me, she thought, could be some poor soul in trouble. *There, but for the grace of God . . .* that was her mantra. Daft, she wasn't religious – not in the *old bearded fellow looking down,* sense. But she did believe in the innate goodness of humanity, however deeply submerged, it was in there somewhere. When she chatted with stressed-out people – and she did a lot of that in her café – she could see how the sludgy layers built up. But what puzzled her was the *intelligent creative energy that held the essence of all things safe*, which Sophie and Nick talked about. She liked the phrase and she could understand the metaphysics, but *safe*? Why then, did it dole out joy and disaster in such a haphazard way? Intelligent it might be, but didn't it have any feelings? Take the recent heart-breaking Indian Ocean tsunami . . .

Anyway, it seemed she couldn't cope with the needy right now. Hadn't she just drawn her blind over the sight of a peering, pale face? What had happened to her capacity to care? Perhaps her heart had shrivelled. She slid her hand under her left breast to check. Goodness, her body felt hot. She tucked her pale coppery hair behind her ears, undid the top buttons of her white shirt, and fanned her damp face with one of the new menus. Gourmet Italian dishes flashed before her eyes – *cotoletta alla valdostana, agnello rustico, melanzane alla parmigiana* – oh, those sensuous words; how they'd seduced her.

'Please, hurry up, Sophie,' she muttered, aware that it was Saturday afternoon, and she was intruding on Sophie and Nick's day off. But Rachel desperately needed to talk to her, and it was going to be difficult. The last thing she wanted was to demolish her friend's honeymoon happiness. But Sophie was on her way from Blue Slipper Bay and had to be told – after all, she had a stake in the business. Rachel felt a fresh surge of tears, her watery gaze sweeping over glossy white paint, gleaming stainless steel, and glass shelving. Her emotions were veering between grief, anger and sheer bewilderment. How was it possible to be feeling like a conned, deluded old bag when yesterday she'd been skipping about like an adolescent high on hormones? And where had her old self gone, the one that was neither of those extremes, that a few months ago was self-sufficient and content?

She blotted her wet cheeks with her black and white striped apron, poured another cup of coffee and sat listening to the wind moaning bleakly along the esplanade, as if it were commiserating. She wondered if the pale-faced person had found refuge. Picking up the menu again she sat reading the enticing list of meals. But the words in her head were being spoken by Sandro in his most seductive voice, rolling the letters over his tongue, gazing at her cleavage with half-closed eyes. She slammed the menu back on the pile.

'How could I have been so stupid?' she wailed.

*   *   *

'Pudden-head,' Fran chided herself, as she rubbed the newborn twin lambs with a rough towel. Beauty, her ageing ewe, was staring at her, dull-eyed. 'I know, Beaut. Ted was right as usual; you're far too old for this malarkey.' Beauty showed no interest in her offspring. 'Come on, say hello,' Fran urged, but none of the three animals seemed eager to bond. Fran sighed, the lambs were small males. The first one – flat and puny – already fading. Fran was sweating, she pulled her dusty aran jumper over her head, dislodging her knot of grey hair, and then knelt down in the straw. She groaned; her back was aching. She was getting too ancient and cack-handed for midwifery. 'In fact, Beaut, we're both too old,' she said. She held up the bigger lamb, trying to encourage it to nuzzle Beauty's udder, which didn't look as full as it should. The lamb's head lolled. Fran was determined to save one of them, and it had to be the stronger. She bedded the dying lamb in the straw near its mother where they could smell each other. Then, she wrapped the other one in her jumper and tucked it under her arm. 'I'll bring him back later, Beaut,' she said, clambering to her feet. 'Have a rest, now.'

Fran went out of the stable and shut the door, glad to be in the open air. How she loved these late January days which smelled of salt and wet

5

grass. She could hear the waves booming below the cliff, like the report of a drowned cannon. She stretched her stiff back, breathing deeply. Heavy grey clouds were lumbering in from the west. The lighthouse beam swept the sky above her, silvery bright in the dull afternoon light. Everything – herself included – seemed to pulse and throb. The raw thrusting of birth still affected her deeply, heightening her senses to the pounding and surging of the wind and sea, and the thudding of her own heart. But surrounded by nature at its most ferocious was when she experienced a deep peace – as if she dropped into a sweet stillness . . . she hadn't the words to talk of it. She lifted the lamb up as if offering him to the world. 'This is a good place to be born,' she said, 'the back o' the Wight.'

Cinders, her collie, came pattering across the cobbled yard to greet her.

'Well, we've got one lamb to look after,' Fran told her. Cinders wagged her tail, her wet tongue lolling as she panted.

Fran walked across the cobbles towards the kitchen door of the stone farmhouse, pausing to talk to her flock of white doves pecking at seed amongst the cracks. 'My lovely-dovelies,' she cooed. A sudden squall of wind gusted through the yard. The doves rose up, scattering and then reforming on the ground like a little corps of ballerinas. Fran stood watching a few pure white feathers drift slowly down in the lull. That's what it would look like – her peaceful feeling. She chuckled. 'Did you see that, Cinders? Wasn't it beautiful?' She bent to fondle the dog's head and ears. 'Right. Well, we'd better find a cosy box for this little lamb.'

*   *   *

Father Ryan stood on the promontory at Mizen Head, bracing himself against the Atlantic wind which tore at his cassock. I stand at the edge of Europe, he thought, nothing between here and North America. Great waves surged and rolled towards him, hitting the land with a mighty crash, throwing dazzling spray high into the air. He felt icy moisture gathering on his face and hair. Was it really possible a huge country existed across that endless lonely sea? Newfoundland . . . that's where

6

he'd like to be. He pictured himself wearing jeans and a red checked shirt, building a cabin of pine logs by a cold green lake, fishing for salmon. He sniffed, imagining the tang of woodsmoke . . . and if he felt like moving on, he could. Solitary, insignificant, anonymous . . . the words gave him relief. It was hard to go unnoticed wearing the garb of a priest. People were always casting him furtive looks, seeking an opportunity to confess sordid things, which they left behind to claw at his skin like demons.

A gust of wind thudded into him as if tossing him inland, back into the arms of Ireland. He'd never left these shores where he was born nearly forty years ago, and he never would. He sighed deeply, his eyes watering. Or could he? It would mean leaving Jeannie behind. Little Jeannie – he still thought of her as his wee sister, even though she was thirty-eight. Would she miss him if he went? Did she still love him? Of course she did. Her love was the kind that would never grow old. He couldn't leave her, or leave here. Just like he couldn't leave off his cassock. He looked down at the black material clinging to his thin body. He didn't have to wear it all the time. Most of the younger priests wore trousers on Saturday outings like this.

Children's voices broke through his reverie and he turned to watch them climbing aboard the coach back to Bantry. He noticed one small girl attempting to wrap a school scarf over her streaming red hair. He felt his stomach lurch. Clare! What had become of Clare? Why hadn't she arrived at the convent in England? Sister Bridget had checked for accidents but would do no more on his behalf. Maybe the girl had been influenced by someone she'd met on the journey; a wicked heathen who'd convinced her she should have an abortion. He should never have allowed her to travel on her own. She was too young and couldn't be trusted. All his discreet enquiries had come to nothing and he didn't know what else to do. Sure, it would be of no use contacting the police. He'd been told all the big cities were full of runaway children that didn't want to be found.

He hadn't the courage to tell Clare's mother that she was missing, unsure of what the woman might do. Fortunately, Mrs Mulligan had been enraptured by his story of her daughter's choice to stay indefinitely at the Convent of the Poor Clares – after the adoption of the baby. *My prayers have been answered*, she exclaimed. *Didn't I name the girl after the blessed saint herself? Surely now she'll be forgiven her sins.* Idiotic woman, he thought, so busy on her knees, eating the altar rail, she forgot to watch her own child. It was her fault as much as Clare's.

Maybe he *should* travel to England and try to trace Clare himself. But how would he do that? England was such a godless place. Wasn't it full of women wearing hardly a stitch of clothing? Suddenly, the thought of leaving his own confined world terrified him. He shuddered so violently that his jaws clamped and he bit his lip. He tasted blood and salt.

'Father! Don't be blown away now,' Sister Constance called, hanging onto her flapping veil.

He peered down at the heaving sea and wondered what would happen if he were to scale the fence and hurl himself forward. Would the Almighty reach down from above and steady him? Or would he just plummet like a discarded black bag of refuse? He closed his eyes and listened within for an answer. But the voice of God was not to be heard; no loving presence felt. He looked up at the livid sky, which suddenly crackled, scored with silver. Was that God's answer – a sign of His wrath? A stab of nauseous pain struck him behind his eyes, as if the small rodent he imagined gnawing inside his skull, had bitten into his optic nerve. He felt the contents of his bowels turning to bubbling liquid. He clenched his buttocks hard until the feeling subsided. Then he bowed his aching head and walked slowly towards the coach. His heavy crucifix thumped against his chest with every step, weighing him down like a tombstone.

CHAPTER

Two

'*The Buddle Inn!*' the driver called. Clare jumped. She had been lulled by the warmth and motion of the bus. 'Nearest we go to St Catherine's lighthouse, love. Straight on down the road, can't miss it. Mind you don't fall off the edge.' Clare struggled to get up; her backpack threatening to topple her. As the bus pulled away she stood in the road, looking at the inn. The windows twinkled with light. She imagined a log fire burning inside, food cooking in the kitchen. OPEN ALL DAY! the sign enticed. But she mustn't stop now. She turned to the road ahead, at least it sloped downhill. She passed a few houses and entered a scary dark tunnel of trees, but soon she saw a *National Trust* sign with a picture of a lighthouse. And then everything opened out, winter fields rose and fell before her and, at last, she could see the white lighthouse, its beam circling, flashing – just as she'd imagined it for so long. A painful sob rose in her throat. That's where Rose said she would be staying – in the caravans near the lighthouse. She caught a glimpse of some flat roofs, just visible, through a clump of swaying trees.

Clare was desperately tired, hunger and thirst making her weak. Her spine felt sore from the rubbing of her backpack, and her arms ached from supporting the baby. He was getting restless, making the bleating noises which meant she would have to feed him, or he'd start wailing, and she couldn't bear that. She needed to do it before she went over to the caravans. She didn't want Rose to see her doing all that stuff, not yet, anyway. It would be so embarrassing, and she felt scruffy and dirty.

She looked for somewhere sheltered to sit down, but there seemed to be nothing but fields around the lighthouse. Then she spotted a group of tall rocks, like the standing stones back home. That would

9

do. There was a narrow, rutted track leading down there. It was hard not to trip, she was feeling so unsteady. When she reached the stones she realised they formed an entrance to a driveway. There was a notice which said ROCKEN EDGE FARM. It was nailed to a dilapidated wooden gate which was propped open. She stepped awkwardly over a cattle grid and crept a little away along. Ahead there was a thicket of bent-over thorn trees, silhouetted against the sky, pointing spiky fingers at her. She didn't like the look of them, but the path tunnelled between the trees so she hurried through. For a moment she thought she'd come to the edge of the land but then realised that it fell away sharply, sloping down towards some stone farm buildings which were hidden from above. Further on there was a rambling old house. She stood still, listening, but all she could hear was the drone of the wind driving the sea, and the agitated grunting of the baby. The place seemed deserted, spooky, surely no-one lived there. A flock of white doves flew up to perch on a barn as she approached, the sudden whoosh of wings startled her, but no dogs barked. Her heart was thumping fast. The baby let out a thin wail. She shouldn't have come down here. Why hadn't she gone straight to the caravans? Rose wouldn't have minded, she would have understood. But now she was here she might as well give him a quick feed, to settle him.

She pushed open the creaky door of what looked like a stable. It smelled horrible inside – of animal poo. The light was dim, shining through one dusty window, but she could see bales of straw stacked up. She unzipped her jacket, lifted the baby out and put him on the bales. Her breasts felt wet and heavy, aching as if they were bruised. How disgusting all this was. She painfully shrugged off her backpack, picked up the baby, and sat down in the small patch of light, glad to rest her breaking back against the wall.

She looked at him. His tiny red face was all screwed up, he was about to start yelling. She pulled up her sweatshirt. The milk was oozing from her nipples. The baby thrashed his head back and forth and then clamped his hard gums onto her breast. The pain made her cry out. The ball of worms inside her seemed to somersault and she felt sick; the baby stopped sucking and gagged. She noticed this breast looked red and lumpy. She turned him round and gave him the other one. After the initial, unbearable tugging he settled and sucked rhythmically, making little gulping noises. Clare pushed back his pink bonnet. She could see the soft skin on the top of his head pulsing up and down as he fed. Mother told her to be careful of that spot. It made Clare nervous. She imagined she might accidentally push her thumb through it, like the paper tops on the jars of jam her mam made. His downy hair was stuck to his scalp. It smelled sour and his body felt damp through his stinky woollen clothes. He hadn't been changed since Mother brought him to her for the night feed. Clare hadn't thought about searching for nappies in her panic to run away. Mother always did all the cleaning up stuff, carrying him off as soon as he was fed.

Clare knew that Mother didn't want her to see the baby's bottom because she was pretending it was a girl. But Clare had seen it clearly when he was born. Mother had held the baby up briefly and then screamed and dropped it on Clare's belly where it slid down between her legs, wailing. Mother rushed from the room leaving Clare dazed and shaking with shock. She thought the worms must have come out with the baby and frightened Mother. She tried to raise herself up to look, but she was too weak. Later, Mother crept back, her white face and cowl streaked with blood from the birth. She wrapped up the baby and thanked the Blessed Virgin for the gift of the girl child. Clare was too exhausted to care; the child belonged to Mother, anyway. She watched Mother gather up a ball of bloody stuff and throw it in a cardboard box. Was that the worms? Had they gone? But Clare woke later with the familiar churning and knew they were still there. She cried bitterly; Father Ryan had been right. Mother promised to let her see a priest, after the birth, if she was good. All Clare had to do was pretend the baby was a girl, and feed it, as part of her penance and redemption. But weeks went by, and the priest never came.

Now, sitting on the prickly straw in the stable, she didn't have to pretend, but she had to go on with the feeding, even though it hurt so much. Mother told her if she didn't feed the baby it would die, and then

Clare would have murder to add to her list of mortal sins. Clare observed the two swollen breasts suspended on her bony ribcage as if they were someone else's. The nipple on the sore one looked as if it were cracking open again. Maybe that's where all the badness inside her would come oozing out. She shuddered. Where had her own small breasts gone – the ones she tucked into her white cotton bra, and buttoned under her blue school blouse each morning at home? The only familiar thing about her breasts was the gold crucifix which hung between them. She felt for her plait, and pulled it over her shoulder. The bright ginger hair glowed faintly in the gloom. She brushed the end of it across her face, her comfort since she was little. But now it felt harsh and spiky – like a paintbrush that hadn't been washed. Tears welled then ran down her cheeks, dripping onto the baby's head. She felt hot now, and sweaty, but sort of chilly too. She wished he would stop sucking and fall asleep so she could get moving again before it was too dark.

The low moan of the wind was soothing; it was the sound she heard from her bedroom at home. She wanted to doze but forced herself to stay awake by chewing at her fingernails. The baby was falling asleep now, his mouth hanging open. She adjusted his bonnet and shawl, pulled down her sweatshirt and clambered up. Her head reeled and she staggered. She dumped him between the bales, squatted down and retched painfully. She hoped she wasn't going to be ill just as she was nearing the end of her journey. She didn't want to be sick when she met Rose – like she was on the boat from Ireland. Rose might think she was always being sick. She'd planned to comb her hair and look tidy and clean, but there wasn't much she could do about that now. The nausea subsided, but her stomach was gurgling. Hunger – that's all it was.

After the struggle to pull on her backpack, she looked down at the sleeping baby, dreading having to pick him up again and feel the pressure of his body against her throbbing breast. But it wasn't far to go now – just across the fields to the caravans. Once she found Rose, everything would be all right. Wasn't Rose the kindest person she'd ever met? After a drink of water and a rest and all, she'd be able to clean up the baby and herself, and wouldn't Rose be sure to help her?

12

A rustling sound came from a dark corner and her heart started to pound. There was an animal in a pen, a sheep or a goat, or something. She could see the whites of its eyes. Creepy – it was scary in here. Clare shivered; feeling sick and dizzy again. She'd better get outside quickly and breathe some fresh air before she fell over. She needed to find Rose, needed some help.

She stumbled along the tracks and across the fields, guided by the lighthouse, its brilliant beam piercing the sky as the light faded. The wind was cold, but she could feel sweat running down her body. As she drew near the thicket of trees, she could see, through the weaving branches, long caravans clustered together and a big yellow digger. This was definitely it – Rose had told her the students were helping rebuild a hotel. Thank goodness! She couldn't walk much farther. Some people were throwing logs on a bonfire, sparks showered into the air like fireworks. She staggered towards them. They stopped talking and watched her as she approached. They seemed young, perhaps they were all students like Rose.

'Looking for someone?' one of the boys called.

'Rose. I'm looking for Rose.'

'Sure you've got the right place?'

Clare felt as if her heart were dropping down inside her chest. She nodded. 'I met her last July . . . on the ferry from Ireland.'

The young people gathered together, peering at her. One of the girls spoke. 'Do you mean Rose from *Cormorants*, Patrick's girlfriend?'

Clare nodded. She remembered Patrick. He hadn't spoken much, and seemed sad. But he'd given her a lift in his car, all the way to Hereford.

'Patrick!' someone yelled. 'There's a girl here asking for Rose.'

He walked towards her, taller than she remembered, he was wearing motorbike leathers. He stood and stared at her, unsmiling.

'Rose isn't here,' he said. 'She's working in Africa with her grandmother.'

Clare felt her last bit of strength and purpose seep away. Her head started to spin and a high-pitched squeal filled her ears – surely the baby didn't need feeding again. And then her legs seemed to disappear. She felt her body crash into someone, just before the ground rose up to meet her.

*　　*　　*

'Poor Rachel.' Sophie rummaged in her bag for a packet of tissues and slid them across the table. 'And you didn't have even a tiny gut feeling that Sandro was leaving?'

Rachel blew her nose, it was getting sore, she hadn't cried this much for years. She shook her head. 'Not a clue. And I can't think of any reason why he would. It was his idea – the Italian restaurant plan. And he was so keen, so confident that it would succeed.'

Sophie shuffled her chair closer to Rachel's and took her hand. 'Well, I can't believe Sandro would disappear without a very good reason – he's much too nice. Perhaps an emergency . . . something back in Italy . . . '

'But why didn't he say?' Rachel's chest heaved. 'The staff at the hotel in Shanklin don't know anything. It's like he's vanished without trace.'

Sophie clucked her tongue sympathetically and sat pulling at a tendril of her dark hair, regarding Rachel with soulful brown eyes. Rachel gazed around the newly decorated café which was littered with half-unpacked crates and stacked shelves waiting to be fixed. Suddenly she threw up her hands, a dramatic gesture she'd picked up from Sandro – she'd have to stop doing that now. 'And we're meant to be opening for Valentine's weekend. It's only a couple of weeks away.'

There was a loud rap at the glass door.

'It's Jill,' Sophie said, getting up to let her in.

'Does she know?' Rachel felt defensive; Jill would have something scathing to say.

Sophie nodded, biting her lip. 'She rang just as I was leaving. I can tell her to go if you like.'

Rachel shook her head. 'Don't bother. Everyone will know soon enough.' I'll be joke of the month, she thought.

14

Jill strode in, her high-heeled black boots clacking on the tiles. A cold stream of salty air managed to sneak in with her. She unwound a long pink and purple scarf from her neck.

'Well?' she demanded. 'Has the toy-boy shown up?'

Rachel shook her head. She noticed Sophie frowning at Jill as if warning her to curb her tongue.

'Thought not. It's like a morgue in here.' Jill sat down at the table and helped herself to coffee. 'I've had a shitty day and I'm short on sympathy. If you ask me, Rachel, you're better off without him. I never liked Sandro, he was a big drip.'

'Don't hold back,' Rachel said. She didn't know whether to feel comforted or insulted by Jill's bluntness.

'Did he get into your bank account as well as your knickers?'

'No.' Rachel put her hand on Sophie's arm. 'But we've invested a lot in this venture.'

'Too bloody right. Let's hope you don't regret it.'

'Jill! Don't be so heartless.' Sophie leaned protectively against Rachel. 'I hope you have a little more empathy with your clients.'

'That's different. You're my friends, I care about you two.' She took a swig of coffee and wrinkled her nose. 'This is cold. Look, Slippery Sandro was a bull-shitter. Believe me you get a nose for it when you spend all day listening to the crap that comes out of some people's mouths.' She grinned. 'Okay, I grant you, he had a certain sexiness, that Latin thing. But you were a bit nauseous, the pair of you – like sodding Romeo and Juliet.'

'Hardly.' Rachel gave a shaky smile. 'More like Richard and Judy.' She flipped a white linen napkin from a stack she'd just unpacked and used it to dab at her streaked mascara. 'But it's so perverse isn't it? When you're an adolescent the thought of old wrinklies having sex is disgusting. Then suddenly you're forty and you realise you can still feel like a randy teenager.' She scrunched the napkin into a ball and hurled it across the café where it flopped over a glass jar of multi-coloured pasta. 'It's as if our primal urges can't keep pace with our ageing bodies. Or vice-versa, I think. Oh, I don't know what I think anymore.'

15

'Well, I understood all that,' Sophie said, nodding emphatically.

Jill grunted and got up to replenish the coffee pot. 'Consider yourselves lucky.' She inspected her distorted reflection in the bright steel appliances, sucking in her stomach, running her hands over her curvaceous body in its fitted black suit, her gold bracelets jangling. Then she groaned and slumped against the marble-topped counter. 'Can't remember the last time I felt even mildly titillated, let alone randy.'

Rachel suddenly sat up straight. 'Who was it sang that song about *Robert De Niro – talking Italian?*' She looked from one to the other of them for an answer. Sophie gazed back, her face concerned but blank. Jill skewed her mouth to one side, drumming her vermillion fingernails.

'Wasn't it something to do with bananas?' she said.

'That's it – *Bananarama*.' Rachel sniffed. 'Well, I know what they were on about now. It was such a turn-on, all that *amore*.' She blew her nose again. 'Sandro and I . . . we used to make love listening to Andrea Bocelli – full blast.'

'How sad,' murmured Jill, sitting down and pouring the coffee.

'And look what's arrived today.' Rachel jumped up and began ripping at sheets of corrugated cardboard. She stood back so that Sophie and Jill could see the brand new double-sided menu board, designed to stand outside the café in the evenings flanked by two olive trees in terracotta pots. It was hand-painted with bunches of purple grapes and Chianti bottles and *Sandro's Italian Restaurant* gracefully scripted across the top.

Jill got up to inspect it. 'Send him the bloody bill.'

Rachel sighed and dropped back onto her chair. 'I would if I knew where.'

'He's probably back with the wife and six kids in Italy.' Jill draped a piece of cardboard over the sign as if she were trying to make it vanish like Sandro. 'And good riddance. He didn't deserve a wonderful woman like you.'

Rachel glanced up, surprised. She always imagined that Jill looked down on her a little from *Cormorants,* her Victorian mansion high above Ventnor Bay. But then, Jill had taken some knocks these last few months. Strange, she thought, looking at the two of them. Sophie seemed to have settled more comfortably into her body since her long holiday in New Zealand with Nick; her olive-skinned face appeared less angular, as if she'd been smoothed. And Jill, always well-rounded and confident, seemed edgy and brittle, as if dealing with her busy practice, battling kids, and errant husband, had sharpened her features. She seemed unable to keep still. Right now she was leafing through the pile of menus as if she were counting them, obsessively. Wasn't that what she was supposed to cure her clients of? Perhaps it was contagious.

We women, Rachel thought. How we rise and fall and bolster each other up again. Looks like it's my turn now.

'It just makes me so angry.' Jill started pacing up and down again, shaking her dark auburn hair from its clasp, deftly twirling and re-clamping it. 'Men can be such rotten—'

'Not all men,' Sophie interrupted.

'Well, your Nick's an exception. He's actually a grown-up – rare for a male.'

'And there's Neptune and Kyp and Chas – all nice guys,' Sophie continued. 'Not to mention Rachel's boys and—'

'Father Michael,' Rachel said, 'and that lovely man that delivers my—'

'Okay, OKAY!' Jill yanked out a chair and sat down. 'So, there's a small minority. Anyway. What are you going to do without your Italian chef? You've already advertised the opening night. We need to think.'

They sat in silence for a while, sipping coffee and making steady progress through a catering-sized box of *After Eights*. Rachel was finding it hard to concentrate on finding a solution. All she could think about was big, warm, noisy Sandro, talking Italian, engulfing her with his *amore*. She'd never had a lover like him before. And that's how she thought about him – as her lover. She didn't have designs on him as a live-in partner. It had been so exhilarating having this energetic man – almost ten years her junior – doing extraordinary things to her body, breathing against her neck at night. She let out a pent-up sob. Sophie's arms immediately enfolded her. What a comfort it was having friends

17

who understood what it felt like to be betrayed. And God knows all three of them had experienced that.

Jill cast doleful eyes towards the wine rack. 'Too early for a drink?'

'Well, this *is* an emergency situation,' Sophie colluded.

Rachel gestured towards the automatic corkscrew and then blew her nose with a final flourish. She picked up her Andrea Bocelli CD, snapped it into its plastic case and frisbeed it across the café. It crashed against the wall, then dropped onto the expensive black and white tiled floor. The lid of the case fell open revealing a picture of the smouldering singer nuzzling the petals of a red rose with a stem a yard long. 'Bloody *romanza*!' she yelled.

*   *   *

Fran paused the video at the precise moment in the pas-de-deux where Nureyev draped Fonteyn over his shoulder as effortlessly as if she were a silken cloak. Fran felt weightless, as if she herself had been dancing. It always took her a while to get back into her own body. She sat gazing at the frozen tableaux – like butterflies pinned under glass, she thought. Who'd believe Margot was in her fifties dancing as Juliet to Rudolf's Romeo? She looked like a young girl, so slender and supple in her floating chiffon. No middle-age spread or hot flushes or aching joints. Well, maybe she did – but not middle-age spread, obviously. Fran looked down at her own square body, her bunioned feet, and her veined, large-knuckled hand stroking the huge Persian cat on her lap. Sighing, she lifted the cat and lowered her gently to the floor. The cat blinked up at her, orange eyes glowing reproachfully out of the mass of white fluff.

'Sorry, Sugar Plum, too hot,' Fran said. The Aga was belting out heat, making faint gargling noises as if it were cooking up a nourishing stew in its dark caverns instead of waiting to warm up her individual steak pie and oven chips. Perhaps she should peel a couple of Ted's carrots tonight, if she could raise the energy to haul herself from the depths of the armchair. She turned off the video. She'd heard that it wasn't good to hold tapes on pause for too long, and she didn't want to damage her precious film. Maybe she would watch *Swan Lake* later,

18

while she ate her pie.

Sugar Plum yawned, revealing the glory of her pink mouth inside the snowy fur. She walked stiffly over to the Aga, stretching her back legs as she went. She sniffed at the cardboard box at the base of the oven, shouldered her way between it and the snoring Cinders, and claimed her place on the threadbare rug. She started to wash, burying her face deep into her long hair and tugging at it, releasing the smell of wet fur.

'You'll get hairballs,' Fran muttered, heaving herself up. She squatted down beside the box, hearing the clicks in her knees and back and briefly wondered how many cardboard boxes had sat here over the years. How many young animals had snuggled down, recovering, roasting themselves, filling the kitchen with the smell of damp and scorching fur? Perhaps she herself had snoozed in one when she was a baby. She pulled back the piece of flannel and laid her hand on the tiny animal curled inside. 'How're you doing, wee lamb?' she said. The lamb twitched its flank at her touch. The cat paused in her washing and the dog raised her head, letting out a questioning yap.

Fran got up to fetch the feeding bottle and squirted milk from the black rubber nipple into her own mouth to test the temperature. She lifted the lamb from the box and sat at the kitchen table. Holding him under her arm, she gently prised open the hard little jaw to insert the teat. This was its first attempt at sucking. She'd given it colostrum earlier through a tube. Now she wanted to make sure it would suck before returning it to its mother. The lamb shook its head and gave a snort but showed interest in the taste and started to thrash its head around spattering milk until finally latching on. 'Easy, easy,' Fran encouraged. The lamb felt warm and had a reasonable layer of fat, it should survive. A bit small, but not as skinny as its twin, which was probably dead by now. She'd replace it with this one soon, now she was confident it would live.

Fran rocked the lamb as she fed him, humming *The Dance of the Cygnets*. She felt relieved. It had been risky getting her ancient ewe to lamb in January. But poor old Beauty was almost past it, this could be her last, pity it was a male. Fran couldn't bear the thought of not having at least one lamb to fuss over. The rearing of sheep was in her blood,

19

her family's blood. She could almost hear her younger brother, Phillip, scoffing from the Australian outback where he'd emigrated years ago to raise *serious* sheep. He'd laugh at what was left of Rocken Edge Farm – *the family farm*. Fran still called it that, reduced as it was to her few pets and chickens. The remaining pasture – Bleak Field – was rented out to Blackgang Ted, to graze his waning herd.

Fran tucked the lamb back in its box, filled Sugar Plum's bowl with coley and clanged a steak and kidney pie into the oven. She couldn't be bothered with peeling carrots. Frozen peas would do.

Cinders got up, shook herself, and wandered over to the door, ears pricked. She snuffled along the bottom of it, as if trying to sniff out what the weather was up to, and then looked at Fran and whined. Fran grinned – another pee needed – good sign the dog was pregnant. She was looking forward to having another litter of pups heaped in front of the stove. When they were weaned she would take Sugar Plum for a tryst with Ted's burly tomcat. About time she was initiated into motherhood – that should cure her vanity. She bundled her grey hair up under her woolly hat, put on her duffle coat and wellingtons and opened the door. 'Come on then,' she said to the eager collie.

The wind was getting up, pitching a mournful note, carrying a tang of frost which seldom truly arrived down in The Undercliff. The sky was clearing, revealing a sprinkle of stars. Waves sloshed rhythmically, rattling the rocks below. The lighthouse beam illuminated the white crests as it swept the sea. She breathed deeply, filling her lungs full of crisp, salty air. She'd better go and check that her ewe was comfortable. The birth had been difficult. Fran had been on the verge of phoning the vet, but they'd managed in the end.

She walked across the yard to the stable, leaving Cinders to sniff out the right spot to pee. The wind had blown the door open. Fran couldn't have fastened it properly. That was careless – leaving the animals in a draft, a new lamb prey for the fox. Beauty was standing motionless in her pen. Fran scratched the ewe's head and ears. 'There, there, old girl,' she murmured. The twin lamb was lying in the straw between its mother's hooves. Fran picked it up. It dangled stiffly. She put it by the door and went back to the house to fetch its brother. She mingled their smells by rubbing their fleeces together then held the substitute lamb, warm and bleating, against the ewe for a good sniff. Beauty quivered and the lamb nudged at her. Fran encouraged it to nuzzle around its mother's teats and take a few sucks, then tucked it deep into the straw to make sure the change in temperature wouldn't be too drastic. She smiled, remembering that her father had sometimes taken a ewe indoors, as well as the lambs, in extremely cold weather. She went outside, listened to her lovely-dovelies cooing in the cote, secured the hens in the barn and filled the water bucket. Cinders was still snuffling about. She bounded back into the stable with Fran and gave a sudden bark.

'Stop it,' Fran said, filling the trough. The dog started a low growling, searching around in the straw. Must be that dead lamb, Fran thought. But then she heard a mewing sound. 'Ah, cat is it? Come away, don't frighten it. It'll only be mousing.' Cinders gave a sharp yap and the mewing got louder. 'Strange noise.' Fran felt in her pocket for the torch. 'Is it hurt?'

She swung the beam around the stable. Cinders was jumping up at the bales. She went over to look. There was indeed something moving in there. She focused the torch slowly, not wanting to terrify the poor creature any more than it was already. She stared and then looked away, not believing what she was seeing. But when she looked back it was still there – a mass of pink wool surrounding the tiniest face she had ever seen. She felt a tingle of shock pass through her body. 'I'll be darned,' she whispered.

*   *   *

Father Ryan was feeling exhausted after the day trip to Mizen Head. He locked the front door of the presbytery, lit the fire that Mrs Mulligan had laid for him, then turned off the lights, so that any callers would think he was still out. He especially wanted to avoid Mrs Mulligan. She often dropped by to see if everything was to his satisfaction – and to ask if he'd heard from Clare. He wished the woman would leave him alone. Hadn't he done his best for her – and her daughter?

He unlaced his black shoes, covered himself with Jeannie's old red shawl, and lay back in his winged armchair to listen to his cassette of Tudor church music. Oh, how he loved the purity of those soaring voices. A Tallis Scholar – that's what he should have been. He sighed. Why hadn't anyone spotted his potential when he was young? Why had he ended up as choir master to an ungrateful rabble that wasted his time? No wonder his poor head was always aching.

He'd had to bear the pain all through the journey home, sitting at the back of the coach with the boys. Sister Constance sat at the front with the girls – and didn't they have a better time with their sweet chatter, and their pretty songs? They reminded him of Jeannie; she used to sing softly to him, under the bed covers at night. The boys had their fun by telling smutty jokes. Father Ryan had closed his eyes to shut out the light and feign sleep. But still he could hear them – and smell them. That disgusting O'Leary had blasphemed, and called the other boys *feckin' eejits,* when they didn't believe his ridiculous sexual fantasies.

When they arrived back in Bantry, Father Ryan had grabbed young O'Leary by his greasy collar and hauled him behind the coach. He put his mouth close to the boy's ear. *Those things that you do to yourself in your bed,* he hissed, *it's the devil himself that's got inside you.* He felt the boy stop wriggling in his grasp and grow limp. *He can become a maggot which lives in your private parts and feeds on your dirty thoughts and spits them back out.* O'Leary stared at him with wide frightened eyes, his wet lower lip wobbling. *CONFESSION!* Father Ryan said, as he let him go and watched him scuttle away. It never did any harm to put the fear of the devil into the little blighters. Wasn't it his own father that had told him his headaches were caused by a rodent nibbling at his bad thoughts inside his skull? Fear was a good tool for ramming lessons home. Indeed, the children took much more notice of him when he locked them in the cupboard, one by one, during their catechism lessons, to help them understand purgatory.

Father Ryan felt better after an hour of the divine music. He'd even added his own voice to the harmonies from time to time. Ah, Tallis and Byrd, Taverner and Cornysh – how they elevated him and restored his faith. 'Would you listen to yourself,' he murmured, 'faith in what?' He rubbed at his eyes and his hard cheekbones. What sort of a question was that for a priest to be asking himself? But he was always asking it, and could never come up with an answer that wasn't a platitude. He held Jeannie's shawl to his mouth and nose, inhaling, imagining he could still smell her. He'd stolen the shawl from her locker the first time he'd been to visit her in the residential hospital. He thought she wouldn't miss it, and he needed something of hers. He folded it carefully. Red was such a comforting colour.

He could hear the wind bellowing outside. Hailstones clattered against the window panes, and a belch of yellow smoke curled down the chimney. He coughed and got up from his chair to light a lamp and coax his meagre fire back to life with a couple of peat briquettes. He thought he might slice some barm brack, and heat up the mutton broth that Mrs Mulligan had prepared. And then he had the scores of Josquin and Allegri to study. The gale lifted his dustbin lid and sent it clattering down the garden. Good, he was unlikely to be disturbed on such a night. Sometimes these long winter evenings could be quite pleasant.

CHAPTER

Three

Clare dreamed she was back home in Bantry Bay. Her mind drifted with the slow rhythm of the silky green sea which patiently nurtured the mussels in their beds. She felt a wave of sadness for the poor deceived creatures nestling in their safe grey shells. But the sea was so soothing; the salt breeze barely stirred the whispering grasses. She brushed the comforting end of her plait back and forth across her cheeks. She wanted to stay there, sitting on the dune, chin on knees, watching, but her mam was calling her, insistently. *Clare! Would you come here this instant! You'll be late for the choir and Father Ryan will not be pleased with you.*

Clare could see herself clearly in the dream. She was watching from the outside, but feeling from the inside, all at the same time. She was much younger, just a wee girl. Something was digging into the palm of her hand. She looked down at the tiny silver statue of Our Lady that she was clasping. Father Ryan had given it to her after he'd measured her chest for the first time. The stiff tape felt uncomfortable, pressing her thin vest against her tender places. Father Ryan wrote something in his notebook and smiled. *There now, put your blouse back on and run home. You'll be catching a chill, and your mother will be after me.* It was then he gave her the little statue. *Don't be telling the others – they'll all be wanting one.* His eyes sparkled as he patted her on the head. *It's pretty red hair you have, young Clare.*

When her mammy asked her what she'd done at choir practice, Clare told her about the chest measuring. Mam turned to look at her, her eyes travelling over Clare's face and body. Clare blushed, feeling she'd done something wrong. *And why was that?* Mam asked. *To see if our chests are expanding after our breathing exercises,* Clare explained;

although the other boys and girls had not been there. Mam nodded. *Then you must do as he says. You're a lucky girl to be chosen for the choir.* She turned back to the picture of St Francis she was polishing. *Father Ryan is a good man, a fine priest.*

Clare could never understand why she'd been chosen – she couldn't sing, at all.

Clare watched her dream-self put the statue in her blouse pocket, swing her plait over her shoulder, and begin nibbling her nails, until her mam called again. Then she got up and shook the sand from her navy school skirt. For a few moments she watched the herons poised in the shallows, wishing she could wade out into the cool water with them. She sighed and turned away.

As she walked up the path to her house, through the grove of myrtle trees, she let her hand brush against the rusty-brown bark peeling from their trunks. She breathed deeply, relishing the sweet smell of the tiny white flowers. But suddenly, the sweetness turned putrid, and her young self disappeared. Her throat seized up, trying to prevent something rotten entering into her. Or was it trying to force its way out? She knew if she didn't breathe she would die. What would happen to her then? She held her breath until she felt her ribs would splinter. Bright lights sparked and flashed behind her closed eyelids. She had no choice but to let go.

And then she wasn't dreaming anymore. She blinked and looked up. A woman was gazing down at her with pale blue eyes, watery like the sea. Clare felt the warm pressure of hands on her chest. She tried to cry out, squirm away; she didn't want to be touched. But the woman gave a beautiful smile; she swayed over Clare and something silvery shone around her. Clare wondered if she was seeing the Blessed Virgin herself. She wanted to ask her something immensely important. Surely the Mother of God would be able to tell her . . . but she couldn't form the words, or keep her eyes focused. Deep inside her body the knot of worms contracted painfully, and then released itself and grew quiet as she fell back to sleep.

*   *   *

Fran placed the baby nervously on the kitchen table. It was squealing and grunting, rubbing its little fists around its face trying to get them into its mouth. What should she do, call the police? She looked at the phone on the sideboard. It would be sensible to check the baby over first, make sure it wasn't injured in any way. She unwound the pink shawl. The baby was dressed in a pink knitted matinee coat, bonnet and leggings. They were grubby, the leggings damp and stained.

'Poor wee lamb,' Fran said, wrinkling her nose at the smell. 'Just look at this, Cinders.' The dog was sniffing the air with curiosity. 'Who would take the trouble to knit all these clothes, and then abandon the little mite?' At least the child was warm, apart from its tiny red hands. 'Thank goodness you heard it cry, could have been out all night, might have died of cold. Dear, oh dear, I can't abear to think of it.'

Fran took off her own coat and hat, bunched her hair into an elastic band and rolled up her shirt sleeves. Then she started, tentatively, to remove the baby's clothes. She'd never done this before. Was it all right to straighten its tiny arms to get them out of the sleeves? Perhaps she *should* call the police and let them take care of it. But she couldn't leave the poor little thing in this state. It might take ages for them to get here. The police were always busy with drugs and violence weren't they? Anyway, the person who left the baby might come back any moment. Unless they'd kidnapped it. Oh dear! Now *she* might be accused of kidnapping. 'Calm down, Fran,' she told herself. 'You're getting all flummoxed.' She rewrapped the child in its shawl, cushioned it in the armchair, and scribbled a note to say it was safely inside the farmhouse. Then she dashed out to the stable and placed the note on the bales.

She burst back into the kitchen, breathless. The baby was still grunting, mouthing at its fists. She filled the sink with warm water, laid the infant on a towel on the table, and carefully removed all the woollen clothes. Next, she took off the leaking rubber pants and unpinned the sodden nappy – a rough towelling thing – not one of those disposables that folk chucked away these days. She paused in surprise. 'I'll be darned. It's a boy. Who would dress a boy in pink woollies?' Cinders yelped as if she too were astonished. Fran dropped everything into a bucket to sort out later. She fetched a toilet roll from the cupboard under the sink, dipped a wodge in the water, and began cleaning the caked faeces from the child's bottom. 'Just look at this little bum, so sore.' The baby began to whimper. Fran felt tears well in her eyes. Who could leave a helpless young creature in this state? He started to cry, an unhappy wail, showing his pink gums and quivering tongue. She picked him up and slowly lowered him into the warm water. The baby's face showed momentary surprise and he stopped crying. Fran felt the tiny body tense, and then relax, as he got used to the sensation. She wondered how old he was. His cord was gone, his belly button healed. Compared to the pups she'd raised, he looked to weigh about eight pounds.

She lathered her hand with a bar of soap and then smoothed it over his body. She could feel her heart hammering with anxiety in case she hurt him, or let him slip. How hard should she rub his skin? It wasn't like bathing one of her tough little animals; his skin was soft and tender looking. She gently eased a soapy finger into the folds of the child's neck and the creases of his elbows and knees. 'That's better, my lamb, isn't it?' she crooned as she worked. The baby stared at her with dark blue eyes, unsmiling. Perhaps he was too young to smile. Anyway, he didn't have much to smile about at the moment. She lifted him from the water and wrapped him in a clean towel from the rack above the Aga. 'There, is that nice and warm?' She sat on a kitchen chair and inspected his body more thoroughly to see if there were any injuries. His clean skin seemed unblemished, apart from the sore patches on his bottom and another under his chin. She patted his hair dry; it was fair and silky with a reddish glint. She sat rocking him. He was trying to get a grip on his hands with his mouth again. He was obviously hungry. Now she would have to call someone, she couldn't feed him. He started to whimper and then let out a frustrated yell as his hands evaded him. Perhaps she should give him some water; he might get dehydrated by the time help arrived.

She got up to put the kettle on the hot plate. The packet of lamb's formula was on the sideboard. She read the instructions. Of course she knew it wasn't for human consumption. But in an emergency, diluted, better than starving. She fetched a fresh cardboard box from the backhouse, lined it with clean flannel and bedded the baby down in front of the Aga. 'There, you're a real little lamb now,' she told him. She put a bottle, and the newest teat she could find, in a saucepan to sterilise. She suddenly remembered her pie and took it from the oven, burnt to charcoal. The baby started whimpering. Fran felt a rush of panic reddening her cheeks. She went outside to the yard and stood listening. There was only the whining of the wind; nobody calling for help. She hurried to check there was no-one in the stable or the barn – an injured mother perhaps, lying unconscious. But there was just the ewe and her offspring, huddled together.

The baby was crying vigorously now, his little face red, his lower lip trembling. Fran made up a bottle of milk, cooled it, and offered it to him. He behaved much like a young animal, hungry but resisting, snuffling and sneezing, eventually managing to swallow a little. She had to wash his face and neck again afterwards, and she found some zinc and castor oil in the medicine cabinet to apply to his sore chin and bottom. She put a wad of cotton wool between his legs and wrapped him in another clean towel, thank heavens she always kept a supply for the animals.

The baby felt warm and relaxed, his eyelids drooping, his mouth slightly open. Fran stroked his little hands, inspecting the minute pink fingernails. She decided to let him rest and recover for a while before she phoned. He deserved that after his ordeal. Come to that, so did she, she felt fagged out. She couldn't face the police all flustered like this. She needed to steady herself and be clear-headed for when they arrived. Otherwise they might accuse her of whatever it was they accused people of these days. She'd heard that innocent people ended up in prison for defending their own property.

She put a video in the player, and sat down in the armchair, cuddling the baby. 'This is *The Nutcracker*,' she told him, 'a nice ballet for little children.' Sugar Plum sat blinking at her resentfully, before jumping up to settle on the arm of the chair. Cinders yawned and curled herself in front of the oven. Fran sat gazing at the baby. The dancers leaped and pirouetted unheeded on the screen as she watched him fall asleep. His eyelashes were fair, glinting like gold thread as they lay on the peachy skin of his cheeks. Something inside her throbbed, as if it were radiating tenderness – the feeling was almost too much to contain. She wondered if this was how it felt to give birth and have your newborn child placed in your arms.

*   *   *

Rachel brewed herself a mug of chocolate, put on her comforting winceyette pyjamas, and snuggled up on the window seat. From her flat above the café she could see the whole length of the esplanade. It was getting late, deserted down there. Another few months and the holidaymakers would be wandering around in search of Saturday night entertainment, hopefully spending loads of cash in her romantic Italian restaurant. Moonlight played on the sea and beach, highlighting the frothy edges of the waves as they spread over the sand.

A few sips of the scalding drink, and a fleeting thought of Sandro, caused a small pulse of heat to expand throughout her body. She didn't know whether it was a hot flush or simply a physical reaction to thinking about him. She opened the window a crack so she could cool down and hear the rhythmic swoosh of water, a sound which always made her feel peaceful.

She was at home alone. Both her boys, Aidan and Patrick, were staying over at Wraith Cove in one of the caravans. Patrick practically lived there now he was employed as foreman, supervising the casual workers on the building site. Rachel didn't know whether this was good or not. He'd done well at university. She hoped he would embark on his career as a geologist. But jobs in that field were scarce. At least he was taking on responsibility and earning a wage. Aidan was working there too, during school holidays and most weekends. Patrick always looked out for his younger brother, and the nights they stayed away had been convenient for her relationship with Sandro.

Rachel felt restless, anxiety niggling at her mind. The sea wasn't doing it for her tonight. And that wind – it was positively growling.

She slammed the window, got up, and started pacing around her sitting room, picking up framed photographs of the boys, dusting them on her sleeve. Perhaps she should never have allowed herself to agree to this Italian restaurant venture. She'd been doing perfectly well running her sparkling seafront café, serving wholesome homemade food. She'd built up a good reputation with the holidaymakers and the locals. But Sandro had made the proposition seem so exciting – *Rachel's Café* by day, *Sandro's Italian Restaurant* by night. Perhaps, in retrospect, it had been Sandro who'd excited her the most. But she'd had a proper business plan drawn up; she would never have offered Sophie a partnership without one. Oh, God. Was it all going to go pear-shaped now?

'Come on, Rachel,' she told herself firmly. 'You've always bounced back, don't let this beat you.' She went into her bedroom, put on her towelling dressing gown, belted it firmly, and went downstairs to the café. She switched on the lights and looked around assessing the chaos. She rescued her CD, fitted the case back together, and planted a kiss on Andrea Bocelli's handsome brow. 'Sorry, gorgeous,' she told him. 'Not your fault.' She grinned. 'But you could do with a shave.'

She slipped the CD into the mini-stereo behind the counter, and set it to play. Swinging open all the cupboard doors in the kitchen, she began rearranging her flowered daytime china to make room for the new evening set. She rolled up her sleeves, slit open boxes and unpacked the white dinner plates, bowls and coffee cups. Then, up to her elbows in suds, she washed and polished and stacked, until all was gleaming and orderly.

She sang along with Andrea until he began singing *Con Te Partiro – Time To Say Goodbye*. 'Oh, Sandro,' she whispered, feeling the desolate pang of loss. Suddenly exhausted she realised it was long past midnight. Sunday – what would he be doing? She sat down for a rest, and the boost of a strong cup of coffee.

She wanted to laugh at herself for her infatuation with Sandro, but she had to admit she was struggling. Why couldn't she just let go, like she'd done before? She'd had several lovers since her husband, Connor, walked out when the boys were small. None of them had been that serious, and she'd never considered having another man as a permanent fixture in her home. She sighed and poured herself another coffee. It was because she didn't understand – that was why. She knew it wasn't boredom, or their age difference. And he only paid lip-service to his Catholic guilt over sex outside of marriage. She had no doubts that he adored her body, her feminine roundness. He'd inspected and kissed all her mature bits as if he'd actually written *Shirley Valentine*. And she'd loved his simplicity, as well as his large swarthy physique. He could pick her up, swing her round, and before she knew it, she was desperate to get her knickers off – didn't even bother to put them on sometimes. And what a chef! He sang – in Italian of course – as he tossed pizza dough and rolled fresh pasta, demonstrating his skills for her. He was like a puppy, innocent and playful, incapable of deception – she didn't agree with Jill's harsh opinion of him. She just couldn't let him go without finding out why. She would have to visit the hotel where he'd worked, again, and try to find someone who knew him well, just to satisfy her curiosity.

Feeling better that she'd formulated a plan of action, she stamped on the empty cardboard cartons and piled them by the back door. She looked around the café; it was beginning to look smart. She'd just get that set of shelves up, and unpack the rest of the table linen, and then the floor area would be clear for her and Sophie to assemble the rest of the heavy wrought iron, mosaic topped tables on Monday. And then she could concentrate on her other dilemma. She needed to advertise for another Italian chef. She doubted whether she would find one in time for the opening night, two weeks away. At least Sophie looked Italian, even though she couldn't speak the language fluently. Maybe they could shove all that rampant hair of hers under a chef's hat, and pretend she was Sandro.

Rachel smiled to herself as she rummaged in her tool box for rawlplugs and the right sized drill-bit. What a great friend Sophie had become. She remembered the day – almost nine months ago now – that Sophie sat down in the café, poured out her heart, and then accepted the summer job Rachel offered her. Rachel expected it to be temporary, a

31

few weeks maybe, until Sophie decided to return to her husband, and her career as a mental health specialist in London. But Sophie loved the café, and then she met Nick who was recovering from his own trauma. They fell for each other in a big way, with a little final shove from Rachel and Jill. *A second chance,* Sophie and Nick sighed rapturously, nestling into their beach house in Blue Slipper Bay. And, Rachel realised, she was becoming increasingly fond of Jill whose veneer had cracked enough to reveal her vulnerability in her own marriage. What a leveller that was between women.

Rachel marked the position of the shelves and plugged in the drill. She needed to put the Sandro episode to rest. Closure – wasn't that the American expression? And then her focus would become clear again. The drill whizzed satisfyingly into the plaster.

*　　*　　*

Father Ryan wondered if he had a brain tumour, like Jeannie. The doctors had said there was no genetic factor, but that was a long time ago. Medical science had progressed rapidly – like a tumour. Perhaps he should consult a specialist. His head seemed to ache continuously, especially when he lay in his narrow bed, trying to sleep. It was a gnawing pain, deep inside, where he couldn't press his hand, or rub. It was easy to imagine a small animal curled in there, nibbling at his grey matter. He shuddered, turned on his side, and reached for the switch on the bedside lamp. Five o'clock. He always seemed to wake at the same time, not that he slept much anyway.

He sat on the edge of his bed and placed his feet on the cold lino. The wind and rain had died down, he couldn't hear a sound. Perhaps he was afloat on an ark – the last human left on earth. What would that be like? No more baptisms and confirmations and weddings and funerals to conduct, with false sincerity. No more struggling to produce another empty sermon. Best of all, no more filth would pour into his ears, through the grille of the confessional. There would be no reluctant choristers either. Would he miss the children? Not the cheeky older ones, especially the boys, like O'Leary. The little girls were nice. But they grew up too soon these days – before he was ready.

His body began to grow cold as he sat watching the bulge in his pyjamas subside. He wondered whether to get dressed and walk across to the church. Perhaps an early morning contemplation, before Sunday mass, would quieten his pain, help him face his day. The church would be cold too; bitter in fact. What comfort could he find there? Cold flagstones, cold statues. Where was the living God that he'd given his life to – a warm loving God that gathered His children to Him? That's what he would do if he were God.

Father Ryan stared at his thin white fingers that looked just like his mother's. Her fingers had been cold too. He got up, hurried down the stairs, and returned with his sister's red shawl. He climbed back into bed, stuffing the shawl under the covers with him, then turned out the light.

CHAPTER
Four

'You really are a pudden-headed old woman,' Fran muttered as she attempted to give the baby some more of the diluted lamb's formula. It occurred to her that he might have been breastfed. He kept twisting his head to one side nuzzling at her, the rubber teat slipping out of his mouth. He was getting frustrated, so was Fran. She desperately wanted to see him settle contentedly with a full tummy. He'd cried a lot during the night and she'd fed him small amounts. But it wasn't right, what she was doing. She should have got help straight away. She could be in serious trouble now. If he was a breastfed baby then his mother must have cared for him and not meant to abandon him. So where was she? Perhaps she had stumbled in the darkness and fallen over the cliff.

'We'll make a plan,' she said to Cinders. 'This is what we'll do.' The collie pricked up her ears. 'I'll go up to the village and buy some baby food. No, that's no good, everyone knows me; they'll ask questions. Right, I'll put his clothes back on, drive into Ventnor and take him to the police station. But I'll buy some supplies first, the police won't have anything to give him.' She positioned the baby over her shoulder and patted his back. 'I'll have to tell a lie . . . I'll say I found him this morning.' The grandfather clock started to chime in the hall. Fran counted. It was only seven o'clock. The shops wouldn't be open for ages. She got up and walked around the kitchen feeling the baby relax against her shoulder.

During the night she'd remembered the shallow straw basket that her mother had used to store flowers and herbs – her flasket, she'd called it. It was hanging up in the backhouse. Fran lifted it down, cleaned it, and cut up a blanket to pad it. The basket's smell reminded her of autumn days. Fran sniffed deeply, remembering running across the field

34

down to Watershoot Bay to hunt for crabs in the rock pools. Phillip would often go with her. They got on well together as kids, before he got restless, wanting to be somewhere bigger than the southern tip of this tiny diamond-shaped island. Fran had never felt as he did. She couldn't imagine wanting to go to another country. She had everything she loved here – the farm, wild cliffs, the ever-changing weather and sea. She couldn't envisage anything more boring than living like Phillip, in vast open country with day after day of blazing sunshine.

Fran stopped pacing and eased the baby from her shoulder. He was asleep but still making sucking movements with his mouth. He was so beautiful. She felt she would do anything in her power to make him feel secure and comfortable. She tucked him gently into the basket. 'Then you'll do the right thing and take him to the authorities,' she said sternly. The cat and dog both looked up at her as if wondering what they'd done wrong. Authorities, Fran thought, that word had a dreadful, cold ring to it. Supposing the boy's mother was dead – who would care for him? She thought about him being shunted around between foster parents and children's homes. Her eyes filled with tears. She picked up Sugar Plum and buried her face in the cat's soft fur. 'Well, let's get you lot fed first,' she said.

She filled the bowls for her animals' breakfast. Sugar Plum ate delicately, as if she didn't want to soil her fur. Cinders gulped her food down as if she were trying to beat a world record. She licked her chops and went to the door and whined. Fran checked the baby. He was sleeping restlessly, grunting and moving his head from side to side. Maybe the lamb's feed was giving him colic.

She put on her coat and boots. It was cold outside, still dark. She lit her torch and went over to the stable to check the ewe and the lamb. She'd looked in on them once during the night to monitor their progress. Beauty had seemed fine, the lamb suckling. 'Morning, Beaut,' she called. 'How are things going?' The ewe was standing with her head down, the lamb lying in the straw. Fran shone her torch on it and knew immediately all was not well. 'Oh, no,' she cried, picking up the lamb. Its legs were rigid sticks, its eyes staring blankly, the same as its

35

brother's yesterday evening. 'Oh, no, Beaut, what happened?' Fran felt guilt rising up in her chest – it was her fault, she'd been so distracted by the baby. She should have given the lamb more colostrum. She assumed Beauty would have enough, but she was an old ewe and Fran had been neglectful. She should have checked more often, made sure the feeding was established. She took the lamb over to the door of the stable and put it with its brother, covering the small woolly bodies with straw. She'd examine them later. 'Leave them, Cinders,' she commanded. The dog whined and sat down. Fran returned to the ewe and stroked her head and ears. 'I'm so sorry, Beaut,' she whispered. 'I won't make you do this again.' Fran wiped her tears away with the back of her hand. 'I'll spoil you rotten and you can spend the rest of your days as a pampered old lady.'

Fran went back indoors and scrubbed her hands. She felt suddenly fearful. If she could let a lamb die, then what might she do to a child that she understood nothing about? She took off her coat. She had to get him to someone who knew how to care for babies, not an ignoramus like herself. She felt the woollen clothes that she'd washed during the night. She'd placed them on a towel on top of the Aga to dry. Such strange clothes they were; gave off a funny smell, like beetroot. The dye had poured out of them in the water. Perhaps his mother was one of those natural organic people. But why pink, for a boy? Was it some sort of statement of equality? They were knitted in different shades and uneven textures. Some of it bobbly and coarse, like inexpertly home-spun sheep's wool. Even the tiny vest. It was a wonder the poor child didn't have sore skin all over his body wearing that scratchy stuff. She didn't want to put them back on him. Anyway, they were still damp. She would have to swaddle him in blankets and put the clothes in a bag to give the police. She should go and start the Land Rover, warm it up. The old rattletrap took ages to heat.

Fran felt panic stirring inside her again. What if the mother came back when it got light? What if she had simply got lost and was desperately looking for her child? She scribbled another note to say that the baby was safe and had been taken to Ventnor police station.

36

She hurried outside and replaced the old note, stopping to murmur more condolences to Beauty. Then she started up the Land Rover and switched on the heater.

*   *   *

Clare woke as something thudded against her back. She sat up. Where was she? The thud came again. It was the wind gusting against the wall she was pressed against. What wall? She rubbed her eyes. The light was dull, flickering. It was coming from a gas mantle above her head. She was in a room, like a cabin. A caravan – that's what it was – where Rose should be. But Rose had gone, far away, to Africa. That's all she could remember.

Clare felt numb. She looked around the shadowed room. There was no-one there. The door was open, leading to a dim kitchen. She was sitting on a bunk bed with a heavy grey blanket over her. She was wearing her tracksuit, but no trainers or jacket. Had someone stolen her things? Her backpack contained everything she owned in the whole world; her money was hidden in an inside pocket.

She jolted wide awake. Blessed Mary, where was the baby? Heat seared through her body and she started to sweat. She swung her legs over the edge of the bunk and stood, trembling. Her breasts throbbed; they were hard, full of milk. In the gloom, she could see a mound on the opposite bunk. That must be him. She tentatively put out a hand. It was her puffa jacket lying there. And her backpack was underneath it, her trainers on the floor. What had they done with him?

Clare flopped down on the bunk trying to remember what had happened. Her mouth was so dry, it was hard to move her tongue. There was a bottle of water standing on a shelf. She wondered if anyone would mind if she had a drink. She would pay for it, leave some money. She got up; the floor of the caravan creaked.

'You okay in there?' a girl's voice called.

Clare jumped. 'I'm fine.' She tried to pinpoint where the voice was speaking from.

'The loo's just outside if you need it.'

The voice seemed to be coming from beyond the kitchen – there

37

must be another bedroom. Would the baby be in there? Why wasn't he crying? Something was wrong. Clare fought the impulse to lie down and pull the blanket over her head. She drank some water, and tried to think. She remembered feeding the baby in the old stable. She remembered feeling sick, desperately needing air, stumbling outside. It was all a blur – but she didn't recall having the baby with her as she staggered across the fields. She'd left him behind! The people who'd let her use this bed wouldn't have known. Had she been asleep for a few minutes, a few hours? It was still dark, so it couldn't have been long. But he might be getting cold. She hadn't meant to leave him. She pulled on her jacket and her wet trainers. Her tracksuit trousers were soaked round the bottom of the legs. She could leave her backpack here. He couldn't be more than a couple of fields away. She'd only be gone a few minutes.

A gust of bitter wind nearly tugged the door of the caravan from her grasp as she opened it. The bonfire was still alight and she could see the other caravans grouped around. Then she saw the lighthouse beam flash. That was the direction she should go. The cold air was reviving her, clearing her head. She tucked her plait inside her jacket and zipped it, trying to ignore the throbbing in her breasts. She set off across the field, battling against the wind. There was a stile to climb over, and then another field. She couldn't remember walking this far last night. She wondered what the time was and stopped to look around. The sky was glowing faintly over the horizon. Day must be dawning. Oh, God. She must have been asleep for ages.

In front of her was a stone wall. How did she get over that last night? She must have come a different way. She didn't remember hearing the waves crashing so loudly. She followed the wall until she came to a place where it had tumbled. Just as she was about to climb over, a bright light shone out of nowhere and she heard the sound of an engine. She ducked down; she must be quite near the lane to the farm. She waited for a Land Rover to rattle past before going over the wall. Now she could see the dark shadows of the big rocks and the bent trees. Her insides were squirming – she tried to shut out all the bad thoughts about what she'd done.

There was the old stable, the familiar wooden door. She pushed it open, remembering the creak. This was it; the stench of animals filled her nostrils. But it was so dark, she couldn't see anything. She couldn't hear anything either – the baby must be asleep. She held her hands out before her, feeling for the straw bales. Yes, there they were. She groped around in the darkness, nothing. This must be the wrong place after all. She stumbled back to the door and pushed it open wider to let in a glimmer of light. Her eyes were becoming more accustomed now. She heard a rustling noise, saw a faint movement. That animal was still there, penned in the corner – so it was definitely the right place. She went back to the stacked bales of straw. There was nothing there. She brushed her hands over the whole area. Something fluttered down to the ground, but it was only a scrap of paper.

Clare clasped her hands in front of her face as if she were praying. What was she to do? Someone must have found him, heard him crying and taken him away. The thought gave her a moment of relief. He would be somewhere warm, being looked after, which was more than she had done. How wicked she was – up to her neck in mortal sin. She briefly remembered her vision of the Blessed Virgin when she'd woken in the night. She hadn't looked angry with Clare; she'd been smiling, beautifully. It must have been a dream – Our Lady would surely be *very* angry.

Clare backed away from the bales. She would have to return to the caravan to collect her backpack and decide what to do. She turned towards the door and tripped over a metal bucket which sent her sprawling. The pain in her shin felt so bad. A penance, it was no more than she deserved. She lay on the ground, crying bitterly. Her whole body seemed to ache. What was she going to do about her breasts? Would they just keep filling up until they exploded?

She put out a hand to lever herself up. It touched something solid under the straw. Clare froze. She was feeling wool – rough wool, covering something small and cold and stiff as bone. She drew her shaking hand away and looked down. It was too dark to see, and she couldn't bring herself to uncover it. She could just make out something glinting up at her that looked like an eye. Sobbing with terror, she staggered to the door and fled.

*　　　*　　　*

Fran stopped the Land Rover in Hambrough Road, opposite the lane that led up to Ventnor police station. She didn't turn off the ignition, not wanting the vehicle to cool down. And the baby seemed to like the rhythm of the engine. He'd stopped crying as soon as she started driving. Tucked in his basket, he was securely wedged between bales of straw in the back, watched over by Cinders.

So, this was it. She was going to have to let him go, give him up to the authorities. And she hadn't been able to buy a supply of baby milk and nappies for him. *Somerfield* didn't open until ten o'clock; she'd forgotten it was Sunday. She glanced up and down the road. There was nobody about, the day dull and overcast, barely light. She sighed and reluctantly switched off the engine. She wound down her window a little, and opened the door.

'Cinders! Guard!' she said. The dog sat up, her ears pricked. Fran shut her door and peered through the side window at the baby in his nest. She could just detect a slight rise and fall of the blankets. She would leave him there while she went into the police station so he wouldn't get cold. At the entrance to the lane she saw a blue sign fixed to the stone wall stating opening hours. Nine-thirty until ten-thirty, for enquiries. Surely police stations should be open all the time. What did people do in an emergency? She looked at her watch – it was only just gone eight. She hurried back to the Land Rover and climbed in. The baby was starting to whimper. She switched on the engine and drove down to the esplanade. She parked in the road and looked at the sea. It was pounding, quite a swell today after last night's wind. Spray and a light rain began to obscure the view.

The baby was hers for almost another hour and a half. Fran was aware how fast her heart was beating. She felt as if she'd been given a reprieve. She put her hot forehead on the steering wheel, and listened to the baby's small noises. What should she do now? If she didn't start to drive he might begin to cry. She'd brought a bottle of boiled water

40

with her, wrapped in a towel. She didn't want to give him anymore of the lamb's formula. He'd been sick after the last lot. But she couldn't feed him here, someone might see. 'This is what we'll do, Cinders,' she said. She would drive out of Ventnor and find somewhere deserted to stop. And then she'd head for Ryde. The big *Tesco* there was bound to be open, and she could buy everything she needed.

*   *   *

Rachel was woken by the sound of a noisy engine running, outside in the road. Who would be doing that so early on a Sunday morning? Why couldn't people turn their engines off while they sat and watched the sea or read the morning papers? She yawned and looked at the clock. It was gone eight, late for her. Of course – she'd been downstairs half the night, sorting out the café. Well, she deserved to be lazy. She would get up in a minute, make a cup of tea and bring it back to bed for a while. Then she'd have a long hot bath and indulge in a bit of pampering. Maybe she would have her hair cut next week, shorter, a bit trendy. And she'd seen some stunning, floaty clothes in the window of *Rita's Boutique*. All this grief had made her look rather frowsy lately. It would give her self-esteem a boost to have a new image.

Rachel stretched out her arms and legs luxuriously. There was something to be said about having a big warm bed all to yourself. But then she caught a lingering whiff of Sandro. She sniffed at the duvet – there it was, still clinging. Sandro was fastidious about hygiene, both with his cooking and his own personal stuff. But his large body was always hot, and Rachel could still smell the enticing fragrance his skin gave off. She lay there breathing him in, her skin almost able to feel his touch. Wasn't this what bereaved people did when they buried their faces in the clothes of the dead? What was she doing? She threw back the duvet, got out of bed and began stripping it. 'Enough!' she said loudly, bundling the linen into the laundry basket.

She thought about the day ahead. Later, she was going to walk along the coastal path to Blue Slipper Bay and have lunch with Sophie and Nick. She was looking forward to that. What did she have to moan about, really? She thought again of the thousands of people who'd lost

41

their loved ones and homes and livelihoods, to the tsunami. *'That's suffering, Rachel,'* she told herself. *'There but for the grace of God . . .'* She felt grateful that she could talk to Sophie and Nick about such things. How else could you make sense of it? If there *was* any sense to be made, of course. But they had intriguing perspectives, and they weren't scared to share them. Father Michael, bless his heart, hid behind the *sacred mysteries* of his faith. And Sandro would never question such issues. Rachel grinned, imagining them all round one table. Now that would be interesting. Just how many motives could be attributed to this *One God?*

She went to the window to see what the weather was doing, and who was polluting the air with exhaust fumes. She pulled back the curtains and peered out. The day was dismal, leaden clouds over choppy grey sea, wind blustering and rain pattering on the panes. There was the culprit – a Land Rover parked opposite with someone sitting in the driving seat. Wasn't that Fran's old vehicle – the woman from Rocken Edge Farm? She sometimes came into the café with Blackgang Ted who also farmed in The Undercliff. Rachel had always admired Fran; there was a rugged beauty about her. She seemed like a woman unafraid of living a harsh solitary life, in tune with the turbulence of nature. A little bit dotty perhaps – called her animals by silly fluffy names. But so what? Rachel liked eccentrics who lived their lives unaffected by other people's opinions.

As Rachel watched, a car drove along the esplanade with its headlights on. The interior of the Land Rover was briefly illuminated, and Rachel could see Fran. She knew it was her because of her thick bunch of grey hair fastened loosely behind her head. Fran was sitting with her forehead resting on the steering wheel. That was odd. Perhaps she was feeling ill. Rachel hunted around for her dressing gown. She'd better go outside and make sure Fran was all right. But as she tied her belt, she heard the engine rev and Fran was pulling away.

*   *   *

Father Ryan sat in his kitchen eating his porridge, whilst listening to a tape recording of the school choir singing *The Hallelujah Chorus*.

He tapped his spoon on the wooden table and then waved it in the air, as if conducting. Not bad, a long way to go, but they were improving. Trouble was, the older more experienced choristers kept leaving, and he had to persuade the younger children to give up their free time, when they would rather be playing computer games. He shook his head and winced with the pain. Not so long ago, parents regarded it as an honour to have their child selected for the choir. And they'd have stood no nonsense from their brats. Occasionally there was a mother or father who still revered it – Clare's mother for example. It was easy for Father Ryan then.

He shifted irritably on his hard chair and turned off the cassette. He should have been a professional music teacher. He wondered what his life would have been like if he'd been strong enough to resist his parents' insistence that he was destined for the priesthood. He wouldn't have all these onerous duties to attend to. He could concentrate on doing the thing he enjoyed. And he was good at it. He especially liked teaching the very young children with their clear innocent voices. But they were becoming increasingly difficult to find. Even with the strict discipline of the Catholic school they were insolent at a much younger age. He sighed, imagining a choir of sweet pale girls, like Jeannie. She had been such a darling. So had Clare – before she started to grow up and get ideas.

Someone knocked at his front door. He jumped up, his heart pounding. 'Will you calm down, now?' he whispered. 'You're only eating breakfast at your own table.'

'Are you there, Father Ryan?' A woman's voice called, through the letter box. It was Mrs Mulligan – had she come to ask about Clare, again? 'I'm sorry to disturb you, Father. Could you spare me a moment to look over the cleaning rota?'

He pressed his finger tips against his temples, but the throb inside his head continued. A brain tumour might be the best thing that could happen to him.

CHAPTER
Five

Clare tried to let herself into the caravan quietly, but the door handle rattled, the hinges squeaked, the floor creaked, and as she reached for the bottle of water her trembling hand knocked it off the shelf. She stood, shaking, waiting for someone to appear from the bedroom beyond the kitchen. But no-one came, or called out – they must be sound asleep. She took off her muddy trainers, tip-toed to the sink, and poured the contents of the water bottle over her hands, rubbing and rubbing at them until they were bright red. She raised them up in front of her face and stared. Was there anything clinging there? Any straw, any pink wool? She wiped them on her trousers.

The caravan was cold; the gaslight had gone out. She looked at her backpack lying where she left it on the other bunk. She should grab it and go – get out of here before they came for her. But what was the point? She felt paralyzed, numb. There seemed no direction for her to take. She couldn't go back home, and with no Rose, there was nowhere to head for.

Still wearing her jacket, she lay down on the bunk and pulled the blanket over her, screwing her eyes shut. She was aware of her clammy body; her throbbing breasts, the stinging pain in her shin, and the soreness between her legs where she was still bleeding slightly from the birth. But it was as if it all belonged to someone else. Even the worms were quiet. She was no longer Clare; she had changed into another girl – a cruel, heartless girl with no feelings at all. A girl who could leave a baby to die. At the thought of him she felt a surge in her breasts and a trickle of milk soaking into her sweatshirt.

*　　*　　*

Fran sat in the passenger seat of the Land Rover in Smuggler's Haven

44

car park, feeding the baby boiled water. He seemed eager at first, but soon realised it wasn't milk and pushed at the teat with his tongue, puckering his face in disgust.

'I don't blame you, little lamb,' Fran sympathised, putting him over her shoulder. 'But it's just to keep you going until I can get you some proper food.' Cinders gave a low growl. Fran glanced up. A man was emerging from the trees which bordered the parking area. He looked towards the Land Rover and stopped. Fran felt her heart start to race again. What if he were a plain clothes policeman on the lookout for a kidnapped baby? 'Stop being so ridiculous,' she muttered. 'He's at least eighty, and you're not doing anything wrong. You're simply caring for an abandoned child whilst waiting for the police station to open.' The man called out, and a labrador trundled out of the bushes. They hobbled away together.

Fran let out a long sigh. But she *was* doing something wrong, at least in other people's eyes it would be considered wrong. She just couldn't let the baby go until she she'd done right by him. She'd been responsible for causing suffering to an elderly animal, and possibly the deaths of two lambs. She needed to feed and clothe and care for this one. And love him.

The baby belched on her shoulder. Fran smiled, delighted. 'There, that's better. Let's tuck you up, and we'll go and buy you some tasty milk, won't we, Cinders?'

*   *   *

Rachel finished eating a heap of buttery scrambled eggs on toast and was about to enjoy her coffee and peruse the Sunday paper, when she heard Patrick's motorbike roar up outside. She might have guessed the boys wouldn't consider that she was having a peaceful morning to herself.

'Hi, Ma.' Patrick strode in bringing with him the smell of sea-air, leather, and engine oil.

'Thought you might be lonely.' Aidan followed close behind.

'Whatever gave you that idea?' Rachel watched as they struggled out of their huge psychedelic crash helmets and complicated biking gear.

Amazing how two young men could disrupt an entire kitchen in a couple of minutes.

Patrick laughed. 'He's lying. We ran out of food at Wraith Cove.'

'So you thought you'd pop home and ask your old mother to whip up a dish of bacon and eggs?'

'As if!' Aidan spiked up his fair hair with his fingers. 'You just carry on enjoying yourself, Mum, and we'll fend for ourselves.'

'Good,' Rachel smiled, flicking through the pages of the colour supplement.

'Wouldn't mind some coffee though.' Patrick glanced at Rachel's cup.

Rachel pushed the empty pot in his direction. 'I'll have some more, if you're making it.'

Patrick sighed. 'Things aren't like they were in the old days.'

'Thank God,' Rachel muttered.

The boys bustled about, searching the fridge as if they had no idea in which compartment the bacon and eggs were kept, let alone where the bread bin resided. Rachel pretended to read, but as usual found herself enjoying their play-acting, amused by their quick wit. She knew it was all done to entertain her. She'd brought them up to be pretty self-sufficient – for sons. And they were trying to cheer her up. They'd been surprised and sorry about Sandro's disappearance. They'd both liked him.

Patrick expertly flipped the fried eggs, his dark good looks reminding her of his dad, Connor. But Patrick wasn't unlike Sandro either. She'd always been attracted to the tall, dark, handsome type. Even Father Michael – strictly out of bounds and balding – was of the same variety. She wondered if Aidan would grow as tall as Patrick. He was more like her with his light, copper-tinged hair and stockier build. Patrick slid the eggs on top of a heap of grilled bacon that Aidan was arranging on two plates.

'There you go, kiddo, someone's got to look after you.'

'You know,' Aidan started shovelling down the food, 'we could really manage without women.'

'Agreed. Except for one thing,' Patrick said, pouring the coffee.

Rachel rattled the paper. 'Let's not go there, boys, please.'

Patrick looked indignant. 'Mother! I was only going to say that women are better at . . . like . . . women's things.'

'Define women's things,' Rachel said, imagining a list which would include items such as irons, ovens and vacuum cleaners.

'Well, you know, like when girls are upset and stuff,' Aidan said, his face serious.

'That's right.' Patrick dolloped brown sauce over his bacon. 'A girl just turned up yesterday evening in a real state. She actually passed out. I just managed to catch her. I hadn't a clue what to do. But the girls took her off to one of the caravans. Haven't seen her since.'

'Really?' Rachel hadn't expected that. She sipped her coffee. 'Do you know who she is?'

Patrick shook his head. 'A student, I think. She was looking for Rose. I vaguely remember giving her a lift somewhere, last summer. Rose befriended her on the ferry from Ireland.' He shrugged and heaved a sigh. 'You know what Rose is like – always has to chat to everyone.'

'Looked awful,' Aidan commented, his mouth full of toast. 'White as your dressing gown.'

Rachel felt her usual reaction of concern for the young. 'Did anyone call a doctor?'

'As I said, she was whisked away by the girls.' Patrick wiped his plate with a hunk of bread. 'But I did see Marguerite walking up from Wraith Cottage. Someone must have gone to fetch her.'

'Ah, that's okay then.' Rachel felt immediately reassured. She imagined Marguerite appearing in the caravan, silver hair shimmering, placing her healing hands on the sick girl. Incredible woman, Marguerite.

Rachel got up and went over to the window, wondering whether she should walk or drive over to Blue Slipper Bay to see Sophie and Nick. The wind and rain were still having fun out there. Normally, she would have enjoyed donning boots and raincoat and joining in the game, but she *had* been up half the night. She gazed down at the esplanade, not many people around this morning. Patrick's powerful motorbike was parked on the pavement in front of the café.

As she watched, a man in a black hooded jacket sauntered over and stood looking at the bike. Then he scanned the café. It was obvious it was shut, the blinds pulled down, the CLOSED sign in full view. But he walked up to the door and tried the handle, rattling it hard. Aidan and Patrick both looked up from the sports section of the newspaper.

'Who's that?' Aidan asked.

'Don't know.' Rachel stepped back from the window as the man walked into the road and stared up at the flat. She felt a sense of unease. It seemed to her as if he were searching for someone. Patrick got up and came over to look. 'A friend of yours?' Rachel asked.

Patrick shook his head. He placed his hands on the window sill and put his face close to the glass, peering down. The man gazed back up for a few seconds then pulled his hood forward and walked away.

'Do you want me to go after him? See what he wanted?'

'No, he was probably hoping someone would let him in for a cuppa. Happens all the time.'

'Git,' commented Aidan.

'Didn't like the look of him,' Patrick muttered.

'Harmless, and lonely, I expect,' Rachel said, stretching. 'Right, lads. I'm off to wash my wonderful body. You won't mind clearing up my dishes when you do yours, will you? I have spent the best years of my life raising you two from puking, shitty little infants.'

'Language, Mum!' Aidan said.

*   *   *

Fran hated supermarkets. She did most of her shopping in Niton, avoiding the big stores as much as possible. The bright lights made her feel confused as soon as she passed through the huge doors which swept open before her. But even this enormous *Tesco* hadn't been open when she arrived at nine-thirty. She had to sit in the Land Rover for another half hour, tempting the baby with the water, which was almost cold, resorting to letting him suck her finger – after she'd washed it, of course, with the remains of the water. The grip of his little mouth around her finger had been surprisingly powerful. He must be so hungry.

'Cinders! Guard! I'll be as quick as I can,' she commanded. She'd parked the vehicle in a remote corner of the big car park, in case someone decided to nose in. There weren't many other cars around on this gloomy morning and she knew that her dog would bark a warning if anyone came close.

She scurried along the aisles looking at the baby supplies. But there were so many different milk products, how could she know which was the right one? She put on her glasses and picked up a brand which claimed to be closest to breast milk. That should do it. She then realised she didn't have a basket. She was getting hot and panicky, sweating inside her thick duffle coat. There was one of those big trolleys nearby, full of empty cardboard boxes. Fran lifted them out, piled them on the floor, and began filling it with tins of powder and cartons of ready-mixed milk. And what about bottles and teats? Dazzled by the choice, she settled for some which advertised themselves as mimicking the breast. She found packets of disposable nappies for newborns, cotton wool, sleepsuits and vests. There were no baby blankets or sheets, so she grabbed a stack of white towels. If only she wasn't in such a hurry she could browse through everything, but all she could think about was the hungry baby wailing outside. She tried not to be impatient with the dozy lad at the check-out, and just remembered to buy a newspaper.

She lugged the carrier bags back to the Land Rover. Nobody was peering in the windows. Cinders was on full alert. As she suspected, the baby was yelling. She got in and started the engine, but he didn't stop crying this time. He was too hungry even for the magic of the engine to soothe him. Ryde or Newport police station? Indecision gripped at her insides. What if his mother had returned for him? Well, she would have found the note and gone to Ventnor police station. But what if she was too scared and was hiding at Rocken Edge?

Fran found herself driving home. It made sense to check if his mother was there. If she was, and Fran could help her, they might not have to involve the police at all. And if the mother wasn't there, Fran would feed the baby and dress him properly, and then she could part with him with a clear conscience, even if she was going to be in trouble. The welfare of the little one was the most important thing.

She drove as fast as she dare along the speed restricted roads. After a while the baby stopped crying. 'Not long now, little lamb,' Fran kept calling to him. As The Undercliff came into view she scoured the lane and the fields as she drove, but noticed nothing different – just the usual walkers. No police cars with flashing blue lights were surrounding Rocken Edge Farm when she arrived. She parked the Land Rover in the yard and dashed into the kitchen, tearing open packages and putting a bottle and teat in a saucepan to boil. Then she rushed back outside, fed the chickens, scattered seed for the doves and checked Beauty. The stable door was open again; she would have to check the catch. The note she left had fluttered down to the floor in the draught. Oh, dear, she still hadn't inspected and disposed of the dead lambs. She'd do it later, when the baby was fed.

She peeped in the Land Rover. Cinders was looking expectant, the baby was stirring. Fran went back into the kitchen, scrubbed her hands and lifted the boiling bottle from the Aga. Then she let Cinders out, carried the baby inside and shut the door.

'Now then,' she said, taking off her coat. 'Out the way, Sugar Plum.' Fran pushed the cat with her foot. Sugar Plum, affronted, took refuge on the armchair. Fran poured one of the cartons of ready-mixed baby milk, into the sterilised bottle, fitted the teat, and stood it in a jug of hot water to heat. Then she lifted the desperate baby and as soon as the milk was warm she touched his lips with the teat. The poor little boy frantically moved his head from side to side. Fran sat on a kitchen chair, held him on her knees facing her and gently grasped his head with one hand until he grew steady and latched onto the teat. And then he started sucking hungrily, drawing it deeply into his mouth. Fran heaved a huge sigh, feeling a wave of relaxation spread through her body as he fed. 'There,' she said. 'That's it, my lamb, that's it.'

She had no idea how much she should give him, she simply let him suck until he released his grip and the teat popped out of his mouth.

His eyes were half closed and his head lolled, drunkenly. She walked up and down the kitchen, with him over her shoulder, patting his back and talking to him until he burped. Then she tucked him in the basket. 'When you wake up, I'll give you a nice warm bath and you can try on your new clothes,' she said.

Fran made herself some tea and sat down at the kitchen table. Looking at her sleeping animals, and the baby, she wondered why she didn't feel more tired herself after her sleepless night and panic-driven morning. She heard the clock start to chime. It was midday. She got up and fetched the biscuit tin and scoffed half a dozen custard creams. The kitchen was a mess. If she got to work, she could get it cleared up and do her chores before the baby woke again, and then she'd be ready to bath him. She rolled up her shirt sleeves, vacuumed the animal hair, mopped the flag-stoned floor, scrubbed the sink and draining boards and the wooden kitchen table, wiped down the Aga, washed up dirty dishes and unpacked the baby's supplies, piling them on one end of the clean table. She smiled; what a mountain of stuff for such a tiny person. And he was still asleep, despite all her bustle and activity.

She went outside to check on Beauty and feel her udder. She seemed to be all right so far, no sign of mastitis. Fran mucked out the pen, laid new straw, screwed up her note, and then collected the dead lambs. There didn't seem to be anything obviously wrong with them, apart from their immaturity. She would have to put it down to Beauty's age and her own mismanagement. She took them behind the barn, lit a fire in the incinerator and placed the lambs in the flames. She should have done this last night. It wasn't good husbandry to leave dead animals lying around. Back in the courtyard, the lovely-dovelies flew down and cooed around her feet. Fran sighed with pleasure and went back indoors.

She scrubbed herself clean, sterilised more bottles, mixed up the correct strength of feed and put several in the fridge. 'You won't go hungry again, little one,' she said. 'Not with Fran looking after you.' But I won't be, she thought. I'm going to give you up; I'm going to take you to the police. The baby was stirring. Feeling like a traitor, Fran

51

filled the sink with warm water and laid fresh towels on the table. She bathed him and dressed him in a soft white vest, a disposable nappy and a blue sleepsuit with a puppy embroidered on the front. Fran lifted him up. 'Look, Cinders. Look, Sugar. Doesn't he look handsome? Better than those nasty pink things—'

Then Fran froze, holding the baby suspended in mid-air. Behind her, the kitchen door was opening.

*　　*　　*

Clare's eyes ached from the strain of squeezing them closed. She was aware of movement in the caravan, faint music, water running. She sensed someone standing watching her. Did they want her to go?

'You awake?'

It was a girl's voice. Clare felt her eyelids flickering.

'I brought you some tea.'

Clare opened her eyes. A girl was bending over her. She was wearing a red fleece zipped up under her chin, her brown hair pinned up haphazardly. She was holding a white mug. Clare struggled to sit up and she took the mug with trembling hands.

The girl smiled. 'I see you put your jacket back on. Sorry it got so cold in here, the gas ran out. I've changed the cylinder, it'll soon warm up.'

'Thanks,' Clare murmured. She sipped the hot tea. It was nice. The girl was holding a packet of chocolate biscuits. She sat on the end of Clare's bunk and offered them to her.

'Hungry?'

Clare nodded, suddenly feeling ravenous. 'Thanks.' She took one.

'No problem.' The girl sat, munching. 'I'm Kate, by the way. Feeling better?'

Clare wiped her mouth; her tongue felt like it was loosening with the tea. 'I think so.'

'You were in a bad way last night. Passed clean out. Patrick caught you, we carried you in here and fetched Marguerite.'

'Marguerite?'

52

'Medicine Woman. You don't remember? She's a healer lives down at Wraith Cottage – owns all this land and stuff, with her sister, Jane.'

Clare blushed with shame that she'd thought the Blessed Virgin had come to her. She felt the ball of bad things tighten and squirm.

Kate crunched another biscuit. 'You're not from round here, then?'

Clare shook her head, trying to think where she might say she came from.

'Patrick said you're a mate of Rose's.'

'Yes,' she nodded. 'I am.'

'We thought you sounded Irish.'

Clare wondered if she'd said anything last night, or whether Kate had picked this up from her mumblings. 'Well, originally . . . my parents . . . ' Clare bent to put the mug on the floor. She pushed back the blanket. 'Thanks for looking after me. I'd better be going now.' She swung her legs over the side of the bunk and stood up, feeling dizzy and weak. Kate watched her.

'There's no hurry. You still look pretty crook to me.'

Clare flopped down on the bunk as a wave of heat washed over her and she felt sweat break out on her face. She unzipped her jacket.

'Are you diabetic or something?' Kate asked.

'No.' Clare tried to think of an explanation. 'I've had tonsillitis. I'm better now, just a bit weak and all.' Kate was looking at her sweatshirt, which was stained with breast milk and pink dye from the baby's shawl.

'Oh, that's been going around. I had it a while back. Have you seen a doctor? You look feverish.'

Clare pulled the edges of her coat together and folded her arms across her chest. She shook her head.

Kate went to the kitchen and came back with a pack of tablets and a glass of water. 'Do you want to try this anti-biotic? Cleared mine up real quick. I didn't bother to finish them – I know you're supposed to.'

Clare took one of the tablets, her eyes filling with tears at Kate's concern. 'Thanks,' she muttered. 'I can pay you.'

'No worries.' Kate stood looking down at Clare. 'I'm going to fix lunch with the others. You're welcome to join us – or you can just rest up. Later, I'll take you down to see Marguerite—'

'No! I don't want to be a bother—'

Kate reached out a hand as if to touch her forehead. Clare flinched. Kate looked uncertain, her smile faded. She had a nice face – Clare wished she hadn't jumped back from her like that. But she couldn't help it, when someone got too close. She looked down and started to bite her nails.

Kate shrugged. 'Okay. You can have a bath and stuff later, if you want – before you go.' She turned away.

Clare heard her go out of the door. Maybe it would be nice to rest for a little longer, and it was weeks since she'd had a proper bath.

*　　　*　　　*

'Good lord, Fran. Whatever have you got there?'

Ted! Why hadn't she thought of that? It was Sunday. Ted always called in and they would walk over to Wraith Cove, call for Marguerite, then hike to Windy Corner to see if The Needles were visible, or the peregrines flying. They usually ended up at The Buddle Inn for a beer and roast dinner.

Fran lowered the baby, cradled him against her chest, and turned around. She felt completely dumbstruck. She knew if she told Ted the truth he would bundle her into the Land Rover and accompany her to the police station. Blackgang Ted was as straight as they came – except for the occasional tax fiddle to make ends meet.

'It's a b . . . baby,' she stammered.

'I can see that.' Ted closed the door and dumped a cabbage wrapped in muddy newspaper on the table, amongst the baby's things. He propped his stick against the wall, took off his tweed cap and unbuttoned his waxed jacket. 'What's it doing here?'

'It's er, it's a visitor.' Fran felt as if her brain were seizing up.

'A visitor's baby, did you say?' Ted rubbed his chin.

Fran nodded and turned away, trying to regain her composure. She swaddled the baby in a towel and put him on the armchair, hoping

54

Ted would forget about him. But Ted's hands were agitated, he was thinking, talking to himself, his hands automatically following the sign language he'd learned long ago in order to communicate with Eddie, his deaf son. Fran began casually clearing up the bath things, trying to appear normal. But Ted walked over to the armchair and stood looking down at the baby.

'What visitor is that then?'

'Phillip.' It was the first name that dropped into her mind.

'Good lord.' Ted sat down at the kitchen table. 'You mean Phillip from Australia?'

Fran nodded and started hanging the wet towels on the rack above the Aga.

'Darn me,' Ted said. 'Bit unexpected, wasn't it? You didn't say he was coming when I saw you yesterday morning.'

'No, it was a complete surprise.'

'I bet it was. Haven't seen him for years. Where is he?'

'Who?'

'Phillip. Who'd you think?'

'Oh, he's gone out for the day.'

Ted nodded slowly, obviously flummoxed. 'Hold on – Phillip's way too old to be having babies. He's our age.'

Fran forced a squeaky laugh. 'Don't be daft, Ted. His grandchild, I mean.'

'Grandchild, eh?'

'Mmm. I'm babysitting for a while.'

'Left him with you, already? Don't let him take advantage.'

'Oh, I don't mind.' Fran hoisted the clothes airer up. 'He's a lamb.'

'Sam, did you say?'

'Sam? Oh, yes, that's right.'

'Well, I'll be darned. So how many of them are over here?'

'How many what?'

'Relatives. I presume Phillip didn't come on his own – with a young baby.'

'Oh, no, Phillip's not here. Just his son – Young Phil. And his wife, er, Ann, of course.'

'Where are they staying?'

'Here.' Fran spoke before she had time to think.

'Here! Bloody hell, you'll have to do some cleaning up then.' Ted chuckled. 'Parts of this house ain't seen daylight for years.'

'I mean here – on the island – Ryde.' Fran felt as if she were sinking deeper and deeper into a treacherous bog.

'Well, you're obviously pleased about it.' Ted got up. 'It suits you. You look all flushed and handsome.'

'Get away with you,' Fran scolded. Ted had been a widower for years and often proposed to her – mainly in jest these days.

'Suppose you won't be coming for a walk to The Buddle then?'

'Not today, Ted.'

'Well, I'll get on over to Wraith Cove and see Marguerite. We'll just have to rub along without you.'

'You'll manage.' Ted had met Marguerite – also deaf – at *Cormorants* where he did a bit of gardening. They had struck up an instant friendship, hands flapping and swooping, like gulls over a shoal of sardines. Fran opened the door as he buttoned his coat and put on his cap. She handed him his stick. 'Pull your collar up, mizzling out there.'

Ted did as he was told. 'Mind you eat that cabbage. I'll call in again to see Young Phil – be nice to see Phillip's boy.'

'I don't know what their plans are.'

'I'll stop by anyway.' Ted loitered outside, watching the doves. 'Beauty's lamb arrived yet?'

'Twins – both died.'

'Oh, lord. What a pity. Well, we thought she might be coming to the end, didn't we? Still, looks like you've got your hands full. See you tomorrow.'

Fran shut the door and leaned against it, breathing deeply. 'We've done it now, Cinders.' She walked over to the armchair and picked up the baby. He gazed at her. She slowly bent her head and kissed his cheek. It was the sweetest, softest touch she'd ever felt. 'Sam,' she murmured, 'I think Uncle Ted's just christened you.'

*   *   *

Rachel decided to drive to Sophie and Nick's. It was still raining – that fine rain that swirled in the mist, obliterating The Undercliff. Normally she liked the mystery of it – the way it blurred the edges of everything and made the Botanic Gardens even more exotic. But dusk fell early these dull January days, and she didn't want to walk home along the dark cliff path later. She parked up on the road and walked down to Blue Slipper Bay, pausing to take in the sight of the three pastel-coloured cottages on stilts, alongside Kyp and Evie's fish restaurant. It still amazed her that Sophie and Nick could be so nonchalant about living here, so close to the sea. It could thunder in with considerable force on a spring tide driven by a strong southerly. She smiled; those two, they wouldn't notice if a hurricane lifted their beach house and put it down in Cowes, as long as they were together.

She walked along the concrete path which was littered with sand and shingle, and knocked on the lavender door of *Sea Spray*, the middle of the three cottages. Nick's head appeared over the balcony rail above. Rachel was still surprised to see him with hair, accustomed as she'd been to his shaven scalp. But Sophie had softened everything about him.

'Hi, Rachel. Come on up,' he called.

Rachel climbed the wooden stairs; Sophie was standing at the top, ready to hug her. She was looking gorgeous in a long, embroidered, khaki thing that would have made Rachel look like a jacket potato.

'Nice schmutter,' Rachel commented, fingering the rich material. 'From New Zealand?'

'Yes, but made in China,' Sophie laughed, handing Rachel a glass of red wine. 'Come and get warm.'

Rachel nudged Commie, the big tabby, from the centre spot of the bright rag rug, and toasted herself in front of the wood burner. How warm and inviting everything was. She remembered Nick's spartan place – *Fair Wind* – the cottage next door, which belonged to Kyp and Evie. They were refurbishing it as a holiday let, since Nick had renounced his monastic life and moved in with Sophie.

Nick, padding backwards and forwards barefoot, carrying dishes,

57

paused to look at her. 'You haven't stopped yawning since you got here, Rachel. Are you okay? Hope you're not bored with us already.'

'You two are the least boring people I've ever met,' Rachel laughed. 'No, I've been up half the night, working on the café.'

'Well, don't overdo it. We'll come over and help anytime, you know that.'

'Of course we will,' Sophie said. 'It's my responsibility too, don't forget. Come and eat.'

Rachel sat down at the table in front of the French windows. The gusting wind chucked sandy rain at the glass. All she could see outside was moody grey waves throwing up white-caps. 'I think you should re-name this place, *Noah's Ark*.'

Nick laughed, his calm face expressing delight. 'Sophie's always saying one morning we'll wake up and find ourselves floating past foreign shores.' He passed Rachel a wooden platter piled with crispy golden potatoes. 'So, why have you been working all hours, and not asking your friends for help?'

'Oh, just to prove to myself that I don't need a man.'

'Did it work?' Sophie heaped roast chicken onto Rachel's plate.

'A bit. I don't know what it is – or was, about Sandro. Can't get the soppy great oaf out of my mind.'

'Still no news of him?' Nick asked.

Rachel shook her head. 'I'm planning to go to the hotel in Shanklin, just to ask around. Someone must know something.'

Sophie sat back in her chair, her dark eyes scanning Rachel's face. 'Are you sure you want to do that? I'll come with you, if you like.'

'No, honestly. I'll be all right. There's no Mafia on this little island.'

'As far as we know,' Nick said. 'But what about the restaurant?'

Rachel shrugged. 'I just don't know what to do. If we can't get another Italian chef, then we're buggered. We'll have to delay the opening.'

'We could try and manage,' Sophie said.

'How? Even if you and I could cope with the cooking – which is doubtful – who will wait on the tables?'

'I'll help,' Nick said. 'And there's Aidan and Patrick.'

Rachel tapped Nick's arm. 'That's really kind of you. But it won't be *quite* the same as having an authentic Italian chef singing arias and wielding pasta, whilst Sophie and I schmooze with the customers. Sandro was a real show-piece.'

They ate in silence for a while. Rachel relished having a cooked meal placed in front of her for a change. She wasn't going to worry about her figure today; she'd lost weight with all this angst over Sandro and meant to indulge in another helping of those delicious spuds.

'I've tried really hard to take your advice about not getting hooked into thinking about Sandro,' she said, between potatoes. 'But I just can't stop the thoughts coming. And before I know it, I'm off again. It seems impossible.'

'It is impossible, when you're in the middle of it,' said Nick. 'Don't try and do what I did, and shove all your grief behind an iron curtain. It won't work. Once it's been triggered, it has to be acknowledged—'

'And accepted,' Sophie interrupted, 'before you can hope to watch your thoughts more dispassionately.'

'But I thought . . . this is where I get stuck. I don't understand when to watch the thoughts – or not. I mean, imagine telling the poor victims of the tsunami to *watch their thoughts*.'

'Believe me, Rachel, I *know* what you're talking about,' Nick said. 'I battled with that dilemma for years, until I met Sophie, and she taught me to stop denying my feelings—'

Sophie smiled. 'Not just any old feelings. Otherwise we just become a self-indulgent, pain-in-the-arse, foisting our dramatic egos on anyone who happens to be available.'

'But how do we know the difference?' Rachel stopped eating. 'I mean, I can hardly compare being jilted with losing a family and home, can I?'

'It's all relative; and different for everyone,' Sophie said. 'I think it depends on how much the issue is affecting our ability to live our lives. Some people might need a good bawl, others may need years of grieving.'

Rachel sighed and sat back, replete. 'I've done quite a lot of bawling.'

'Feel free to do some more,' Nick said. 'You're amongst friends.'

'I tell you what would help,' Rachel said, 'a slice of that great big apple pie lurking in the kitchen. With, maybe, a little cream.'

'Sounds like a good remedy for—' Nick began, and was interrupted by a loud knocking at the door.

'Heavens,' said Sophie. 'A smuggler perhaps?'

Nick got up and ran downstairs. 'My goodness,' he called. 'Look what the tide's washed up. It's Kyp and Evie and the Water Babies.'

Rachel could hear big Kyp panting up the stairs. He beamed into the room looking larger than ever. Evie followed behind, her raw-boned face was tanned, her cropped hair sun-bleached. Nick carried little giggling Mila, and Jack hurled himself down beside Commie on the rug.

'I didn't think you were coming back just yet,' Sophie cried, hugging everyone.

'Well, we were missing you good people, can't think why,' Kyp said, inspecting the remains of their lunch. 'Food all gone? Can I have this chicken leg?'

'Pig,' Evie said. 'Actually we were bored with Milos – all that sunshine, white sand and turquoise sea. We wanted to get back to the grey stuff – and press on with renovating Fair Wind.'

Nick unwound Mila's arms from his neck and went to fetch the apple pie. 'Think it will just about stretch to seven,' he said.

'It could feed most of Ventnor,' laughed Rachel.

'Or just Dad!' Jack yelled, and toppled Mila down on the rug with him. Commie got up, shook a front paw and retired to a safer spot on one of the sofas.

'Right, we want all the gossip,' Evie said, sitting down beside the cat, burying her face in his thick fur. 'Hello, Commie. We missed you.'

Sophie told them about her New Zealand trip with Nick, her

60

face exhilarated. Rachel followed with the glum news about the Italian Restaurant.

'No problem,' Kyp said. 'I'll be your Italian chef. Anything the Italians can cook, Kyp can cook better.'

'But you're Greek, Dad,' Jack said.

'I am aware of my ancestry, young man,' Kyp said. 'And as a chef I am second to none. If anyone glimpses me in your kitchen, Rachel, all they will see is an extraordinarily handsome profile, and dark hairy hands doing wondrous things with food.'

Rachel looked at Sophie, not knowing whether this was just a joke. Sophie smiled and raised an eyebrow.

'That's a great idea,' Evie said. 'You could easily do that, Kyp – until they find someone permanent.'

'But what about your fish restaurant?' Rachel said.

'Not opening until Easter. And as my good wife has just pointed out, you will have it all sorted by then.'

'But we couldn't pass you off as an authentic Italian, could we? I mean, doesn't that clash with the Trade Descriptions Act, or something?' Sophie said.

'One taste of my cuisine and they won't care if I'm from Outer Mongolia.' Kyp kissed his fingers.

Rachel found herself wondering if they could pull this off. A chuckle suddenly rose up in her throat and she started to laugh. It felt good – perhaps she'd done enough bawling.

*   *   *

Father Ryan pushed his plate of cold ham and potatoes away from him. Cold food, cold weather, even his cup of tea had gone cold. He almost wished he'd accepted Father Christopher's invitation to Sunday lunch; *his* table would have been heaped with hot food *and* alcoholic beverages. But then he didn't have a big appetite these days, and he'd have been the butt of Father Christopher's puerile jokes about being back in the dark ages of Catholicism. Father Christopher always wore casual clothes on a Sunday afternoon and behaved as if he were an ordinary man who didn't have to adhere to Catholic principles outside church walls. And wouldn't it be *Ryan this and Ryan that*, as if they were the best of friends and not Fathers of the Church at all?

But Father Ryan sometimes felt he'd be glad if nobody called him Father ever again. He was sick of the word. Sick and confused. He was sick of the word mother too.

Mothers, fathers . . . Our Father who art in heaven . . . Holy Mary, Mother of God. Brother was just as bad. Fathers, brothers, seminaries full of them. He thought briefly of his own father, stiff-backed, authoritarian. Was there any comfort to be had from fathers? He would have liked to call his father Daddy or Da like some of the other boys at school called theirs. But that wasn't allowed. Daddy, mammy, little sissy, were nice words, easy to feel something about. You couldn't touch a mother or a father – not even a brother. They were all special words, belonging to religious people. Untouchables. People called him Father too. But he couldn't relate to it. What did it mean that the people in this village – some of them much older than him – called him Father? How could he be a father to them?

He got up from the table and opened the back door to his garden, not much more than a square of rough grass with a path around it. In the centre stood a white plaster statue of the Madonna and Child. He breathed the dank air and looked up to the heavens. More grey clouds were piling up.

'Forgive me, Father, for I have sinned,' he intoned, wondering what kind of father he was invoking. Suddenly, a small bird plummeted out of the sky from nowhere and perched on the Madonna's head. It gave a few surprised cheeps, as if it hadn't quite meant to land there. Its little red breast barrelled over its stick legs. Father Ryan stared, transfixed. A strange feeling invaded his chest, as if the red glow and the white plaster ignited something inside him. And it occurred to him, that maybe he *was* a father – a real father of a real child. He didn't know what this meant, or what he should do. His limbs had a jittery energy coursing through them. He had to find out about Clare. What had happened to her? The times he'd thought of her, since she left, had been with a paralysing fear that she would come back and accuse him publicly of what he'd done. He could deny everything, of course. Her mother would be the first to believe him. He'd told her in secret that Clare had confessed the father of her child had been a foreigner, a casual fisherman long vanished. But if Clare took it in her head to accuse him herself, well, they could do tests these days, and he could be sent to prison. It would be the end of his priesthood.

The bird put its head on one side as if listening. It regarded Father Ryan with a black bead of an eye. And then it flew away, with a little whirr of wings, as if it knew exactly where it was going. Such freedom. How he wished *he* could do that. He clasped his aching head with his hands.

Prison! But wasn't he already in prison?

CHAPTER

Six

Clare felt someone shaking her shoulder. Kate was bending over her.

'Clare? Sorry to wake you, but if you want to get cleaned up and head off before it gets dark then you should get started.'

Clare didn't want to wake. Sleep blanked out everything in her mind. She wanted to stay unconscious, forever. But she couldn't – Kate was waiting. She struggled up and bent to put on her trainers, still feeling dizzy.

'Your name *is* Clare, isn't it?' Kate asked.

'Yes,' she responded automatically. Too late, she remembered she'd planned to call herself Tess. She was going to ask Rose to call her that. She thought it would be like making a fresh start. Rose and Tess. And it would make her harder to find, if anyone from home came searching for her. But now that had all changed. It would be the police looking for her.

'You weren't making much sense last night,' Kate said, handing her a glass of water. 'You said Tess at first, but then insisted you were Clare. Strange what a fever does to you.' She handed Clare the pack of tablets. 'Take one now, and one later – you should be over the worst by tomorrow morning.'

Clare obeyed, gulping down the whole glass of water. Her mouth was parched, she must smell awful. She looked at Kate apologetically. 'I'm sorry,' she said.

Kate gave a wry smile. 'Look. I know how rotten it is to feel ill away from home.' She picked up Clare's backpack. 'C'mon. I'll show you where the bath house is, and then it's up to you.'

Cold air hit Clare in the face as they left the caravan, making her gasp. It was raining, the wind blustery. Kate strode off across a field;

the lighthouse beam circled above their heads. Clare struggled to keep up, panic rising inside her.

'Are we going to the farm?' she called, wondering how she might be able to wrench her backpack from Kate and run.

Kate slowed down. 'Farm? No, just down to Wraith Cottage – Jane and Marguerite let us use their old outhouse to have baths. The showers in the caravans are a bit meagre. There's a washing machine there too.'

Clare could see the thatched roof of a long low cottage. It was surrounded by a garden, right at the edge of the cliff. They went down a path, through bushes and shrubs to a shack-like building at one end. Kate opened the door and pulled the light cord. There was a white bath and a sink and toilet. Kate switched on the wall heater.

'There's usually plenty of hot water. Have you got some soap and stuff? If not, there should be some in the cupboard. Jane and Marguerite keep it stocked up. Washing machine's behind that screen.' She put Clare's backpack on a wooden chair and pointed to a door. 'But don't go through there, otherwise you'll end up in their kitchen. Right, I'll leave you to it. Can you find your own way back? That's if you want to come back. If not, good luck.' She went out without waiting for an answer.

Clare ran the bath whilst turning out the contents of her backpack. She sorted out some knickers and socks and another grey tracksuit. The clothes were creased and not clean, but less stained than the ones she had on. Mother hardly ever did any washing in the abbey; it took ages to heat water over the fire. Clare wished she had a bra. She'd outgrown her own bras months ago. Mother should have got her one, especially for the breast-feeding. It was awful, walking around like this.

Her wash bag contained a soggy bar of soap and smelly flannel. She looked in the bathroom cupboard. There were several big plastic bottles of stuff in there. She poured bubble bath under the running taps, then stripped off, unplaited her hair, and stepped into the scented foam. It felt so good. She lowered herself into the hot water and lay with her eyes closed, feeling the pain in her breasts throb then ease. After a while she sat up and looked at them. They didn't seem so red and lumpy now, just huge and repulsive. Perhaps they would gradually go down. She raised her sore leg. Her shin was cut and bruised from her collision with the bucket.

She fitted the rubber shower spray onto the taps and washed her hair several times with the shampoo, which smelled of herbs. She began to feel better. If she could have a proper meal, maybe she could get her strength back and decide what she should do. She lay in the bath until the water began to cool, then reluctantly got out and dried herself on her towel, which was so damp and musty, she felt reluctant to use it on her clean body. She dressed, wiped the bath and emptied out the rest of her backpack.

She arranged her belongings into three piles. The first was her heap of dirty clothes and towel. Maybe she could put them in the washing machine; they'd be done in an hour or so, damp but at least clean. The second pile consisted of her toiletries, her brush and comb, and her diary and books. She opened her diary to check that the money Father Ryan had given her was still tucked inside. Thank goodness she had thought to do that. Her purse had been stolen out of her pocket on the boat from Ireland.

She took out the photo of her parents, with Clare as a baby, standing outside the house in Bantry Bay. Her da was big, her mam small. Da had red hair. He was from Scotland, a fisherman. He drowned when Clare was little. That's what Mam told her. Years later, one of the kids at school said it was a lie; he'd run off with a bad woman, his mam said so. Clare knew that was impossible. He would never have left her. Clare rushed to tell Mam. Mam turned white with rage and told Clare never to mention Da again. Clare had gone to find Father Ryan. He said he wouldn't lie to her, it was true – her father had committed mortal sin. Clare cried and he comforted her and told her she must be a good Catholic girl and obey her mother, and himself, so that the sins of her father wouldn't be handed down.

Clare stared at the picture, then put it back in her diary. She picked up her tattered copy of *Tess of the d'Urbervilles* – the book she'd been reading before all this happened. She liked reading – it helped her forget things for a while, and quietened the worms. She flicked through the pages. She used to think about Tess all the time; even spoke to her – inside her head – like an imaginary friend. That was before she met Rose. But Rose had gone, and Tess was her only friend now. She placed the book back on the pile, along with her bible with the mother-of-pearl cover that she'd been given at her confirmation.

She started to sort through the third bundle. There was a tiny dress and jacket, a pair of mittens and boots, all made with Mother's knotty pink wool. Clare imagined she could hear the clicking of Mother's knitting needles as she sat in front of the smoky wood fire in the annexe of the vast empty abbey. While Mother knitted, Clare heated barley soup over the flames and spread jam on stale crackers for their meals. A grubby white prayer book was folded inside the clothes, and a yellowed bone teething ring with a tarnished silver bell, which had belonged to Mother's little brother, who'd died of diphtheria. She looked at the things blankly, as if they had nothing to do with her. But she would have to carry them with her, for now. There were some plastic carrier bags hanging on a hook on the back of the door. She put the baby's things into one and pressed the bag into the bottom of her backpack. Then she took it out again and added the photo out of her diary. And then, as an afterthought, her bible. It couldn't help her anymore.

She bundled all her dirty things into the washing machine and scooped in some powder from a big plastic container which stood on a shelf. Surely those women, Jane and Marguerite, didn't supply all this for free. There were no notices pinned up about prices. She would have to remember to leave some money. She watched as the machine began its cycle, the revolving clothes mesmerised her. She felt as if her mind was going round, and wished she could wash away all her thoughts so easily. She'd have to come back later and collect her clothes. Tonight, she would ask Kate if she could pay for some food, and she would try to act as if she were a normal girl – until they came for her.

*   *   *

Rachel parked her car on the esplanade and leaned for a while on the

67

railing, watching the lamp-lit waves stretching themselves on the sand. She hadn't meant to stay out so late, but her visit to Sophie and Nick had developed into quite a party after Kyp and Evie and the kids arrived. She'd listened to the travellers' tales, eaten too much, and they'd tossed ideas around about the restaurant. And best of all she'd laughed until she had almost wet her knickers. It felt so good to be laughing again. She would get through this heartache of hers. Sophie and Nick were right – grief and suffering shouldn't be denied, or glossed over. They needed to be safely expressed. But how fascinating to be open to the idea that human angst was only a small part of a much greater reality. Sophie and Nick seemed to be piecing together the two halves of the equation. Sophie had so much experience of dealing with unimaginably traumatised people, and had felt frozen by it. Whereas Nick had attempted a spiritual quest, whilst ignoring his own blocked-out pain. They'd defined each other's philosophies. Rachel's; *there but for the grace of God.* Nick's; *are we not more than this?* And Sophie's; *our holiness is held in trust, while we wear out the old shoe of ego.*

'Great stuff,' Rachel said, as she walked round to the back entrance of her flat. The boys were out, there were no lights on. She felt for her key with its little torch attached, before climbing the stairs. Suddenly, the hairs on her body stood up on end. A man stepped out of the shadows beneath the stairway.

'Know a bloke called Sandro?' he demanded.

Rachel stood, silent. She could hardly see him. He was dressed in a dark hooded coat. She briefly wondered if it was the same man who was looking up at her flat that morning.

'Sandro. Know him?'

Rachel shook her head.

'Who was that looking out the window this morning then?'

'My son. Not that it's any of your business,' Rachel said. 'He's inside now, if you want to speak to him.'

The man glanced up at the flat. 'Sitting in the dark is he? Where's Sandro?'

'I have no idea. And I wouldn't tell *you* if I did.'

The man shuffled his feet and sank his chin down behind his zipped up collar. 'Look, lady. I've got no argument with you – just want to talk to the bloke, that's all.'

'Well, let me know if you find him. I'd quite like to talk to him myself.' Rachel felt angry. She switched on her torch and shone it in the man's face. He flinched, turned and hurried away. Rachel ran up the stairs and let herself into her flat, panting. Her knees felt weak. 'Oh, Sandro,' she said aloud, 'what have you been up to?'.

*   *   *

Fran wiped the grime from the old radio and plugged it in. She worked her way through the stations attempting to tune it to something recognisable. It was very crackly, probably full of dust on the inside too. She listened intently, but she didn't hear any news reports about a missing baby, kidnapped, abandoned, or lost. Not a word – even on the Isle of Wight station. She hadn't found anything in the newspaper either.

She sat down at the table, ate a corned beef sandwich and drank a mug of tea. She'd be losing weight if she carried on rushing about like this, forgetting to eat anything. She sighed and looked around her. The kitchen looked cleaner and tidier than it had done for years. The baby's next feed was ready in the fridge for when he woke. Sam's feed, she thought. Cinders and Sugar were curled up in their usual place in front of the Aga. Beauty was recovering, bedded in fresh straw and eating well. The lovely-dovelies were in their cote, the biddies clucking contentedly in the barn. She knew she should be feeling bad, very bad indeed. But she didn't, she felt calm and contented. Even though she knew this experience could only be a brief episode in her life, she was relishing it.

She got up, put the video of *The Nutcracker* in the player, lifted Sam out of the basket and sat back in the armchair. Sam was sleeping soundly; he had a tiny white blister on his top lip where he'd been sucking so avidly. 'I've got some wonderful stories to tell you,' she whispered to him.

*   *   *

Clare was dismayed to find the caravan empty when she returned from her bath. She'd been hoping Kate would be in, so she could ask about paying for some food and another night's lodging. She looked out of the window. It was raining, water trickled off the roof into a muddy puddle. No bright bonfire lit up the area this evening. There were some lights on in the biggest caravan, but no sign of movement, no music playing. Perhaps everyone had gone out somewhere to eat. Or perhaps they'd sneaked away to fetch the police; someone must have discovered the baby's body by now. She explored the little kitchen. There was no food in the cupboards and even if there was, she wouldn't have dared take anything without permission. She sat down on the bunk, shivering. It was warmer in the caravan now, but her hair was wet, she could feel it dampening the back of her tracksuit top. Her mam always used to dry her hair for her when she was little. She used to brush it until it shone, and then she'd plait it tightly to stop Clare being vain. But Clare knew Mam liked it – she'd have a little smile on her face, and sometimes she would stand Clare in the sunlight to *bring out the colour*. It was nice when Mam smiled. Clare felt lonely thinking about her home. She wished she could make things better so that Mam would forgive her. But how could she?

There was a sudden roar of sound outside. She jumped up. This was it! She went to stand by the door, shaking, but relieved that it was almost over. Then the noise stopped and she could hear voices and laughter. It wasn't the police, not yet. The voices faded and she heard doors opening and shutting. Tentatively, she went outside. A huge motorbike was parked in front of the big caravan, more lights were being switched on and music started playing. She wrapped her arms across her body and stood watching. The door opened again, and Kate came out and dumped a bag of rubbish in a bin. She looked up and saw Clare.

'Hi there. Thought you'd gone.'

Clare attempted a smile. 'I . . . I wondered if—'

'Sorry, can't hear you in this wind. Come inside and join us?'

Clare nodded gratefully and followed Kate inside. This caravan was bright and warm, more modern than Kate's. Some kids were opening huge cardboard cartons containing pizzas. They smelled delicious; Clare's mouth filled with saliva. She looked at Kate, feeling her face flush with embarrassment.

'Can I have a wee bit – if I pay?'

Kate grinned. 'Course. We always buy far too much – we're all pigs here. Help yourself.' She waved a large knife at the others. 'Patrick, Aidan, Billy, Jules – meet Clare.'

'You look a bit better than last night.' Patrick grinned at her.

'He was the one that caught you as you fell,' Kate remarked, hacking large slices of pizza and handing one to Clare on a piece of kitchen paper.

'Likes to play knight-in-shining-armour,' the younger boy with the spiky light hair commented. Aidan, Clare thought, trying hard to remember their names. Her attention was riveted on the slice of pizza she was holding.

'Thanks,' she murmured, sitting down at the bench beside the table, taking a bite. Cheese and tomato had never tasted so good before. She wanted to cram it into her mouth without having to talk. She tried to restrain herself. Her mam always told her she mustn't start eating before everyone was ready. Kate was filling plastic cups from a giant bottle of lemonade. Clare gulped some down and hiccoughed loudly. The others laughed.

'You must be starving,' Patrick commented. 'Take it easy.'

Clare felt mortified, but the others didn't seem bothered by her bad manners. They carried on talking and joking as if she were one of them. She sat quietly, eating and drinking, observing. This caravan had electricity, there was a glowing heater, and a rock band was playing on a small television. Jules was fiddling with Billy's dreadlocks while he rolled straggly tobacco into thin cigarettes.

Clare became aware that Patrick was watching her.

'I remember you vaguely from last summer – that hair,' he said. 'You made friends with Rose on the boat from Ireland, didn't you? And then we gave you a lift. Hereford, wasn't it? Or Worcester?'

Clare recalled her confusion when she'd realised the address of the Convent of the Poor Clares had been in her stolen purse. She was quite certain that she remembered it correctly, but when they arrived, there was no sign of a convent, just a group of new houses. Patrick and Rose had dropped her outside a police station to ask directions. They were going to wait for her, but Clare assured them she would be fine. After they'd driven away, she walked to a bus station and talked to an old woman sitting there who said that Hereford and Worcester were often lumped together. *I think the place you want is in Worcester, my dear. That's the only convent I can think of that has those strict nuns. An old abbey, it is.*

'Hereford,' Clare mumbled to Patrick, her mouth full.

Patrick smiled. 'Sorry, you're eating. Pity you missed Rose. But if you hang around here she might be back soon. I'm waiting to hear from her.'

'How soon?' Clare managed to say. Yesterday, before she left the baby, that news would have filled her with joy, but now it caused a spasm of anxiety. What if Rose should appear and start to question her? What would she say? Would Rose understand, or take her to the police?

'A few weeks, maybe,' Patrick said.

'Poor bruv,' said Aidan. 'Lovesick?'

'Rose is nice,' commented Billy, who was now sprawled in front of the television. 'I fancy her myself.'

'Out of your league, man,' Jules swished her blonde pony tail. 'She's a posh bird. Anyway, she's Patrick's.' She got up from the table, tugged at her short denim skirt and slumped down beside Billy, who immediately tried to roll on top of her. 'Get off, I want to watch Robbie Williams,' she said, shoving him.

'Rose is her own person,' Patrick said, firmly, pushing the pizza box towards Clare. 'So, what have you been doing since then? You obviously haven't been in contact with Rose, and it seems an odd time to turn up here – most students come for the summer.'

Clare realised they assumed she was a student. She must look older than she thought. 'I've been travelling around,' she said.

'Lucky you,' said Aidan. 'That's what I want to do, have a gap year and just go off.'

Clare folded her arms across her chest. She was worried that her breasts might start to leak, they felt so full. She had put on two sweatshirts to try and soak it up. Suddenly, Aidan reached out a hand to her. Clare went rigid and tried not to flinch. Aidan gently touched her hair and then took his hand away.

'Great hair,' he commented. 'Have you just washed it?'

Clare nodded, her heart pounding.

'Red hair and green eyes,' he said.

'You shouldn't go outside again until it's dry – won't do your sore throat any good,' Kate said. She re-filled Clare's cup with lemonade. 'So, have you decided what you're going to do?'

Clare shook her head, wishing they would leave her alone. She knew she could eat all the remaining pizza in the boxes. This was the first time she'd felt truly hungry since she had the baby. They all seemed to be looking at her. Oh, Blessed Mary, at any moment the police could arrive. What would they think of her then? 'I, er, wondered if I could stay – just one more night?'

'No worries,' Kate said. 'It's nice having another girl around.'

'Sure is,' Jules called, still trying to disentangle herself from Billy.

'I can pay,' Clare added, hurriedly.

'We can sort that out in the morning.' Kate yawned. 'I'll take you down to meet Jane – she deals with all the rent and stuff.'

'Rose should have let you know she was going away,' Aidan said, frowning. 'Some friend, getting you all the way here for nothing. Are you from Ireland? Are you a Catholic? My mum's ex-boyfriend was a Catholic – and my dad.'

'She might have tried to contact me,' Clare said, swallowing hard, trying to find her way through this barrage. 'I haven't been home for a while.' She suddenly felt like crying. 'It wasn't Rose's fault.'

She didn't want them to think badly of Rose. Rose was always kind. Clare pictured her concerned face. *Are you pregnant?* she'd whispered, after witnessing Clare's continuous retching and nausea on

73

the calm crossing. Clare felt unable to lie to Rose; there was something so open about her. *I know where you can get help,* Rose continued. *You don't have to go through with this. Things are different in England.* That's when she wrote down the directions to this place on the Isle of Wight. *This is where I'll be . . . in a few weeks . . . there's something I have to do first.*

'Clare? You'd better have another of those pills I gave you. You're still looking pretty crook.' Kate was talking to her. 'Clare?'

Clare nodded, miserably.

'We'll take you to see Marguerite tomorrow,' Patrick said. 'She'll soon have you feeling better.'

Marguerite – that name again. Clare wondered what had passed between them in her confused state last night. 'Did . . . Marguerite say anything about . . . what was wrong with me?' she asked.

Patrick smiled, his face looked kind. 'Marguerite? No, she doesn't speak – well, only with sign language – she's deaf.'

Kate got up, opened a drawer and took out a hair dryer. 'Look,' she said. 'Let's dry you off, and get you back to bed. You'll feel better after a good night's sleep.'

Patrick got up too. 'Right, kiddo,' he said to Aidan. 'I'm going to run you home. School tomorrow.' They began pulling on their motorbike leathers. 'See you guys in the morning,' he said as they went out. 'Early start – lots of painting to get on with.' He smiled at Clare. 'Don't worry, you'll pull through.'

Clare shuddered as Kate lifted her hair. How could she pull through? There was nothing to hold onto.

* * *

Father Ryan rose from his knees and slid between the cold sheets, glad that another Sunday was over. He lay shivering, rubbing his frozen feet together. He had never known the warmth of another human body in bed. At least, not since he was a child, and Jeannie got into the habit of crawling into his bed for a cuddle. She would wriggle her soft arms inside his pyjamas to get warm and they would lie there, listening to the bitter fights that went on downstairs.

There had been plenty of bed-sharing at the seminary. Music was played loudly in the dormitories to drown the cries of the orgasms, and the men took it in turns to act as lookouts. Not all the seminarians were involved, of course, and neither was he. Men and boys had no appeal for him. But he never wanted to fantasize about women either. At least not grown-up women that had no innocence about them. They seemed to lose that beautiful quality when they embarked on adolescence. They grew powerful then, and everything was reversed. They looked at you with a kind of mockery, as if they possessed a secret knowledge that could ensnare a man and make him weak and dependent.

Father Ryan pounded his pillow, trying to find a soft place for his head. The trouble with celibacy was that it ruled out the possibility of intimate human contact. He didn't want to hug his parishioners, like some of the more liberal clergy did these days. Neither did he want to cuddle their babies. Holding them at baptisms, dribbling and wailing over the font, was about as much as he could tolerate. He thought longingly of Jeannie. She'd had such a trusting nature, she believed everything he told her, would do anything he asked. They had a special bond. He supposed it was to do with a shared apprehension of the unpredictability of the mood of their parents. He recognised that quality in some of the girls that he picked for the choir. It was a reticence that usually responded quickly to any gesture on his part to make them feel special in some way. It was something small to begin with – a little gift perhaps, joking with them not to tell the others. So harmless, the children enjoyed it, he watched them blossom. There was a new girl, Maria; very shy, he was just beginning to win her over. He could sense her loneliness. He knew she didn't get the love she needed at home. He loved to touch her and draw her to him. *Suffer the little children to come unto me.*

It was only Clare that had posed a problem. She'd reminded him so much of Jeannie. And he'd let it go on for too long.

CHAPTER

Seven

Fran battled to close the barn doors as the rain swept in a horizontal gust through the yard. She stood for a moment feeling the icy needles pricking her cheeks. It was so invigorating, this weather. Couldn't understand why people moaned about January. This was just as it should be. And there was the contrast of the warm kitchen to enjoy. She looked around for Cinders, hooked a finger and thumb in her mouth and whistled. Cinders came panting and bedraggled from around the side of the house, her whole body wagging itself with delight. Fran laughed, maybe only her dog could understand how she felt. She opened the kitchen door, kicked off her wet boots and gave Cinders a rub with a towel. The dog headed for the Aga, stepping over Sugar who hissed a protest. Fran went over to the armchair to look at Sam in his basket.

'Are you still asleep, my lamb?' she whispered, and gently laid a hand on his soft hair. She couldn't believe how little trouble he was; much less demanding than her animals. Now that she could feed him properly, he just slept and woke when he was hungry. She rather wished he would wake more often so she could play with him. Perhaps he had some catching up to do after his ordeal. She wondered again exactly what he had been through. But if she started to think those thoughts, she would have to question what she was doing, and that seemed an impossible task. She would just have to let things take their natural course.

She looked around the kitchen. Last night she slept in the armchair so she could watch over Sam. She hadn't got much sleep; she seemed to be listening to every breath he took. And he had only woken twice, drunk his milk and gone straight back to sleep. She wondered what to do. The kitchen was the only warm room in the house, but she couldn't keep sleeping in the armchair – her back was already suffering. And she was beginning to feel a bit disorientated, losing track of time. She looked at the calendar pinned on the backhouse door. It was Monday, the thirty-first of January. Well, her life had certainly changed in the last couple of days. She yawned, her eyes watering. Maybe she could put a heater in her bedroom and take Sam up there with her tonight.

Fran climbed the creaky wooden stairs, noticing how threadbare the red carpet was becoming. It was worn thin along the length of the landing too. She opened the door to her bedroom, the smallest of all the rooms, just big enough for her brass bedstead, a mahogany wardrobe and chest of drawers. The walls were covered with faded Degas prints of dancers, tying on their satin shoes. She had slept here since she was born, not wanting to change for a larger room because of the particular way the west wind prowled around this corner of the house. Her childish imagination believed she could hear voices in that sound. She would burrow under the bedclothes, fascinated and terrified. She smiled and shivered. But it was cold in here, too cold for a tiny baby.

She went along the landing, peering in at the other rooms. Her parents' – much larger, the furniture covered with dustsheets. Phillip's – still containing his boyhood trophies, crashed balsa wood planes in mangled heaps on the floor, some still hanging by their threads from the ceiling, supported by cobwebs. The bathroom looked as if it were about to disintegrate – the brittle brown lino cracking under the huge clawed-feet of the bath, white tiles with their glazing crazed, khaki runnels under each green-coated brass tap. Goodness knows what would happen if she attempted to turn anything on. Just as well there was another bathroom downstairs. The box room was stacked to the ceiling with crates left behind by Phillip when he'd emigrated. It was as if he tried to slough off his past life, but had not quite managed to destroy it completely. She didn't know what should be done with his stuff. It was probably full of nesting mice and moths. A heater – that was what she was looking for. Perhaps the guest room. It was at the other end of the landing, the biggest room with the best view of the sea and the lighthouse. Not that they'd ever had many relatives to stay. But after Fran's father died, her mother had let this room as a family bed and breakfast, to earn some extra money. Very popular it was too. Fran and Phillip had to be quiet in the mornings and eat in the kitchen. They sometimes peeped in at the guests, who were eating bacon and eggs and sausages off the willow pattern plates, on the oak table in the dining room.

Fran hadn't thought about that for ages, she didn't dwell on the past. *A woman who lived for the moment*, Ted said. She laughed, Ted was right; parts of this house hadn't seen the light of day for years. She didn't need all these rooms. But she couldn't think about letting it go and moving to a plastic bungalow. So she'd shut it off and forgotten about it.

She pushed open the door of the guest room, which gave an agonised squeal. Fran stopped, surprise catching her breath. It struck her that this was a beautiful room. A blue patterned carpet covered the sloping floor, leaving a wide border of mellowed oak boards. The bed was a huge four poster with carved black posts and tea-rose curtains. The mattress was covered with yellowing sheets; the furniture antique, ornate. Fran wandered around the room, wiping a finger over the dusty surfaces. Behind a curtained corner was a wash-stand, and in the walk-in dressing room were stored two folding single beds, and a dismantled wooden cot.

Fran's mind was tumbling over itself with ideas. Her heart was beating fast. She leaned on a window sill and hummed a few bars from *Giselle* to calm herself, then rubbed at the glass with her sleeve. The rain had stopped; a pale shaft of sun was highlighting a patch of grey sea turning it silver. She heard a panting sound and a scrabble of claws. Cinders appeared at the door and stopped, looking at her expectantly.

'This is what we'll do, Cinders,' Fran said.

*   *   *

Rachel stood in the café staring at the phone, waiting for the answering machine to finish recording another inquiry about Valentine's weekend. Valentine's Day fell on a Monday this year, so she and Sophie and Sandro, had decided to make the whole weekend a romantic celebration, and use it to launch *Sandro's Italian Restaurant*. Now minus the *Sandro*.

'We're going to have to make a decision,' Sophie said, scratching her head with a screwdriver.

'I know. We can't go on ignoring the calls. We should cancel all the Valentine's bookings—'

'Unless we take Kyp's offer seriously.' Sophie dropped the screwdriver into the toolbox. 'Help me turn this table over. We need to sit down and talk.'

The mosaic tables were heavy, but they looked beautiful, little cubes of turquoise and sea green and white, swirling and glinting in the morning light. Rachel sat down and ran her hand over the surface. Sophie was watching her. Even though they were in this together, Rachel sensed that Sophie was waiting for her to take the lead, respecting the fact that the café was Rachel's livelihood.

'Right.' Rachel took a deep breath. She felt so unsure, so reluctant to pull out of this venture, but so fearful of failing and disappointing Sophie – not to mention the financial loss. Sophie waited, her dark eyes unblinking. Rachel suddenly sensed an energy coming from her. It was as if she could feel Sophie's positivity radiating – and it was just raring to take a risk without minding the consequences. Rachel felt a smile stretching her mouth. 'You want to go for it, don't you?'

Sophie grinned, and nodded vigorously, stray curls jiggling around her neck. Rachel leaned back precariously in one of the new wrought iron chairs.

'Okay. Let's do it.'

'Yes!' Sophie leaped up and jumped up and down a few times, arms in the air. 'We can do it, I know we can. I have such good feelings about this.' She gave Rachel a resounding kiss on the cheek and sat down again. 'We've got two weeks. We'll have a practise run. A proper evening – arranged with Kyp. Nick's up for it, and we can coerce Patrick and Aidan. And we can drag in Jill and Ash, Jane, Chas and Marguerite, and anyone else we can bribe to be our customers.'

Rachel laughed. 'You had this all worked out, didn't you?'

'Nick and I have been plotting. But we didn't want to put pressure on you.'

'Then we'd better make a shopping list.' Rachel took a pad and pencil out of her pocket. 'And we'll start answering the phone again.'

'Okay. We could get the supplies this afternoon.'

79

'Actually, I'm having my hair done, and then I was going to Shanklin—'

'Oh, Rachel,' Sophie reached across the table to grasp her hand. 'Is that wise?'

'I just want to ask once more, that's all. If nobody knows anything, then I'll call it a day. Sandro's gone and that's that.'

Sophie nodded. 'Would you like me to come with you?'

'No, spend some time with your Nick – we'll sort out the food tomorrow.'

Sophie looked pensive. 'I can understand how you feel. Nick and I had to finalise a lot of things before we could truly move forward.'

'But yours was serious stuff – death and betrayal. I don't know how you got through.'

'Nick is special.'

'Don't underestimate yourself, Sophie—'

'But he has this spiritual thing – he seems to be able to come at life from a different perspective.'

'But how does that work in a *gotta-earn-money-eat-wash-socks* sort of way?'

'It's actually quite down to earth – being present with what *is*, instead of living, mentally, in the future or past. I'm so intrigued by his philosophy. Sometimes I think we're stuck as a human race. Or, maybe evolution is just so slow it's hardly discernible.'

'Going backwards, I would say.'

Sophie grinned. 'I think what we were both ready for is the understanding that nothing can be held onto, nothing stays the same. Or, as Nick says, *beware, all physical structures are destined to crumble.*'

'Sounds sad.' Rachel felt a sudden emptiness yawning, like a void, inside her.

Sophie squeezed her hand. 'We're living in this unstable place – the land slips and slides, the cliffs fall, even the houses creep about. I don't know – everything changes right in front of you – even our minds – from moment to moment.' Her voice felt soothing to Rachel, quiet and calm. 'But accepting it makes life easier. It's simpler than fighting against it; and it makes room for something else.'

'For what?'

Sophie shrugged. 'What we were talking about yesterday, I suppose. The peace that lies within, undisturbed by the mad plans of the ego.'

'I could do with some of that. But I need to let go of Sandro first, and then maybe I—'

They both jumped as someone rattled the handle on the door. It was Jill, stamping her feet outside like a Spanish dancer. Sophie let her in.

'Can't stay,' she said looking round. 'Looks great in here.' She rubbed her hands together and blew on her fingers. 'I'm perished. Just got back from Ryde – shopping.' She pulled up a chair and sat down. 'You'll never guess who I saw.' She looked from one to the other, eyes wide. 'I was sitting in a café, when across the road there he was – just disappearing into a bar.'

'Who?' Rachel and Sophie spoke together.

'Sandro.'

Rachel felt heat rush into her face. He was still on the island then. Unless Jill was mistaken.

'By the time I dashed outside, and nearly got myself run over, he'd vanished. I went into the bar but there was no sign of him. I hung about a bit – in case he was in the loo. But nothing.'

'My God,' Rachel said, feeling as if she'd been winded. 'Are you absolutely certain it was him?'

'Positive. But look, if he wasn't in the loo, where was he?'

'What do you mean?' Sophie said.

'Well, he could only have gone behind the bar, or out the back somewhere. So – he must work there.' She got up. 'Have to go, got a client coming. Fancy a Monday night out? We could pay a visit to Ryde this evening and see if we can track the bugger down.' She grabbed her bag and headed for the door. 'Phone me,' she called out.

Rachel sighed. 'Inner peace will have to wait.'

*   *   *

Clare stuck her hand inside the washing machine and felt around to check. But it was obviously empty. She searched the laundry area, and went back into the bathroom – no basket of clothes anywhere. Had someone crept in and stolen them during the night? She stood, biting her nails, trying to calm the panic rising in her chest. She'd put everything in the machine, except the things she was wearing.

She would have to go and find Kate and ask her. But she wanted to leave while the others were working. She'd woken late, feeling better, and found a note propped against a box of cornflakes saying Kate would be working in the stable block. Clare planned to collect her clothes, leave some money and go. Now, she realised, she'd left her backpack in the caravan with her money in it. If there was a thief about . . .

The door opened. A woman with dark bobbed hair stood there, smiling.

'Are you Clare? I'm Jane. I expect you're looking for your clothes. Someone else wanted to use the machine, so I hung yours up in my kitchen to dry.' She held the door open. 'Come through and collect them.'

Clare tried to smile, feeling her mouth quiver with nervousness. Was this a trap? Had they taken her clothes last night so she couldn't escape? Were the police waiting in there? Jane was looking at her, expectantly. Clare had no choice but to follow her through the door.

She found herself in a low, beamed kitchen. It was hot and smelled of baking. A big black range was against one wall, just like the one her mam had at home which was hardly ever lit. A wooden clothes rack was suspended above it, on which Clare's clothes were hanging.

'They're all dry.' Jane lowered the rack and began lifting off the socks and knickers, piling them on the table. 'Here, I expect you'd prefer to fold them yourself.'

Clare grabbed her towel. 'Thank you,' she muttered, feeling her face turning red with embarrassment at the sight of her socks with holes in them, and the baggy navy school knickers that she had stretched to fit over her belly.

'Cup of tea?' Jane asked, lifting an iron kettle off the stove.

'Well, I, I have to go soon,' Clare stammered.

'Have one before you set off – it's cold out there.' She looked

Clare up and down. 'Goodness, you look too young to be travelling around alone. Or is it me getting old?' She filled a big brown teapot and set it on the long wooden table, next to a plate of scones. 'Marguerite baked these this morning – they're good.' She picked one off the pile and cut into it, spreading it with butter. She held it out to Clare. 'Come and be bad with me.' She patted her hips. 'Shouldn't, but can't resist. You'll make me feel less guilty.'

Clare felt she could eat the whole pile. She reached for the scone. 'Thank you,' she murmured, sitting down.

Jane sat opposite her. Clare watched her eating. She was about Mam's age, but her face looked soft, as if she cared about keeping it smooth. Her hair was shining under the light, dark brown like her eyes. Clare didn't know what to say. She glanced around the cottage. What a strange place. It was so untidy, books and papers were piled everywhere and the shelves heaped with seashells. She looked up at the beams and the weird driftwood shapes that hung from them. Her mam would have all that junk cleared out in minutes. Clare's home was scrubbed, austere like the convent where Mam spent much of her time on her knees, praying or cleaning for the sisters. The only ornaments at home were the statues of the Blessed Virgin and the crucified Christ on the mantelshelves. The pictures on the walls were of Jesus exposing His bleeding heart, and the framed, cross-stitched bible texts that Mam had worked.

'Mess, isn't it?' Jane said. 'I'm an author, a novelist. This place has the right atmosphere for me to write. That's why I never disturb it.'

An author – Clare pictured murders and detectives. Jane might be looking for clues, trying to catch her out with questions. Perhaps she worked for a newspaper as well.

'So,' Jane said. 'Kate told me you came here looking for Rose.'

Clare nodded; her mouth full of scone.

'What a pity. She had an opportunity to go to Niger with Stephanie, her grandmother, who is a doctor. She treats girls and women who've had disastrous experiences, mainly with childbirth.'

Clare felt her face go red again. Why had Jane said that? She must know something. But Jane was calmly pouring mugs of tea.

83

'But if you're wanting some work, there's plenty here. My sister and I have ridiculous plans about restoring Wraith Cove Hotel, and its grounds, back to their former glory. We like to offer the work to youngsters and students, knowing how hard up they usually are.' She smiled. 'And my husband has a never ending supply of nephews and nieces and their friends. There aren't many of them here at the moment, they like the summer best. They're painting the stable block; it's too wet to do anything outside. Or, if you like gardening, you could do what Rose was doing – helping our gardener, Nick, catalogue all the old plants. It's a big task and he's missing Rose. We all are.'

Clare noticed a movement out of the corner of her eye. She looked towards the other end of the room. Logs burned brightly in a big fireplace and a black cat was lying on its back on the hearthrug, stretching its legs. Clare wanted to stroke its glossy tummy. She felt herself smiling slightly. It was very warm and cosy in here.

'That's Surfer,' Jane said. 'She was my aunt's cat – came with Wraith Cottage.'

'She's nice.' Clare tried to think of something else to say. But she wanted to avoid any talk of university and a gap year; she couldn't bluff her way through stuff she didn't understand. She'd simply met Rose on the boat last summer. Rose had befriended her, like Kate was doing now. Clare wondered if – in her loneliness and desperation – she'd made it too important. She attempted to speak, crumbs caught in her throat and she started to cough.

'Are you still feeling rough?' Jane sounded concerned.

Clare shook her head but couldn't prevent her eyes filling with tears.

'Oh, dear. And here I am pestering you with questions. Why don't you go and have a long soak in the bath?' She got up and finished folding Clare's clothes. 'Marguerite should be back by the time you've finished. She wants to see you.'

Clare looked around frantically. 'Where is she?'

'Marguerite? Oh, she's out fishing with Neptune.' Jane peered out of a little latticed window. 'You can just see them in the bay.' She laughed. 'Mad, the pair of them. But they catch good fish.'

Mad, Clare thought. Everything seemed mad to her. Neptune –

who or what was Neptune? Were these sisters witches or something?

'We're going away this afternoon, for about a week,' Jane said. 'She wanted to see you before we left.'

'What about?'

'Marguerite will tell you – in her own way. She has a gift of diagnosing health problems. I expect she wants to help you get better.'

Clare got up and grabbed her pile of clothes. 'I'll go back to the caravan and get my washing things, shall I?'

'Good idea.' Jane looked at her watch. 'She won't be back for at least an hour or so. Take your time – have a bath and then come and sit by the fire, if you like. There are plenty of books to read.'

Clare went outside and started to run back to the caravan, her sore breasts throbbed with the pressure of the milk, but not quite as painfully as yesterday. She gasped for breath, feeling unfit. She used to be able to run for ages. The rain had stopped, the weather was brighter. Clare didn't want that to happen. She liked the dark brooding clouds and mist. She felt more hidden. And other people kept their heads down and folded themselves inside their coats and scarves, without looking around. She could see the long stable block beyond the caravans where the others were working. She must get away quickly, before Marguerite came looking for her.

*   *   *

Fran stopped outside the house in Cowes and checked the address she'd copied down. She'd spotted the advertisement in *The County Press*. This was it. It was huge, glass fronted, looking towards The Solent. It must belong to a millionaire. There was a big yacht on a trailer in the drive, and a Mercedes parked outside a double garage. She took a deep breath.

'Look after Sam, Cinders,' she said. 'I won't be long.'

She knocked on the front door, suddenly conscious of her scruffy clothes. She tucked strands of hair back into its bunch. A young woman appeared around the side of the house wearing a red padded sailing jacket and green wellingtons.

'Yes?' she said, sharply.

'I've come about the advert,' Fran said, 'for the baby stuff. I phoned earlier.'

85

'Oh. You must have spoken to Nanny.' The woman looked annoyed, as if Fran had interrupted her at something important. 'You'd better come and look. It's all in the garage.' She took a device out of her pocket and one of the garage doors slid soundlessly open. Fran followed her inside. 'This is it,' the woman said, pulling back a sheet of plastic. 'Travel system, moses basket, and all the other stuff – practically unused. We're off abroad – not worth taking it all. Cheaper to buy it again out there.'

Fran looked at the piled equipment. She wondered if she should ask to inspect it – but if it was almost new . . .

'Travel system?' she ventured.

'You know, the buggy and car seat thingy – all-in-one contraption. I suppose you want to see it?' The woman glanced at her watch.

'Well, if you're sure it's all in good order . . . '

The woman looked relieved. 'I *am* sure. Look, to be honest with you, I'm pushed for time this afternoon, a million things to sort out. You can have the whole lot for a hundred, cash.' She pointed to two huge laundry bags. 'Boy or girl?'

'G . . . girl,' Fran said, cautiously. Poor Sam – he'd grow up confused if this carried on.

'Pity – there's loads of boy's winter clothes and stuff – won't be needing them where we're going.'

Darn it, Fran thought, missed out there.

'Can you take them, anyway?' the woman said impatiently. 'I expect some of the things will be suitable for a girl – they all wear dungarees these days. They'll only go to the charity shop.'

Fran pulled her money from her pocket and counted out a hundred pounds. Ted always paid his rent for Bleak Field in cash. The woman was hardly looking, as if the money wasn't important at all. She took the notes and stuffed them in her pocket as if they were loose change.

'Can you manage on your own?' she asked, already walking away. 'Only, the au pair's gone out.'

'I'll manage,' Fran said. She ran down the drive, backed up the Land Rover and piled everything in as fast as she could. There was no sign of the woman. Fran could have packed half the contents of the garage if she'd wanted to. She drove away fast, smiling. 'Well,' she said over her shoulder to Cinders. 'That was a bit of luck, wasn't it?'

*   *   *

Clare was walking to Ventnor. It hadn't seemed far on the bus, but now it felt like a very long way. The road was narrow, dangerous for a walker. Darkened by tall trees which dripped rain on her, and bordered with stone walls, there'd be nowhere to go if a car came too close. She passed gateposts at the head of drives leading to unseen houses, reminding her of Rocken Edge Farm. Her trainers were splitting, her heels sore. She felt weary, but at least she could put her hands in her pockets and it was so much lighter without having to carry . . . she shoved the thought deep down into the ball of bad things. She mustn't think about it. Not until she was forced to.

There didn't seem to be any clothes shops along the high street, but there were some charity shops, for lifeboats and animals and all. She went into each of them, looking at the clothes, holding things against herself, trying to gauge whether they would fit her. She found bras and pants, socks and tee-shirts, and jeans with a stretchy waistband. A few months ago she would have hated to wear second hand underwear, but now it seemed amazing that she could buy these things so cheaply. She discovered some big woollen jumpers and even a pair of decent black leather boots. There was a shop which sold sets of hats and gloves and scarves. She bought a black set – she needed to cover her hair. It would be easy to see, if people were looking for her. She kept her plait tucked inside her puffa jacket and pulled on the black hat.

In a newsagents, she bought some chocolate and read the front pages of the papers. There was nothing about her crime in the headlines. But she bought a paper in case it was inside. Now, if she could find a café, she could change into her new clothes in the toilet and then buy some hot food and decide what to do next. But she might have to take her hat and coat off if she got hot indoors – someone might spot her.

She walked down the steep hill to the sea front. The café that she'd looked in before – *Rachel's Café* – was still closed. She peered

87

through the window. There was nobody in there, no lights on. There was another café open further along. She bought a bag of chips and sat on a bench to eat them. They were cold and greasy, but she ate them all, ignoring the seagulls that stood watching. Next, she munched her way through the whole bar of chocolate. Mam wouldn't have allowed that at home. Clare watched a long ship, piled with containers, sail slowly across the sea. Where was it going? She imagined herself as a stowaway, crouched in a corner of the deck. Where would she end up? Maybe she could work on the ship and one day, when she was grown up, she could sail back to Ireland and go to see her mam. Would Mam be pleased to see her? Maybe, if lots of years had gone by . . . Clare took a deep breath and glanced through the newspaper – but there was no story in there.

She walked back up the hill to the high street and stopped outside a hairdressing salon. Perhaps she should get her hair cut short, like a boy. She looked through the window. There weren't many people inside. On an impulse she opened the door. The hot air smelled strongly of hairspray and perm solution. A girl was sitting at the reception desk writing in a book.

'How can I help you?' she said.

'Could you cut my hair?'

'Have you got an appointment?' The girl eyed her, curiously.

Clare shook her head. Another girl was styling a woman's hair. She looked up. 'I could fit you in, if you come back later. What exactly did you want?'

'I . . . er, just a cut.'

'Excuse me a moment,' the girl said to her client, and came over to Clare. 'When you say, *cut* . . . can you be a bit more specific?'

'A few inches.'

'Can I look – just so I know how much time to allow? We close early on Mondays. ' She lifted her hand as if she were going to remove Clare's hat. Clare grabbed at it in panic realising she hadn't thought this through. The three women were all staring at her as she backed out the door. 'I . . . I've changed my mind,' she said.

*   *   *

Rachel watched as the youngster went out. Slight concern nagged at her mind. The kid seemed extraordinarily pale and agitated. She'd be worried if Aidan came home looking like that.

'Weird,' the receptionist said, returning to her appointment book.

'Probably on drugs,' the hairdresser said, running her hands up the back of Rachel's head. 'This is going to really suit you, you know? It'll knock ten years off you.'

'I could do with some knocking off,' Rachel laughed.

'Couldn't we all,' the receptionist giggled.

Rachel sat back in the comfortable chair, enjoying the feeling of being pampered in the sweet-smelling salon. She'd already had a facial and manicure, and bought a beautiful skirt and jacket in *Rita's Boutique* in her favourite shade of faded blue. She was planning to wear it tonight for her trip to Ryde with Jill and Sophie. They had decided to make an evening of it and treat themselves to a meal, whilst trying to track down the elusive Sandro. *Even if we don't have his balls*, Jill said, *we'll make sure we have a bloody good time.* Rachel hoped Jill would leave the talking to her, *if* they confronted Sandro. *Don't worry*, Sophie reassured her. *Jill's a wise old bird under all that brash talk. She'll know when to back off. If she doesn't, I'll just have to flatten her.* Rachel smiled to herself, imagining gentle Sophie standing over a prostrate Jill.

She studied her transformed hair in the mirror as the hairdresser continued to tweak it. It was as good as a facelift – all those perky little ends flicked up behind her ears. She'd had that old swept-back bob for years. She found herself wondering if Sandro would like it.

*   *   *

'I have a child, Jeannie,' Father Ryan told his sister. He wanted to know how it felt to say the words aloud. Jeannie gaped at him, a long string of saliva drooled from her bottom lip. He took a tissue from the bedside table and wiped it away. He looked round the ward to make sure nobody was within earshot. 'At least, I might have,' he added. What if Clare *had* got rid of it? She could have done anything once she'd stepped off the boat onto foreign shores. Weren't Irish women tempted all the time now by the voice of the devil from overseas?

He patted his aching forehead with the wet tissue and studied Jeannie's face. Was the shape of her head the same as his? She had the same fine brown hair, which slipped forward easily, just like his. He pushed her hair back – her brow was high and smooth and white like his, too. Maybe it *was* hereditary; perhaps he was developing the same type of brain tumour that had struck her down as a girl. But hers had started when she was much younger – he remembered her having her first fit when she was preparing for her confirmation. He'd never had a fit. He'd better consult his medical book again.

He watched two nurses as they whipped the curtains round a bed on which a woman was thrashing in some kind of seizure. He felt no compassion, no desire to help, or even pray. Jeannie must sit in her chair and watch these incidents day after day. Did it depress her at all? What went on inside her head? Did she still possess the ability to think? Maybe it would have been better if she'd died. But she still had a soul, what was *it* doing? Surely, it must be pure, unsullied. Did it have a vantage point, an overview? Could it see inside his?

Jeannie appeared to be gazing at him, her dull eyes sunken in her thin pale face. He suddenly felt naked, exposed. What an empty sham of a man he had become. And he had the audacity to call himself a priest. He took hold of Jeannie's hand. She always responded to his touch. He felt the pressure of her fingers squeezing his.

'What should I do, Jeannie?' he whispered. 'Ought I to try and find this child and make reparation?' He felt confused in his mind, unsure whether he meant Clare, or the baby. He leant towards Jeannie to kiss her cheek and her head fell forward heavily so that their foreheads clashed. The hardness of bone on bone brought tears to his eyes. He gently propped her head back against the chair, she didn't appear to be hurt. The tears streamed down his cheeks and he felt as if a dam were inside him that might burst and flood the ward. He got up abruptly and left.

CHAPTER

Eight

'This always was a nice room,' Ted said. 'You must have given it a bit of elbow grease to get it looking like this. It's been a few years.'

Fran watched anxiously as he wandered around the bedroom, prodding the freshly made four-poster and running his hands over the polished furniture. She hoped he wouldn't leave finger marks, or drop bits of mud on the carpet from his boots. She grinned. This was new to her, this feeling of housewifely pride.

'Not like you, is it?' Ted commented. 'How long are they staying for then?' He stood staring at the cot.

Fran shrugged and hung a white towel next to the wash basin. 'They're going to be touring around – all over the place. They'll be coming and going, I should think. I told them it was silly staying in hotels when I've got all this room.'

'That was good of you, I reckon. Can't be easy having folk you've never met before to stay.'

'Well, they are relatives. Young Phil is my nephew, and Sam is my . . . er, great-nephew, I suppose.' Fran couldn't believe how easy she was finding it to make it up as she went along. She felt as if the old Fran were watching the new one with interest.

Ted shook a finger at her. 'Don't you go letting them take advantage, now. You could end up doing a lot of babysitting.'

That was just what Fran wanted to hear. 'I don't mind,' she said. 'Besides, it's unsettling for a baby to be travelling around all over the place.'

'Christ almighty, Fran. They've just carted the nipper half way round the flaming world.'

'I know, I know.' She grinned. 'But I'm enjoying myself. You know I'm a sucker for looking after young ones.'

'Animals are different,' Ted said. 'They aren't the same responsibility. And it's not like you've had kids of your own.' He chuckled. 'Wouldn't have minded trying though.'

Fran laughed. 'They're not so different. They all need feeding, cleaning and a warm safe place.' But Ted was right. It was different. The love that she felt for her animals was enormous, but Sam was arousing feelings in her that she never dreamed possible. She wanted to cry and laugh all at the same time when she held him, and she felt she could easily kill anyone who threatened him. He was sleeping now in his new pram, which she'd pushed into the backhouse when she heard Ted stamping his feet outside. She was hoping Sam wouldn't cry, but Ted probably wouldn't hear him anyway.

'Nice and warm in here, too,' Ted commented, looking around.

'I fired up the old boiler.'

'Have you gone mad? You could have blown the place up.'

'It was always serviced properly when Mum was alive.'

'That was years ago.' Ted shook his head. 'Coming down The Buddle for an early evening pint, then?'

'Won't, if you don't mind. I'm shattered after all that cleaning.'

'Go on. Do you good.'

'No, I need a bath and I'll put my feet up and watch TV.'

'Another of your ballets? Soppy old thing, you are.'

'Better than those miserable soaps people watch. Any . . . er, gossip, down the pub?'

'Gossip? About what?'

'I don't know. Anything happened in the village?'

'Didn't think you were interested in gossip. That's why I like to talk to you. You've got more about you.'

Fran suddenly felt sorry for him. She knew he was lonely by himself over at Blackgang since Janet died and Eddie left home. Normally she would have invited him to stay for a bite to eat. But not tonight. She faked a yawn.

'Best be going then,' Ted said. 'I'll look in tomorrow, bring you a nice cabbage.'

Fran thought guiltily of the last cabbage that was mouldering in the backhouse. She would have to start eating properly now, she needed to keep herself healthy. 'Good,' she said. 'I'll cook it with some chops – come over to supper and share it with me. Young Phil might be back by then . . . with Ann . . . and the baby.'

*   *   *

Clare changed her clothes in the public toilet. The bra was tight, but hopefully her breasts would shrink some more. She should have asked Kate if she had a tape measure, then she could have found out what size she needed.

Clare shuddered at the image it provoked. She'd got used to Father Ryan measuring her chest; her mam said she must do as he said. After a few weeks he started measuring and checking other parts of her body too. *You see, Clare, boys and girls both change here,* he said, passing the tape around the tops of her thighs. *But with girls it's more subtle – that's why I have to check thoroughly. There now, isn't that nice?* She still believed he did it to all the children. And there was something comforting about the way he put his arms around her, and a familiar smell. She couldn't quite remember what it was, but it made her want to lean against him. And he was always so pleased with her progress.

Clare caught a glimpse of herself in a shop window. In the jeans and dark jacket and hat, she could be mistaken for a boy. She had thrown her old clothes into a rubbish skip. She'd wandered all around the town, up and down the side streets. She'd bought a torch, and a pink plastic watch, and a guide book. She felt as if she were waiting for something to happen. Those women in the hairdressers had seemed a bit suspicious. Would they report her? But nothing happened; people were doing ordinary things, just living their lives, not noticing her at all. The shops were closing now, and it was getting dark. She didn't want to stay in Ventnor. There was a map in the guide book – she took the road to Shanklin.

Why was everything uphill? The second-hand boots were too big, rubbing her sore feet, and the tiredness was overwhelming her again. She sat on a wall and took another pair of socks out of her

93

backpack to pad out the boots. As she set off, she noticed a sign that pointed down a little lane to a church – a Catholic church. She stood, biting her nails. She knew she wasn't worthy to go inside. Mother had kept telling her she had to make a full confession first. But when Clare had begged to see a priest, Mother told her she was unworthy. It was so confusing. Maybe it had been Mother's way of telling her she had been cast out – excommunicated. But she needed to know. What if she were to go inside this church and find a priest to ask? She could say she was inquiring for a friend. Wouldn't that be better than walking around like this, cold and scared and full of badness? Even if she could never be forgiven, at least she'd know the worms would be inside her for ever. She would have to accept that.

She walked down the short lane and entered the stone porch, half-hoping the door would be locked. But it wasn't. The heavy iron handle turned and she stepped inside. It was dim and it took a while for her eyes to adjust. She could see the light switches but didn't want to turn them on. She hesitated before dipping her fingers in the holy water and crossing herself. She stood listening. It was so quiet. A tiny red light glowed on the altar and the spicy smell of incense hung in the air. She tiptoed around looking at the fourteen Stations of the Cross. She always liked the one where Our Lord met the women of Jerusalem who cared so much for him. She closed her eyes and absorbed the peace. It felt comforting, part of her life. She moved to the head of the aisle, genuflected briefly, then crept to a pew near the front and knelt down. She bent her head and clasped her hands in front of her face but no words formed in her mind. It seemed such a long time since she'd done this. But how could she even begin to pray? She'd never seen Mother pray at the abbey – she often used to disappear into one of the locked rooms off the corridor and Clare had thought there must be a passageway in there that connected with the main part of the abbey where the other nuns lived. That's where the priest must go, to give communion and hear their confessions. When Clare asked about this, Mother told her not to ask impertinent questions. Clare had tried to pray in her room, kneeling beneath the wooden crucifix nailed to the wall. But it was so cold and it was awkward when she grew big.

Clare remembered her rosary and took it out of her pocket. She tried running it through her fingers but her mouth wouldn't whisper the familiar *Hail Mary*. Perhaps she was being prevented by some unseen force, an angel of God, who stood between her and any connection with the Blessed Ones. Or maybe it was because she hadn't confessed. That could be it. She needed to see a priest before she could pray. Her knees were hurting; she rose and sat on the pew. Did the priest live near to the church, in a presbytery, like Father Ryan? She felt apprehensive. Maybe the priest would refuse to hear her. Perhaps he'd sense straight away that she had tempted another priest with her wickedness and almost brought him to ruin. It would be best to go. She needed to find somewhere to stay tonight, and it was a long way to Shanklin.

Clare heard the door creak open behind her. She stayed hunched in the pew hoping she wouldn't be seen in the gloom. The person stayed silent for ages. Was it the priest? She wondered if the lights would be turned on. Then she heard footsteps, coming down the aisle. A man walked past, up to the altar, and stood there with his head bowed, as if praying. He was wearing a long black overcoat with the collar turned up, like Father Ryan's. After a while he moved to one side, picked up a candle, lit it, and placed it in a holder. Clare saw him look around. She bent her head lower, but she knew he'd seen her. Was he the priest? She heard his footsteps come close.

'Scusi,' he said, hoarsely. 'You know where priest is?'

Clare looked up and shook her head. He wasn't wearing a white collar. He sat down beside her.

The man cleared his throat; she could smell garlic on his breath. 'You come here for confession? What time?'

'I . . .I don't know.' Clare slid back along the pew. He was too close. He looked scruffy and needed a shave. He stared at her, blinking his red-rimmed eyes. His nose was red too, as if he had a cold.

'You are a young lady, si? I thought you were a boy.'

Clare thought he sounded Italian, like one of the sisters that taught at her school.

'You live near?' he asked.

Clare shook her head. The man rubbed his hands over his face, then lifted his arm, indicating the church. 'Why you sit alone in dark?'

'I . . . was waiting for the priest.'

'Ah, you want confession too?'

Clare nodded and looked down at the rosary in her hands. She felt the man's gaze on her.

'Scusi. You are in trouble?'

Why had he asked her that? Clare wanted to get up and run, but didn't know what he might do.

'Always people who are troubled sit alone in dark church.' He sighed loudly. 'I am in trouble too.' He let out a harsh bark of laughter. 'It take one to know another. Isn't that how they say it?'

Clare looked at him with fresh interest. Was it possible there could be another person in trouble – wanting a priest, like her? But he was a grown-up. She nodded. 'Yes, I am . . . in trouble.'

'Mi dispiace.' The man nodded, turning the corners of his mouth down. 'Maybe we help each other.'

'How . . . how can we?'

'I want to leave here – this island. But first I have to get something – from a hotel. You could get it for me.' He turned his face away, coughing, his shoulders heaving. Clare waited until he turned back to her.

'Why can't you get it?'

'Because, someone there – a man – want to harm me.'

Clare didn't like the sound of this. She should tell him to go away. But she couldn't help asking. 'Why?'

'I do something bad . . . with his wife.'

'You want me to get something – from him?'

'No, no. I hide my papers – passport and things – behind the wardrobe in my room – and I forget them when I very quickly leave.'

Clare shook her head. 'I can't do that.'

'Per favore. I help you in return, si? Whatever you need . . . money?'

Clare thought about the money Father Ryan had given her. She'd been dismayed at how quickly the notes had disappeared today, just

96

buying things in charity shops. She hadn't even bought a proper meal. What was she going to do when it ran out?

'I want to leave the island too,' she said.

The man smiled. 'We go together. Once I have my cards – I buy a car. I take you where you want to go . . . in return.'

Clare felt tempted. He could take her to England, to a big city where no-one would know her. She could have her hair cut and dyed. 'But what if someone catches me going into the hotel?'

'There is back stair to staff rooms. If somebody ask, you are old friend looking for me.' He pulled a brochure out of his pocket. 'This is the place – in Shanklin High Street. And there, see, is where you go to backstair. My room is first inside. Feel behind wardrobe.'

'What's your name – if someone asks me who I'm looking for?'

The man's eyes shifted around, nervously. 'Angelo . . . no, no, Sandro. But, per favore, tell no-one I'm here.'

He wasn't smiling anymore – he looked anxious, his eyes were watering. 'Is it a mortal sin? What you did?' she asked, hoping it was, so she wouldn't feel so alone.

'Non importa.' He took a handkerchief from his pocket and blew his nose. 'But you – little one – what is it you have done?'

'I ran away from home.' It was almost true – she mustn't tell a lie in church.

'Why?'

Clare bowed her head and sat silently. She couldn't tell this man, this stranger, who wasn't a priest.

'Tell me tomorrow. I meet you in Shanklin.' He took a pen out of his inside pocket and drew a map on the brochure. 'Here, si? I wait in morning, by this pond.'

Clare nodded. She needed to think about this. She didn't have to do anything he said.

'Grazie, grazie. And then we leave, at once.' He got up. He seemed very big and tall, looking down at her. 'What is your name?' he asked.

'Tess,' she said, standing up. It sounded strange, as if someone else was saying it.

It was dark when they got outside. Clare stood shivering, watching Sandro hurry up the lane and turn towards Shanklin. She wondered where he was going to spend the night and half wished she could go with him. He seemed almost like a friend, someone else in trouble. A car turned off the road and drove down the lane towards her, its headlights blazing. She scurried round the back of the church and found herself amongst gravestones. She heard the car stop, someone opened the church door. Perhaps it was the priest. She no longer felt the need to talk to him. Not now she had found Sandro.

He'd seemed unsure about telling her his real name. He said, Angelo, at first – that must be his surname. His uncertainty had made her remember to call herself Tess. How strange. Angel Clare was Tess's husband in *Tess of the d'Urbervilles*. But not for long, not when he found out, on their wedding night, that Tess had borne a child to another man. Tess's baby had died too. But babies died easily then. It hadn't been left to die . . . murdered by its mother. Tess had loved her baby . . . . *Sorrow* she'd named him, and baptised him before he died. Clare's baby hadn't been baptised. Mother kept saying she would arrange it with the priest. What happened to unbaptised, illegitimate babies, if they couldn't go to heaven? A vision of a fiery devil holding a pronged fork flashed into her mind. She put her hands over her face. She didn't want to be alone.

She ran along the lane, back to the road. She could catch a bus and return to the caravan tonight. Marguerite and Jane would have left by now. Tomorrow she'd attempt to do what Sandro Angelo wanted, and then leave the island with him.

*   *   *

'Your hair looks fabulous, Rachel,' Sophie said.

'Knocks years off you,' Jill added.

Rachel patted her hair. 'I'm surprised it's still clinging to my head after that wind.' A gale had propelled them up Union Street so fast, they'd almost taken off.

Jill ran her hands through her own windswept mop. 'Ah, but it's the sort of hairstyle that looks better messed up.'

'Messed up? That's me,' Rachel said.

'No you're not,' Sophie said. 'It's Sandro that was messed up. You are just temporarily confused.'

'I'm confused by this spaghetti.' Rachel was trying to twist it round her fork but the whole lot lifted off the plate in one lump. She hadn't really wanted it, but thought that Sandro might somehow manifest – like a pantomime genie – if she ordered something Italian. But looking at the sticky mess, she knew Sandro would never dish up something like that. 'Perhaps it's the chef's night off,' she said. 'Monday's not a busy night, especially in January.'

Sophie was inspecting her lemon sole, frowning. 'One of us could ask.'

'I'll ask.' Jill stopped sawing at her steak to take a gulp of red wine.

'Hold on.' Sophie looked wary. 'What will you say?'

'Is that bastard, Sandro, skulking about in your kitchen?'

Rachel grimaced. 'I think not. Anyway, it should be me that does it.' She couldn't imagine that Sandro was behind the scenes, cooking up these grotty meals in this unremarkable pub. But she had a palpitation every time the door to the kitchen swung open. Perhaps Jill had been mistaken when she thought she saw him earlier. Or maybe there was another exit, although Rachel hadn't seen one when she'd snooped around on her way to the ladies.

'I'd swear on my children's lives it was him,' Jill said, as if picking up Rachel's doubts.

Rachel pushed her chair back; she was feeling a bit braver after two glasses of wine. 'Right. I'm going to ask.' She strode up to the bar, her nervousness returning. Suppose he was in there and someone called him out. What would she say? Perhaps this wasn't such a good idea after all.

'What can I get you?' the girl behind the bar stopped inspecting her nails, and glanced up.

'Oh, er, I just wanted to ask about the cook—'

'Food lousy, was it? I'll call him.'

'No, no.' Rachel held up a hand. 'I wondered if you have a chef called Sandro working here.'

'No, just a couple of blokes.'

'Sandro is a bloke.'

'Is she?'

'He, actually. Italian.'

The girl laughed showing a silver ball sticking in her tongue. 'Whatever. Italian? Dunno. Only started here a couple of days ago myself.'

'Could you, er, ask someone?'

The girl sighed. 'Brian!' she called to a man clearing tables. 'Can you come here a mo?' She resumed her nail inspection.

The man ambled over, wiping his hands with a cloth. 'I was just enquiring if you have an Italian chef called Sandro working here?' Rachel said.

'Who wants to know?' The man looked around furtively as if she were accusing him of employing illegal immigrants.

'I'm a friend, just trying to trace him, that's all.'

'Sandro, was it? No. We had one called Angelo – daft names – only lasted a few days – just disappeared. Pity, he was good. I thought things would pick up with him cooking. But the gooduns never stay. Get poached, you see.'

Rachel nodded. 'Thanks, anyway.' She ordered drinks to take back to the table with her. Brian leaned on the bar, looking her up and down. 'From Ryde are you?'

Rachel shook her head. 'Ventnor.' She picked up the tray of glasses.

'Nice,' Brian muttered, peering at her cleavage. 'Sorry couldn't help you. Good chap, Angelo was, bit like that blind opera singer – Andrew somebody.'

Rachel tried not to drop the tray. 'Do you mean Andrea Bocelli?' This was too much of a co-incidence.

'That's him. Marvellous voice.'

'Where did you say this, Angelo, went?'

'Didn't. He just vanished.' Brian was obviously getting bored with this talk about another man. He swished his cloth over the bar.

'Someone else was in here asking for him the other day.'

'Who?'

'Some bloke.' Brian grinned at her. 'Not as good looking as yourself.'

Rachel forced a smile. 'Did he say what he wanted?'

Brian shook his head. 'Same as you, I expect. Everyone's desperate for good chefs around here.'

'They are, indeed.' She walked carefully back to her table. Sophie and Jill had obviously heard every word. Rachel handed out the drinks and sat down.

'So he's disappeared from Ventnor, Shanklin and Ryde.' Sophie frowned. 'How odd.'

'Odd, my arse,' Jill commented. 'He's up to no good. Must be, if all these people are on his trail.'

'It might not be lots of people. It could be the same man who accosted me,' Rachel said.

'Who, or what, *is* this Sandro? A con man? An extortionist? A gambler?' Jill said.

'He's just not bright enough to be a real criminal.' Rachel sipped her wine. 'Do you know, it's just occurred to me that he's a lot like my ex-husband – Connor. Perhaps I'm just one of those women that choose crap men.'

'In what way is he like Connor?' Sophie asked.

Rachel realised she'd never really spoken about him much. Her marriage was filed away, along with the divorce certificate. 'It took me ages to sum Connor up. So many people liked him – they couldn't understand why I was always so stressed out. He was fun and sociable, and nice looking. But . . . '

'A serial adulterer – like my ex?' Sophie asked. Rachel noticed her glance at Jill. Sophie and Jill had been through a difficult time last year and Rachel had often wondered . . . ah, well, their friendship seemed to have survived. But Sophie was much more assertive with Jill than she used to be – thank goodness.

'A boring old bag of bones – with a dark side, like Ash?' Jill said.

Rachel laughed. 'No. Not even a gambler, or an alcoholic. He was just bloody irresponsible.'

Jill gave up hacking at her steak and pushed her plate away. 'Irresponsible, how?'

'Well, he was the kind of person that would see a couple of cute puppies in a pet shop, and bring them home – without giving any thought to the fact we lived in a flat. Let alone their care and the expense. And he'd be dumbfounded and hurt by my lack of enthusiasm.'

'Are we talking real puppies here?' Jill asked. 'Or metaphorical puppies, such as your two boys?'

'The boys, pets, cars, everything. He was always getting sacked from jobs because he wouldn't stop talking.' Rachel stuck her fork in the top of the congealed mound of spaghetti, where it stood unaided, like a TV mast. 'He hadn't just kissed the Blarney stone – he was born under it.'

'Where is he now?' Sophie asked.

'Back in Cork – single – unchanged. Patrick went to visit him last summer.'

'With Rose,' Jill said.

Rachel nodded. 'With Rose. I was as surprised as you, believe me, Jill.'

'It was a seriously surprising few months – for all of us,' Sophie said, as if she were setting a boundary beyond which it would be unwise to go. 'So what is all this Catholic connection about, Rachel? From Irish Catholic Connor to Italian Catholic Sandro? But you're none of the above.'

'I know. It's odd. And they were extremes. Connor paid vague lip service to it – trotted it out of the closet when it suited him, tried to get me to agree to bring the boys up in the faith. And Sandro – he was steeped in guilt and all the trappings – went to mass – but just went along with his urges. That's what I mean about them being basically the same.' She leaned back in her chair and laughed. 'The funny thing was, Father Michael – Connor's priest – turned out to be one of my greatest friends. He told Connor that Catholicism wasn't a tool to manipulate people with, and in our case it would be better for the boys to decide for themselves when they were older.'

'Michael? I know him,' Jill said. 'He's all right – good sense of humour – nice looking too.'

'Oh, yes,' Rachel nodded. 'I often tell him that if he wasn't celibate, I'd slip that little black dress off him in no time.'

'Do you really say that to him?' Sophie's eyes were wide.

'No! But I think it. He's a lovely man.'

'Odd thing, religion,' Jill commented, lining up her peas on the edge of her plate. 'One God, supposedly, yet umpteen denominations and sects, all killing each other to be right. What's that all about?'

Rachel chuckled. 'God knows.' She tapped Sophie's arm. 'And Nick, of course.'

'Well, he's not into religions as such. He thinks – like you, Jill – they are grossly misinterpreted by power-hungry humans. But they also have their esoteric essence – a mystical aspect – the *be still and know* stuff. The secret is to *feel it*.'

'*It!* What is *it?*' Jill said, piling the peas in a heap and starting to sort them again.

'An experience – you can't intellectualise—'

'Look, girls,' Rachel said. 'Can we return to the reason we're here?' She waved a dismissive hand at the half-eaten food and empty glasses. 'Let's face it; Sandro doesn't want to be found. I've had enough of this *ladies detective agency* stuff. Let's go to *Yelf's* and buy a glorious pudding – a sticky, oozing, hip-thickening delight. And then, my friends – get me pissed!'

*   *   *

Father Ryan locked the door of the church and stood looking at the bright stars. The wind and rain had died away and the evening was cold and clear, with the bitter edge that suggested frost.

'Father?'

He jumped. Oh, God! It was Clare's mother. What was she doing creeping around the churchyard at this time of the evening? 'Is it you, Mrs Mulligan?' he said.

'Pardon me for intruding on your thoughts, Father. Only, I was just wondering if you'd heard anything from the holy Sisters about

Clare recently. She doesn't write to me, you see.'

Father Ryan forced his mouth into a smile. 'I thought you understood. The Sisters said it would be best if there was no communication from her, until the time is right.'

Mrs Mulligan nodded vigorously. 'So you did, Father. So you did. It's just that it's been quite a while since her . . . since her confinement.'

'Sure, it's really not long. Maybe the, er, confinement, was late.'

'Oh, but I thought they'd told you when—'

Father Ryan slapped his hand to his forehead. 'Of course, of course. I was forgetting. I have so many things to think about.'

'Forgive me, Father. I shouldn't be troubling you.' She tightened her headscarf and turned away.

'I'll let you know if I hear anything further,' he said, watching her pick her way along the dark path. 'Mrs Mulligan,' he called. She stopped and turned. 'There's a possibility I might be going over to England soon. I'll maybe pay a visit to the Poor Clares, and I'll see for myself how the girl is getting on.'

Mrs Mulligan's face was a pale blur in the moonlight. 'Thank you, Father. That's very kind of you. She doesn't deserve such attention.'

'Goodnight, now,' he said, moving away in the opposite direction. He didn't want to walk along with her, even though he'd have to re-trace his steps when she'd gone.

He'd surprised himself with his impetuosity. Why had he suddenly blurted out that he was going to England? That news would be around the village in no time. And he hadn't even applied for leave of absence yet. He leaned on the churchyard gate feeling the damp from the grass seeping in through his thin shoes. He realised he hadn't eaten since breakfast, but his stomach felt distended with fear. England. It seemed such a long way to travel. But his mind was made up. He had to go. If he didn't find out what happened to Clare, he would have to live with this fear every moment. Any day she could reappear and ruin his life. He was beginning to hallucinate, imagining her pale face framed by her red hair, appearing at a window of the school, or popping up amongst the rows of children in the choir. He was never going to be free of her, unless he did something.

He had no idea of what he would do if he found her. He didn't even know where to start looking. She'd never so much as written. He saw this as a sign that she didn't want to be found. And he hoped this was true. But he had to know. His tentative plan was to try and follow in her footsteps by booking a passage on the same evening ferry and heading for the convent of the Poor Clares to visit Sister Bridget, his cousin.

He could go to his house now, and start making arrangements. He realised a part of himself – that he didn't really yet know – was excited by the possibility of escape. It might be good to get away from the choir for a while. That wee girl, Maria – he was finding it difficult to win her trust. It was the first time he'd not been able to reassure a child with his special ways. It was all Clare's fault. She was the one that made him lose confidence in himself.

He smiled as he walked along the church path. Let Father Christopher take over the choir for a while. Then the children would be so glad to have himself back when he returned with little presents from abroad.

*   *   *

Fran rocked Sam in his buggy, to and fro, to and fro. She yawned and wondered what to do next. He'd been fed and changed and winded. Maybe it was the different milk – but he wasn't drawing his knees up with colic. She'd tried to settle him in his cot upstairs, but he didn't seem to like that. His arms flailed around in the big empty space as if he were searching for someone. She'd brought him back down to the kitchen and put him in his moses basket, but still he wailed. What did he need? He'd not been this upset before, even when he'd been starving. She had so little experience with human babies. Animals usually settled easily once they'd been fed. She vaguely remembered when she was about three, and Phillip had been a baby. She recalled a big rubber dummy and gripe water. She could also remember herself and Phillip being squashed between their parents in the big double bed.

She looked at Cinders and Sugar Plum asleep by the Aga. At

night, Sugar dropped her airs and graces and curled up against the dog's warm belly. And Cinders obligingly draped a paw over the cat. She watched as Cinders twitched her tail and Sugar twitched a leg, as if in response. They seemed part of the same body. Fran lifted Sam out of the pram. 'This is what we'll do,' she said.

Upstairs, propped against pillows in the four-poster bed, Fran held Sam cocooned against her chest. She could feel his downy head under her chin as she sang softly to him. He seemed to like the theme from *Swan Lake*. His tiny hands scrabbled against her nightgown. She rocked and patted him until she could feel him begin to relax. He yawned several times and then grew still. She held him until she felt he was so deeply asleep that he wouldn't wake. Then she slowly transferred him to the moses basket beside her on the bed. She had warmed it with a hot water bottle. She left one small lamp on so she could see the rise and fall of his chest, and then settled herself down. She patted his tummy a few times to reassure him that she was still there. He looked peaceful. Fran wondered what was going on in his poor little head. Now that his basic needs were satisfied, was he feeling the distress of his ordeal, his abandonment?

'There, there, sweetheart,' she whispered. 'Fran will never leave you.'

*   *   *

'Back again,' Kate commented, when Clare knocked tentatively on the door of the caravan. 'Never know whether you're staying or going. Come in, then. You've missed supper, I'm afraid. I'm off to bed.'

'Sorry.' Clare dumped her backpack on the bunk. 'I needed to go and buy some things.' She gestured towards her new outfit. 'I had to wait ages for a bus back this evening.'

'You could have called in at the stable block and told us your plans,' Kate said, filling the kettle from a water container. 'Marguerite came looking for you. She wanted to see you before she left.' She wiped her hands on her paint-spattered dungarees, frowning.

'I didn't want to trouble anyone,' Clare said, realising how rude and ungrateful she must seem. 'I'm feeling so much better now. It must be the tablets you gave me. Thanks.' And she *was* feeling better, she realised. The redness had calmed down in her sore breast and although they still leaked at times, they both seem to be deflating. She was still very tired, but not shivery anymore.

Kate shrugged. 'No worries.' She struck a match and lit the gas ring. 'I'm making hot chocolate, want one?'

Clare nodded. She'd eaten fish and chips, huddled in the shelter, waiting for a bus. 'If I could just stay one more night . . . I promise I won't be a bother to you.'

'I've told you before, if you want to stay and work, you can.'

Clare felt Kate's gaze upon her as she took off her hat and coat and searched in her backpack for her money. When she finally glanced up, Kate's face seemed kinder, concerned.

'Why not take a couple of days to sort yourself out. You seem to have a lot on your mind. And I don't blame you for not opening up – after all, you don't know us. Just give us a few quid for food and stuff, then come and go as you like, until you've decided what you want to do. Okay?'

Clare felt her eyes fill up with tears again. How could anyone be so kind to her? She took the mug of chocolate Kate was holding out.

'I'm really grateful to you,' she whispered.

CHAPTER
Nine

Father Ryan had been granted compassionate leave. He'd lied and said that an elderly aunt was seriously ill in England and asking for him. Last night, after he fought down his fear of not being believed, he made the phone calls, and everything had been arranged, quickly and simply. Nobody, it seemed, would be put out by his absence.

He backed his Morris Minor out from under the corrugated plastic roof which served as a garage. He'd risen, even earlier than usual, to have time to check the oil and water, and give her a final polish, before he set off for the port. She needed warming up, the windscreen was frosted, the wipers stuck. He sat in the driver's seat, intoning the *Miserere*, while he waited for the temperature gauge to rise, trying not to think about driving on busy roads, through towns and cities, and then boarding the ferry. And what about when he arrived in Wales and then England? At least they drove on the same side over there. He wondered whether his old car would survive all those miles. He never drove much more than ten in any round trip in his parish. But she'd been serviced every year, and hadn't Finbar, at the garage, always said she was good for a few miles yet? Even so, it had been a big decision to drive. But it gave him confidence to think that he would have his own private place where he could lock himself in, if the fear got too much. And what if he decided not to come back? He'd be able to go anywhere; other people did it, why not him?

Father Christopher crunched up the frosty drive, and stood laughing at him.

'You look like something out of an old film, Ryan,' he guffawed. 'When are you going to wake up to the twenty-first century?'

Father Ryan looked at him. He was dressed in black slacks and jacket, his paunch bulging over his belt. And look like you, he thought, a man with no standards, a man for whom the children have no respect? He got out of the car, stumbling over his cassock, which made Father Christopher laugh louder.

'You will be taking care of everything for me now, won't you?' Father Ryan said, trying to look unaffected by Father Christopher's behaviour. 'Especially my choir.'

'Oh, especially your choir. I'll teach them some lively songs. It'll make a change from your depressive stuff. They can have a bit of fun while you're gone. Religion is supposed to make them happy, as well as good, man.'

Depressive – Father Christopher was always calling him that – just because he took his vocation seriously. He didn't like the word. 'Don't be filling their heads with nonsense.' Father Ryan fetched his small brown suitcase, and his black briefcase, from the porch, and put them in the boot. He didn't have much to pack – just a few clothes, Jeannie's shawl and his long black, winter overcoat. He thought he'd better take his briefcase and a few official accoutrements – just in case he was called upon professionally. He handed Father Christopher a bunch of keys. 'You won't be needing to go in the house, these are the church keys.'

Father Christopher held out a plump red paw for a handshake which Father Ryan pretended not to see. 'Well, Ryan, have a good trip, old boy. I hope you find your aunt recovering. I'd ask you to ring me, but I don't suppose you know how to work one of these.' He held up his mobile phone, chuckling.

'Now, what would I be needing one of those things for?' Father Ryan forced a grin, as if he were playing along with the joke. He got in the car and backed carefully out into the lane.

'May God go with you,' Father Christopher called as he pulled away.

'Why would He want to do that?' Father Ryan muttered. 'He hasn't bothered as yet.' He checked his watch and noticed the date; February the first. It seemed fortuitous to be driving off into the unknown, on the first day of a new month. He eased the car carefully up through the gears. 'This is the beginning of my quest,' he said. 'When . . . if, I return here, I will know about the child.'

*   *   *

Rachel sat at the kitchen table wondering what on earth had possessed her to drink so much wine last night. But she had enjoyed herself with Sophie and Jill. They'd eaten and drunk themselves silly, men had tried to chat them up, and then they'd tumbled into the taxi like a gaggle of girls on a hen night. But they'd talked deeply as well – before they'd got too drunk – and Rachel felt some of her confusion had cleared away. She realised that all the turmoil over Sandro was triggering something deeper within her – a need to make sense of life. Not just the seemingly random events, but a larger, more meaningful aspect that seemed to be pushing at her consciousness, forcing her to inquire. She'd often heard Nick say, *when the pupil is ready, the teacher appears.* She'd taken that to mean a blazing vision of Jesus or the Buddha. But Nick said the teacher comes in many guises, and we had to pay attention to what was in our path right now – the person, or event, that was forcing change. In her case, Sandro. She smiled, it was hard to see *him* as a spiritual teacher. But, she had to admit, he'd certainly precipitated something.

She'd also realised last night, how much she loved her Irish legacy that Connor had left her. She would never have gone to live for all those years in Cork and imbibed the culture, if it hadn't been for him. Even now she could still hear a slight accent in her voice when she spoke of Ireland. And, if it wasn't for Connor, she wouldn't have her two wonderful sons.

'You look rough, Ma.' Patrick came into the kitchen and shoved bread in the toaster. 'But, sort of interesting. Your hair's good.'

'Not quite sure how to take that, but thanks anyway.' Rachel started opening the mail. It was time to stop hoping that Sandro might have written. 'At my age a few drinks can do wonders for morale, but very little for the ageing process.'

'I'll remember that.'

Rachel tapped him on the head with a pile of junk mail. 'You won't. Youth hath no memory for such matters.'

110

Patrick buttered his toast and stood eating it. 'I'll probably stay over at Wraith Cove for the next few nights. Jane and Marguerite are away and I like to keep an eye on things. The youngsters can't always be trusted.'

Rachel smiled. Patrick was taking his responsibility as foreman seriously. She was pleased. 'Heard from Rose?' she asked.

'Got a text yesterday. She might be coming home soon. Stephanie has been quite ill – some sort of foreign bug. Apparently, she didn't want to give in, but she's become quite weak.'

'Poor Stephanie. Jill didn't say anything last night.' But then Jill was still digesting the fact that Rose had given up her music training in order to go off to Niger with her grandmother. Jill couldn't understand why Rose had developed this deep bond with Stephanie – *my mother from hell*, Jill called her. Rachel thought Stephanie was a marvellous woman – a doctor who worked in atrocious conditions to help young, traumatised women. But relationships were different when you were on the inside. Jill probably experienced her mother as giving all her attention to others.

'It will be nice for you to have Rose back,' she said. Although this was another thorn in Jill's flesh – more Ash's flesh really. His precious gifted daughter going out with a café owner's son.

Patrick shrugged. 'We'll have to see how things are,' he said. 'People change when they travel and experience different ways of life.'

Rachel felt a protective maternal wave wash through her. She knew Patrick adored Rose. She hoped he wasn't about to have his heart broken. That was so hard to bear, even at her age.

'No sign of Sandro?' Patrick asked, as if reading her thoughts.

'Nope. We did a bit of detective work last night but he's given everyone the slip, it seems.'

'Can't understand it. Does he owe money, do you think?'

'I really don't know.'

'Just seems odd that he's still hanging around. Why?'

'Maybe he's on his way back to Italy.' Rachel looked out at the day. It was brighter, a clear blue band of sky on the horizon. 'Anyway, I

111

feel differently since last night. I think my self-esteem is returning. I'm going to make a success of this Italian thing – I won't be beaten.'

'Good on you. Anything I can do?'

'I was wondering if you would be a waiter. And you might mention it to the young ones at Wraith Cove. It would be just for the Valentine's weekend celebrations.'

'Kate and Jules might be interested. And the new girl, Clare, is still around. Billy's a bit scruffy, but might scrub up.'

'I was wondering . . . do you think Rose might play her violin for the guests – something classical, or romantic – if she's back?'

Patrick laughed. 'She'd probably rather play folk music. But, if she's here, I'm sure she'll oblige.'

They went downstairs together. Patrick kissed her goodbye. Rachel let herself into the café. 'Right,' she said, pulling up the blinds and assembling her apparatus. 'How difficult can it be to make fresh pasta? It's only flour and water.' She put her Andrea Bocelli CD on the bottom of the pile and slid an Irish compilation in the slot. '*I wish I was in Carrickfergus,*' she sang.

*   *   *

Clare crept up the stairs at the back of the hotel. She had taken her hat off and tucked her hair inside her coat. She'd hidden her backpack behind the big dustbins. She didn't want anyone thinking she was a burglar. The fire exit door at the top was propped open, just as Sandro Angelo had told her. Her heart was thudding. Why was she doing this? Because it had seemed like a plan, a direction to move in. If Sandro didn't want to be seen, then he would know how to get away from here, undetected. She had no idea where she wanted to go; she'd have to think about that later. Maybe Sandro would advise her. He seemed desperate – he'd *done something,* with another man's wife. Did he mean sex – or a robbery, maybe? He'd acted as if he were a murderer – like her.

There was no-one about. Clare tried the first door on the landing, but it was locked. It had an engaged sign on it, like a bathroom. She tried the second door and it opened. It was just like he said – a bed, a chair, a chest of drawers and a wardrobe. It looked uninhabited, no

112

possessions lying around. She tiptoed over to the wardrobe and slid her hand into the gap behind it. She could feel a small ledge, but nothing was wedged behind there. She tried from the other side, but there was nothing. Someone must have found it. Perhaps the room had been cleaned, but her hands were covered in dust. She looked round desperately. There was only one wardrobe. She grasped the side of it and shunted it forward slightly. Anything lodged behind would surely fall out. She peered into the gap. Nothing there, except spiders' webs. It hadn't been moved for ages. She pulled the chest of drawers forward, nothing behind there either. She looked under the bed and the armchair. But he'd definitely said the wardrobe.

Suddenly, she heard footsteps coming up the stairs, walking along the landing. Suppose someone came in, what would she say? She held her breath; a key rattled and a door opened close by. She waited for a while and then let herself quietly out of the room and ran down the fire escape. Sandro Angelo wouldn't take her with him now – she'd messed up her half of the arrangement. Why did everything go wrong?

She'd have to meet him by the pond in the park to tell him. But what was the point? She didn't have the wallet. But maybe – if she explained – he'd have another plan.

*　　　*　　　*

Fran finished putting the baby clothes into the chest of drawers. She couldn't believe how fortunate she'd been, buying all these things from that rich woman. They looked expensive and hardly worn. There were lots of dungarees, and tops with diggers and animals on them. They were tiny, but still much too big for Sam. He would have to stay in his sleepsuits for now. He was lying in the middle of the big bed, waving his arms and legs about. She smiled at him.

'What a smart little chap you'll be,' she said. She picked up the pile of pink clothes that he'd arrived in. 'What am I going to do with these?' The clothes seemed to have shrunk and distorted in the wash. So much dye had run out they were now a shade of sludgy brown. She sniffed them; they still smelled of vegetables. She straightened them out as best she could and put them in the bottom drawer of the chest.

If Sam's mother had made these for him, then Fran had a duty to keep them. He would need to know, when he grew up. What would he make of it? She sat down on the bed. How easily she was drifting into this way of thinking.

'Fran!'

She got up quickly, picking up Sam. It was Ted. She didn't want him to come up here.

'Coming,' she called. She hurried down the stairs, holding tightly to the banister in case she should trip. Ted was in the kitchen inspecting the pram.

'Smart contraption,' he said, tapping the wheels with his stick. 'Did they bring it with them?'

'Oh, yes,' Fran said, wondering if it was possible to bring such a thing on an aeroplane.

Ted came over to look at Sam. He reached out a calloused finger; Sam curled his tiny pink ones round it. Fran resisted telling Ted not to touch the baby with dirty hands. But Ted's hands were always grimy, even after he'd scrubbed them. She'd never minded before.

'Look at that,' Ted grinned. 'Strong little chap.' He put his head on one side. 'Reckon he looks like old Phillip, you know.'

'Oh, Ted,' Fran laughed. 'You've not seen him in years. Anyway, Phillip's his grandfather.'

'Well, likenesses run in families.' Ted gave her arm a squeeze. 'He'll do okay if he looks like you.' He took his cap off and looked around. 'Where is everyone?'

'Oh, they've gone off – for a couple of days.'

'And left you with the nipper?'

'I really don't mind. They were reluctant, but I insisted.'

'You're a saint.' Ted shook his head. 'Suppose that means you won't come to The Buddle this evening, then? We could wheel him up there.'

For a brief moment Fran had a vision of herself doing it. How lovely it would be to show him off. But what if people asked difficult questions that she wasn't prepared for? And maybe there had been

114

news of a missing baby or an injured mother found wandering. For the first time that day she felt a pang of remorse. There might really be a distressed woman somewhere, looking for her baby. 'Too cold out,' she murmured. 'And there's the smoke. Perhaps another day, if the weather bucks up. One lunch time – we could sit outside.'

Ted was looking at her. 'You all right, Fran? Something I said? You're looking mighty serious.'

Fran shook her head impatiently. 'Has, er . . . has anything happened out there, Ted?' She knew he always had Isle of Wight radio playing at home.

Ted looked at the kitchen door. 'Out where? In the yard?'

'No. In the village, out in the world.' Fran couldn't understand it. Why weren't the police knocking on doors?

'You getting enough sleep?' Ted scratched his head. 'Can't think of anything. Nothing much happens this time of year. Everyone hibernates. Wait a minute though. I have just thought of something.'

Fran's heart seemed to trip over itself inside her chest. She held Sam tighter. Ted reached out and gave her arm a pinch and punch.

'It's the first of February,' he chuckled.

CHAPTER

Ten

Clare found Sandro Angelo in the park at the edge of Shanklin. He was hunched on a bench beside the pond. The collar of his black overcoat was pulled up and he was hiding behind a newspaper. He glanced up furtively as she approached. He looked awful – his eyes were bloodshot, his stubble thicker than ever.

'Ciao,' he said, thickly, without smiling. 'You got it, si?'

Clare bit her lip and shook her head.

'No! Why no?' He dropped the newspaper and staggered up. Clare backed away.

'I'm sorry. I did everything you said, but it wasn't there. There was nothing behind the wardrobe. I checked everywhere, behind the chest of drawers, under the bed—'

'Wait. You say *chest of drawer*?'

'Yes, just in case I misunderstood—'

'No chest of drawer in my room. You go in first room?'

'The one after the bathroom, yes.'

'Bathroom?'

'The one with the *engaged* sign on the door.'

Sandro slapped his forehead with his hand. 'Si, si. Occupato – that was my room.'

'But I thought . . . it looked like . . . '

Sandro stared at her and sighed. 'Va bene. You go back . . . yes?'

Clare felt exhaustion draining her. She'd got up so early to catch the bus and had nothing to eat or drink. 'I can't . . . I was scared . . . someone came up the stairs . . . I can't go back.'

Sandro held up his hands. 'But is easy. You know where now, si?'

'Why can't you go?'

'I tell you. A woman I work with there – her husband want to kill me.'

'Why?'

'You very young . . . ' Sandro stood, pouting out his bottom lip as if thinking. 'Okay, this woman become pregnant, she have abortion. Her husband find out. He search for me everywhere. I don't blame him. I will go away, but I need my passport and documents.'

He sat back down on the bench and grabbed Clare's arm, pulling her down beside him. He leaned towards her. She could smell his stale breath. His voice became urgent. 'We are Catholic, no? I am so shamed. I go back home to see my priest.'

'Did you know – about the abortion?' Clare asked.

'No, no.' Sandro shifted on the bench as if trying to wriggle away from unpleasant memories. 'She tell me after.'

Clare wondered briefly what her life would be like now, if she'd made that decision. 'Perhaps she was right,' she murmured.

'What you say?' Sandro glared at her. 'You a Catholic, si? You know where soul go of not baptised baby? You understand *Limbo*?'

Clare tried desperately to find a nail to nibble, but they were all bitten down. Was she still a Catholic? She needed someone to tell her. Sandro was scowling.

'What have *you* done?' he demanded. 'If we help each other – you tell me.'

Should she tell him? Maybe he would understand, after what he'd just told her. She didn't know what to do. Tears started to run down her face and drip off her chin. Sandro put a hand on her shoulder.

'Scusi. I sorry . . . you just a child.' His voice sounded softer, more sympathetic.

'I've done something terrible,' she sobbed.

'Si? You steal something? Drugs?'

'Much, much worse.'

He lowered his voice. 'Maybe you have abortion too?'

'No . . . I gave birth to a baby.'

Sandro made a strange sound in his throat. 'You have baby? But you so young. Where is it?'

Clare wondered if he believed her. He was looking around as if
she might have hidden it in the bushes.

'I . . . left it . . . in a stable.'

'A stable?' Sandro looked mystified. 'Non capisco.'

'Like a shed. I didn't mean to. I was ill.'

He lifted his shoulders. 'What happen to it?'

'I went back the next day . . . ' Clare's whole body was shaking.

'The child . . . it was still there, si?'

Clare nodded. 'But . . . it was dead!' She looked at him, horrified
that she'd said it.

Sandro jumped up as if something had hit him. 'No! You lie!
You not do that!'

'I did, I did! I didn't know what I was doing.'

'When this happen?' Sandro demanded. 'You been in prison?'

'No, no. It was last Saturday.'

'Saturday! The police let you go?'

'Nobody knows.'

'Someone must found it and called police.'

Clare thought about the stable. There'd been a sheep or something,
penned in a corner. The farmer would have been in to feed it. And the
baby . . . it was under the straw. Who had put it there? Perhaps a wild
animal – a fox – they hid things, and came back for them later. Oh, God.
She couldn't bear it. She stared at Sandro.

'Please, help me,' she whispered. But Sandro was backing away
from her. He held up a hand as if to ward her off.

'So terrible, terrible,' he muttered. 'I not help you.'

'Let me go with you, please.' Clare clasped her hands together.
'I'll go back to the hotel, I'll try again.'

Sandro was shaking his head, moving further and further away.
'You go to the police *now*,' he called. He turned and hurried off.

Clare sat, stunned. She had told someone and they'd reacted
with horror. Another Catholic – a man who'd also done something bad.
She sat for a long time until she began to feel cold. Her head felt clearer

118

after her outburst to Sandro. She had to face up to what she'd done. The baby's body must have been discovered by now. And Sandro would surely tell the police about her – an anonymous phone call, perhaps. She decided to walk back to the town to find out where the police station was. She got up stiffly from the bench and reached for her backpack. And then she realised, with despair, that she'd left it behind the dustbins outside the hotel.

She walked quickly back to the high street, her tiredness forgotten. All her possessions were in her backpack – how could she have been so careless? She crept round the side of the hotel. There was a door open downstairs and she could hear voices and the clank of pots and pans. She sneaked past and peered behind the dustbins. Thank heavens, it was still there. Just as she was about to pull it out she caught sight of the outside staircase. Supposing she dared make another attempt to retrieve Sandro's wallet? If she could get it, she could go back to the park. Perhaps he'd return and he might forgive her and change his mind about taking her with him.

She hurried up the stairs and in through the fire exit. She tried the first door on the landing. It opened this time. She knew straight away that someone was inside. She could feel warmth in the air, and the smell of stale cigarette smoke. The room was dim, the curtains half-closed. There was a mound of blankets heaped on the bed. Someone was sleeping there, she could see the rise and fall of breathing. She wanted to back out of the door and run, but she had nothing to lose – even if she was caught. She tiptoed to the wardrobe and slipped her hand behind it. She slid it up and down and immediately her fingers connected with an object. She carefully pulled it out – it was a big leather wallet.

Clare felt as if she might burst out laughing – or crying, as she crept from the room. Was she a thief now as well as a murderer? She silently closed the door and walked down the stairs. She lugged her backpack from behind the dustbins and strode away.

Back in the park she wandered around and around until her feet began to ache. The park was deserted. She stood watching the ducks on the pond, her elation at finding the wallet turning to desolation.

Sandro wasn't coming back – she knew it. She sat on the bench and took the wallet out of her pocket. What should she do with it? She could hand it to the police when she went to give herself up. But then she might land him in trouble. She looked inside, feeling guilty. There was a passport and money and loads of credit cards, and some photos of groups of happy people in a place that looked hot and sunny. In one of them, Sandro was standing with his arm around the shoulders of a smiling woman. Was she the man's wife that had the abortion? Clare recognised the place they were standing outside. It was the café in Ventnor – *Rachel's Café* – the one that was always closed whenever she looked in. The woman was wearing a striped apron – she must work there. They looked as if they were good friends. She might know where he was hiding and could get the wallet to him.

Clare decided to catch a bus back to Ventnor. She could take the wallet to the café – it felt like a small act of reparation, to help poor Sandro. And then she would go to the police and give herself up.

*　　*　　*

Fran wanted to go out. It was a bright, cold afternoon and it was difficult for her to stay confined to the house. She liked to walk along the cliffs most days. It kept her healthy. She was always telling Ted this when he nagged at her about her slovenly diet. She gazed at Sam asleep in his pram. She would love to just push it outside and along the cliff path. It looked as if it could cope. It had three wheels that could tackle rough terrain – or so she'd read in the instructions. But she would feel so conspicuous. Not that there were loads of people around in early February, but there were always the regulars who walked their dogs, and she didn't want to explain too many times about the baby. Someone might have heard something and be suspicious of an elderly woman pushing an infant in a pram.

It was getting late, maybe she could venture outside without the pram – she could carry Sam. But would that be fair on him? Supposing she tripped and fell? And then she remembered – there was one of those harness things amongst all the stuff she'd bought. She went upstairs and took it out of the wardrobe. It looked complicated, but she was used to

120

fathoming straps when she'd had the horses. She found a warm outdoor suit for Sam. It took ages to get him dressed and strapped to her chest. He didn't seem to mind being jiggled about, just stared at her with wide dark eyes.

'I'm worn out,' she told him. 'I need two pairs of hands to cope with this contraption.' She pulled on her big duffel coat and just managed to get a couple of toggles fastened over the top of everything. Cinders was sitting by the door, panting with anticipation. Fran selected one of her father's old walking sticks that still stood in the rack. 'Let's do it,' she said.

She walked carefully down to the beach at Rocken Edge, glad that she'd thought to bring the stick to steady herself. The path was muddy and slippery, rutted by the hooves of Ted's cattle. She paused on a grassy ledge above the beach, enjoying the cold freshness of the air. The tide was nearly out. Rocks and boulders were piled, glistening with seaweed. A piece of orange fishing net flapped in the branches of a grey-limbed tree which had been heaved onto the beach by the sea. Flotsam and jetsam had accumulated in the recent storms. She usually came down here with Ted, and a few of the locals, to clear up the debris in the spring. There were plastic bottles and matted ropes and wooden pallets and the usual collection of old shoes. Water tinkled from the landslip down to the sea and half a dozen cormorants stood on rocks in the shallows, their strong beaks pointing skyward, as if they were listening to the weather forecast.

Fran continued scanning the shore. She was looking for a body. They washed up here occasionally. Sometimes grey and bloated, a suicide perhaps, or a boating accident. Sometimes they were skeletal, a few tatters of skin and rags clinging to the bones. The coroner said they were sea burials that hadn't been sealed and weighted properly. It made his job difficult, should be made illegal, he complained. When they were kids, she and Phillip had seen it as something exciting and scary. But with age had come the realisation of tragedy and what it might mean for relatives, waiting for news.

There were no bodies here today. Fran wondered if this was good news or bad. If there had been a young woman lying there it would more than likely be Sam's mother. But at least she would know. Dead or alive, she wondered. Are you dead or alive? She turned away. Perhaps she'd look further along, towards Wraith Cove. She whistled to Cinders who was foraging amongst the debris.

Fran kept close to the cliff edge until she came to the lighthouse, then she had to turn inland where the path dropped away. She hadn't seen a soul so far. She walked across the fields to the stone wall that bordered the grounds of Wraith Cove Hotel. She could remember the grand hotel being there when she was a child. It had been closed down because of a fire, and later gradually demolished. Sometimes she and Phillip had squeezed through gaps in the walls and played in the overgrown gardens. They'd also known that someone lived in the cottage on the edge of the cliff. It used to be so hidden you wouldn't know it was there, apart from the little plume of smoke from the chimney. They pretended it was a wicked witch who captured children and boiled them in her cauldron. They scared themselves silly sometimes, even though their mum said it was only the fishermen. It was quite recently that Ted had found out that Marguerite had grown up there, a recluse. Fran would have loved to know more, but Ted never bothered to find out. A man of the earth, was Ted.

Fran could see a man in the garden of Wraith Cottage now. It would be Neptune, from Puck's Bay. He spent much of his time at Wraith Cottage. The story was that he was Marguerite's father. But Ted had always disagreed. A man's man, he called him, chuckling to himself. Fran wasn't quite sure what he meant by that. Well, he certainly was a man of the sea whatever else he might be. Anyway, Jane had put a stop to those rumours. She was Marguerite's sister, and their old father had met his death along this cliff path.

Fran watched Neptune working. He would know if anything had washed up. She pulled her coat firmly over sleeping Sam and walked down to the brambly hedge surrounding the cottage garden. Neptune was repairing a lobster pot. He looked up as his small terrier, Loot, started to yap at Cinders who was scrabbling through the hedge.

'Afternoon,' Fran said.

'Keep yer dog away,' Neptune said. 'Unless she wants 'er legs nipped.'

'Cinders!' Fran called. The dog bounded back wagging her whole body with excitement. 'Sit!' She smiled at Neptune. 'Over-friendly.'

Neptune nodded and tipped his cap back. He didn't return her smile. But that didn't mean he was hostile, it was just his way 'What brings you down here?' he said. 'Haven't seen you in a while.'

'Just walking. Is Marguerite about?' Fran knew perfectly well that Marguerite had gone away.

'Off gallivanting again, with Jane.' He shook his head disapprovingly and stared down at the lobster pot.

'Caught anything?'

'Couple of little 'uns. I put 'em back.'

'I expect you catch all sorts in those.'

'Less and less worth having.'

Fran walked a little closer to him, still on the other side of the hedge. The land was crumbling down the cliff face here. She gestured towards it. 'Anything interesting washed up lately?'

'Not that I've noticed.'

Don't believe that, thought Fran. They all kept a watch for anything useful that might come ashore, especially after a heavy sea. Smuggling was in Niton folk's blood. 'No bodies lately then?' Sam suddenly wriggled and squealed. Even though Neptune's eyes were sunken deep in his head, Fran could feel his gaze on her coat.

'What you got in there, a pup?'

Fran nodded and turned away. 'Bit cold for it really. I best be getting back.'

Neptune grinned suddenly. 'Mind it don't pee on you.' Fran waved over her shoulder and walked away. She followed the stone wall of the hotel. There appeared to be a lot going on in there. The stable block was looking just like it used to before the old place fell into disrepair. Big caravans were parked for the work force to live in. Rachel's boy, Patrick, was in charge. Fran liked Rachel, she had often chatted to her in The Buddle during the quiet season when Rachel wasn't busy with her café. She saw Patrick coming out of one of the caravans. He spotted her looking over the wall and waved.

'Hi! Fran, isn't it?' Cinders started to bark madly. Quick as lightening, Patrick was through the gate and kneeling beside Cinders, stroking her.

'Good dog,' he was saying. He looked up at Fran, smiling. 'Come and see the stable block if you want to. It's almost finished and we want to show it off.'

He bounded away with Cinders before Fran had a chance to say anything. She followed. 'Keep quiet,' she whispered to Sam. But she knew, up close, nobody was going to miss the fact that she was carrying a baby under her coat.

The stable block was indeed impressive. Patrick showed her around and introduced her to a nice girl called Kate, who immediately spotted Sam, and called another girl over to see him.

'Is he your grandson? He's so cute, so tiny!'

'He's my great-nephew, actually, visiting from Australia.' Fran felt herself smiling with pride as the young people gathered around to admire Sam. Even a boy with ratty hair was cooing over him.

'Oh, a little Ozzie! I've just got back from there,' Kate cried. 'Whereabouts is he from?'

'Can I hold him?' another girl asked, giving Fran an excuse not to answer questions.

'Well, I have to get him home, he's getting hungry,' she said, backing away. These kids were nice, but noisy, and they talked and moved so fast.

'I'll walk you to the gate,' Patrick said, putting a protective hand on her shoulder. 'It's getting a bit murky out there, wouldn't want you tripping over any of our building materials.'

What a nice lad, Fran thought, as they walked. I must make sure Sam grows up to be well-mannered.

'How many youngsters are working here?' Fran asked.

'It varies,' Patrick said. 'Not many at the moment. Some have gone back to university and others are too soft to work here when it's cold. They like the easy life.'

'Are they all students?'

'No. Mostly locals and layabouts this time of year.'

'And do, er, strangers just turn up looking for jobs?'

'Not really. It's too remote. They're usually kids that Jane and Chas know, or friends of them.' He opened the gate for Fran. 'Take care,' he said.

Fran set off across the field; she could see her breath, cloudy on the cold air. 'Wouldn't be surprised if we have a bit of frost tonight, Sam,' she said. 'Better get you in the warm for some milk.' She heard Patrick call out, she turned and looked back. But he was calling to another youngster in jeans and a big black jacket who was walking down from the direction of the road.

'Clare,' he yelled. 'Are you lost? There's a gate here.'

Nice lad, Fran thought again, seems to look after people. She trudged on, relieved. No bodies washed up, then. No strangers lurking around Wraith Cove. Nothing to report from anyone.

'What shall we do this evening, Sam?' she said. 'We could watch some more of *The Nutcracker*.' She kissed the top of his head through the hood of his blue suit with the teddy bear ears. 'Or I could show you some of your grandfather's old aeroplanes that he made when he was a little boy.'

CHAPTER

Eleven

Rachel had invited some friends to supper to sample her homemade pasta. She leaned back in her chair to survey the cosy café and her guests, sitting talking around the table. The blue blinds were drawn, shutting out the cold blackness. The appetising smells of the meal they'd eaten seemed layered in the warm air. Sandro always said neutralising the smell of cooking was a mistake – the tantalising aromas of fresh ingredients worked the salivary glands into a frenzy.

'That was delicious,' Nick said. 'Thank you, Rachel.'

Rachel wiped her mouth on her serviette. 'But lasagne and pasta dishes and pizza – they're so ordinary now. When they were first introduced into this country they were considered foreign and adventurous. Now, they're like curry – part of our nation's everyday diet.'

'Ah,' Ash said, holding his glass of red wine up to the light and peering at it, 'but cooked authentically, taste the difference.'

'I think Ash is right,' Sophie said, patting her flat stomach with a sigh. 'We do need to have dishes everyone is familiar with as well as more exotic ones. That way we'll cater for all tastes.'

Jill was making an intricate pattern on a dish, with olive stones that she'd collected from everyone's plates. 'And you'll soon get to know which ones are most popular with your particular clientele. You can adjust the menu accordingly.'

Rachel groaned and reached for one of the menus. 'It took us ages to design these, and they were bloody expensive.'

Nick took the menu from her and perused it. 'I don't see why these need to be altered. Everything you and Sophie have cooked so far has been great.' He smiled at Rachel. 'Maybe you ought to show this to Kyp so he can tell you which dishes he has more expertise with.'

'That's right.' Sophie ran her hand down Nick's arm. 'Between us we might be able to produce everything on the menu.'

'And then we could invite a good mix of people and see if we can cope with anything they order.' Rachel laughed, she was beginning to feel a bit heady with relief that this meal had been so positively appraised.

'You need to get on with it, not much time left until Valentine's weekend.' Jill was frowning at her olive stones as if they'd failed to come up with the pattern she had in mind. 'Who will you use as guinea pigs?'

'It isn't medical research,' Ash commented.

'Kyp and Evie, obviously. The Water Babies could be bedded down upstairs. And Jane and Chas and Marguerite, if they are around. What about Neptune – do you think he could be prised out of Puck's Bay?'

Nick laughed. 'Unlikely. He gets more like a limpet everyday. It's hard to get two words out of him – he's turned monosyllabic. But if it's an assortment you want, there are always the youngsters working at Wraith Cove—'

'Christ,' Jill commented. 'Hope they wash themselves and comb their dreadlocks, otherwise we'll all have lice when we get home.' She scratched her head.

'Jill! For goodness sake,' Ash said, straightening his long spine and glaring down at her over his beaky nose, like a hawk.

Jill swept her olive stones into a pile. 'Joking,' she said. 'I was joking. And the Water Babies can muck in with our kids at Cormorants. Give the nanny something to do. She's an idle bitch.' She reached for her lipstick-stained glass.

Rachel suspected it was time to start winding up the meal; a few bottles of wine had been sunk and some liqueurs tested. She started to get to her feet. 'Coffee?'

Nick put a hand on her shoulder, pushing her down. 'You've done enough. I'll make it.'

'You're a lucky cow, Sophie.' Jill sprawled back in her chair and with a dramatic gesture unclamped her generous hair from its clip and let it tumble down to her shoulders. Rachel saw it had been freshly streaked with gold and black amongst the auburn. She suspected Jill

127

wanted to show it off.

'I know I am,' Sophie smiled, her dark eyes glowing as she watched Nick walk towards the kitchen.

Rachel noticed she felt envious too. Sophie and Nick certainly had chemistry. She forced her mind back to the topic of food. 'What about Blackgang Ted, and Fran from Rocken Edge? They enjoy a meal out. They often go to The Buddle Inn.'

'Good idea,' Ash said. 'Ted's coming over to tidy up the garden tomorrow. And we could ask the staff from *Cormorants* – the health practitioners. And the doctors and nurses from the surgery. That will be a good mix.'

'Great!' Jill rolled her eyes. 'And my mother will possibly be home from darkest Africa to introduce a tropical disease into the brew.' She looked at Ash. 'I daresay Rose might play a spot of Vivaldi, with a red rose between her teeth, if Daddy asks her nicely.' She turned to Rachel. 'I could be a waitress, if you like. I quite fancy dressing up.'

'No, no.' Rachel hastily racked her brains for a reason. 'I want you as an appreciative customer.' She noticed Sophie's alarmed expression and knew what she was thinking. Jill would have no qualms about tipping a dinner over an unfortunate punters head, if they criticised the food.

'So who will wait on the tables?' Jill asked.

'I will,' Nick called from the kitchen. 'And Patrick and Aidan. And I'll have a word with the kids at Wraith Cove to see who has any experience. There's a new girl called Clare who seems polite.'

Rachel felt herself relaxing, anticipating coffee. There was still a lot to plan, but it was taking shape. And what did she have to lose? She got up and wandered around, thinking. She noticed the post-box on the café door was stuffed with junk mail. She pulled it out and something heavy fell on the floor. She bent to pick it up. It was a large leather wallet.

'What's this?' She carried it over to the table. Everyone watched as she opened it. 'Why would someone put it through my door? If they found it, they should have taken it to the police station.'

'Too far to walk,' Jill said.

Rachel glanced in the different compartments. There was quite a lot of money in there. And a passport and some official looking documents. At least there would be some identity to get it back to its owner. She pulled out the passport and opened it.

'Oh, my God!' She sat down with a thump. The photo inside was of Sandro.

Sophie got up and hurried round the table to her. 'What's the matter? What is it?'

'This is Sandro's.' Rachel looked at the post-box, wondering how long the wallet had been in there. 'Who would have posted it?' She took out some more of the papers and a photo fell out. It was of her and Sandro standing in front of the café. 'So that's how . . . but why?'

*   *   *

Father Ryan congratulated himself on leaving so much time for his journey to the ferry at Rosslare. That would teach Father Christopher for laughing at his caution. The journey had been interesting too. Slow but sure, always the best way. And his car had run well. He stopped frequently, just in case the engine overheated, but the old Morris Minor stayed cool. The radio still worked – once he felt confident with his driving, he tuned it to Radio Three and enjoyed Bach's *Third Brandenburg Concerto in G Major*. He'd eaten his sandwiches and drunk his flask of tea at various viewpoints, contemplating the Irish scenery which was brushed with a light layer of snow in places. How little he'd seen of his own country.

But on the evening ferry, he'd begun to feel overwhelmed. It was far larger than he expected. Caught up in the queue of snarling traffic he managed to embark and find his way to a lounge. But there were so many noisy bustling people. He went outside, in the dark, to be by himself, but as soon as they set sail, an icy wind blasted the breath out of his body and he was forced to head back inside. People were eating at tables and sitting around drinking alcohol. It was more like a hotel than a ship. The constant movement made it difficult to walk straight, and caused him to feel nauseous.

He perched on the edge of a long padded seat, turning away from the other people sitting there. He opened his black briefcase and

129

rummaged through some papers, trying to look busy, just in case someone spoke to him. Maybe he should have worn trousers and pretended to be an ordinary man. But he wanted to ask a few people – members of staff – if they remembered Clare, and he was sure that no-one would take any notice of him without his clerical garb. This was the ferry she'd travelled on. He wondered how she'd coped – a little Irish girl who'd never been much further than Bantry. He shrugged his shoulders. She was young and resilient, and hadn't he arranged it all for her? All she had to do was sit on coaches, and the boat, and have everything taken care of at the end of her journey. Except, she hadn't reached the end, had she? And he had to find out if she'd been on this boat.

Father Ryan took a photo out of an envelope. It was a picture of the school choir; Clare stood out well, because of her long red plait which was pulled over her shoulder and hanging down her front. She'd obviously been showing it off for the camera. Such vanity. He glanced around. The only members of staff he could see were serving food and drink. He wished that he'd saved some sandwiches. He was feeling quite sick and didn't want to join the queue for food. He got up and wandered shakily around the big lounge. There were some vending machines, but they only offered crisps and chocolate and fizzy drinks. A young man in uniform was thumping one of them. Father Ryan waved the photo under his nose and asked if he could spare a moment. The youth looked annoyed, but then noticed the dog collar and adjusted his expression.

'Her mother is so worried about her, you see,' Father Ryan added to his explanation.

The boy peered, then shook his head. 'There are so many people . . . ' he gestured around. 'See for yourself. It's hard to remember one girl – so far back.'

'But,' Father Ryan waggled the photo, 'her hair . . . '

The boy shrugged. 'Ask the band.' He pointed to a small stage where musicians were arranging themselves. 'They've been playing on this run for ages.' At that moment the band launched into a lively Irish jig and people began cheering and whistling. The noise was unbearable. Father Ryan tottered to the other end of the lounge and found a men's cloakroom. He sat down in a cubicle for a while; someone was retching in an adjacent one. When he ventured out, a steward was mopping the floor. Father Ryan showed him the photo.

'Only just started here, mate. Can't imagine why I did.' He stared ruefully at the mess on the floor. 'Go and ask the bar staff.'

Father Ryan swayed back to the bar and squeezed his way to the front of the throng. The bartenders passed the photo along to each other, barely glancing at it. He retrieved it and bought himself lemonade and crisps and found a place to sit.

'Feeling rough, Father?' A large woman wearing a blinding red and white outfit shuffled along the seat towards him. 'What are you drinking there?'

'Lemonade,' he mumbled.

'That's no good if you're feeling queasy.' She reached across the table for a bottle. 'Have a drop of this. It'll settle your stomach.'

'Oh, er, is it alcohol?'

The woman and a couple of inebriated men laughed uproariously.

'Medicinal!' she yelled. 'It'll do the trick.' She poured some into a glass and proffered it. 'Here you go, Father.'

Father Ryan took a gulp. The liquid burned its way down his throat to his stomach. He gasped and coughed and sat feeling shocked, his eyes watering. But it was true, he did feel better. He took another sip, and another. The heat inside him felt good. He found himself smiling around at the company.

'So, where is it you're heading?' asked the red and white woman.

'I'm looking for a missing child,' he said. 'In England. She travelled over on this boat.'

'It's a good man, you are, and all.' The woman turned to the other people. 'Would you pay attention to this fine priest, giving up his time to look for a wee girl?' He pointed out Clare in the photo and it went from hand to hand. More and more people seem to be joining in. The band stopped playing after a while and joined them for a rest. The photo was passed to them. Father Ryan began to feel concerned that it would be destroyed with all the handling.

'Sure, I remember her,' one of the fiddle players said.

'Go on wid yer, Jo. You wouldn't remember a girl if she sat on yer head,' the woman laughed.

'I would an' all. Well, maybe not her face,' Jo smirked.

Father Ryan wondered if he should move away from this raucous bunch of people. But he was starting to feeling exhausted and everything seemed blurred and dreamlike.

The photo was passed round again.

'Give it back here,' Jo said, grabbing at it. 'I swear I remember her. She was with that gorgeous girl with the wild hair and big tits – sorry, Father –you know, the one who joined in with us – on the fiddle. Bit of a posh bird, but up for it.'

'No, she was all alone,' Father Ryan managed to say, 'very young, only thirteen.' Thirteen. Was she really only thirteen? She must be fourteen by now. But old for her age, too old by far.

'What's her name, the little one?' the woman asked.

'Clare.'

Jo shook his head. 'Can't remember. Didn't speak to her. Just seem to recognise her, maybe not. The hair just reminded me . . . the posh one had a boyfriend.' He turned to another young man who was gulping a huge glass of Guinness.

'Carl, you surely remember that girl who played wid us? She was a good musician.'

Carl belched loudly. 'I never forget a girl who plays with me,' he laughed. 'When was this?'

'Last summer, end of July.' Father Ryan managed to get the words out – his tongue felt thick and dry. 'But it's not that girl I'm looking for.'

'People do join in, we invite them. Usually rubbish.' Carl sat, tapping his fingers on the table. 'We sometimes get the occasional star.' He turned to Jo. 'Good tits, you say? I remember the one with the messy hair – all tied up and half falling down. I thought she might get it caught in the bow.' He looked at Father Ryan. 'Does that sound like her?'

Father Ryan was feeling exasperated with these young brash men with their straggling hair and unshaven chins. But he was unable to raise the energy to explain further. He took a deep breath. 'No,' he said. 'Definitely not.'

The musicians lost interest, turned away and soon went back to the stage to resume playing.

'Rose,' Carl shouted over the din. 'I'm sure her name was Rose.'

'God, give me strength,' Father Ryan slurred. His heavy eyelids closed, and he vaguely remembered resting his head on a red and white shoulder as he fell asleep, still clutching the photo.

CHAPTER
Twelve

Clare sat on a little wooden stool in the porch of Wraith Cottage. She'd had another long soak in the bath and then wandered around the cottage garden knowing that Jane and Marguerite had gone away. She thought they wouldn't mind. She wasn't doing any harm, sitting there, sheltered from the cold wind. The clouds were moving fast across the sky and there was a faint orange glow of sun behind them. Earlier there'd been a sparkle of frost, but it had melted now. The garden in front of her stretched to the edge of the cliff, which wasn't far. She could hear the waves dragging the stones on the beach below. What a strange place to live. Everything seemed jumbled up, as if someone had created a garden from whatever oddments of wood and rope they could find. It wasn't like her mam's garden with its straight rows of lettuces and potato plants.

She pulled her hat on over her wet hair and zipped up her coat. She knew that something had changed inside her. Yesterday – after posting Sandro's wallet through the door of *Rachel's Café,* she had found the police station and it was closed. Her mind seemed to go blank. In the absence of any other idea she'd returned here. She'd tried to avoid meeting anyone by sneaking along the hotel wall to where the caravans were parked. But Patrick had been at the gate talking to a woman. Clare tried to duck down, but he spotted her and called out, as if she were lost. She had no choice but to walk towards him. Fortunately the woman had hurried off. It was then – as she was walking – that she decided not to run away again. What was the point? Why had she so desperately wanted to go with Sandro? She might just as well stay here and wait. If people were looking for her, they would find her, no matter where she was.

She had given Kate some money and helped cook a supper of baked beans and fried eggs. Nobody spoke to her much because there was an important football match on the television. She'd gone to bed early, and this morning told Kate she needed another day to rest, and then she would help with the painting.

After her bath she'd inspected her body in the mirror and decided she was much better. The afterbirth bleeding had stopped and her breasts were smaller and softer, the leaking less. She was still tired, continuously yawning. Her face was deathly white – her freckles seemed paler. It was as if everything in her body had drained out, even the nest of worms was still. All she had to do now was wait.

Clare looked down at the flagstones in the porch of Wraith Cottage and was reminded of the church at home. Her mam was always scrubbing the entrance. Why did she bother? The stones just got dirty again as the congregation trudged across them with their muddy shoes. But the flagstones seemed of great importance to her mam – far more important than Clare. Mam would get cross, as if she expected people to somehow leap over them. And Daddy used to get angry with Mam for being cross about the dirt. He shouted that she cared more about dirt than she did for him. And Mam used to shout back that he *was* dirt – a dirty, filthy Scottish man! Clare would put her hands over her ears and run down to the shore where she would sit and cry. She thought her da was right, but she didn't want them to fight about it.

Did Mam miss her? Was she lonely living on her own? She wouldn't have anyone to make her a cup of tea when she came in tired from sweeping the church in the evenings. Would she have heard yet that Clare had run away from the abbey? Father Ryan must know – Mother would have written to him. Clare had once asked Mother if she had ever met Father Ryan. Mother had looked bewildered, as if Clare had asked a stupid question. *You're not to talk about all that,* she said, blinking at Clare, with eyes reddened by the smoke of the fire, and the steam from the pan of beetroots she was stirring to make dye for the baby's clothes. *I don't have anything to do with men, and neither should you. This is a place for women, and it's your home now.*

But Clare couldn't help thinking about her old home. Should she have written, or tried to phone? Mother said she wasn't allowed. Did Father Ryan mean her not to return? He hadn't said so. But then he hadn't really told her anything about what she was supposed to do after the birth. He *used* to tell her things – before she told him about the baby. He told her about his little sister, Jeannie, and how they once lived in a log cabin beside a big lake and slept in a bed together covered by a red shawl. Clare wondered where the lake was and wished she could go there with him. He told her about catching fish, and swimming, and running about without any clothes on. He said Clare reminded him of Jeannie, and then he'd hold her really tightly. Her own daddy had cuddled her in his big arms – not in the same way as Father Ryan – and *he'd* told her she was a good girl too. And then, when she was four, her daddy disappeared. That was when Mam said he'd drowned in an accident on the fishing boat. Mam never smiled again, indoors. She never talked of Daddy either, except if Clare had been bad, and then Mam would say she was just like her father.

Clare wondered what her father would have done if he'd been there when Father Ryan told Mam about the baby. Would he have hit her across the face, like Mam did, when she burst screaming into Clare's bedroom?

Clare put her hand to her cheek as if she could still feel the stinging blow that made her jaw ache for days. Suddenly, she heard footsteps crunching on the pebble path. She stood up, knocking the stool over. A man in yellow waterproofs came into view. He stopped abruptly.

'What do you think you're doing?' he demanded.

'I, er, was looking for Jane.'

'Where did you come from?'

'I'm working on the hotel – with the students.'

The man pushed his cap back. He was very old. 'You'd best be getting back then, hadn't you?'

'I came down for a bath – Jane said—'

'Bath house is round the other side. This is private.'

Clare turned away. 'Sorry,' she mumbled.

'Told 'er not to let them youngsters run wild . . . ' Clare heard him muttering as she hurried away.

*   *   *

Fran felt a sense of pride as she pushed Sam in his buggy around *Mothercare*. She'd spent ages deciphering the manual on how to secure the car seat into the Land Rover, and then onto the pram chassis. Also, she'd agonised about where she should go to shop. Niton and Ventnor were too local, she still felt nervous about being seen with Sam. Newport was more anonymous. Poor Cinders had been left behind, drooping and mournful. Fran always took her on excursions. But she didn't know whether she'd be able to manage a pram and a dog at the same time. As it happened, the buggy was easy to manoeuvre and she began to feel confident. Nobody eyed her suspiciously, and anyone she spoke to in the shops assumed she was the baby's grandmother.

She'd already been to the supermarket to stock up on nappies and babyfood, and was now wandering around simply for the pleasure of it. She didn't really need more clothes for Sam, but she felt as if a completely new world of interesting equipment had been presented to her, that he might possibly need in the future. He doesn't have any toys, she thought. Filled with a childlike happiness she bought soft, rattling, squeaky things and cloth books. They were such nice textures and bright colours. She couldn't believe how expensive everything was. She would have to go to the bank and draw out some more of her meagre savings. She stopped outside *The Early Learning Centre* – maybe just a quick peep. And then she would have to go home – she couldn't carry many more bags, and Sam would be waking for a feed soon.

On a sudden impulse, she walked along to the police station. A couple of young women were standing outside, smoking. Fran ducked her head, preparing to pass by, but the girls ground out their cigarettes on the pavement and moved away. Fran stopped and glanced at the notice boards, half dreading that she would see a poster about a missing baby. She still couldn't quite fit together all the pieces of this mystery. If the mother had gone to the police it would have been because she had no memory of leaving Sam in her stable. And surely the police

137

would have been able to tell, with all the tests they could do, where she had been wandering. They would have searched every farm building on the island by now. Maybe her body had been swept far out to sea. The only other possibility she could think of was that someone had stolen the baby and then got scared and abandoned it. But wouldn't that have provoked a huge search? People would be talking about it, newspapers would have blazing headlines, the radio would be discussing it non-stop. So, had Sam simply been abandoned by a mother who didn't want him? But why in her stable? Because it was so remote? And where was she now? Surely someone must know her and question what she'd done with her baby.

Fran felt anger pulsing inside her. I won't give him up to a woman who could leave him like that, she thought, don't care if she is his mother. She doesn't deserve him.

'Fran?' A woman's voice spoke beside her. Fran, lost in her thoughts, jumped and grabbed tightly at the handle of the buggy.

'I thought it was you.'

It was Rachel from the café. Fran stared at her, not knowing what to say.

'Not used to seeing you pushing a pram,' Rachel laughed. 'Have you got a baby in there, or some lambs?'

Fran swallowed and attempted a smile. 'My great-nephew,' she managed to say.

Rachel came closer and peered inside the pram. 'Oh, he's teeny-weeny. Is he new?'

Fran nodded. 'One month,' she said, thinking this might be about right.

'Gorgeous,' Rachel cooed. She looked around as if wondering where the parents were.

'I'm waiting for my nephew,' Fran said, glancing at her watch.

'Oh,' Rachel seemed slightly uncomfortable. She looked at a large brown wallet she was holding, then gestured towards the police station 'Is he in there?'

Fran nodded. 'Lost his passport,' she said vaguely.

'Really? How strange,' Rachel said. 'Where is he from?'

'Australia.'

'Australia!' Rachel looked amazed. 'Fancy travelling all that way with a new baby.'

'Sleeps well,' Fran said.

Rachel was shifting the wallet from hand to hand. 'I'm glad I bumped into you. I was going to invite you to try out my Italian menu at the café, on Saturday evening. I've asked a group of friends to give me feedback.'

'I, er—'

'No charge, of course. You'd be doing me a favour. Bring Blackgang Ted.'

Fran nodded towards the pram. 'I'm not sure what my visitors are doing.'

'Bring them all – if they'd like to come. I'd welcome some Australian palates.'

'Well, the baby—'

'Bring him too; his mother can use my flat. The more the merrier.' She glanced towards the police station again then shoved the wallet into her bag. 'I must go. Give me a ring.'

Fran watched Rachel hurry away until she was out of sight. It was beginning to rain, cold and sleety. Flocks of gulls swooped and screeched overhead, seeking the warmth in the centre of the island. She fastened the raincover on the buggy, pulled up the hood of her duffle coat and headed for the car park. She was looking forward to getting back to Rocken Edge with Sam, and settling in for a cosy afternoon. Cinders might be getting anxious. She smiled as she walked. There was something in her that seemed to overrule the surges of anxiety. It took command like the ocean absorbing the power of a wave. Quite a few people knew about her great-nephew now. I wonder, she thought, I wonder if I dare take him to Rachel's. The smile gradually faded from her face. Soon, she was going to have to deal with the problem of the missing relatives.

*   *   *

On Wednesday evening, Father Ryan sat at a little table in the window of the guest house he'd spotted in Abergavenny. He was enjoying his supper of home-baked shepherd's pie, broccoli and carrots. The pie had a crisp cheesy top and the vegetables tasted fresh. Pity Mrs Mulligan couldn't cook like that. There was only one other couple in the dining room and they were engrossed in each other. The landlady bustled in and out with the dishes and seemed too shy to talk to him. He ran his finger under his clerical collar, thinking how easily his uniform provided a way in to people's lives; and a way out when necessary. He thought back over his exciting day.

After he'd disembarked from the ferry at Pembroke, well after midnight, he'd driven a few miles and parked in a lay-by. He slept for several hours, surprisingly well, on the cramped back seat, covered with Jeannie's shawl and his overcoat. He woke without a headache for the first time in ages. Could it have been the whiskey that awful red and white woman had given him? He got out of the car and stretched his stiff limbs. He had to defrost the windscreen – the grass and trees sparkled with hoarfrost. It was a grand morning to be travelling. He checked his map to make sure he was on the right road and set off.

He stopped for breakfast at a scruffy roadside café with enormous lorries parked outside, probably on their way to the docks. He ate bacon and eggs and drank strong tea out of a huge thick mug. The lorry drivers created a dense atmosphere with their smoke and body smells and he heard a few ribald vicar jokes, obviously intended for his ears. He found he didn't mind. He didn't have to deal with these men. He was a foreigner. He'd driven the breadth of Ireland and sailed across the Irish Sea to this land – a place of hills and valleys where people talked with a lilting accent. It hadn't been as frightening as he'd anticipated. Cork had scared him the most, but caught in a line of traffic, he just had to keep going. And tomorrow he would drive across the border into England. As he thought about it, his confidence grew. The lorry drivers made crude remarks about men in dresses. He grinned back at them and followed them into the lavatories, joining them in the line at the urinal. He'd show them he was a real man.

Later, he'd stopped at a supermarket and bought himself a bottle of whiskey. He took occasional sips as he drove through Wales and his relaxed mood stayed with him. Perhaps this was the answer to his troubles. He might not have a brain tumour. He just needed something to take the tension out of his body. Why had he never discovered this before? Maybe there were other things he could try that he'd never dreamed of.

And now, in the guest house, he was relishing his supper. He smiled at the landlady as she served him a mound of red and yellow trifle, the creamy top sprinkled with children's sweets. She blushed and hurried away. He almost wished she *would* talk to him; he felt as if his words might flow easily. He looked down at his briefcase propped against the table leg. His heart warmed at the thought of the bottle of whiskey in there. He would have to be careful though, it wouldn't do to be caught with alcohol on his breath, driving a car.

He forced down the last spoonful of trifle, feeling his belly straining against his belt. Flopping back in his chair, he became aware of a small face staring at him. A little girl was peeping round the door of the dining room. Her head was heaped with a mass of blonde curls. Father Ryan smiled at her. Shyly, she came into the room. She was wearing pink and white pyjamas. Her feet were bare. She was clutching a furry toy to her chest. She looked around the room and back at Father Ryan. He smiled again, encouragingly. The child didn't smile back, but she sat down on the carpet and smiled at the toy instead, bouncing it up and down in her lap, glancing up at him from time to time. Father Ryan knew she wanted him to watch her. That's what little girls were like. He sighed. She was entrancing. He was suddenly reminded of a book he'd read at school. It was about an old miser who had his pot of gold stolen but found a little girl with golden hair in its place. He took her into his house and cared for her and they adored each other. *Silas Marner* – that was it. He'd always envied that man.

The landlady came into the room. 'Beth!' She yanked the little girl to her feet. 'You know you're not allowed in here. Go back to bed.'

Why were women so awful? Father Ryan wondered. And to think

141

he'd been wishing she would talk with him. He picked up his briefcase and got up from the table. There was a television in his bedroom. He might just see what was on, and maybe have a wee night cap.

*   *   *

Rachel sat at a table in The Buddle Inn with Sophie and Nick. The huge log fire was blazing and Allan, the resident musician, was strumming *Country Roads,* his mellow voice soporific. Everyone was overheated and yawning over their drinks. Rachel's thoughts drifted towards the mysterious appearance of Sandro's wallet, and the anonymous person who'd posted it through her letterbox.

'Could have been anybody,' Sophie said, as if reading her thoughts. 'At least it was someone honest, who recognised you – or the café – in the photo.'

'Why didn't they take it to the police station though?' Rachel said.

'Never open,' Nick commented. 'And they obviously thought you would know the owner.'

'You'd have thought they would knock, wouldn't you – with something that valuable?'

'Perhaps they did, and we didn't hear them above the clashing of saucepans and the warbling of Andrea Bocelli,' Sophie smiled.

'No one could ever accuse him of warbling,' Nick laughed.

'Hadn't you noticed? I've given him up. It's back to my Irish folk music from now on.'

'Except on Italian nights – that won't create the right ambience for the customers,' Nick said.

'So, what are you going to do with the wallet?' Sophie asked.

'I don't know. I nearly took it into Newport police station this morning. I thought Sandro might go there to see if it had been handed in.'

'But?' Nick prompted.

'But – I just couldn't bring myself to do it. I mean, he's in some sort of trouble, isn't he? I might make things worse if I give it to the police. And I didn't want them to have the photo.'

'Why not? You've got nothing to hide,' Sophie said.

'Yes, but . . .oh, I don't know. I can't be rational about this. I just

142

couldn't do it.'

'But now you're lumbered with it,' Nick said.

Rachel nodded and let out a long sigh. 'You're right. I should have handed it in. I'll do it tomorrow.' She got up. 'My round.'

She went up to the bar. Deep down inside she knew she'd clung on to the wallet because it felt like a little bit of Sandro had come back to her. But *he* didn't know that, obviously. So there wasn't much point.

Blackgang Ted was leaning on the bar, sorting out the world with a couple of local men.

'Good evening, Rachel,' he said, taking off his cap. 'Nice to see you brightening up The Buddle.'

'Hello, Ted. I was talking about you this morning with Fran, met her in Newport.'

'Ah, I can't get a look in at the moment. All in a flummox about her visitors, she is. Anyone would think the royal family was staying, the fuss she's making.'

'She was waiting for them when I saw her – proudly guarding a baby in a smart pram. I thought at first it might be a new lamb.'

Ted guffawed. 'That'd be more like her, wouldn't it? Can't believe it, the way she's taken to childminding. That family of hers . . . I told her . . . don't let them take advantage. Haven't seen them, meself – they're always out, leaving her with the kiddy . . . at her age. Did you say she was talking about me?'

'We were. I invited you both to dinner at my café, on Saturday evening. A trial run for the Italian cuisine.'

'She won't come. Not with her folks staying.'

'I suggested she bring them all – baby as well.'

Ted grinned. 'That should do it then.'

'Do you happen to know if Jane and family will be home by Saturday?'

'They're not due back until Monday – but you never know – they often change their minds. Marguerite doesn't like to be away from Wraith Cove for too long.'

Rachel carried the drinks back to the table. Sophie and Nick

143

were leaning against each other, the firelight adding to their look of contentment. Allan was playing a Buddy Holly medley, *everyday, it's a gettin' closer* . . . .How nice it would be to stop time for a while and have nothing to do. She yawned. Was it worth all this frantic activity just to keep the physical body peddling the bike towards the Grim Reaper? *Goin' faster than a roller-coaster* . . . Was there a purpose to all this? She looked at Nick who was gazing at Sophie. Did love make it all worthwhile? She couldn't think of another question that made sense.

'We need to do a headcount for Saturday,' she groaned. 'The numbers are rising. Thursday tomorrow – not much time left.'

'I sense a huge shopping list shaping up,' Sophie mumbled sleepily.

'*Please* let your woman get some sleep tonight,' Rachel said to Nick. 'And can you do some recruiting tomorrow at Wraith Cove? We're going to need those students of yours.'

CHAPTER

Thirteen

If there was one thing Clare knew how to do it was paint walls. Ever since she'd been strong enough to hold a paintbrush her mother had started her on a routine of wall painting. If it wasn't in their own house, it was in the church buildings, or the convent. *We must keep everything pure*, her mam told her, as she scrubbed and polished. *White walls reflect good Catholic souls, and don't they show off the pictures and statues nicely?*

Painting a wall, without any drips or runs, was one of the few things that Clare received praise for. The other things were: obedience, and singing nicely in Father Ryan's choir.

The paint that Clare was using on the wall in the stable block was whiter and creamier than her mam's watered down stuff. It covered the area with satisfying strokes, and didn't keep running down the brush and dripping on the floor. Kate was painting the opposite wall, and Jules and Billy were in adjoining rooms. She could hear them calling out to each other and laughing. Music was playing on a little radio in the corridor. Kate was singing as she worked, *you're the one that I want . . . oooh, hooo, hooo . . .*

Clare wished she could just stay here like this, painting walls. Kate had stopped asking her questions now she was better. Jules and Billy didn't appear to be at all interested in her, and Aidan wasn't around. She supposed he was at school. He was the one that worried her. She noticed him watching her last night at supper, and he seemed to take every opportunity to sit near her and talk. He'd even touched her plait of hair and told her it was fabulous when it hung loose. He talked about going to university next year and asked her opinion about taking a year off. He obviously thought she was the same age as Rose. Clare had made an excuse to go back to Kate's caravan and have an early night.

She lay in her bunk reading *Tess* but, remembering Tess's miserable end, she tucked the book deep into her backpack and fell asleep.

She felt much better painting the wall. Her arm seemed to be working automatically at the familiar task. She remembered another wall like this, in a similar room, where Father Ryan kept his vestments, and the choir their robes. She had gone after school, on her mam's instructions, to check the wall was dry, so that the clothes could be hung back up. *We mustn't disrupt the Father's routine,* she'd said. *He'll be wanting to get dressed for evening mass.*

Clare had been aware that Father Ryan was watching her as she stretched up to the hooks. *Let me help you, there,* he said. He was always so kind to her. Clare knew her mam would disapprove – Clare should be doing the tasks, not him. But he'd come up behind her and clasped her shoulders. His hands felt cold through her school blouse. She didn't know what to do, so simply stood there. And then he'd bent and kissed the top of her head. *Sweet girl,* he murmured, *always looking after me.* He slid his arms around her from behind, wrapping them across her tender chest. *Let me give you a little cuddle for being kind to Father.* He pulled her against him and swayed with her gently from side to side. Clare had no choice but to lean back and sway with him. *This is nice,* he murmured. The swaying became faster; Clare could feel his whole body pressed against her back. She felt anxious, wondering if she was meant to know about this – should she be doing something? But suddenly the swaying stopped and he let go of her so quickly, she almost fell. She looked round at him, but his face was turned away, he was bending over, breathing fast. Clare didn't know what to do – was he feeling ill? But then he straightened up. *Go now,* he said, sharply. *I'll finish hanging up the clothes.* Clare wondered if she'd displeased him. *Thank you, Father,* she whispered. He turned to her. *Now, why don't you come back at the same time tomorrow?* His face looked pink and his eyes were glittering. *You could help me sort out my clothes.* Clare couldn't understand how his clothes might need sorting. They were hanging up, just like they always were. She didn't know what to say. *I might have a little treat for you,* he said, smiling, waiting for her to speak. *If you*

146

don't want to, I'll ask one of the other wee girls. A strong feeling that she was about to lose something rose up in her. *I, I'll come,* she said. *I'll tell Mam.* He reached for his stole. *Do that,* he said.

That night Clare had lain in bed thinking about Father Ryan. She recalled the feeling of his arms around her. It had confused her when he hadn't let go, but a bit of her had enjoyed it too. She liked the smell of him, and she never got cuddles from her mam, like she used to from Daddy. She missed that. She wondered if she should tell her mam, but it seemed a secret thing, somehow. She was aware of a little feeling of excitement inside her as she fell asleep.

Clare dipped her brush in the paint and sighed. It all seemed such a long time ago. She was a little girl then, who didn't know anything. She didn't understand she was being wicked. Perhaps Father Ryan should have realised and sent her away. But he wasn't to know about the feelings that were going on inside her.

'Nice job.'

Clare nearly dropped her paintbrush. Patrick had come into the room and she hadn't even noticed.

'Gather round, guys,' he called. Jules and Billy appeared – Billy had white paint daubed in his dreadlocks.

'She did it,' he said, pointing at Jules.

'Okay, little children,' Patrick said. 'Listen up. Have any of you had any experience waiting on tables in cafés or restaurants? Or, to put it another way – who would like to earn some extra dosh on Saturday evening?'

'I've worked in a posh hotel in Australia,' Kate said.

'I've done a *McDonald's* stint,' Jules grinned.

'Not me, man,' Billy said. 'Hair too long, and stuff.'

'Couldn't disagree with that,' Patrick said. 'How about you, Clare?'

She shook her head.

Patrick looked from Billy to Clare. 'Could you two manage some table clearing and washing up?'

'Sure. How difficult can that be?' Billy said.

Clare had a brief moment of panic. She would be amongst strangers; anything might happen. But then, wasn't that what she was waiting for – something to happen? She nodded. 'I'll do it.'

'Great. I'll tell my mother.' Patrick gave Billy's hair a flick as he went out. 'You'll need to scrub up – it's a smart restaurant.'

'Your mum's café? Smart?' Jules shouted after him.

'Wait until you see it on Saturday. The transformation into Italian restaurant will amaze you,' he called back.

'Where is this place?' Clare asked.

'Ventnor. *Rachel's Café,*' Kate said. 'Patrick and Aidan's mother is turning it into an Italian restaurant in the evenings, and she's having a trial run.' She lowered her voice. 'Trouble is, the man Rachel was in partnership with has run off and let her down. He was Italian – a fantastic chef, apparently.'

Rachel's Café! Clare turned back to her painting. Rachel was Patrick and Aidan's mother. That's where she'd posted Sandro's wallet. Was she the woman in the photo? But Sandro had told Clare he worked in the hotel in Shanklin where he got someone's wife into trouble. Perhaps he'd worked in both places and had to run away from everyone. That would mean Rachel wouldn't be able to give him his wallet. And Clare had thought she was doing a helpful thing. It seemed she couldn't do anything right. Her brush swept across the wall. What did it all matter anyway?

*　　　*　　　*

Father Ryan sat in his car looking at his pocket book. He wanted to phone Sister Bridget, to arrange his visit to the convent to talk about Clare. He turned the pages back and forth. How odd, he'd written the address in twice. Now, why had he done that? He resisted the temptation to have a swig out of his precious bottle. It might clear his head, but he was driving, and he certainly didn't want his breath to smell of alcohol when he arrived. He looked again at the identical addresses and phone numbers. He remembered copying them out. Of course he had; he'd copied the address for Clare. But why hadn't he given it to her? He'd meant to tear out the page. But there *was* a page torn out – the ragged edges were still there.

Holy Mary, Mother of God! He'd torn out the wrong page. He'd

148

given Clare the address of the convent before it had been moved to a new site. Was that why she was missing? Had she simply gone to the wrong address? But that couldn't be true. Surely the girl would have had enough sense to ask someone where the new convent was situated. He shook his head – the tension seemed to be creeping back. Just one little sip wouldn't do him any harm. He took the bottle from his brief case. He could always suck a peppermint.

Stupid child, he thought. He'd always known she was stupid. He should never have trusted her. Now what was he to do? Maybe he should drive to the old convent and see if anyone still lived in the place. He remembered the address quite clearly. Perhaps it was used for another purpose now. And someone might remember seeing Clare around.

It wasn't far to the outskirts of Hereford. But there was no sign of the convent where it should have been. Half a dozen new houses had been built on the site. He walked along the unmade road and knocked at each of the doors. At one of them a curtain twitched, but the inhabitants didn't appear. They probably thought he'd come to preach at them – as if a man in his position would do such a thing. There was no-one in three of the houses. The other two were answered by women with snivelling kids clinging round their legs. They looked at Clare's photo but said they hadn't seen her.

He walked back to the car and sat with the engine running, trying to warm himself. Perhaps Clare had never been here. Maybe she was still back in Ireland. But somehow he didn't think so. If the wicked girl had planned to run away and get an abortion, she would have come to England. He felt at a loss. He'd had no help, either from the mad people on the ferry or from these vague housewives. Wasn't it turning out to be a waste of time? Maybe he should go and visit Sister Bridget and discuss it with her. Perhaps she would be able to think of something. He couldn't go home without knowing the truth. How could he spend the rest of his life in fear of Clare's accusations? Sudden anger flared up inside him. Maybe he should have realised she would break her promise to him. He was too trusting by far. He should have dealt with her, somehow, an accident . . . why hadn't he thought of that? But then, there would have been a post-mortem . . . he took another sip of whiskey and then popped a mint in his mouth.

He studied his map. Maybe he wouldn't bother to phone Sister Bridget, he would simply turn up. After all, she was his cousin. Not that relationships should mean anything to a nun in an enclosed order – they were all married to God. But he knew what women were like. She'd surely experience the sin of pride that her cousin – a priest – had come to visit her all the way from Ireland. And she'd be permitted to receive him in a guest room.

It was harder to gain entrance to the new convent than he thought. He had to make his request for a visit through a grille to unidentifiable women. But, as usual, his status got him through. Sister Bridget met him in a small modern library which smelled of wax polish. Another nun was flicking a duster at the books, quite unnecessarily acting as chaperone. His cousin looked the same as he remembered her, although he hadn't seen her for years, since she was a novice. Her serious face was smooth beneath her black veil and she looked a bit stouter where the cord was knotted around her waist. She fingered a black bead rosary while they talked. Father Ryan sensed she was annoyed that he'd turned up like this. She appeared to sniff the air between them. He wondered if she could smell the whiskey. Too bad, he thought, she hasn't been much help in all this. And he could always say it was cough medicine, if she commented.

'I really don't know what else I can do,' she said. Her voice was calm, distant. Father Ryan could detect barely a trace of her Irish roots. 'I find it hard to believe that you could have sent her to the wrong address – such a young girl – on her own. It was most careless.'

'Ah, you didn't know her. Very grown up, a wilful girl.'

'Nevertheless, young and inexperienced – and vulnerable – in her condition.'

Father Ryan let out a short laugh. 'As I say, you didn't know her.'

'Neither did you, it seems,' she said, coldly. 'Anything could have happened to her. As I said, we checked the hospitals and we also asked the Salvation Army – they do the best work with missing youngsters.

This isn't the sort of situation I usually deal with. The foster family we'd arranged for her were really upset. And you did ask me not to inform the police.' She folded her hands in her lap. 'I can't think why.'

'Her mother wouldn't allow it. She didn't want the scandal.'

Sister Bridget leaned forward slightly, her eyes looked fierce. 'You should have overruled her. Clare is a child, a minor, in need of protection.'

Father Ryan sighed, what did this woman know about young girls? He was finding this meeting unpleasant. He'd expected Bridget to be compliant. Had she forgotten her vows of poverty, chastity and *obedience*? He wondered what her Mother Superior would think of this display of opinionated self-will. He wasn't going to be made to feel guilty, as if he were to blame. 'So, what would you have done in Clare's position? I mean, arriving at that address and finding nothing there?'

'I cannot imagine myself in such a tragic dilemma, Father Ryan.' She rattled her rosary. 'But I think Clare might walk to the nearest place where she could inquire as to the whereabouts of the new convent and how to get there. But, seeing as she didn't arrive here, I assume she didn't do that. Unless someone misdirected her.'

'What do you mean – misdirected her?'

'People are always on the lookout for stray children. Who knows? Maybe someone took her in – another church, perhaps – but the Salvation Army would probably have known about that. There are some religious cults about too.'

A bell sounded in the distance. She rose from her seat. 'I must go. It's been . . . pleasant.' She looked past him to the door as if wishing him gone. 'If I were you I would inquire at the other convents and monasteries in the county. There aren't many. She may have called in at one of them. Although I doubt it, I'm sure I would have heard. I pray to God you find her safe and well. Good bye.'

Father Ryan walked back to his car feeling cold and hungry. What a miserable woman Bridget had become. He thought he might have been offered lunch, or at least a cup of tea. At home the women would have fallen over themselves to feed him. Maybe he would drive into Hereford and visit the cathedral; he'd heard it was a fine building. He'd find someone to talk to there and get some information about other religious institutions in the area.

*   *   *

'Good cabbage, Ted.' Fran chewed a mouthful enthusiastically. She knew it would give her terrible cramp and wind later. But she felt guilty about the number of Ted's cabbages she fed to her animals, or composted.

Ted was cutting into a pork chop. 'Can't beat a Savoy – full of goodness them.' He waved a fork at her. 'And you need good sustenance at the moment with all this goin' on.' He nodded towards the moses basket on top of the sideboard, in which Sam was sleeping. 'Can't have you getting worn out.'

'I'm enjoying it. Don't you worry, I can look after myself.'

'You don't though, never have. You'd be suffering from malnutrition by now if I didn't bother to bring you decent food.'

Fran patted her plump body and laughed. 'Do I look malnourished?'

'It's quality, not quantity,' Ted remarked, piling more cabbage on her plate. 'Mind you, I like your quantity.'

'Stop. I'll explode if I eat that lot. Anyway, I've never been ill in my life – not really ill. I get plenty of exercise with my walk every day.'

Sam started to stir in his basket, making little squeaks. Fran put her knife and fork down.

'Eat your dinner,' Ted snapped. 'You'll spoil him if you pick him up everytime he squawks. He's not crying proper.'

Fran had never heard Ted so snappish. It occurred to her that he was jealous. How silly to feel like that about a baby. But then, men were silly sometimes. She remembered Phillip sulking for days if he wasn't the centre of attention. Mum always seemed to be running around trying to keep the men of the family happy. Fran was left to sort herself out. But she'd liked that. It meant she could sneak off to be with the animals and nobody missed her. But Phillip had been allowed to go to cubs and scouts and even on a school holiday to France. All Fran had ever

152

wanted was to have ballet lessons. Her parents had laughed at that and said it would be a waste of money, given her physique. Anyway, they couldn't afford it. So Fran had kept her fantasies to herself and learned to be content with her pictures of ethereal creatures wafting through surreal landscapes. What a joy it had been when she acquired the old video player at a car boot sale. Now she could sit and indulge herself as long as she pleased.

'Been working at Cormorants?' she asked, thinking a change of subject would be a good idea.

'Not much to do up there – just a bit of tidying. Everything's either sodden or frozen. Bulbs are coming up though. That garden will look a picture this year. Should do, money they've spent on it.'

'Doing all right then, the health centre?'

Ted nodded. Fran watched him chomping on a piece of pork fat. If anything was unhealthy that surely was.

'Marguerite is kept busy. And she says Ash and Jill and the others are always booked up.'

'Is she happy there – Marguerite?'

'She is now. Between you and me, there was a bit of trouble last year. Ash got himself involved in some odd psychic stuff. And their eldest girl, Rose, got friendly with Rachel's boy and walked out of her posh music college. But it's all blown over.'

'I saw Patrick the other day at Wraith Cove – nice, polite young man. So, where is Rose?'

'Went off to Africa with her grandmother – Jill's mother, Stephanie. She's a doctor. But they're coming home soon.'

Fran sat back in her chair, hoping Ted wouldn't notice the amount of cabbage she'd left. She pushed his glass of beer towards him. 'You're becoming quite a fount of knowledge since you started gardening up at Cormorants.'

Ted took a swig of beer. 'Hope you don't think I'm gossiping.'

'No, I enjoy a yarn.' Fran had never been that interested in the doings of Ventnor before, but now she felt she had her ears pricked – like Cinders – for everything. If there was any talk of a missing baby,

153

Ted was bound to have heard by now. 'What do you think about this dinner at Rachel's, on Saturday?'

'Could give it a go.' Ted was picking his teeth with a cocktail stick. 'Italian's not really my cup of tea. I'd like you to come with me though.'

'Not sure, Ted.' Fran glanced toward Sam's basket.

'Rachel's invited everyone.' He waved towards Sam. 'His parents can look after him for the evening – or they can bring him along, if they want.'

'I don't know if they would come.'

'Why not? Be nice for them. Don't they want to meet the folks who lives here? Young Phil's roots are in this place, and Sam's. Are they snobs or something?' Ted's hands were flapping, a sign he was getting agitated.

'Calm down. Of course they're not.'

'Well, they're certainly in no hurry to meet anybody. They arrived last Saturday and now it's Thursday, and I haven't clapped eyes on them.'

'I expect they'll come.' Sam was starting to whimper, Fran got up. 'They'll be back soon. I'll ask them.' She lifted Sam out of the basket. 'I'll come anyway.'

'Good.' Ted watched her as she went to the fridge to get Sam's bottle. 'I suppose you've been left to do the feeding again.'

'They said they'd try to get back in time, but they've gone up to Newport, to see a play.' Fran lifted the Aga lid and put the kettle on. 'I told them not to rush.'

Ted got up. 'I'll get going then and leave you to it.' He put on his jacket and cap and picked up his stick and torch. 'Don't seem right, somehow,' he muttered, 'leaving such a young baby all the time.'

Fran laughed, anxiety building up inside her. How much longer could she bluff her way through this? Ted was getting irritable and that wasn't like him. She'd noticed him looking around for signs of Sam's parents. Fran had placed a few old things of Phillip's around the place – wellingtons and a cap and jersey, and she'd unwrapped a new pink cardigan that someone had given her, and hung it on the back of a chair. But she knew, day by day, it was becoming more difficult. Maybe she

154

should just confess everything to Ted. But the thought of him making her go to the police was more than she could bear.

Anyway, Sam needed feeding and that was the most pressing thing right now. 'I told you, I'm enjoying it. Won't be for long. Might not see them again for years.'

'Suppose you're right.' Ted kissed her cheek and patted Sam's head before opening the door. Cold air seeped in. 'It'll be rimy out there by morning,' he said.

Fran tested the milk and sat down to feed Sam. For the first time it occurred to her that she could go away. Ted would look after the animals. She could tell him she'd been invited to travel a bit with Young Phil and Ann, and while she was away she could think up what to do next. The thought of leaving Rocken Edge terrified her. But what was the alternative? She watched Sam feeding. His eyes were locked on hers and one tiny hand clasped her finger as she held the bottle. He was the most precious thing she had ever possessed. She looked around the warm, scruffy kitchen, the animals sleeping in their usual place against the stove. The wind was quiet tonight; she could hear the murmur of the sea. This was her life, her world. But everything had changed now, and she realised she would give it all up for the joy of keeping this child.

*   *   *

Rachel was in Kyp and Evie's beach house, *Sun Spot,* at Blue Slipper Bay. She sat at the table, awaiting Kyp's verdict on the Italian menu, half listening to Evie reading *The Lamb-a-roo* to Jack and Mila. She looked around the big cosy room – the beach houses were those *Tardis*-type places that were so much larger inside. The walls were covered with Evie's seascapes and the kids' bright paintings. Rachel wondered what it would be like raising two children in such close proximity to the mighty ocean. But then, the Water Babies had been born in the sea – perhaps they were half merfolk and would one day swim away.

'Who devised this menu?' Kyp had been studying it for ages, it seemed to Rachel. She was looking forward to his comments, proud of the list of delicious food that Sandro had concocted. She smoothed her hand over the thick cream paper of the one she was holding. It was beautifully printed, really upmarket, designed to fit into black leather covers. It had cost her a lot of money, but Sandro had assured her it would impress the customers.

'It is ridiculous.' Kyp dropped the menu on the table and threw himself back in his chair. Rachel was stunned. She felt the smile of satisfaction fade from her face. Was he joking? Kyp was always joking.

'Kyp!' Evie extricated herself from the sofa where she was tucked in between Jack and Mila. She picked up the menu. 'What do you mean, ridiculous?' She glanced at Rachel.

Kyp gestured at the menu as if waving it away. 'The man is having a joke. It would take a whole team of experienced chefs and a kitchen three times the size of yours, Rachel. I am sorry. It is impossible.'

Rachel stared at him in horror. 'Do you mean it? Are you sure?' She looked at Evie to see if she could pick up a clue. But Evie was now frowning and biting her bottom lip as she perused the menu. 'I see what you mean . . . it certainly does look complicated.'

'Complicated! What's his name? Sandro? Was he insane?'

Rachel recalled that Kyp and Evie hadn't met Sandro. He had come . . . and gone, while they were away. 'He was very experienced. He had a restaurant in Italy – a family business.'

'I think he should have stayed there. That's what this needs – a whole family of cooks.'

'But he said it was all going to be easy – once we got into the swing of it.'

'The man was giving you bullshit.'

Jack and Mila started to giggle. 'Time for bed, you two,' Evie said, 'before your dad teaches you a few new words to take to school.' She smiled encouragingly at Rachel. 'Back in a mo. I'm sure we can work it out.'

'We can't,' Kyp said. He leaned towards Rachel after Evie left the room.

'How much did you know really – about this fellow?'

'Well,' Rachel sighed, knowing she was going to look foolish, again. 'He seemed very ambitious, confident, keen to start the restaurant.'

'A con man? Did you give him money? You can tell me.'

'No. I didn't give him any money – well, not much, just odd treats.' Come to think of it, those odd treats probably added up to quite a sum. But she'd felt well-treated in return. 'I think he genuinely thought he could do this. And I truly believe he was fond of me.'

Kyp patted her shoulder with his big hand. His heavy-lidded eyes looked concerned. 'I'm sure he was. Why wouldn't he be?' He tapped the menu and sighed. 'Maybe just a dreamer.'

'I think that's right, Kyp. Now I look back on it all – he was a fantasizer. I don't think he truly set out to con me or let me down.'

Kyp smiled ruefully. 'You're a generous-hearted woman, Rachel.'

Or a mug, she thought. Why hadn't she realised that Sandro was carried away by his own unrealistic plan? She'd always been so sensible, never taken risks with her finances, always put her security and the boys' interests first. But still, a good lesson learned, she supposed. For the first time she felt glad that Sandro had disappeared. Maybe she would have become so overwhelmed by lust, she wouldn't have noticed that she was being drawn further and further into chaos.

There was a knock, and Kyp got up to let Sophie and Nick in. They'd only come from their beach house, *Sea Spray,* next door but their faces were red with cold. Rachel guessed they'd been standing outside enjoying the night.

'Wonderful weather,' Nick said. Rachel knew by the exhilaration on his face that he meant it. 'Have you seen the stars? Incredible display.'

'What's wrong, Rachel?' Sophie asked immediately, in that uncanny way she had of detecting angst. The psychic detective, Nick called her.

Evie came down from the kids' attic bedroom. 'Kids want kissing,' she said to Kyp.

'So does Kyp,' he said, getting up and grabbing her.

'Daft bugger,' Evie said fondly. 'When you come down you can make some of your wonderful coffee.'

'Yes, Captain,' Kyp said, saluting and heading for the stairs.

Rachel told Nick and Sophie about the problem with the menu.

'But we've ordered all the meat and fish, and everything,' Sophie said. 'It's arriving tomorrow.'

157

'I suppose we'll have to force it into the freezers,' Rachel said.

'Not all of it, surely,' Nick said. 'Maybe just a pared down menu – the basic stuff, like you did before, and a small selection of the gourmet choice.'

Rachel had a sudden vision of her glorious Italian restaurant suddenly fading into yet another pizza and pasta house. It was all going to be so special, a must-visit place, the authentic Italian experience of the Isle of Wight, bringing tourists to Ventnor, upgrading the little Victorian seaside town. She felt as if her energy was fading with the vision. And with the feeling came an intense loneliness, heightened by the presence of these two lovely, happy couples. Sandro had gone, her boys were cutting the ties, a life-time of monotonous drudgery watching people stuff their faces with ordinary food in her ordinary café loomed before her.

'Rachel?' Sophie's gentle voice roused her. 'What do you want to do?'

Rachel looked around at her friends' concerned faces. 'Do you know, at this moment, I would like to turn my back on the whole thing and run away. It just seems like one problem after another. I don't know if I can summon the energy to deal with all this. Maybe I should cancel the trial run, and the Valentine's celebration, and delay the whole thing until the summer. I might manage to find another chef by then. If not, I can always revert to simple *Rachel's Café.*'

'No!' Sophie said, sounding unusually vehement. 'This is my project too, remember. And I know we can do it.'

Kyp came in carrying a large wooden board piled with cheeses and hunks of fluffy bread. The smell of coffee trailed behind him. He was humming cheerfully. 'Of course we can do it,' he said. 'It just needs a bit of re-thinking that's all.'

CHAPTER
Fourteen

Clare had started bleeding again. What was happening to her now? For months her body had seemed like an alien being – it just did things without her understanding why. How did it know what to do? Was it doing things right, or was there something wrong with her? So much stuff seemed to have come out of her – but not the worms. She didn't feel ill; just tired. Perhaps this was an ordinary period. Perhaps her body had rid itself of all the baby stuff and decided to start all over again. She wondered if she should see a doctor. There was no-one she could ask – not even Kate. The only person she could talk to was Rose; maybe she would come back soon. She planned to tell Rose the baby had been adopted.

Clare emptied the big cans of tomato soup into a saucepan. It was her and Jules's turn to get lunch for everyone. Jules was hacking at a loaf with a blunt bread knife. She hadn't stopped talking since they started the preparations.

'Billy's such a pain, you know? But, like, he's quite sweet, so I don't know how to tell him to get lost. I mean, we all live here, and I don't want to hurt him, and then have to go on working with him. Do you see what I mean? You're lucky, Aidan fancies you. I wish he fancied me – he's really nice, you know, more mature. Billy hasn't grown up – we're the same age, but with boys that means younger, doesn't it?'

Clare smiled. 'Aidan doesn't fancy me, at all.' She hoped he didn't, she would feel even more self-conscious. But that was stupid. Why would he fancy her – a pathetic, scrawny kid who hardly spoke to anyone?

'He *so* does. Like he's always talking about your gorgeous hair and eyes. He's dead keen. Personally I think he's too young for you – I think girls go for boys at least a year older than them.' She sighed. 'He'd be just right for me.'

Clare shook her head and stirred the soup. She didn't want to hear this. Gorgeous hair? She really should get it cut. Father Ryan was always asking her to loosen it – it was a bother having to plait it again, before she went home. But she had liked him to stroke it and tell her how lovely it was. Later, when he turned against her, he told her it was the colour of hell. Clare shuddered at the memory of her shock.

She couldn't understand how someone so tender had suddenly become so rough. For years he'd been gentle, everyday he would cuddle and kiss her and sometimes press himself against her back to sway with her. She always went home feeling so special, so loved. She couldn't wait for the next day to come so she could see his loving eyes. And she'd grown used to the intricate journey he made over her body, assessing her growth, her ribcage, writing down her measurements, asking questions about her private parts. *It's important, if you want to be a good singer,* he assured her. Her mam never talked to her about growing up, and Father Ryan was concerned – in the absence of Clare's daddy – that she should know everything. And she grew eager to learn. It felt safe to be taught by him. And Mam continually told her to do as Father Ryan said. It was ages after that the roughness started. He'd begun pushing himself at her tender skin, and eventually right inside her body. It had hurt and she wanted to tell him to stop, she didn't like it. She couldn't help crying, but he rocked her, and told her it was just the way of men, and it was because he loved her so.

It was when she'd started her periods that he began to change. He didn't want her to come to the vestry every day. And often there would be other children around doing chores when she was there. It was only on the occasions that she went to him, unexpected, that he seemed like his old self and was unable to send her away. But even then – after he'd done what he wanted – he'd get angry and call her a Jezebel, a temptress. He was so changeable, so different. Clare was always confused, not understanding what she had done wrong. It wasn't until her periods stopped that she fully realised the implications of what she was doing. It wasn't that she didn't know how babies were made. But she trusted so deeply in Father Ryan's love and she genuinely believed he would never let anything bad happen to her. It was only afterwards that she understood it had been her own fault. Father Ryan said all girls were told the story of Adam and Eve as a warning, and she'd let it go unheeded. Women had always been the downfall of men since the beginning of time.

'What do you reckon?' Jules was still talking. 'I can tell Aidan you think he's too young, if you like. He's too shy to ask you.'

'Ask me what?' Clare realised the soup was sticking to the bottom of the pan where she'd forgotten to stir it.

'If you're interested in him. Dah! You're a real dreamy cow, you are. Dunno what he sees in you.'

'Sorry. I don't want a boyfriend right now.' If ever, she thought. I'm never going to go through that again. Anyway, I won't get the chance. I'm going to spend the rest of my life in prison. Clare wondered what Jules would think if she'd spoken those words aloud.

The door of the caravan opened and Kate, Billy and Patrick came in bringing a rush of cold air. They dumped their boots in a heap inside the door and took off their coats.

'Dish up that soup, Clare.' Billy sat down at the table and picked up a spoon. 'I'm freezing and starving.'

Clare ladled the soup into bowls hoping it wouldn't taste burnt. But she didn't think they'd notice. Patrick had switched on the television and Kate was leafing through a magazine. They all seemed to do more than one thing at a time. But at least it stopped them talking and asking questions.

She sat down to eat her own share. The slightly lumpy tomato soup reminded her of being in the abbey with Mother. Tinned soup was their everyday food, mainly pearl barley, or Scotch broth, watered down and tasteless. They ate it with stale crackers. Mother grew a few vegetables in the garden but all she seemed to harvest were a few rock hard beetroots which she used for dying wool, and some potatoes which turned out to have worms inside, just like Clare.

The first time Clare had seen Mother was through a rusty grille in one of the abbey gates. Mother was digging a hole in the ground. She

161

lifted a spade of earth and threw it over her shoulder. It was then she spotted Clare looking at her through the gate. She'd seemed terrified. Clare supposed it was because of it being an enclosed order. The nun had brandished her spade. *Go away!* she croaked. *Go away! I'll set the dogs on you. I'll call the police.* Clare was sobbing with fatigue. *Please!* she begged. *Are you Sister Bridget? I have a letter for you from Father Ryan.* She pushed the envelope through the grille. The nun stared unblinking at the white square on the dusty ground for a while as if it might explode. Then she bent over, brandishing the spade in front of her like a soldier in combat, as she crept forward to pick it up. If Clare hadn't been so distressed she might have laughed. The nun made a grab for the letter and backed away. She tore open the envelope and read, glancing up at Clare intermittently. Then she dropped the spade and ran up the overgrown path to the door of the abbey. She disappeared inside and slammed the door. Clare was mystified. Perhaps she'd gone to fetch someone, the Mother Abbess, perhaps. Then the door opened a crack and Clare could see the nun peeping out as if to check she was still there. Slowly she opened the door and came out. She walked down the path as if on tiptoe. Clare could see that one side of her mouth was turned up in a slight smile. *You'd better come in,* she said. *But you must only go where I tell you. Everywhere else is out of bounds to a girl like you. We can't have the Sisters defiled.*

They'd had great difficulty shifting the gate. It didn't seem to have been opened for years. Once inside the grounds, Clare looked around. The abbey was enormous. It had taken her ages to find a gate in the outside wall, much of which was behind a corrugated iron fence and barbed wire. Even this bit was like a building site. Bricks and rubble were piled everywhere and the garden was completely overgrown with brambles and nettles. The nun led Clare inside the abbey, along the gloomy hallway, then through a curtained entrance into a dark smelly passage. She opened another door into a small room where a smoky wood fire was burning in a grate. Clare was glad of it. The place seemed freezing inside, even though it was July. The nun made Clare take off her backpack and her jacket. She stared at Clare's stomach with interest.

Sit down, she said. *I'll make you some tea.* Clare watched as the nun balanced a tin kettle on a metal rack over the fire. The woman seemed a bit bewildered; she was searching around as if looking for a clean cup. She took one out of a pile in the sink and wiped it with a grubby cloth. Clare noticed she was using powdered milk. *The electricity has gone off and I don't have any sugar,* the nun said.

Clare wondered what she should call her. *Are you Sister Bridget – Father Ryan's cousin?* She hadn't expected her to look like this, short and plump. She thought she would be taller, slender, like Father Ryan. *Call me Mother, my child,* she said. *I will be like a mother to you now.* She made the tea before the water had boiled and handed a cup to Clare. *Thank you,* Clare said, remembering to be polite. *You were expecting me then? I got lost. I went to the old Poor Clares' convent by mistake and someone directed me here.* The nun sat down in a rickety armchair which looked as if might collapse under her weight. She clasped her hands together; they were still earthy from the garden. A grubby rope was tied around her middle, from which dangled a wooden crucifix and rosary, and a bunch of big keys. She nodded. *That's right, that's right.* Clare took a sip of tea trying not to make a face. *But I thought this was supposed to be a new place,* she blurted out. The nun looked around the room, up at the flaking ceiling. *It's being rebuilt – you saw all the mess outside. But this is a wonderful old building.* The nun grinned, showing discoloured crooked teeth. *You mustn't go out though. It's dangerous, you might have an accident.* Clare felt disappointed. *Where are the other nuns?* The nun frowned. *You ask too many questions. You won't see them. I have a special dispensation to look after you.* Clare's heart sank. Was she going to have just this nun – Mother – for company? *Won't I see them at all? Even at mass?* The nun looked away. *You wouldn't be allowed.* Clare realised then how bad she must seem in the eyes of the nuns. She lowered her eyes. *Will a priest come to see me? I need to confess.* The nun got up. *I will arrange everything. Stay here and rest after your journey. I'm going to make your bed.*

The nun went out of the room. Clare sat back in the chair feeling nauseous from the foul-tasting tea awash in her empty stomach. She thought she was going to be sick. Where was the toilet? She went to the door and turned the handle. It was locked . . .

'Clare!'

Clare snapped out of her reverie.

Jules was laughing. 'What are you on? God, I've never met anyone as dozy as you in my life. I've asked you three times if you want anymore soup.'

'Sorry.' Clare felt her face go red. 'I was thinking about something.'

'Oh, right. There is someone at home then. So?'

'Oh, no more thanks.'

'At last,' muttered Jules.

Clare collected up the bowls and started the washing up. She really must stop this daydreaming. Trouble was, things reminded her of stuff she'd blocked out, and once it started she found it hard to stop.

*   *   *

Father Ryan was fed up with asking people for information. He'd already wasted the morning on futile journeys. First he'd been directed to Belmont Abbey, near Hereford, and discovered it was a male Benedictine order. And then he'd driven to Bartestree Convent – right across the other side of Hereford – only to find it was now a hospice. But he had enjoyed wandering around the beautiful buildings. He especially liked Hereford Cathedral. It was a pity the Anglican churches were so liberal in their views. Christian or not, there were some boundaries that could never be crossed – their misguided sacraments for example. He'd sat for a while in a pew admiring the carvings, feeling the vastness arching above him. But people were wandering around sight-seeing, schoolchildren were swarming all over the place whispering loudly, and messing about with brass rubbings. Never would he want to kneel and pray here.

Now he was having lunch in yet another church, All Saints – right in the centre of Hereford. He'd seen the notice advertising the café and assumed it was a disused building. But standing in the queue for his bowl of soup he realised, with horror, that an actual service was taking place at the far end. A vicar in full vestments was praying, a small congregation intoning the responses. His first thought was to walk out, but the girl behind the counter was handing him his soup. He sat down at a glass and aluminium table and began hurriedly spooning the scalding carrot and coriander into his mouth, his hand trembling. The congregation began leaving, thank goodness, he could slow down, he wanted to enjoy his lunch. The young vicar was shaking hands with people, smiling and joking. He looked barely more than a youth – how dare these youngsters assume ordination gave them the right to try and change an institution as powerful as the Church.

He tore the coarse seeded bread into small chunks – it looked as if it might be indigestible. He blew on his soup – at least that had been worth coming in for. As he ate he watched a group of people start to move all the chairs into a circle. Perhaps there was going to be some sort of public meeting. They lit candles and sat with their eyes closed for a while, and then they started to chant – one of those *Taizé* things that Father Christopher liked. And there was a woman leading the chanting. Father Ryan nearly dropped his spoon – she was wearing a white stole around her neck and he could swear – even at this distance – that it was embroidered with the symbols of other religions – Islam, Jewish, Sikh – others he didn't even recognise. What was going on? He shuffled his chair around the other side of the table to turn his back on them. So much was wrong here. But the soup was delicious, and so was this flavoursome warm bread. And, he had to admit, the acoustics weren't bad.

He took some leaflets out of his briefcase. He'd visited the library earlier, pored over some old history books, and made notes about possible monasteries and convents to explore. He'd decided to be self-reliant from now on and not be led on any more pointless expeditions by people who obviously didn't know the history of their own country. The music was soaring; it was really quite good – as a background to having lunch.

He bought a pot of tea and a huge slice of fruit cake and sat thinking. He reasoned that Clare, who'd never travelled before, becoming lost, would have sought directions as to the whereabouts of an enclosed order. What else could she have done in her condition? Unless, of course, she hadn't even got as far as the Poor Clares' convent – simply run off. And then there would be no hope of finding her. This was the only course he had to pursue. If it all turned out to be a dead-end, he would return to Ireland and try and live with the fear of the unknown. He'd have to invent a story to tell Clare's mother. She would believe him, whatever he said – probably be glad to be rid of her. He was beginning to feel some sympathy with the woman. How awful to have your only child turn out like Clare. He thought of Jeannie, sitting by her bed in the hospital. She would never have done such a thing. If she'd grown into a normal woman she would have come to live with him. They'd have cared for each other – she would never have messed about with men.

He looked at the notes he'd made. One thing he'd learned was that Hereford and Worcester use to be referred to as one county. That widened his search. There was a big convent near Worcester – Stillwater Abbey. Not Poor Clares, but they had a retreat centre where lay people could stay. Maybe Clare had been directed there. It was possible she could have stayed for a while before moving on. It wasn't much to go on, but at least it seemed like the next step he should take.

He finished his lunch and walked back to the car park. He supposed he should phone Father Christopher to see how things were at home. But a pang of fear gripped him. Suppose Clare had arrived back there – with or without a child? What would he do? His journey would be at an end, so might his life as he knew it. He started his car. Maybe he wouldn't go back at all.

*   *   *

Fran pulled the suitcase down from the top of the wardrobe in her parents' bedroom. Dust floated in the air making her sneeze. She dumped the case on the bed; the catches were rusty and stiff. It was full of photographs and old family souvenirs that her mother had hoarded. Fran emptied everything into the bottom of the chest of drawers. Maybe, one day, she would look through it all and show Sam his family history.

She carried the suitcase along the landing to her and Sam's room. Sam was lying on the bed, asleep. She stood gazing down at him. He was so tiny, so innocent and dependent on her. How could she even think of lying to him about his family history? But what was he going to say when he found out the truth? She shook her head; it was so far into the future. And she was beginning to get quite good at telling lies –

166

starting to believe them herself.

She began putting her clothes into the case. She might have to get another one down from the attic – Sam would need all his things for the journey. She didn't know where she was going to end up. She would start in the New Forest and stay at quiet hotels and come back when she was sure there was no search going on for the baby. She had considered going abroad, but the idea terrified her. And then she'd thought of all sorts of complications, like passports and the fact that she didn't have Sam's birth certificate. And money – she didn't have much put by. Her small savings had rapidly diminished since she'd had Sam; and her pension and the rent from Ted for Bleak Field didn't amount to much.

She planned to go to the Italian dinner with Ted tomorrow and ask him if he would tend the animals for her while she went off travelling with Young Phil and Ann. It would be so much easier to concentrate on Sam if she was away. And she could have some peace to think about what she would do next. She had lain awake half the night, between Sam's feeds, wondering if she could make up a story about a car accident – Sam becoming orphaned – but it all sounded ridiculous to her. Ted would never believe that. She was going to have to move away altogether – maybe pretend she was going back to Australia with them.

Her eyes filled with tears. How could she think about leaving Rocken Edge? But how could she think about giving up Sam?

*   *   *

Sitting in her café, looking over her lists, Rachel felt calmer. She and Sophie had just checked the necessary ingredients for tomorrow night's trial run. Kyp had selected a few of Sandro's exotic dishes that he felt confident to cook, and Sophie had typed a new menu which they'd printed out on Aidan's computer. Jane had phoned to say that she, Marguerite and Chas were heading home tomorrow and would come to the meal if they were back in time. Sophie and Nick – being teetotallers – had arranged to transport the young ones from Wraith Cove.

'So.' Sophie shuffled a pile of paper. 'We're all ready to roll. You and I can deal with the basics, Kyp can cook the exotics. We have waiters, washer-uppers, and most importantly,' she counted names, 'around

167

twenty-five customers of assorted ages and backgrounds. Perfect.'

'Okay.' Rachel looked around the café. 'Let's get cleaning and organising and then we can make some of the freezables.' She looked at her brightly painted board announcing *Sandro's Italian Restaurant,* and gave it a mournful pat. 'This can go out the back for now, until I have time to get it re-painted.'

CHAPTER
Fifteen

Clare opened her eyes, wondering what day it was. Saturday. A whole week since she'd arrived on the island and abandoned the baby. It seemed like a lifetime – a dreadful, nightmarish, lifetime. Poor baby. Clare found herself thinking about him sometimes, now that she was feeling better and calmer. She knew he was dead; she'd felt his stiff limbs. She shuddered. She hoped that he'd been *really* dead before . . . before the animals had got at him. That's the only reason she could think why no-one seemed to have discovered his body. Even if the farmer had found a few tiny bones, he would probably have thought it was those of an animal. She closed her eyes again and tried to pray to the Blessed Virgin to help the soul of the baby. She knew she had no right to pray for herself, but she didn't like to think of him, unbaptised, in Limbo. She hadn't wanted him, but she didn't mean for that terrible thing to happen.

Clare had kept asking Mother, and Mother had promised she would fetch the priest to come and baptise him. *He says he's very busy this time of the year, with funerals*, she'd said. *He'll come when he's ready.* Mother took the baby from her. Clare covered her sore breasts. *When did you see him? You promised I could ask him to hear my confession.* Clare was near to tears. She thought she was going to be able to leave the abbey as soon as the baby was born. Mother had said she could. Clare told her all about Rose and her plans to go to the Isle of Wight. She hadn't realised she'd be expected to feed the baby for weeks, as part of her penance. The only thing that had kept her sane from day to day during her pregnancy was the thought of her escape at the end of it – and then she would go to find Rose.

It had been like being in prison, staying in the abbey all those months as she grew bigger and bigger. It grew freezing cold as winter set in. There was no heating, except in the little room where she sat through the strange dark days with Mother. The electricity had been turned off. Mother didn't seem to know why. In the evenings she lit candles. The water was from a well. At least Mother had stopped locking the sitting room door. No-one came to the convent, although Mother talked about the nuns who still lived in the main part of the abbey. *This is the old retreat house,* Mother told her. *It's the only place where girls like you are allowed to stay. But don't worry; you will be quite safe and comfortable.*

Sometimes, during the boring days, while Mother dozed over her knitting, Clare crept out of the stifling room and wandered around, trying the handles of the doors. Some rooms were locked; others were stacked with broken furniture and old wooden spinning wheels. The outside doors were locked too, apart from the big front door which wouldn't close properly. Mother had stuffed the cracks with bundled up sheets to keep out the wind. Everywhere felt dank and unused. Down the steep stone stairs at the end of the passage, she discovered an enormous kitchen with a long wooden table in the centre. Huge cold pipes ran along the walls and up the stairs to the passages. The large store cupboards were filled with tins of soup and beans and ham and peas. And there were enamel bins full of packets of biscuits and dried milk and boxes of teabags and sugar. This was the food they lived on. Clare didn't mind, she felt sick most of the time. The shelves and floor were sprinkled with mice droppings. There were racks full of dusty white plates and bowls, and cupboards packed with cups and saucers. The big refrigerators contained decaying food. The smell was disgusting. Mother's footprints criss-crossed the grimy quarry tiles to the red-stained sink where she soaked her wool. Clare wondered if it was the stench from the kitchen that had seeped upstairs and was mixed up with the boiled beetroots and smoking fire. Mother smelled too; Clare had never seen her wash. Clare tried to keep herself clean, and launder her clothes, but it was so difficult.

From the small window of her tiny bedroom, Clare could see the back of the abbey. She never saw any sign of activity, however

170

long she watched. She hoped she would see a priest; she might be able to get outside and speak to him. But as the weeks rolled by and the days shortened, she stopped looking and became more and more lethargic as her belly grew huge. She could hardly be bothered to wash herself properly. Mother didn't seem to mind. She spent most of her day dragging bits of wood in from outside, or sawing up the furniture to feed the fire. At certain times of the day she would hurry off to pray. Clare asked to go with her, but Mother said she wouldn't be allowed to do that until after she had the baby.

Clare once asked, before the lethargy set in, if she could go out for a walk, maybe outside the abbey grounds. Mother had been really angry then. *My instructions from Father – what was his name? – were very strict.* Clare wondered why Mother couldn't remember his name. *I thought you were cousins,* she said. *We give up all that sort of thing, once we take the veil. My job is to keep you out of temptation's way.* She smiled at Clare and stroked her hair. *I'm your Mother. We will soon have a baby – a little holy girl. And then everything will be all right.* Clare tried to work out Mother's moods before asking questions. *Do you . . . do you know anything about the adoption arrangements?* she ventured. *Don't worry about that,* Mother snapped.

So Clare hadn't worried about it. She went to bed early and got up late. She stirred soup in the pot over the fire, and held Mother's lumpy skeins of wool while she wound it into balls. She re-read *Tess of the d'Urbervilles* twice, and sorted through a box of old towelling nappies and smelly rubber pants that Mother told her had been used before, for the babies of bad girls like Clare. *Are you expecting more girls?* Clare asked hopefully. It would be nice to have some young company, and compare her progress with others. Mother dropped her ball of wool in the ashes in the grate. *No! Now look what you've made me do.* Clare retrieved the wool and dusted it off. *Why?* She persisted. She could see Mother's lips trying to form words *You ask too many questions. Curiosity is not a nice quality in Catholic girls. I'm doing this as a favour . . . to my cousin . . . special dispensation. Now be quiet. I can't concentrate.*

Clare was getting used to Mother telling her that everything she did was a special dispensation. Who from? Pope John Paul? Clare had noticed there was a picture of him down in the kitchen with its face turned to the wall. Had he died? Surely Mother would have told her. Apart from the wooden crosses in the otherwise bare bedrooms there were no religious ornaments or pictures. Clare would have liked to follow Mother to see where she went to pray but she didn't dare . . .

Clare was jolted from her daydream by someone knocking at the caravan window above her head.

'Clare!' she could hear Billy's voice calling her. 'Get up you lazy cow. Aidan's just arrived, and we're all going down on the beach for a kick-about.'

Clare sat up. On the beach, in this weather. Could she do that? Could she mess around with other kids? Surely she was much younger than them, but they didn't know that – and she felt so much older.

*   *   *

Father Ryan stood outside Stillwater Abbey. He stared in disbelief at the corrugated iron and barbed wire surrounding the perimeter. Another wild goose chase – he wasn't going to find Clare here. To be sure, he only had himself to blame this time. The history book he'd consulted in the library was very old. And hadn't he felt proud of himself finding his own way? What was going on in England that all these beautiful old buildings were being demolished, or requisitioned for other uses? He'd thought the church was a wealthy institution. But here in England he'd heard that young people no longer felt called to give their lives to God. The convents and monasteries were full of ageing men and women who were probably not going to be replaced at all, as they died.

He managed to find a small gap in the fence where he could peer in. The pinkish abbey looked magnificent with its gothic spires and turreted roofs. But there were piles of rubble everywhere, as if it were being demolished. The grounds were wild, tangled with briars and rampant shrubs. He could see stained glass windows glinting tantalisingly in the winter sun. Frost sparkled in the grassy hollows. Rooks and crows and jackdaws called harshly from the tops of oak and beech trees, whose bare branches were silhouetted against the pale gold sky. The birds rose and skirmished and landed, wings clattering

172

in the quiet afternoon air. How he'd love to go in there and take a look around. He wondered if there was anyone about, a caretaker or security guard, but the place looked deserted. Oh, well, he had one more place, at Tewkesbury, that he wanted to see before it got too late. And then he would need to find a place to stay the night.

'Shame, isn't it?'

Father Ryan jumped away from the fence. A man was walking towards him, leading a brown and white spaniel.

'Beautiful old place; pity they can't save it.'

'Indeed,' Father Ryan said.

'Too far gone. Or so they said. But I expect you know that, being a man of the cloth.'

'Oh, no. I'm a stranger here, a visitor.'

'From Ireland, by the sound of it.' The man chuckled, reminding him of Father Christopher. He was portly too, with a purple nose; obviously far too fond of his food and drink.

Father Ryan nodded. The English were so nosy. He wasn't going to give anything away.

The man looked around. 'Nice crisp day, good to see a bit of sun, isn't it?'

Why did the English always want to talk about the weather? Father Ryan thought he'd better say something; the man seemed to want to talk. 'How long has the abbey been closed down?'

'Oh, quite a while. The few nuns that lived here were very elderly, to be honest. Most of them went to a Catholic rest home. The retreat house was used by lay people a fair bit. Even after the nuns went, there were usually a few strangers hanging about.' He sniffed. 'Down and outs mainly. We wondered – us in the village – if some of them were recovering from alcohol or drugs. Glad to see the back of them, to be frank. The nuns were the only people who had any time for them.' He yanked his dog away from sniffing at Father Ryan's shoes. 'Wouldn't want your job, vicar. I'd lock 'em up, and throw away the key.'

Father Ryan managed a smile. I'd probably agree with you, if I was allowed, he thought.

The man leaned a little closer. 'Wouldn't be surprised if there was still a bit of illegal activity going on in that retreat place. Lights have been seen in there, and smoke from one of the chimneys. I wanted to inform the police, but you know how it is – you'd probably end up with a brick through your window. And they don't bother us. It's pretty isolated out here.' He looked around as if he were making sure nobody was listening. 'Anyway, rumour has it the whole place is coming down soon. The nature people have been delaying things for years with their badger setts and whatnot.' He laughed. 'Leave it much longer and the place'll fall down on its own.'

'What a pity.' Father Ryan looked at his watch. 'Well, now. I must be going. Good day to you.'

The man raised his hand to his cap in a brief salute and trudged off. Father Ryan pretended to be tying his shoe as he watched him go. He didn't want to have to walk back to the car with him, and listen to more of his inane chatter. The late afternoon sun was fading; the temperature dropping. He pulled up the collar of his overcoat and decided to take a stroll around the perimeter of the fence, to see if he could get a better view of the abbey. There might even be a place where he could enter. The barricade seemed pretty solid most of the way and the grounds were extensive. Soon, however, the fence stopped, revealing the high brick wall – it really was like a prison. There was a heavy gate with a grille in it where the nuns would have received visitors. He peered through the rusted bars. There was an overgrown path leading to a door. This building was separate from abbey, although there did seem to be some kind of covered way with the glass roof caved in. Perhaps this was the retreat centre, where the dossers came. If he could get through, he might be able to gain access to the abbey. He felt daring; if Father Christopher could see him now, he wouldn't be so quick with his taunts. The gate was open slightly; he managed to squeeze through and walked up the path to the door. He was surprised to see that it was also ajar. There couldn't be any vagrants in there now – they would be frozen.

He shoved at the heavy door; bundled up sheets fell out of the opening. He stepped inside the dark hallway and stood, listening. It was gloomy. He tried the light switch but it didn't work. There were some rooms off the hallway, stacked with furniture, dirty and neglected. At the end of the passage, stone stairs led down to an enormous kitchen with no sign of habitation, just a strong smell of decay and rot. But there was also another smell in the air, like something singeing. He started to feel nervous. He went back up to the hall and then climbed the main staircase to the upper landing. There were two bedrooms that looked as if someone might have slept in them recently, the beds dishevelled, a few bits and pieces scattered around. Most of the other rooms were locked. Those that weren't were empty, or contained a single bed base, with broken springs. There were two bathrooms, which hadn't been used for ages judging by the dead spiders and green stains in the baths. He went back downstairs. He must have missed something. If this was a retreat house there would be a chapel for visitors. Indeed he had overlooked a door – it was covered with a tapestry curtain. It opened onto another dark corridor. This was where the smoky smell was coming from. There were more locked rooms along here. The last one was slightly open, revealing a small sitting room. Perhaps this was the warden's quarters.

He coughed and then called out. 'Excuse me, is there anyone at home? I am a priest come to visit.' Silence – just a few distant creaks. He pushed the door open further, and there was the fire smouldering in the grate, filling the room with smelly fumes. There was nobody there. He went inside. The place was filthy; dirty cups were on the floor and chairs. Packets of sugar and cereal spilled over the table. He put his hand over his mouth and nose. The stench in here was nauseating. The local man had been right; this place was being used by squatters. Heaven knows where they were, probably full of drugs in one of the locked rooms. He was feeling anxious now. He needed to get out of here – there could be someone dangerous lurking, watching him. He turned to go out and let out a yell of fright. There, in the doorway, stood a short plump nun. Her arm was raised above her head and she was holding a spade. She ran at Father Ryan, but before she got to him, the weight of the spade unbalanced her. She tripped on her habit and fell heavily to the floor in front of him.

175

It took him a moment to recover from his shock. Then he bent down and picked up the spade, holding on to it, unsure of what she might do next.

'I'm sorry I frightened you,' he said, his voice shaking. 'I'm Father Ryan, just called in to visit.' The nun raised her head slightly and seemed to be staring at his shoes. 'Are you all right?' he said.

The nun nodded without looking at him. He placed the spade against the wall, within reach, and reluctantly put a hand under her arm and helped her to get up. Then, he recoiled from her in disgust. Her hands and face were filthy. Matted bits of hair stuck out from under her grimy veil. Her breath smelled fetid. He swept the rubbish off a sagging armchair and pushed her into it.

The nun sat staring at him with eyes bloodshot by the smoke. 'I thought you might be a murderer.'

'I'm sorry,' he repeated.

'So, you're him. Are you on your own?' she croaked.

He nodded.

'Will you give last rites?'

'Last rites?'

'You are a proper priest aren't you? *She* said you were.'

He touched his collar. 'Of course.' He had his briefcase in the car with his bible and holy water and all the stuff he needed for the sacrament. But he probably wouldn't need them – he suspected she was senile. 'And you are?'

'Sister Benedicta. Come with me.' She got up with difficulty and limped out of the room into the corridor. She selected a key from the big bunch dangling from a dirty rope around her middle and opened one of the doors. It led into a small chapel. Candles and incense were burning in there, but they couldn't disguise the terrible smell. She led him into a small ante-room. Father Ryan felt his stomach wanting to force its contents up into his throat. But he followed her. There was a bed in there, and in the bed was a body. He put his hand to his mouth, trying to hold his breath. He approached slowly.

'This is Sister Agnes,' she said. 'Agnes.' she put her hand on the nun's chest and turned to Father Ryan, smiling. 'I think she's ready for the last rites.'

Father Ryan felt sweat break out and run down inside his clothes. He caught hold of Sister Benedicta's arm and pulled her roughly from the room. He felt the blood draining from his face, nausea rising up in him.

'For the love of God,' he hissed. 'She's been dead for a long time, as you well know.'

Sister Benedicta looked sly. 'But I knew you'd come; I've been waiting. Do this, and I'll tell you about *her* – she's gone you know.'

'Of course, she's gone.' He was going to vomit, he tried desperately to remember where the bathroom was – upstairs. No time. The kitchen sink. He staggered towards the hall. The nun was stumbling after him, her habit getting tangled up with his cassock in the narrow space.

'I knew you'd come looking for *her*,' she wailed.

Father Ryan tried to push her to one side. 'Who?' He was poised at the top of the stairs leading down to the kitchen. Bile was beginning to escape from his lips. He couldn't hold it much longer. He lurched forward. The nun grabbed at his sleeve.

'I know all about you. Do it!' she yelled. 'Do it for Agnes!'

'I can't!' Bile erupted from his mouth and down the front of his black coat.

'Then I won't tell you about *her*, I won't tell you about Clare.' She growled like a dog and shoved him in the back. Taken by surprise at her strength, he fell forward, his hands clutching wildly. He caught hold of her habit and managed to grasp the handrail on the wall. He regained his balance and clung on only to see the nun toppling forward. She grabbed his sleeve. He could have reached out and steadied her. There was no rail on her side. But he didn't. He prised her filthy fingers from his sleeve, one by one, and watched her fall headlong down the steep stairs.

She lay in a crumpled heap of black and white clothes at the bottom. His nausea had subsided with the shock. He tried to think about what she'd said. Had she really mentioned Clare, or had he misheard? She said she knew all about him, she was waiting for him. What did she mean? What did she know? He slowly made his way down the stairs; his legs felt as if they had no bones in them. He knelt down beside her;

she was breathing shallowly. He thought that he shouldn't move her. Not that he cared if she lived or died. He put his mouth to her ear.

'Where is Clare?' he said, loudly.

The nun's eyes flickered.

'Is she here?'

Sister Benedicta licked her lips. Dark blood was seeping onto the quarry tiles from underneath her veil. 'Gone.'

'Where?' he shook her shoulder.

'To her friend, Rose,' she gasped, 'on ferry . . . Island.'

'Ireland!' Father Ryan exclaimed. Oh, God. She had gone back home after all.

'When?' he demanded. The nun didn't respond. He shook her again, roughly. 'Did she have the child? Did she take it with her?'

The nun seemed to be falling unconscious. He slapped her grey face. 'I don't care if you die, you stupid old woman. Just tell me what happened.' Her breath was shallow, puffing one corner of her mouth. Father Ryan stood up. 'I'll call an ambulance,' he muttered, looking around for something to put over her. He wasn't going to give up his own coat. He walked over to the sink and ran water, sluicing the sweat from his face, the slime from the front of his coat. Something dangled above him. He looked up; long skeins of pink wool were hanging from hooks over the sink. He yanked them down and draped them all over the nun's body until he could hardly see her.

CHAPTER

Sixteen

'It's not that I mind looking after the animals,' Ted was saying from the back of the Land Rover. 'It's just that I'm surprised you're going away. Never expected to hear you say you wanted a holiday.' He laughed. 'You always say your life is one big holiday, living here.'

'I know, but this is different. It's a chance to be with my family.'

Ted sat in silence for a while. Fran could almost hear him thinking things through. 'So where did you say they are now?'

'Oxford.'

'And they expect you to go across on the ferry on your own – with the baby – and drive all the way there?'

'It was my suggestion. Seemed silly them coming back here, if we're going to stay in Oxford.'

'I dunno,' Ted muttered, 'seems like a liberty to me.'

'It will be an adventure.' Fran tried to sound enthusiastic. 'I was getting set in my ways.'

'Thought you liked your ways.'

'I do. But it's good to do new things as we get older, otherwise we'll just settle into old age.' Ted made a noise which she couldn't decipher. 'I am a little worried though, Ted.'

'What about?'

'I think there may be something wrong with Young Phil's wife, Ann. I know they've been consulting specialists in London, and now in Oxford. That's one of the reasons they came over here.'

'Do you know what's wrong?'

Fran shook her head. 'But I've a feeling they're going to tell me when I get to Oxford.'

'Oh, well that puts a different light on it,' Ted said, 'if they're in trouble. Why didn't you say before?'

'They didn't want me to say anything to anyone. I don't think they know what the problem is themselves.' Fran parked on the esplanade outside *Rachel's Café*. She could hardly bring herself to look at Ted as he helped her unstrap Sam's seat and lift it out. How could she lie like this to dear, kind Ted, who she'd known all her life?

*   *   *

Sophie photographed Rachel standing proudly amongst the tables in the restaurant. Kyp came out of the kitchen, beaming. He was dressed in snowy white chef's gear.

'I'll take one of both of you,' he said. 'It looks fantastic – and so do you two in your sexy black dresses.'

'Thanks, Kyp.' Sophie handed him the camera and went to join Rachel.

Rachel smiled broadly and gazed around. It really did look stunning. The candles were lit in their crystal holders, crisp white napkins stood to attention in polished glasses. Pink carnations enhanced each table. The gentle light made the mosaic table tops glow like jewels. The cutlery sparkled. Easy-listening songs played softy. Rachel had decided against Andrea Bocelli – she didn't want any trace of her feelings about Sandro to be connected to this evening. She'd stood the olive trees outside, either side of the door. She glanced at her watch.

'People will start arriving soon. Thank heavens it isn't raining for once. We won't have loads of wet coats to deal with.'

The door opened and Nick came in with Kate, Jules, Billy and the girl she hadn't met before.

'This is Clare,' Nick said.

'Right,' Rachel grinned at the gang. 'Let's get you sorted with aprons. I don't need all of you serving at once. You'll be falling over each other. Two of you can sit down and eat with everyone else, and then swap over. I want your young palates to sample the food.'

'We were hoping you'd say that,' Kate laughed.

'We've been starving ourselves for days,' Billy commented.

Rachel distributed the black and white striped aprons and sent

180

the kids to the cloakroom to scrub their hands. Eventually she was going to have her staff wear black and white clothes, but she thought this was too much to ask of them for the trial run tonight.

'Now, the rules. Number one – politeness at all times – I've asked for feed back from the customers, so don't take anything personally. Number two – hygiene. Wash hands frequently, don't use anything that has been dropped, and don't touch the food. Any problems, ask me or Sophie. Clare – you can do first stint on washing up duty.' She took them into the kitchen to show them how things were organised. 'Now don't forget, the customers can glimpse you working between the shelving that separates the restaurant area. So best behaviour – no nose picking!'

'Gross!' Jules commented.

'Has to be said,' Rachel laughed. She turned to Clare. 'I expect Kyp and Sophie have some pans to wash up. Let's get you started.' Clare gave Rachel a small smile. The girl looked awfully pale, but she had that skin that goes with red hair and green eyes. A striking, sweet, serious face. Rachel remembered Aidan and Patrick saying that Clare had arrived at Wraith Cove feeling poorly.

'Are you all right?' she asked, gently.

Clare looked slightly alarmed. 'I'm fine.'

'Good. We'll have to cover that hair of yours with a cap, while you're in the food area.' Rachel helped Clare pin up her long red plait. The back of her neck looked so white and tender, Rachel thought she should be tucked up in bed with a mug of hot chocolate and a teddy bear, she seemed incredibly young. How could her mother let her go off travelling on her own? But these kids – look at Rose – if they wanted to do something they went ahead and did it. Aidan would be off soon. It seemed different with a boy, somehow.

'There,' she said, poking a wisp of hair inside the cap. 'Not glamorous, but you can take it off when you sit down to eat.' Clare smiled shyly. There was something about her . . . something vaguely familiar. 'Have you been in my café before?' Rachel asked.

'No. I . . . er, no.'

'I thought I recognised you,' Rachel said.

181

The door opened. The first customers were arriving – a group of doctors and staff from the GPs' surgery. They made appreciative comments as they sat down. Nick hung up coats and opened bottles of champagne for them. Jill and Ash arrived next with Evie. The Water Babies had been dropped off at Cormorants where they were bedding down with Jill and Ash's kids, under the care of the nanny. Rachel noticed how everyone had dressed up for the evening and felt pleased. Evie wore a simple white dress that showed off her Grecian tan. Jill was in her usual black, but with pink accessories bright enough to set eyes watering. Ash looked elegant in a dark grey suit and a red bow tie.

The atmosphere was building, chatter and laughter and exclamations over the décor and menu could be heard. Patrick and Kate were taking baskets of warm panini, and little terracotta bowls of olives to the tables. Rachel felt her anxiety lessening. It was going to be just fine. All she needed now was for the food to be a success. Solveig, the receptionist from Cormorants was coming in the door with Father Michael and some of the therapists. One table was full of local traders. And then, to her delight, Jane, Chas and Marguerite appeared.

'Just made it,' Chas was saying in his deep voice.

Jane was wearing her magenta salwar kameez. She blew a kiss to Rachel. 'Couldn't tempt Neptune, I'm afraid.'

Marguerite smiled and brushed her cool hand over Rachel's hot cheek. She looked beautiful in her flowing dress of sea colours. Her long silver hair shone in the candlelight.

Rachel fled back to the kitchen. 'Sorry,' she gasped. 'I'm neglecting my duties. I'm just so excited.'

Kyp looked up from the complicated set of pans he was managing. 'Good to be excited,' he said. 'Sophie, keep an eye on that sauce, don't let it boil.'

Rachel smiled. Kyp and Sophie, glimpsed by the clientele, really could be mistaken for authentic Italians. 'Right,' she said. 'Are we ready for orders?'

When she went back into the restaurant, Fran had arrived with Ted. They were carrying a little car seat. 'I'm baby-sitting, so had to bring him,' Fran whispered, looking a little flustered. 'He won't be any trouble. Is there a corner table? I can tuck him down by my legs.'

People exclaimed over the baby as Fran and Ted settled themselves. Rachel noticed how proud Fran looked. But then she always had been devoted to rearing the young. How nice for her to have a baby in the family. Anyway, she'd better get cracking with the food.

Kate and Patrick were taking orders. Nick was dealing with the champagne and drinks. Aidan was the general dogsbody at the moment, doing whatever was needed. Billy and Jules were looking very smug sitting with the customers, drinking champagne. 'Don't let the young ones drink more than one small glass,' Rachel whispered to Nick. The last thing she wanted was for them to get out of their heads and cause a problem.

'I'm keeping an eye,' he said. 'I've told them it's fruit juice next – seeing as they're working.'

The food was smelling delicious. Rachel checked the first course for presentation as she handed the dishes to Kate and Patrick to serve. The clatter and chink of cutlery could now be heard. She studied the orders. There seemed to be a good mix of traditional and exotic dishes. Kyp had been absolutely right. His selection was perfect, and there was no way they'd have been able to deal with more than this. What had Sandro been thinking of? But she wasn't supposed to be giving him any thought tonight.

Half way through dealing with the main course, Rachel heard her name, and Sophie's, being called. Patrick came in to the kitchen.

'I think your guests want to toast you,' he whispered.

'Not a good time,' Sophie muttered through a cloud of steam.

'Bugger.' Rachel was drizzling olive oil and lemon juice over lattuga.

'Disaster,' Kyp said. 'But you must go, ladies. Always, the customers' appreciation must be acknowledged. Go. I will manage. But don't be long.'

'Curses,' Sophie was red in the face. She whipped off her hat. She grabbed Nick by the shirt as he went by and handed him a wooden spoon. 'Stir that,' she ordered.

Rachel winked at Sophie. 'Let's go and meet our fans,' she whispered. 'Smile, girl.'

Chas stood up as they walked into the restaurant. 'On behalf of everyone assembled here, we would like to wish you every success in your new venture,' he said, raising his glass. 'To Rachel and Sophie.'

Dear Chas, Rachel thought, he'd been such a help with the business side of all this. Without his expertise who knows what might have happened, given Sandro's – don't think about him.

'Hear, hear. To Rachel and Sophie,' everybody joined in, some of them trying to get to their feet, dropping napkins and clashing chairs.

'And thank you for inviting us to be guinea pigs,' Jill called. Rachel could see she had drunk a great deal already. Maybe she shouldn't have been so generous with the drink.

'You are most welcome,' Rachel said, starting to worry about things in the kitchen. 'Sophie and I would like to thank you all—'

The door burst open and a young woman almost fell in. Astonished, Rachel stopped mid-sentence. It was Rose! She looked distraught, her eyes were wide, red-rimmed. She scanned the restaurant.

'Mum! Dad!' she yelled, seeing Jill and Ash. 'Come quickly! We've just got home, and Grandma's going to die!' She burst into loud sobs.

Ash was by her side in an instant, elbowing people's heads as he scrambled between the tables.

'All right, darling. Calm down. Dad's here.'

'The kids are all screaming and the nanny can't cope,' Rose wailed, her mouth trembling. 'I've been trying to phone you.' She glared at Rachel. 'The sodding answer phone's on.' The customers had fallen silent, every face turned towards the scene. Jill staggered up and lurched between the tables trying to reach Rose. She knocked over her glass of red wine. It shattered as it hit the hard mosaic. Nick grabbed cloths and started mopping up. Patrick appeared from the kitchen carrying wooden bowls of salad.

'Patrick!' Rose yelled, and hurled herself at him. He dropped one of the bowls but managed to hold onto the other. Black and green olives, and tiny red tomatoes, rolled over the floor. 'I don't know whether to call the doctor or an ambulance.'

One of the doctors stood up. 'I'll come,' he said, wiping his mouth hastily on his napkin.

'Marguerite!' Rose sobbed, 'will you come and help my grandma?'

Marguerite got up gracefully and slid through the throng surrounding Rose.

'The kids!' said Evie. 'I'd better come too.'

People were grabbing coats and leaving fast. Suddenly half the guests were about to depart.

'Rachel! Sophie!' Kyp's voice could be heard calling.

'Christ!' Rachel muttered rushing to the kitchen. Kyp was instructing Clare to stir something while he endeavoured to dish up the rest of the main courses. Rachel didn't quite know what to do. Would they come back? Should she try to keep their dinners hot, or give them fresh ones?

'I didn't know Stephanie was so ill,' Sophie was saying, taking over from Clare. 'Jill didn't say. How awful.'

'Can we talk about it later?' Rachel said, feeling guilty as she said it. Sophie had known Jill's mother for years. 'Hell, Patrick's gone with them. Nick!' she yelled, realising she'd broken her rule never to shout at the staff across the restaurant. Fran was at the counter asking, apologetically, for hot water to heat the baby's bottle. Clare was standing at the sink, looking as if she had frozen to the spot.

'Washing up, Clare,' Rachel snapped. Clare looked even whiter, if that was at all possible, her green eyes wide with shock.

'Was that Rose that came in?' she asked. 'Patrick's Rose?'

'Yes! Now let's do the gossip later. We have to get things back on track.'

Rachel flew around clearing the debris and chatting in her sunny manner to the remaining guests, trying to restore the ambience. Fran was giving the baby his bottle. She and Ted were chatting as if nothing had happened. Father Michael, obviously used to pouring oil on troubled Italian dinners, was entertaining Solveig and the health team.

185

In the kitchen she ordered Aidan and Clare to have a break and to send Billy and Jules in.

'I'd prefer to stay in here,' Clare said, nervously. 'I'm not hungry, or tired, or anything.'

'Okay. But let me know when you've had enough.' Rachel handed her a large glass of orange juice. 'Don't get de-hydrated.'

The main course was finished – or wasted. Kyp was taking a break, trying unsuccessfully to phone Evie. The desserts were Rachel and Sophie's speciality. Sophie was clearing work space. Rachel grabbed the bags of rubbish and let herself out the back door to where the dustbins were kept under the stairs to her flat. The night was cold and clear, stars glittered; she could hear the sea. She breathed deeply. Well, she thought, that was an unfortunate interruption. At least it was an emergency beyond her control. Everyone would understand that. Still, she wished it hadn't happened; everything had been going perfectly up to that point. For the first time she thought about Stephanie. Jill had mentioned that Stephanie had picked up a disease in Africa. Rachel hoped it wasn't anything serious. She smiled. Rose, like Jill, did enjoy a drama sometimes.

She put the bags down and opened the bin lid. Suddenly, something moved by her feet. She jumped back and yelped. Not a rat! Oh, God. She could just about see it in the dim light from the windows. It twitched. It was a foot! Was it a drunk slumped there, behind the bin? She should call Kyp. She crept forward and bent down to get a closer look at the person's face, which was in the shadows.

'Rachel,' a man's voice rasped.

She nearly fell over backwards. She knew that voice; it was Sandro! She took hold of his arms and tried to yank him forwards.

'What the hell are you doing here? Are you drunk?' But she could see he wasn't. His eyes were slits in his bruised and bloody face. He'd been beaten up.

'Oh, Sandro,' she whispered. 'Let's get you inside.' She helped him up with great difficulty; he seemed in a bad way. He leant heavily on her as they stumbled up the stairs. Rachel prayed nobody would come looking for her. She unlocked the door to her flat, hauled him

186

inside and down the hall to her bedroom. He fell on the bed. She rushed to the kitchen to get water and a cloth. 'I have to go,' she said. 'Rest here and keep quiet. I'll be back as soon as I can.'

She let herself out and locked the door. She wasn't going to let him escape again until she'd found out what was going on.

Sophie was peering out of the kitchen door. 'Rachel,' she was calling.

'I'm here. Sorry. Had to cool down – hot flush.' She went back inside and started arranging fruit – her hands trembling slightly. What a night this was turning out to be.

*   *   *

The policeman put the phone down and shook his head.

'I'm really sorry, sir. The nun – Sister Benedicta – has died.'

'I am indeed sorry to hear that.' Father Ryan meant it. Damn the woman. He'd wanted to question her further about Clare. Maybe he shouldn't have been so rough with her. But she'd asked for it – hadn't she tried to kill him? But then, if she'd lived, she might have had something to tell the police. He didn't know what lies Clare had told her. The policeman was looking at him with his head on one side, sympathetically. 'Would you like a cup of tea? This must have been a terrible ordeal for you.'

'No, thank you.' He wished he'd been offered a glass of whiskey. The English seemed to think tea was the answer to everything.

The policeman moved some papers around on his desk. 'Would you mind telling me how you came to be there?'

'Didn't I already tell the other officer? I'm touring around, looking at some of the old Catholic institutions you have here – a sort of holiday, I suppose.' He thought it best not to mention Clare, not knowing where that might lead.

'So it was just co-incidence – you finding the Sisters?'

'Indeed it was. I thought the abbey was empty.' He felt like he was being interrogated. Who did these people think they were? He leaned forward and rested his elbows on the desk. 'What were those nuns doing there – so neglected? There appeared to be no electricity or proper heating.

187

Sister Benedicta was out of her mind. It was a disgrace.'

The policeman frowned. 'The situation will be fully investigated – by the police, as well as the Catholic authorities. All I know so far is that most of the elderly nuns had been re-housed – in a Catholic care home. But Sister Benedicta and Sister Agnes insisted on staying where they were, until the time came for demolition. It seems they were overlooked through some mix-up. They unplugged the phone themselves. And the electricity wasn't turned off – just a blown fuse. But they obviously didn't realise.' He wrote a few things on his notepad. 'Now, if you wouldn't mind telling me, again, how Sister Benedicta came to fall down the stairs—'

'All this is in my statement. She took me to see the – er, body. I was shocked and needed water. She went ahead of me to the kitchen stairs and she tripped and fell. I tried to catch her.' Father Ryan bent his head and lowered his voice. He reached for the tissue box on the table. 'I just couldn't quite—'.

'I understand,' the policeman said, averting his eyes. 'You've been very helpful, sir.'

He showed Father Ryan to the door. 'We'll be in touch if we need you for anything. There will have to be a post-mortem on both the Sisters, of course. But I'm sure we won't need to trouble you further.'

Father Ryan drove to the nearest lay-by and drained the last of the whiskey from the bottle. He tried to remember the nun's last words. *Gone to see her friend, Rose, ferry, Ireland.*

'Damn, damn, damn,' he yelled, thumping his hand on the steering wheel. He'd been wasting his time. Why, oh why had he not bothered to listen to those drunken eejits on the ferry? He would have to go back. He would question that band and try to find out where Rose came from. Trust Clare to be so devious. He was going to teach that girl a lesson when he caught up with her. And he still didn't even know about her child.

But first, he had to find a place to stay the night. And even more importantly, another bottle of whiskey.

CHAPTER
Seventeen

Clare got up while it was still dark to make tea and toast. She was starving. She didn't have anything to eat last night at Rachel's dinner. She thought Rachel was the woman in Sandro's photo – she seemed familiar – but she couldn't be sure. She was nice and kept trying to persuade Clare to eat something – there was some delicious food left over. But she'd been so full of excitement that she found she couldn't eat. She waited for the kettle to boil, thinking it over.

First of all she'd glimpsed Marguerite as she came into the restaurant. It was hard to see clearly through the shelves that separated the different parts of the kitchen from the dining tables. The pasta jars, bottles of drinks, and glass ornaments all got in the way. But she couldn't mistake Marguerite's hair. It was definitely her that she'd taken for the Blessed Virgin the night she arrived at Wraith Cove and collapsed. How foolish she'd been. And how she'd dreaded seeing Marguerite again. But now it didn't seem to matter at all. Clare was better. Even if Marguerite had suspected – by the state of Clare's breasts – that she'd recently given birth, she wouldn't know anything about the baby. She probably assumed it had been adopted. Clare just hoped Marguerite wouldn't tell anybody. And then she remembered, Marguerite didn't speak.

But what had amazed Clare most of all, last night, was the sudden appearance of Rose. Clare didn't realise what was going on for ages. She thought it was just general noise from the customers – they'd been so lively. But then she heard Rose's name called. She'd just managed to stop herself from rushing into the restaurant. It was then she realised something was wrong, people were getting up to leave. Patrick was going too. She wanted desperately to know what was happening, but Rachel was getting annoyed and wanted everyone to get back to work.

189

Clare spread butter on her toast and took it back to bed with her. Her bare feet were freezing. She wondered what to do next. Today was Sunday. Perhaps Patrick had told Rose that she was here, and Rose would come to see her. She still hadn't made up her mind whether she should tell Rose the whole story. Would she understand? Surely Rose wouldn't be horrible to her. Not like that Sandro Angelo. Thank goodness *he* hadn't turned up last night.

Clare put her plate and cup on the floor and lay down in bed. Should she tell Rachel about posting the wallet through her letterbox? She could say that she found it in the street and recognised the photo. But there was no point really. And it would mean another lie. She didn't want to lie to Rachel.

Clare yawned. She thought she would stay close to the caravans today – so she wouldn't miss Rose, if she came.

As she started to drift, an image rose in her mind of going into the cloakroom, at the restaurant last night. Rachel had asked her to check that it was clean and tidy. There'd been a woman in there, short and plump. She had her back to Clare and was bending over a child on the changing table, talking in baby language. Clare decided to come back when she'd gone.

She realised now, the woman's shape had reminded her of Mother. Mother used to bend over like that, stirring pots over the fire, talking to herself. After Clare had given birth to the baby, Mother had become increasingly strange. Sometimes Clare felt frightened of her. She'd get so angry when Clare asked questions about when she might be able to leave, or when the priest would come. Mother sometimes threw things at her. Clare felt too weak to protest. She began to watch Mother's movements, trying to work out how she might run away when the baby was weaned. Where did Mother go when she went to pray? Was there a passage that led to a chapel in the abbey? Maybe there were other nuns that Clare could go to for help.

One night Clare decided to try and follow her. She had just been through the torture of feeding the baby, and Mother had taken him back to her own room. And then Clare heard her going downstairs.

She watched over the banisters as Mother opened the door behind the tapestry to the corridor that led to their small sitting room. Clare tiptoed down the dark stairs and followed her. Mother placed her candle on the floor and unlocked one of the doors off the corridor and went inside, leaving it ajar. She always locked the door behind her during the day, when Clare was around. But not that night. She must have been sure Clare wouldn't get out of bed. Clare found herself in a small chapel, plain and bare. Candles were burning – and some foul smelling incense. Mother opened another door. *Agnes,* she called. *Agnes, it's Benedicta, I'm here, dear.*

Clare's heart leaped. Mother's name was Benedicta, not Bridget, and there *was* someone else living here. Mother hadn't lied about the other nuns; but nobody was answering. Clare was confused. Maybe Agnes was a cat or something. She was finding it hard to breathe – perhaps there were several cats and they'd messed all over the floor. Clare moved closer to the doorway, trying to keep in the shadows. Mother was bending over a narrow bed; she appeared to be stroking something – it must be an animal. She sat down and picked up a bible and Clare saw the head and shoulders of a person. Clare put her hands over her mouth and nose to stop herself from retching. The person's eyes were wide open, staring, the mouth grimacing, toothless. It looked like a skeleton covered with yellow skin. *Agnes, dear Agnes,* Mother was intoning, like a chant. *I'll read to you.*

Clare turned and sped silently away. She got up the stairs, clinging to the rail, trying not fall in the dark. She gulped and gulped, attempting to get some saliva into her dry mouth. Mother was mad. She was talking to a dead body. Maybe she had killed Agnes. Perhaps she intended to kill Clare. Clare was frantic. She pulled on her clothes and shoved her belongings into her backpack. She had to get away from here. Mother said she must stay until the baby was weaned otherwise it would die, and Clare would never be forgiven. Her life would be just a matter of waiting for the fires of hell. Clare crept into Mother's room, her legs trembling – she hadn't regained her strength from the birth. She crammed the baby's things into her pack, lifted him out of the drawer in which Mother kept

191

him, and wrapped him in his shawl. She struggled to get her backpack on, and then stuffed the baby inside her coat and zipped it up. She listened on the landing for Mother, but could hear nothing. She tip-toed down and heaved the front door open, just enough to squeeze out into the cold night. Once she'd wriggled through the gap by the heavy gate, she started to cry. Why had Father Ryan sent her here? How could he have done this to her? Her mam always said the Poor Clares were the best nuns on God's earth. Her legs were shaking, her body sore and aching. She needed someone to help her. But there was no-one. She would just have to do the best she could. She started to walk. At least she was outside, and she still had her money. She'd ask someone how to get to the Isle of Wight, and then she would find Rose.

Clare turned over in her bunk bed. And now, Rose was just a couple of miles away, in Ventnor.

*   *   *

Rachel was propped up on one elbow watching Sandro sleep. She wanted to wake him and demand to know what was going on, but she didn't have the heart to disturb him, he looked so hurt. Both of his eyes were blackened and he was snoring through nostrils blocked with clotted blood. His nose looked as if it might be broken.

Thank goodness it was Sunday. She yawned; she was exhausted but too overwrought to sleep. She didn't really know if last night had been a success or not. Everybody was complimentary about the food, but the evening had been so disjointed with all the drama, that it was a bit of a blur. Still, at least the customers had only the one disturbance to deal with. Whereas – she frowned at Sandro – she had this one as well.

Patrick hadn't been seen since he'd disappeared with Rose. Aidan had gone back to Wraith Cove with the others. Rachel gathered he was keen on young Clare. She looked too young to have a boyfriend. If Rachel was her mother, she'd definitely want her home by ten. But if she was a student she was probably older than Aidan. The doctor who had gone to tend Stephanie hadn't returned to finish his dinner, neither had Marguerite, Jill, Ash or Evie. Jane and Chas and Kyp had gone up to Cormorants to find them after the meal was over and they hadn't come back. So Rachel didn't have a clue what was going on.

She got off the bed and went to make coffee. 'It's confession time, Big Boy,' she called, as she returned with the tray. Sandro opened his eyes, as far as he could. He groaned.

'I expect that hurts,' Rachel said. 'Sit up. This will wake you.'

Sandro struggled into a sitting position. She didn't try to help. He reached out a hand to her. She ignored it and passed him a mug of coffee.

'Grazie,' he murmured. He held it with trembling fingers and took a sip. He groaned again. It did look painful, but Rachel had made her mind up not to be sympathetic.

'You'd better explain,' she said, pulling a chair over to sit beside the bed.

'Rachel, I am so sorry.'

The way he said *Rachel* sounded even more sensuous through his swollen lips. She took a large gulp of coffee and said nothing.

'I don't know what to say. I let you down.'

'Big time,' Rachel said.

'Si, si,' he nodded.

'Si, si,' she agreed. 'Why?'

'I have done terrible thing.'

'It looks that way. And?'

'And – I am so sorry.'

Rachel put her mug down. 'Look, Sandro. We're going round in circles here. Just tell me straight what this is all about. And then you can go, and I can get on with my *very* successful life.'

'Bene. I tell you. I have affair with wife of manager of hotel.'

'So, I was just one of many, was I?'

'No, no. We finish – before I meet you.'

'Not sure I believe that. But go on.'

'After I meet you – and we make plans, she come and say she pregnant and need money for abortion. I am Catholic, si? I say, no! But she do it and get sick, so her husband find out. She tell me to disappear. I get out, quick.'

'I bet you did. So, why are you still here?'

'I leave my wallet. I hide it for safety and forget it in my hurry.'

'Where did you go?'

'I get quick jobs. But this man hunt me, and I run on.'

'Looks like he finally caught up with you.'

'Si, si. I go back to get wallet. He catch me and do this.' He pointed to his face, looking at Rachel mournfully. He leaned forward to put his mug down and winced. 'My ribs, so sore.'

'That was a bit risky, wasn't it? Going back there.'

'Si, I meet a girl who try for me, but she go to wrong room.'

'*Another* girl, Sandro?'

'Not that kind, she very young. I talk to her in Catholic church, in Ventnor.'

'And you asked her to do your dirty work for you? Why would she?'

'She in trouble too. Terrible trouble. I promise to help, in return.'

'And did you?'

Sandro looked down. 'I am shamed. No, I did not.'

'What happened to her?'

'I not know. I run away from her.'

'You ran away from her?' Rachel let out a startled laugh. 'A young girl in trouble who tried to help you!' She shook her head. How could such a big man be such a wimp? 'Look, Sandro. We're getting diverted here. Why didn't you come and tell me all this? You disappeared without any explanation. Do you have any idea of the anguish you caused me? I thought we had something special. And then there was all the anxiety over the restaurant. Sophie was let down too.'

'Please, please.' He put his head in his hands. 'I suffer. I too shamed and scared to come back. That man follow me everywhere. I thought he might come here.'

'He did – or one of his morons did.' She sighed. How could she have spent so much time on this weak cowardly man crumpled on her bed? 'So, you've been hanging around, trying to get your hands on this wallet – bribing a little girl to risk her neck for you.' She got up and opened a drawer in her dressing table. She took out the wallet and threw it on the bed.

Sandro's gloom seemed to lift instantaneously, even his eyes brightened. He grabbed the wallet and opened it, searching its contents. 'My passport, cards, money, still here.'

'Yes, there are *some* honest people about,' she commented.

'How you get this?'

'It plopped through my letterbox. Someone obviously found it and recognised me, or the café, in the photograph.'

'Tess! She say she will go back again. That's why it not there when I go.'

'Tess? Another of your girls?'

'No. The little one I tell you about.'

'Okay. You've got your wallet. Go and have a shower and clean yourself up. And I'll take you to the ferry. And that's the last thing I'll ever do for you. Understand?'

'Grazie, grazie.' Sandro clambered off the bed and went into the bathroom. Rachel got dressed. How could she ever have thought she loved this man? A man who would get a young troubled girl to take such a risk, and then run away from her?

'Let's go,' she said, as he emerged from the bathroom looking a bit better. She noticed how much thinner he was, and his clothes were dirty. She opened the door before she succumbed to the thought of cooking his breakfast.

She drove to the terminal on the end of Ryde pier. Might as well put him on the *Fast Cat* – get rid of him as quickly as possible.

'Out you get,' she said, leaving the engine running.

'Rachel,' he murmured. She could hear the tears in his voice. 'I really love you, si? I not lie to you.'

'Sandro, you are a bull-shitter,' she said quietly.

'No, no. I honest. This happen before I meet you.'

Rachel couldn't rid herself of the vision of him running away from a young girl in trouble. She watched the heaving sea and said nothing, but felt tears welling in her own eyes at the sheer mess that humanity was capable of – the pain inflicted intentionally, or otherwise.

'Rachel?'

She looked at him then, his dark eyes brimming with tears. 'That girl, Tess, her name. She birth a baby and leave it in a shed to die. So terrible for a young girl – just a child. What I did is bad also – mortal sin. Her confession, it make me think, I am shit. That's why I blame her, and run away. I have been without honour, si?'

'Si, Sandro. Please go now.'

'If you meet this girl, Tess – she has long hair – rossa. Tell her, I am sorry. Per favore?'

Rachel nodded, feeling her heart was going to crack open if he didn't go.

'Rachel? Forgive me,' he was sobbing.

All Rachel could do was bow her head. And then he opened the car door and was gone.

CHAPTER
Eighteen

Father Ryan sat on an uncomfortable cane chair in the cramped room of a shabby bed and breakfast house. He sipped at his whiskey and looked around. The bed was similar to his own, high and narrow with squeaking springs. The dour landlady had been unwelcoming; indifferent to his status. There wasn't even an electric kettle to make a cup of tea, and the room was chilly. Still, what did he care? He had his new comfort – and Jeannie's red shawl tucked over his knees.

He felt physically tired after his traumatic day yesterday, but his head wasn't aching – the nibbling rodent seemed to be rendered unconscious by the whiskey. And a strange excitement possessed him – as if part of him were relishing all these astonishing happenings. He'd been almost murdered by a mad nun, experienced a macabre death scene, witnessed a fatal accident, and ended up in a police station, being interrogated. He felt like a celebrity. Would he be in the newspapers? VISITING IRISH PRIEST UNCOVERS GHASTLY MYSTERY. He suspected not; in England this was probably an everyday occurrence.

He'd planned to start the long journey back home today but felt reluctant to end his adventure so soon. What else might he encounter on the road? And he didn't know if Clare would be back in Bantry when he arrived. She might be there now – with or without a baby. What would she have told her mother? Would she have broken her promise not to name him? Surely she wouldn't, hadn't he put the fear of hell into her? But still he was troubled by the thought of what Clare might do. He had chosen badly when he'd sent her to Sister Bridget. He should have taken her away himself and arranged . . . something different. He thought about that disgusting old nun tumbling down the stairs. Accidents happened so unexpectedly.

He screwed the cap back on the bottle. It was mid-afternoon. He needed to make a decision. He got up, put his overcoat on and hurried downstairs. The hallway smelled of roasting meat. His stomach rumbled. The old bag hadn't offered him any Sunday lunch. Not that he would have accepted. He didn't want to sit at her table and answer banal questions. He let himself out of the front door and got in his car, wondering if he was sober enough to drive. Sure, he'd only had a few sips, hadn't he?

He found a car park near a railway station where he'd spotted a row of telephone boxes. He fumbled nervously with the buttons, these new-fangled phones were so complicated. Eventually he made a connection.

'Is that Father Christopher?'

'It is.'

The priest sounded sleepy. Father Ryan had obviously roused him from his afternoon nap. 'Father Ryan here.' There was a silence. He held his breath feeling a prickling of sweat break out on his upper lip. Would Father Christopher have something dreadful to tell him?

'Ryan? We've been wondering about you?'

'Have you?'

'What have you been up to?'

'Up to?' His hand felt slippery on the receiver – he wanted to drop it and run.

'Thought you might have phoned before. How's your good aunt?'

Father Ryan breathed deeply. 'She's not so well.'

'You'll not be back just yet, then?'

'I'd like to stay a while longer. If that's all right with you. Can you manage without me?'

'Manage?' Father Christopher let out a loud hoot of laughter. 'We're doing just fine. Don't you be worrying, now.'

'The choir? Is everything in order?'

'The choir is delirious. I've taught them some fine songs.'

I bet you have, he thought. 'Is Mrs Mulligan keeping things spick and span?'

'Everything is scrubbed to sainthood.'

'Would there be nothing to report then?'

'Not a thing. I hope your aunt recovers well. We'll pray for her. Let us know when you're coming back.' He laughed again. 'We'll sober up.'

Father Ryan replaced the receiver and stood staring at it, waiting for his heart to stop beating so fast. Nothing had happened. Clare hadn't returned. Which didn't mean she might not be on her way. But for now . . . maybe he could afford a couple more days of freedom. Perhaps he would go to a concert tonight. He'd seen a poster advertising a performance of Elgar's oratorio, *The Dream of Gerontius,* in Malvern where Elgar had lived. The thought of hearing such dramatic music, live, made him feel shivery all over again.

He drove slowly through the suburbs of Worcester. He stretched his neck to look at his dog collar in the mirror. It wasn't too grubby. He'd brought some spare ones with him – must remember to wear a fresh one tomorrow. It was important to look pristine. He pushed a lock of brown hair off his forehead – a good trim wouldn't go amiss, either.

Now, he had the rest of the afternoon to while away. He was looking for a park where he could sit peacefully and watch the children playing. Parents never minded priests smiling at their little ones.

* * *

'Any of you reprobates need a lift into Ventnor?'

Clare looked out of the caravan window. It was Jane's husband, Chas. She recognised him from the restaurant last night. He was a large man with big ears and mouth, like the jolly giant in her book of children's stories at home. She dropped Kate's magazine – all about celebrities and their weight – and got up from the bunk. The others were already grabbing their coats. Clare pulled on her boots and jacket and rushed after them. They piled into Chas's big posh car with leather seats that reminded Clare of horses.

'Thought you might want to spend some of your hard earned cash,' Chas commented as he started the engine and drove the car up the bumpy path to the road.

'Shops are shut, it's Sunday,' Kate said. She was sitting beside Chas in the front seat. 'But it will be nice to mooch about.'

'Mooch about!' Chas said. 'In my day we had hobbies, like train-spotting and filling in I-spy books.'

'You did not!' Kate laughed. 'You were smoking dope, and paving the road to hell for future generations.'

'That's very astute of you. I do seem to remember belonging to CND and suchlike.'

'You still should.' Billy leaned forward from the back. 'The nuclear threat isn't over.'

'Oh, political are we?' Chas commented.

'We are,' Jules said. 'We stand for a green and peaceful land, to raise *our* young.'

'Glad to hear it. Don't have your young too young, though. Enjoy your freedom first. Do great things.' He glanced around at the back seat. 'What do you think, Clare? What line of study are you pursuing?'

Why did grown-ups always ask those questions? All she could think about at the moment was how she was going to get to see Rose. Patrick and Aidan hadn't been to Wraith Cove today. This lift to Ventnor seemed like an opportunity to get closer to her.

'I, I'm thinking things over, at the moment,' she said. 'Not quite sure – I'm considering horticulture.' She'd picked this idea up from listening to Jane talk about Nick and the restoration of the hotel gardens. The others didn't seem to know much about it and so couldn't ask difficult questions. And it seemed to her like a nice career, working with plants and trees. She always enjoyed digging in the garden with Mam, trying to grow things. It seemed miraculous to her, when she was little, that big plants could burst out of tiny seeds. Maybe she would be allowed to study horticulture while she was in prison.

'Excellent,' Chas boomed. 'So, you're having a year to travel around while you consider?'

'Mm, I am,' Clare said.

'Aidan wants to do that,' Jules said.

'Here we go,' Billy sighed. 'The sun shines out of Aidan's—'

'Preferable to what comes out of yours,' Jules retorted.

'Children, children . . .' Kate said.

200

Clare sank back against the warm leather, listening to the others wrangling, glad she was no longer the focus of attention. Her story seemed to have become established now.

Chas dropped them off on the esplanade. 'I'll pick you up about nine o'clock, outside The Spyglass.'

'Too early,' Billy said.

'Not for me it won't be,' Chas said, as he pulled away. 'And don't have too much to drink. Be ambassadors for your generation.'

The four of them stood where Chas had dropped them. The tide was in, the sky dull and heavy, as if were ready to let loose a downpour. But it was strangely still. Clare remembered this atmosphere back home, as if something unusual was about to happen – like a snowfall. There were a few people striding along, heaped with hats and scarves and thick coats. A crazy black dog was running in and out of the foaming waves fetching a stick for its owner.

'What shall we do?' Billy said, huddling against Jules. 'Is the amusement arcade open?'

'Let's call for Aidan.' Jules was looking along the esplanade towards Rachel's Café.

'Why doesn't that surprise me?' Billy pulled away from her.

'You don't own me,' Jules snapped.

'Now, kids,' Kate warned. 'What would you like to do, Clare?'

'I don't mind.' But she did mind, she wanted to see Rose. She just didn't have the courage to say so.

'Well let's call for Aidan, then.' Kate pulled her hood up and shoved her hands in her pockets. 'It's too bitter to stand here. His mum might let us into the café for a drink.'

Clare walked beside Kate, trying to voice her question. She took a deep breath. 'Do you know where Rose lives?' she asked.

'Patrick's Rose?' She stopped and looked up at the houses that were banked behind the shops and cafés on the seafront. 'The house is called *Cormorants.*' She pointed. 'It's that one with all the balconies. Her parents run a natural health centre there, downstairs. I expect you saw them at the meal last night. Ash is tall and bony, and Jill has amazing dark auburn streaky hair. She's quite old, so I expect it's dyed. They've got two younger children.'

'So who was it that was taken ill last night?'

'Jill's mother, Stephanie. She's a doctor, works in Niger. She's great. Before she went back there last year, with Rose, she used to come and help us at Wraith Cove.' Kate frowned. 'I do hope she's all right. Perhaps Aidan will know.'

The café was closed. They trooped round the back and rang the bell to the flat above. Aidan opened the door.

'Hi, yer.' He ruffled his hair, looking pleased to see them.

'Thought you might be missing us,' Kate grinned.

'Great! Come up, I'll make a drink.'

Aidan had the Sunday papers spread over the table. He put the kettle on and bustled about making tea and coffee and looking for biscuits. Billy and Jules took over the papers. Kate reached for the arts supplement.

'What did you think of last night?' Aidan asked Clare. He seemed nervous. 'Busy wasn't it? Bit of drama thrown in. You coped well – with all that washing up. Are your hands sore?'

'Lots of it goes in a machine. And I wore rubber gloves,' Clare said.

'Have you heard how Stephanie is?' Kate asked.

'She's in St Mary's, intensive care. They're thinking of transferring her to Southampton.'

'What's wrong with her?' Clare asked.

Aidan shrugged. 'She was ill before she left Africa, and got suddenly worse.'

'Have you seen Patrick, or Rose?' Kate said.

'Patrick hasn't been home. He's at the hospital, looking after Rose. He phoned earlier to say he didn't know when he'd be back.'

Clare felt her hopes sink. It might be ages until Rose came home, especially if she went over to the mainland. 'Where is St Mary's?' she asked.

'Newport.'

Clare wondered if she could get a bus on a Sunday. She might be able to comfort Rose while she watched over her grandmother. She imagined Rose smiling up at her – how surprised she'd be. Would

Patrick have told her yet that Clare was here, at Wraith Cove? And would Rose have told him that Clare was pregnant when they met on the ferry? She didn't think Rose would have. She remembered how kind Rose had been. Patrick had been sullen; he didn't speak to Clare hardly at all. And he looked annoyed when Rose got out her violin and joined in with the funny band who played such wonderful music. Rose was terrific. Everybody clapped and clapped as if she were famous.

Aidan handed her a mug of tea. 'Do you want to go for a walk?' he said. 'We could go up to Cormorants, if you like, and see if they're back.'

'Freezing out there,' Billy grumbled.

'You can stay here. Mum won't mind as long as you're quiet. She's having a sleep.'

Jules looked sulky. 'Okay, okay. We know when we're not wanted.'

Clare and Aidan drank their tea and went outside. They walked up a steep side road to Cormorants. Clare wondered if they owned the whole house, it looked so grand with its long balconies, big enough for dozens of people to live in, like a hotel. Aidan knocked on the white front door which had stained glass windows with big sea birds on them. A tall man answered. Clare remembered Ash, Rose's father.

'No further news, Aidan,' he said, stooping towards them, his long face looking tired and serious. 'Patrick said he'd phone you if there was, didn't he?'

Aidan nodded and they turned away. As they walked back down the road, a shiny black car was driving slowly up.

'It's them,' Aidan said. 'That's Jill's BMW.' He waved and the car stopped. Patrick got out.

'Hi,' he said, yawning and stretching. 'I'm knackered.' He put a hand on Aidan's shoulder. 'Are you going home? I'll come with you. Must have a shower and get some sleep.'

'How's Stephanie?' Aidan asked.

'Okay. No change, really. Stable.'

Clare was straining to look at the two women sitting in the front of the car. They were leaning towards each other, talking.

'Is . . . is Rose in there?' Clare asked Patrick.

'She's exhausted. I'd catch her later, if I was you. She's had no sleep since they flew in to Heathrow yesterday.'

But Clare couldn't help herself. She tapped on the car window. A pale face turned towards her and the window slid silently down. Was it Rose? She looked so different, old and white. Her hair was pulled tightly back, the bright streaks and all the little plaits and rainbow beads had gone. She stared at Clare, frowning.

'Yes?'

'Rose? It's me, Clare.'

'Sorry? Who?'

'Clare. From the ferry—'

'Ferry? The Isle of Wight ferry?'

'The ferry from Ireland . . . last summer . . . you asked me to come here?'

'Did I?' Rose yawned, screwing up her face. 'Look, I'm completely zonked. I'll catch up with you all later.' She closed the window and the car drew away, turning into the drive at Cormorants. Clare watched it go, feeling numb. The first snowflakes were starting to fall, swirling like feathers around her face. Patrick was already striding away down the hill. Aidan started to go after him, but came back for Clare.

'Hey! It's snowing. How cool is that?' He tilted his face to the sky, laughing. 'It hardly ever snows here.' He looked at Clare, his smile fading. 'Are you okay?'

'I thought she would remember me.' Clare's eyes were brimming with tears. How could Rose have forgotten her?

'She's worn out, that's all,' Aidan said. 'Let's go for a walk. I'll buy you a drink in *The Spyglass*, we can sit and watch the snow.'

He reached out and caught hold of her cold hand. His touch seemed to trigger a response in her which felt almost violent. She wrenched her hand away, struggling to control herself, while he gazed at her, looking hurt and puzzled.

'Please,' she whispered. 'Please, don't touch me.'

* * *

Fran wandered through the farmhouse, dwelling on its structure in a way she hadn't done for years. This evening, in the twilight, made luminous by the layer of snow, everything seemed to be whispering memories. She was surrounded by the worn and mellowed map of her ancestors. The colours of stone and brick, iron and copper, wood and wool, were muted, the surfaces smooth. But, faded and threadbare, they contained a dense richness, as if their essence had been concentrated and honed.

She didn't consider herself to be sentimental. She was a solid woman who made sense of life from the strong nameless emotions that arose in her in response to the physical events of the natural world. The feelings were ecstatic, sometimes terrifying, and she received them as the direct communication of life itself. She had no use for explanations by the scholarly. She accepted her passion for ballet as part of this rich spectrum – its thistledown quality as essential to her as tossing a forkful of steaming manure.

She climbed the sloping treads of the wide oak stairs, imagining Phillip whizzing down the banister in his grey flannel school pants. The rail never needed polishing. She went into her bedroom. She hadn't slept in it for a week now, not since she'd found Sam. She had thought about transferring her posters – the delicate Degas prints, the big black and white photos of Anna Pavlova and Margot Fonteyn, and the coloured ones of Darcy Bussell and Sylvie Guillem. She'd even pinned one up of the Ballet Boyz, but wasn't too sure about them – they weren't dainty or pretty, but wonderful dancers, nevertheless. And she liked to keep up to date with the ballet world. But you couldn't beat the old favourites. She would never tire of *Giselle* and *Les Sylphides*. She wondered if Sam would share her enthusiasm. She'd heard that more boys were interested in ballet these days, ever since that film whose name escaped her – *Billy something*. And there was even an all male performance of *Swan Lake*. Now, that would be something to see.

She sometimes wondered what life would have been like if she'd been less resistant to Ted's advances, and he'd married her instead of Janet. But she'd been too independent for that. She felt the life she'd led had suited her, even though she'd never married and had children. Anyway, now she wasn't childless – she had Sam. And with him came feelings that she'd never had to cope with before. Looking around the old house was making her feel confused and apprehensive. She couldn't bear the thought of going away. But she didn't have a choice. Her love for Sam was greater than her fear.

One thing was a relief, though. Ted had been mollified, last night, when she'd told him Young Phil's wife was ill. He seemed more understanding now of Fran's willingness to look after Sam. She felt she'd gained a bit of time, without his pestering. Another couple of days, to get used to the idea, and then she would go. She heard a noise outside. It was Ted knocking the snow off his boots in the porch.

'Fran,' he called as he came in. 'Where are you?'

Fran hurried along the landing, she didn't want him to wake Sam. Ted grinned up at her as she came down the stairs. 'I've got this idea, see. I'll come with you to Oxford. You'll need another pair of hands when the nipper wants feeding. You can't drive with a crying baby—'

'Oh, no, Ted. I—'

'Don't fuss. I won't get in your way. Once you're safely there, I can come back on the train.'

Fran sighed. She knew Ted would hate to do all that travelling. And where could she say she was going, exactly?

'I'll get someone to look after our animals,' he said. 'It'll only be a couple of days, afore I'm back.' His ruddy face was so open and honest – a good human being, prepared to put aside his own fears out of concern for her. She stopped on the stairs, gazing down at him.

'Don't be more of a pudden-head than you can help,' he said, unwinding his scarf. 'I'll brew up, while you think on it.'

CHAPTER
Nineteen

Rachel stepped out of the shower and towelled herself vigorously.

'Monday, new week, fresh start,' she told herself. 'I've done with misery.'

When she'd returned from taking Sandro to Ryde early yesterday morning, she fell into bed expecting to sleep for hours. But she hadn't. Her eyes refused to close, her eyelids were forced apart by the torrent of tears that needed to be shed. She didn't quite understand the depth of her misery and where it had all come from. But it insisted on coming out, so she let it. Her mind was awash with images that she'd seen on television. Bereft people tore with bare hands at mountains of rubble that once was their home, searching for loved ones. Faces rose up, old and young, contorted with grief. She saw makeshift mortuaries with rows of shrouded bodies; the living, with expressions of dread, peeping under each sheet, wanting to know, yet not to know. She imagined what it would be like to uncover the bloated vacant faces of Aidan and Patrick. Seas of strained faces scanned pinned-up lists of the missing. Shocked parents queued at desks . . . *have you seen my child . . . two years old . . . curly hair . . .* The visions were never-ending. People plummeted from burning skyscrapers; oceans seethed; ferries rolled over; bodies flew through the air, disintegrating; powerless women were abducted and raped. On and on it streamed. Women wailed, men fought, and still Rachel wept. 'What a world,' she kept repeating, 'what a sodding awful world.'

Gradually, the crying lessened, but her body was still racked by the occasional deep sob. It was then she remembered something Nick had said. It was months ago, before Sophie arrived. He used to come and sit in her café – a troubled soul – they'd talked for ages on quiet days. *I believe there's a universal body of pain, Rachel. It's been built up over millennia and we humans carry it in our shared unconscious.* He ran his hands over his shaven head and sighed deeply. *Our individual pain can precipitate torrents – if we can't contain it.* His sadness was palpable. *We get quite good at repression. Who would want to open the door to all that?*

Rachel's body heaved with a sob. Is this what had happened to her? Had her grief over Sandro set off this huge reaction? Had she inadvertently tapped into humanity's suffering? She thought she had come to terms with Sandro. She had no idea all this sorrow was going to overwhelm her again. She pictured his face as he sat in the car, asking for her forgiveness. In that moment he'd seemed so utterly open and vulnerable. And she hadn't been able to meet that need – after all, she had her own stuff to deal with. Why should she always be the one to give? *He* hadn't even got it in him to help a young girl in serious trouble.

That had been the trigger for all this. Love was so blind, so trusting – she saw eyes beseeching, hands outstretched. She could feel it – her own eyes, her own hands – that desolate heart-rending moment when someone turns away. Didn't we all recognise that instant somewhere in our lives? And what was it that we each searched for? A response of unconditional love from another member of the human race – something that went beyond the crap that appeared on the surface. Isn't that what the search was all about – that understanding that we're all in this together – we all screw up out of fear? *There but for the grace . . .*

She didn't know why this was happening now – she'd experienced other, greater grief in her life. Maybe it was her age, the beginning of a change of life. Now she heard Sophie's voice: *Little hurts pile up and break our hearts, Rachel. One too many drops of water and, whoosh, the dam bursts.*

Well, it certainly had for her. She sighed deeply, the sobs were lessening. She could view it more dispassionately now. And then came a feeling of clarity which seemed to surround the experience. It felt calm and peaceful, as if it recognised the suffering, but possessed a far greater wisdom and compassion than she could understand. Was this the experience Nick and Sophie talked about? She felt herself relaxing, drifting. She could sleep for hours.

And she had. She'd stayed in bed all day. She heard Aidan and Patrick and their mates coming and going. Patrick had knocked once to ask if she was all right and she said she wanted to be left alone to sleep.

Today she felt better. The weeping and sleeping had done her good. At last she knew the full story of what had happened to Sandro. He'd gone and that was the end of it. The positive thing was, she didn't regret anything, she no longer felt like a loser. In fact she realised she had gained something – a shift in her understanding of life that would, hopefully, remain with her forever.

She sat at the dressing table mirror and dried her hair, flicking up jaunty ends behind her ears.

Saturday evening's meal had been successful in spite of the dramas. Now she would concentrate on the run up to Valentine's weekend and the official opening. She'd invited the mayor and the press, and members of the council and tourist board. It was going to be great, she was confident of that. There were a few minor wrinkles to smooth out, some of Kyp's techniques to be mastered, fresh menus to be printed, and the signboard to be repainted. She studied her face in the mirror – not too bad considering she'd wept for the world.

Aidan slouched into her bedroom wearing his school uniform. He slumped down on her bed looking mournful.

'What's up, sunshine?' Rachel asked.

'School,' Aidan groaned.

'Not much longer, sweet. Soon be over and done with.'

Aidan continued to sit there, unmoving.

'You'll be late for the bus.' She turned to look at him. It wasn't like Aidan to be moody. 'Is there something else troubling you?'

'Mum?'

'I'm listening.'

'You know, Clare?'

'Clare – washing up Clare?'

'I, er, really like her.'

Ah, thought Rachel, so that's the problem. My little boy is in love. But he'd already been in love so many times . . . was this something different?

'And?' she prompted.

'She just seems so odd.'

'Odd? In what way?'

'She's like, very quiet and shy, and it's taken ages for me to get her to talk—'

'I thought she'd only been here about a week. Anyway, isn't she a bit older than you? I know she doesn't look it, but . . . ' Rachel didn't have the heart to say that girls of that age preferred more mature boys.

'Well, yes, but . . . anyway, we were getting on really well yesterday, and then she saw Rose and she, like, got really upset? I tried to hold her hand . . . you know, just to comfort her, and she told me not to touch her.'

'Perhaps she thought you were being a bit forward.'

'But she was trembling, Mum. Like, really weird.'

'Oh. So do you think it was you that upset her, or Rose?'

'Not sure. She said she really wanted to see Rose. I think she met her on the ferry. Rose didn't seem to remember *her* though.'

'I expect Rose was exhausted.'

'She was really out of it.'

'Well then, maybe it wasn't you.'

'Maybe. But the look in her eyes, Mum. I thought she was going to hit me.'

'Goodness. Well, perhaps you should just leave her alone for a while.'

'She seems so lonely.'

'She might feel happier in a group – she could be confused about her sexuality.'

'You mean, *lesbian*?' Aidan looked a bit startled, as if he hadn't considered such a possibility.

Rachel shrugged. 'It could explain her distress over Rose. I was going to ask the kids over for an evening, to talk about Valentine's weekend. I'll need them again, and I want to give them a few instructions. Clare might find that less threatening.' She smiled. 'I'll feed the lot of you, and you can play your music. If you would like me to, I'll try and have a chat with Clare – don't worry, I'll be discreet.'

Aidan jumped up. 'Thanks, Mum. Must fly.' He blew her a kiss as he rushed out.

Rachel got up, patted her body and smiled at her reflection.

'Right, world. Things to do, places to go, busy, busy.'

*　　　*　　　*

Clare was painting another wall in the stable block. Tears kept blurring her vision and she wiped them away with the back of her hand. She felt bereft. The small warm nub of comfort that she'd held inside for so long, had gone. That little flame had kept her going through all the long months of despair. Rose had been something to live for; a friend waiting at the end of a bleak never-ending road. It had been bad enough arriving here and not finding her. But to actually see her, and realise Rose didn't remember her, had been devastating. Aidan had tried to comfort her, explain it away. But she knew all he wanted was to get his hands on her, touch her. She wasn't going to fall for that again.

The worms inside her belly seemed to have grown. Perhaps Father Ryan was right and they were vipers after all. Suddenly she couldn't stand the squirming anymore – couldn't stand anything. She dropped her brush into the paint tin and rushed outside.

'Where are you going in such a hurry?' Kate called out. 'It's nearly lunch time.'

Clare ran and ran. She ran through the grounds of the hotel, across the slushy field where the snow was melting, and past the hedge of Wraith Cottage. She stopped abruptly, her heart pounding, her throat burning; she was at the edge of the cliff. The sea was calm, reflecting the grey of the sky. There were no boats passing, no seabirds calling. She felt homesick for Bantry Bay, the mussel beds, the cry of the gulls, and the wading herons. She would never see them again; never see the little brick house where she was born, and the school next to the church, and the familiar kids. How strange, they would all grow up and lead lives that she'd know nothing about. She'd never again smell the incense burning in the church, or the wax polish on the wooden pews. She pictured the children sitting on the little chairs in Sunday school learning their rosaries with the Sisters. She could hear the choir singing, practising their scales, Father Ryan reprimanding them. How young they all seemed. Tears ran down her cold cheeks. And what about Mam? Clare knew her mam didn't want her to go back – hadn't she said the shame had almost

211

killed her? The only way Clare could have made amends would have been to dedicate her life to becoming a nun – a Poor Clare. Then her mam might be proud to say she had a daughter once more. But Clare knew convent life wasn't for her. She'd rather die than end up living like Mother.

Clare closed her eyes and listened to the gentle rippling of the waves which sounded like rain falling. What if she simply fell forward off this cliff? She would go straight to hell; that was certain. She'd be dying in mortal sin, without confession, without the sacraments. Would she see the baby? Would he accuse of her of casting him into Limbo? Would death be preferable to *this* life that she was leading, which seemed like a living hell?

She took a step forward thinking of the muffled quietness that waited just beneath the surface of the sea. The grass beneath her feet felt spongy and slippery. She opened her eyes and looked down at the beach below. The tide was out; the rocks glistened with green and purple seaweed. Everything stood out with great clarity. She imagined her head smashing on the rocks, the blood spilling into a pool. Who would find her? Or would she simply be washed away, without trace, on the next tide?

She took another step. Something dislodged beneath the grass at her feet; she heard the rattle of falling stones. She was losing her balance; there was nothing to hold on to.

She felt a hand grab her upper arm from behind and hold it firmly. Clare knew she could still jump; one hand couldn't prevent her. She leaned forward and the hand increased its grip and tugged her back. Then she felt both arms being grasped.

'Let me go,' she growled. But the hands were insistent. She looked around. It was the old man that had been horrid to her the other day when she was sitting in the porch at Wraith Cottage. His face was brown and wrinkled, his eyes sunk deep into his head. Clare felt afraid of him.

'Easy now, lass,' he said. 'The overhang is very soft here. Come away.' His voice was quiet and slow. He continued to hold her arms, drawing her back from the edge. 'I've known more than one person come a cropper on this cliff.'

212

Clare was forced to move back several feet. And then she felt her arms slowly being released. 'There now,' he said. He gestured towards Wraith Cottage. 'Come inside and have a cup of tea.'

Was he being kind to her, or just trying to get her into the cottage? How could she know if he was telling the truth? She shook her head. 'I'm all right,' she mumbled. 'I didn't realise . . . it was dangerous.' She started to walk away on shaking legs. She could feel the old man watching her.

When she knew she was out of his sight, she sat down, leaning against the stone wall of the hotel grounds. Would she have done it? Would she have jumped if he hadn't stopped her? She closed her eyes, imagining herself falling through the air, tumbling, twisting, grabbing at nothing. Would it seem like a long way, or would it be over in a flash? If that old man hadn't held her back, it could have been over by now. She could always return and try again, further along, away from here, at night maybe. Would it be easier in the dark?

She had a sudden vision of Mother sitting in front of the smoky fire in the abbey, her knitting needles clacking as she told Clare graphic stories of hell. Stories the nuns told her, she said, when she was young. *You're a lucky girl, Clare.* Mother showed her decaying teeth as she smiled. *You could have been sent to a strict home and the baby taken for adoption.* She paused to sip at the communion wine, which she said helped the pain of her molars. Clare thought adoption was supposed to happen, but she'd given up arguing with Mother. *This child was sent here by God and will stay here*, Mother sighed, a look of contentment spreading over her face. *Blessed Clare . . . we will name St Francis as the father . . . and then it will be like a virgin birth. We'll be a family of holy women.* Mother was kinder in the evenings, after her medicine. She was different in the mornings, irritable and spiteful, tormenting Clare with her stories. *You can clear off as soon as the holy child is born!* she would cry. *You! You with your love of men.* And then she'd stomp into another room and begin sawing up the furniture. Clare hadn't argued. All she'd wanted was for the birth to be over, so that indeed she could go.

Clare felt the stone wall digging into her back. She should have left the baby behind. She could see that now. Mother would have found a way to feed him, and he would still be alive. But Clare had killed him, and God wouldn't listen to her prayers for his soul – not her, a mortal sinner.

Clare put her hands on the cold wet grass, digging her fingers deep into the earth. She could feel little stones. An idea occurred to her. What if she could find a trace of him, a bone perhaps, in the stable where she'd left him? She remembered seeing feathers strewn around the yard at home, when the fox had taken a chicken. Supposing a fox had buried the baby under the straw and come back for him later? Wouldn't there be traces of his clothes? If she could find just a scrap, to show he'd existed, then maybe she could take it to a priest – or even bury it herself. She could find a graveyard and look for the place where children were buried. Surely that would help him a little.

She got up and hurried across the fields, keeping close to the walls. She skirted the lighthouse buildings and found the path leading down to the farm. She stood for a long time listening and waiting for any sign of life. But all she saw were white doves pecking among the cobbles and a few chickens scratching outside a barn. She crept across the yard to the stable. It seemed different in the daylight; in her memory it remained a gloomy, half-seen place. She pushed open the door, her heart thumping. The creepy sheep was no longer in its pen in the corner. But the animal smell brought back the horror of that night, the nausea and exhaustion, the pain in her breasts, her desperation and disappointment, and her frantic dash back, only to find the baby's body under the straw.

She bent down and with shaking hands started to rake the straw aside. It seemed fresh, undisturbed on the stone floor. She scrabbled at it, flinging it aside in heaps. There was nothing there – not a small bone, not a strand of pink wool. She stood up, panting. She looked at the bales where she'd left the baby. There seemed fewer than she remembered. She began toppling them from the stack. They were heavy, her arms ached, but the fallen bales revealed nothing. She searched the far corners, kicking the straw in all directions. Her mouth felt full of dust, her eyes prickled. She even poured the water out of the metal bucket. But she could find no trace of him.

Tears poured down her face, stinging her skin. There was nothing she could do for the baby. Unless, unless she could find a priest. A picture of Father Ryan rose in her mind. She hardly dared let herself think about him anymore. But his image grew stronger as if she couldn't stop it. It was almost as if he were there, wanting to comfort her. She wanted to be comforted. He opened his arms. *Suffer the little children to come unto me* . . . Sweat broke out on her body; she could feel the touch of his hands as he started to loosen her hair. Her stomach heaved as she fell on her knees and vomited into the bucket.

*   *   *

Father Ryan had driven to Swansea. He'd been into a large department store and bought himself some grey slacks, a white open necked shirt and a navy blue jacket. Looking in the full length mirrors, he couldn't believe it was him. He looked sturdier, as if there was more of him. What day was it? Monday. He'd been away from home less than a week, and look at him. He wondered if all the experiences he'd been having had made him more substantial. And he'd eaten so much food these last few days. Without his headache he had more appetite. Wasn't it turning out to be a grand trip? He just needed to solve the problem of Clare.

Walking along the high street in his new clothes, he was feeling self-conscious. But, he realised, the public weren't giving him sidelong glances anymore. He straightened his shoulders and raised his head to look around as he walked. Maybe he didn't have to dream about Newfoundland and a solitary life. Perhaps he could be anonymous in the middle of a big city.

He would have to be careful. No longer would people tolerate him smiling at their children, patting their heads. He wondered how he would fit into civilian life. How would he find a way to work with children? He could teach music. Parents would soon get to know him and trust him, just like they did now. After all, he was simply a kind man who knew he could comfort small lonely girls – just like he had with Jeannie. That's all he wanted. Clare had been something different, an aberration. He shouldn't have been so tolerant with her, indulging her teenage crush. He should have been firm and unyielding, dismissing her from the choir if necessary. And God knows he had tried. Not that God cared.

He caught a glimpse of himself in a shop window and smiled. Quite a handsome man, in the prime of life. He knew he was moving towards a decision. He'd first resolve the issue of Clare, and then he would consider giving up his vocation and start a new life.

*   *   *

Fran stared around the stable in horror. Her insides felt as if they were turning to water. Who had done this? She'd only cleaned the place out that morning. She'd put Beauty in the field, and cleared out all the old straw and burnt it. She wanted to go away leaving everything in order. Just because she had Sam, there was no reason to neglect her animals. Cinders was sniffing at the bucket. No animal would vomit in a bucket – it must have been a human. Anyway, she knew she'd definitely fastened the door to stop it banging. Someone must have come in here while she was in Ventnor this afternoon, shopping for her journey, and avoiding Ted.

Why would someone do this? Was it some drunkard who had kipped down for a few hours? Or was it a sick human being? She allowed her deepest fear to rise to the surface. Could it have been the baby's mother who had returned to look for him? But why would she throw everything around? Had she been frantic? But surely she wouldn't expect him to still be lying where she'd left him, more than a week ago? It didn't make sense. Was she ill, or had she vomited with anxiety? Had she knocked on the door of the farmhouse? Why hadn't she left a note? And, even more worrying – where was she now?

Fran ran out of the stable with Cinders at her heels. She rushed into the kitchen and locked the door. It was getting dark. Was Sam's mother out there, demented, watching, waiting? Had she gone to fetch the police? It was hot in the kitchen. She unstrapped Sam from his car seat and began to take off his coat and hat. He opened his eyes, blinked at the light and yawned. She loved it when he did that. It seemed such an unexpectedly grown up thing to do.

'Are you hungry, my sweet?' she whispered, as if someone might hear. She laid him on the armchair while she took off her coat and heated his bottle. Every nerve in her body was alert, straining to hear the slightest sound. She kept looking round as if someone might

216

be creeping up behind her.

By the time she sat down to feed Sam she was in tears. 'This can't go on, wee lamb,' she kept saying. 'What shall we do?'

Sam let go of the teat and stared at her. He gave a little belch and then the corners of his mouth turned up, as if he were smiling.

'Oh, Sam,' she whispered.

He pulled a few faces, as if trying to repeat his new skill. And then, as if the right circuit connected, he smiled again.

'Oh, darling, you're really smiling at me, aren't you?' she felt the tears running freely down her cheeks. 'I'll never give you up,' she sobbed. 'We'll go away this evening. That's what we'll do.' Cinders was looking up at her, mournfully – as if she suspected something. Maybe she could take her – but it would be difficult getting accommodation with a dog as well as a baby.

She finished feeding Sam and changed his nappy and dressed him for the journey. There seemed so much to do and all the time she was tense, listening. As she packed suitcases and all Sam's equipment into the Land Rover she was waiting for someone to loom up at her out of the darkness. She put Sam in the car and came back into the kitchen for a last look round.

She picked up Sugar Plum and buried her wet face in the cat's fur. 'I'll miss you, Sugar,' she wept, putting her on the armchair. She knelt down and hugged Cinders. 'I'm so sorry, but I don't know what else to do. Ted will look after you.' Then she went out and locked the door behind her. She left the key under the boot-scraper. It was eight o'clock now. She planned to phone Ted when she was off the island to explain she'd been called away urgently by Young Phil. Ted would have to come over this evening to let Cinders out.

Maybe she would stay in Lymington for the night while she calmed down and cared for Sam. She could hear Cinders whining inside the kitchen as she started the engine. 'I'm so sorry, Cinders,' she wailed again, as she pulled away.

At the end of the drive she decided she would shut the gates to Rocken Edge Farm, to deter anyone from entering. It was difficult; they hadn't been closed for such a long time, they were sunk into the ground. A sleety rain was falling, her hands were slippery. She heaved and heaved, weeping with fatigue and frustration.

'What are you doing?'

Oh, no! It was Ted! Where had he come from? He never came from this direction. She ignored him and carried on tugging at the gates. Ted caught hold of her arm.

'Fran!'

She stopped, completely at a loss.

'What are you doing?' he asked again.

'I, I'm going.'

'Where?'

'Oxford.'

'Tonight?'

Fran nodded. 'Things have got worse.'

Ted prized her hands off the gate. 'There is absolutely no way you are going anywhere tonight. Look at the state of you!'

'I have to.'

'I won't let you. You're not fit to drive, let alone look after the nipper.' Ted climbed into the driver's seat and reversed the Land Rover back down the drive.

Fran stood watching. Ted hadn't driven anything that wasn't a tractor for years. He walked back to her, took hold of her hand, and pulled her until she started to walk with him. He found the key, opened the kitchen door, pushed her inside and went back to fetch Sam. Cinders was barking deliriously, as if Fran had been away for years.

Ted pulled out a chair. 'Sit down, woman,' he ordered. He competently took Sam's hat and coat off, placed him in her arms and sat opposite her.

'This doesn't add up,' he said. 'I think it's time you told me what's really going on.'

'L . . . lock the door first,' she stammered.

CHAPTER
Twenty

Clare had wandered back to the caravan after she searched the barn on Monday afternoon. She'd got into bed with her clothes on and pulled the blanket over her head. Kate had come looking for her. *What's the matter now?* she said. Clare kept the covers over her head. *Tummy upset*, she mumbled. Kate stood there for a while. *Can I get you anything?* She sounded irritated. Clare wanted her to go. *No, thanks. Just need to sleep.*

And she'd stayed there, right until the next morning, trying to control the squirming ball of worms inside her, which seemed to have resumed full activity. Every time she started to drift into sleep, bodies fell from cliffs and tumbled out of straw. Sometimes it was her body, and she would wake with a jolt before she hit the ground. Sometimes it was the tiny body of a baby.

As dawn broke on Tuesday, she had another idea. She climbed quietly out of her bunk, emptied her possessions out of her backpack and laid them on the floor. She opened the plastic bag containing the baby's things and her bible. She took her rosary from her coat pocket and added it to the pile. Then she unfastened her gold crucifix from around her neck. She looked at it for a while – undecided – she'd worn it since she was little. But then she tucked it inside the clothes and put everything back in the plastic bag. She pulled on her boots and puffa jacket and let herself out of the caravan. Everything was calm and silent; the other caravans in darkness.

She switched on her torch, walked up to the main road, and headed towards Ventnor. She'd noticed a church along this road when she came this way before. It wasn't a Catholic church, but there was a big cross near the entrance – like the Celtic ones at home. *Lest We Forget,* was inscribed on it. She wasn't quite sure what that meant, but it sounded right.

It was further than she thought. The sky lightened, she turned off her torch to save the batteries. A few cars passed by, still with their lights on. She pulled her hat down and kept close to the stone wall until she reached the church. The big wooden gate was open. She walked along the wet grass path, reading the inscriptions on the gravestones. Most of them were ancient, the lettering worn away. There was a bunch of soggy red and yellow chrysanthemums on one grave and some plastic roses in an urn on another. Little patches of snow glimmered here and there. She couldn't see a special place for children, so she chose a spot under a yew tree where a few snowdrops shone in the mossy grass. She sat down for a while to rest, her back against the trunk. She looked up into its dull green branches. A breeze stirred them and cold drops of water landed on her face. High above the church she saw a tower of bells – she wondered if they would ring out a warning, if they noticed her. Two fat birds were perched on top of the tower. They seemed to be leaning on each other with their beaks crossed. Occasionally they shifted, re-crossed their beaks and settled back together. Were they doing it for warmth, or did they love each other?

She hadn't got anything to dig with; why didn't she think to bring a knife or something from the caravan? She hunted around. All she could find was a broken jam jar and some twigs. It took ages to make a hole; the ground was clogged with roots and it was hard to pull them out with her cold fingers. Eventually she was satisfied with the grave. She laid the strange pink clothes in one by one. At least Mother had made them specially. She'd cared about the baby in her mad way. Clare hadn't cared at all. She placed her prayer book, bible, rosary and crucifix on top of the clothes. She knelt down and prayed for her baby who'd died carrying the burden of original sin. She prayed that an angel might comfort him as he lay in Limbo. And then she whispered the prayer of St Clare that her mam loved so much. *May Almighty God bless you. May He look upon you with the eyes of His mercy and give you peace. Here below may He pour forth His graces on you abundantly, and in heaven may He bless you among His saints.*

A strong feeling rose up in her as if something dammed up

inside, that had trickled out from time to time, had found a way through. She wept and wept, her tears falling on the earth and grass as she tried to pack the sticky mud back into the hole. It clung to her hands and streaked her face as she wiped her nose and eyes. At last everything was covered up. She wanted to stamp the grass down, but it didn't seem right to tread on the little grave. She patted and smoothed it, and picked two snowdrops to put on top.

She wiped her hands on the grass, blood was oozing from one of them, but she couldn't feel anything. She looked up at the bell tower, but the birds had gone.

$$* \qquad * \qquad *$$

'I still can't believe you made up all those lies,' Ted said, furiously buttering a heap of toast. 'And I thought I knew you, a good honest woman.'

'I know, Ted, I know. I'm sorry. You can go if you want to. I wouldn't blame you.' Fran desperately hoped he wouldn't go. What would he do?

'No point now, is there? I was sorely tempted last night, I can tell you. I wanted to walk straight out that door and never set eyes on you again.' He bit into a piece of toast and pushed the plate towards Fran. 'Still can't believe you could tell such lies.'

Fran nibbled at her toast. She was still in her pyjamas. Last night Ted had sat her down, forced the story out of her – bit by painful bit – and then put her to bed. He'd taken off his trousers and shirt and climbed in beside her. He held Sam and rocked him to sleep and then tucked him in his moses basket. Fran stayed awake, alert for noises outside, in between Ted's snores. Sam had woken in the early hours for a feed and Ted had gone downstairs to heat a bottle. *I don't want you driving off into the night,* he'd said, handing her the baby. *I dunno,* he scratched his head, looking at her in the big bed. *Didn't think I'd have to go to these lengths to sleep with you.* The small attempt at humour had somehow lightened the terrible weight of her dilemma, and she slept until dawn, and Sam's demand for his next feed.

Ted was staring at her across the kitchen table as if he'd never truly seen her before. His hands had been flying about as he spoke, a sure sign of his agitation.

221

'So why do you suppose this woman knocked on your door and handed you her baby to look after?' he asked again. 'I can't get my head around that.'

'I don't know. Maybe because this seemed such a remote place.'

'But just think about the odds against someone answering the door and saying, *Oh, a baby. Ta very much.* Ted waved his toast in the air. 'Are you positive you didn't recognise her? She must have known you, surely.'

Fran shrugged. She knew how implausible her story was. But it was the best she could do.

'Tell me again, what she looked like.'

Oh, God. Had he asked her that before? She was so tired she was beginning to lose track. 'Foreign-looking.'

'An illegal immigrant? Shouldn't be hard to trace. Not many of them around here.' Ted munched, thoughtfully. 'What was she wearing?'

'It was dark.'

'Didn't she come inside?'

Fran shook her head.

'She just shoved the kiddy in your arms and said . . . ?' He waited.

'Please, look after my baby.'

'And you said . . . ?'

'Ted . . . we've been through all this before.'

'But you need to be clear about this, Fran – when you tell the police.'

'The police!'

'Well.' Ted dropped his toast onto the plate. 'Who *are* you going to tell?'

'I, er. I was simply hoping she wouldn't come back, and that would be that. There's been no news of a missing baby, has there?'

'This is the twenty-first century. Things don't happen like that anymore. Children aren't given away without someone knowing.'

'Aren't they? We don't know everything that goes on.'

'So why were you running away like a fugitive?'

'I told you. I thought she'd come back for him.'

'That's even more reason to stay and find out who she is. It's the best possible solution. If she returns and you can unravel all this, you might avoid being in serious trouble.' He got up and looked out of the window. 'And it seems likely, if she was ransacking the place yesterday, she has come back for him.' He turned round to face her. 'And that doesn't add up either. Why would she be searching in the stable?'

'Maybe she wasn't searching, particularly. The house was empty, locked. Perhaps she felt ill and went in there.'

'And threw straw bales about? Do you think she's a nutter?'

'Possibly.'

'Then I am going to stay around. And Cinders can roam about outside. That way we'll get a warning.' He began pacing up and down the kitchen. 'But this can't go on much longer. If she doesn't show up, we'll have to do something. I'm an accomplice now.'

*   *   *

'We were so sorry to mess up your evening on Saturday,' Jill was saying, handing around the coffee. It was her turn to host a Tuesday morning get-together.

'Don't worry.' Rachel sat back in the soft leather armchair which seemed to sigh beneath her. 'It wasn't the only trauma of the night.'

Jill's eyes widened, her mascaraed lashes flaring. 'Wasn't it? You mean something else happened that I missed?'

'I don't know if I can go through the whole thing again,' Rachel groaned. 'I just want to sit here in your lovely room, Jill, and let all my worries drift away.'

'But we want to know, don't we, Evie? Jane?' Jill insisted.

'Essential, for a novelist,' Jane laughed.

'And a nosy friend,' Evie agreed.

'Sophie knows all about it. She'll probably be kinder, and swear less than me. Tell them, Sophie.'

Rachel half listened while Sophie relayed the Sandro saga. For some reason Rachel hadn't told her about the troubled young girl Sandro met in the church and abandoned to her fate. She was still protecting him a little, she realised, and that bit of the story wasn't really relevant.

223

She relaxed and sipped her coffee. This was an exquisite room with its south facing windows reaching to the floor, and the veranda running along the outside. If it was hers, she'd be sitting out there watching the sea and the beach all year round.

She looked at the women's faces as they listened to Sophie talk. Jill's dramatic as ever, with her maroon lipstick and big features. Evie's shining cropped hair emphasising her amazing cheekbones; fingers moving to her lips as if she were dying for one of the little cheroots that she smoked. And Jane, with her dark brown eyes and glossy chestnut bob, constantly altering her expression. They were enthralled. How women loved intrigue.

'Good heavens,' Jane murmured from time to time.

'Wow,' said Evie.

'Fucking hell,' was Jill's favoured response.

They all turned to look at Rachel. 'So how do you feel about him now?' Jane asked.

'I'm just glad it's all over,' Rachel sighed. 'I feel better than I've done for weeks, to be honest.'

'Yes. It must have been awful, not knowing,' Evie agreed.

'What a weak bastard he was,' Jill said. 'I'd like to get my hands on him. I'd have his balls—'

'I'm sure you would, Jill,' Sophie said. 'But let's leave him intact, and just be glad for Rachel.'

'Yes, but without those appendages some other vulnerable females might escape—'

'The Italian women will have to fend for themselves,' Rachel said. She held out her cup for a refill. 'How's Stephanie today?'

'Better than she was. She's been stabilised. Hopefully they will let her come home soon.'

'Do they know what the disease is she picked up?'

Jill pulled a face. 'You might as well know, but keep this to yourselves. She has AIDS.'

A silence fell on the room.

'Oh, no, Jill. How dreadful,' Sophie said at last, reaching out a hand to stroke Jill's arm.

'There was an accident while she was operating. Somebody tripped, or something, I don't know all the details. But Mum – Stephanie, cut her hand quite badly. It was always a risk with the work she did. She has been HIV positive for some time. That was one of the reasons that she came home for a while last year.'

'Isn't that just the universal law of buggeration?' Evie said. 'She spends her life helping others and gets landed with this.'

Rachel couldn't believe it. Stephanie had always looked so full of vitality. 'Will she get through this, Jill?'

'She's strong, but she'll be seventy next year.'

Another hush fell while they all seemed to be coming to terms with this news.

'Well,' Jill said, 'as they say; life's crap and then you die.'

'Do you want me to tell Marguerite?' Jane asked. 'She will gladly come to see Stephanie and do some healing. Or you can ask her yourself – she's working downstairs at the moment.'

'Marguerite probably knows already, she was there on Saturday. I'll talk to Stephanie when she comes home.' Jill smiled wanly. 'Meanwhile, let's eat chocolate biscuits.'

'There's something else I wanted to ask all of you,' Jane said, taking a biscuit. 'Do any of you know anything about the new student at Wraith Cove – Clare?'

'She did some washing up for me on Saturday,' Rachel said, 'and Aidan likes her. Why?'

'I've spoken to her a couple of times. She looks very young, and she's painfully shy. She was ill when she first arrived. Marguerite went to see her. She was concerned and wanted to see her again. But Clare bolted like a startled fawn when I suggested it.'

'And?' Evie prompted.

'Neptune saw her standing right on the edge of the cliff. He pulled her back, and she ran off saying she didn't realise it was dangerous. But he said he could have sworn she was going to go over.'

'Christ!' Jill said. 'On purpose?'

'So he says. But Neptune does have a bit of a thing about people falling off the cliffs.'

'As in, did she fall or was she pushed?' Jill grinned.

'Well, Aidan mentioned he was worried about her,' Rachel said. 'He thinks she seems over-anxious.'

'Where does she come from?' Evie asked.

'Ireland, but she's a bit vague.' Jane turned to Jill. 'Doesn't she know Rose?'

'Rose knows everyone,' Jill said. 'She's around somewhere, I'll ask her.' She went out of the room and yelled up the stairs. 'Are you up, flower?'

Rose ambled, yawning, into the room. Rachel thought how different she looked since her African trip. She'd always been a childish version of her mum. But now, she seemed grown-up. Her hair had lost all its streaks and ornaments. It was brushed straight back off her face and tied in a bunch. Her face was clear of make up and studs. But she still had that relaxed easy-flowing walk – as if she were happy inside her own body. Rose looked around in surprise.

'Oh, hi, everyone. Didn't know Mum was having a hen party.' She flopped down on the floor and sat cross-legged. 'Did you want me?'

'We were talking about Clare – wondered how you got to meet her.'

Rose clapped a hand to her mouth. 'Oh, God. I meant to go over to see her, but I've been so tired, what with Grandma and jet-lag and everything—'

'Oh, Rose,' Sophie cried. 'We know you have, sweetheart. We're not criticising you.'

'I saw her, for a moment, just when we arrived home on Sunday. To tell you the truth, I didn't know who she was. I met her ages ago – last summer – on the way home from that folk tour I went on with Patrick.' She glanced at Rachel and smiled. 'Patrick was a bit fed up with me talking to her. And then I really blew it by offering her a lift to somewhere or other – can't remember where we were going now. Oh, yes, I do. We were going to visit Grandma in the commune. My grandma lives in a commune when she's here, you know.' She smiled round at the women, as if she were proud of this fact.

Jill raised her eyebrows. 'Was she on her own then – this Clare?'

Rose nodded. 'That's why I sort of befriended her. She was throwing up all over the place and looked so forlorn.'

'Seasick?' Jane asked.

'No. Pregnant. I felt so sorry for her. Her Catholic priest had packed her off all alone to England, to have her baby in some strange convent. She was terrified.'

'Bloody hell,' Jill said, 'I bet she was.'

'And although she said she was sixteen, I didn't believe her. She only looked about fourteen or fifteen to me.'

'Sixteen!' Jane said. 'I understood she was eighteen, having a gap year. But maybe I assumed that because she was a friend of yours.'

'Anyway, I told her she didn't have to go through with all that – things were different in England. I gave her the directions to get here and told her, if she needed any help, just to come.'

'You are *so* like your grandmother,' Jill grumbled.

Rose frowned. 'I was going through a difficult time myself.' She shrugged. 'Anyway, she never showed up, and I forgot all about her.'

'Well, she got here eventually,' Jane said. 'I suppose she must have gone to the convent.' She looked around at the others. 'Do you suppose she had the baby adopted, and then came here?'

Rose did a rapid count on her fingers. 'Possibly. Or maybe she did her own thing – had an abortion.'

'But she would have gone back home afterwards, surely.' Evie said.

Rose made a face. 'To a strict Irish Catholic family? I don't think so.'

'Poor girl,' Sophie said. 'No wonder she's in a state.'

'I wonder just how old she is,' Evie said, her face taut with concern.

'Do you think we ought to talk to her? I'm taking what Neptune said more seriously now,' Jane said.

'Oh, God,' Rachel said. 'And Aidan really was concerned about her, too.'

Rose jumped up. 'I'll go and find her. I expect she's at Wraith Cove. If she'll talk to anyone, it will be me. Can I borrow your car, Mum?'

*   *   *

Father Ryan was at the ferry terminal at Pembroke. He was trying to find out if the band that played on the evening boat had a name. He'd asked several people without success.

'I expect they're all different, mate,' a young man said. 'Casual, you know?'

Father Ryan didn't know. He felt affronted. He'd never been called, *mate,* before. He wasn't sure he liked being a member of the common flood of people milling about the terminal. *Mate*, indeed.

He went back to his car and sat looking at his brief case. He'd made a resolution not to drink while he was driving. But he needed a little drop to clear his head. He had to be careful, wearing his casual clothes. The police wouldn't know he was a priest. Just one sip. He sat thinking. The musicians had talked as if they'd been playing on that evening ferry for months. What could he do – sail across to Rosslare, and then come back? That would be silly. He didn't want to spend all that time on a boat, and it would be expensive. He decided he would return when the ship docked tonight, and see who disembarked. With a bit of luck, the band might stagger off, and he could follow them.

Satisfied with his plan, he drove away. Maybe he'd spend another day touring around. He'd heard there was a wonderful cathedral at St David's. A place that had seen fifteen hundred years of pilgrimage. Imagine that! The largest cathedral in the smallest city, on the western most point of mainland Wales. He couldn't wait to tell Jeannie. Perhaps there would be another concert that he could go to. The Elgar performance had been magnificent. He'd bought a boxed set of CDs, *The Collected Works of Sir Edward Elgar.* It wasn't all religious music by any means – but uplifting to the spirit. He'd never spent that kind of money on himself before. Indeed, he'd never owned a CD before. And he intended to shop for one of those little portable player contraptions that some of the children had at school.

He chuckled. If Father Christopher could see him now!

CHAPTER
Twenty-One

Clare walked back from the churchyard, along Undercliff Drive, like an automaton. She was hardly aware of the traffic until a car hooted, as if she shouldn't be on the road. But there was no pavement, nowhere else to walk. Maybe she would step out in front of the next vehicle. She heard one coming up behind her and could feel herself being drawn towards it. The car swerved to avoid her. She walked on, smiling, waiting for the next one. This was a good game. The drivers wouldn't be able to see her easily in her dark jacket. The trees arching overhead made the light dappled and dull. Another one swerved and hooted, then another. She wished the road was busier. The next driver gave a long and angry blast on the horn and further on screeched to a halt. Clare felt as if she were waking from a trance. What had she been doing? She might have caused an accident and had another death on her conscience.

She stopped walking. The car door was flung open. A woman got out and started running towards her. She was wearing a baggy white sweater and blue jeans. Clare was going to be in trouble, again.

'Clare!' the woman shouted. 'Clare!'

It looked like Rose. What would she be doing here, driving a big car? Clare wondered if she was ill again, hallucinating.

'Clare? It is you, isn't it?' The woman slowed down, panting. 'I recognised your hair. It's me, Rose. Are you trying to get yourself killed? Where are you going?'

Clare stood and stared at her. 'I don't know.'

Rose held out her hand. 'This is a dangerous road to be walking along. And I shouldn't be parked here.' She took hold of Clare's hand, her face showing surprise as she saw the mud. 'You're bleeding,' she said, quietly. 'What have you been doing, Clare?'

'Digging.'

'*Digging?* Okay. Well, we'd better get going I think, don't you?' She led Clare, like a small child, to her car, helped her into the passenger seat and pressed some tissues into her bleeding hand. It was warm inside, the black seats soft and leathery, like the ones in Chas's car. Clare started to worry about making things dirty. She leaned forward.

'Relax,' Rose said. 'A bit of good honest mud isn't going to hurt anything.' She started the car. 'I'm going to take you home with me – I think a hot bath might be a nice idea, don't you?'

Clare went through the next couple of hours in a daze. Everything was so unlike anything she'd experienced before, she found it hard to take it all in. Rose's mother briefly said hello, as she went downstairs to the health centre. Clare vaguely heard her telling Rose that she would let everyone know that Clare was safe. Safe from what? Who was everyone? Upstairs, Rose ran hot water in a big white tub which stood in the centre of the room. She dolloped perfume into it and pointed to the array of soap and shampoo.

'Help yourself, take as long as you like. I'll be downstairs in the kitchen, making soup. Yell, if you want anything.'

Clare sunk her aching body into the water, remembering how good it felt the first time she got into the bath at Jane's. The pale green room was warm, the lighting hidden in the walls. She lay, drifting in and out of sleep, before scrubbing herself clean and showering her hair. Rose kept popping her head around the door.

'Are you all right in there?' she asked.

Clare had said hardly a word so far. She just nodded and said, thank you. Rose, she thought. Rose was here. But what did she want her for? There was nothing she could do for Clare now.

She got out of the bath and dried herself with the soft towels that Rose had put on the hot towel rail. She'd never been surrounded with so much warm softness before. She rubbed her hair and wrapped herself up.

Rose came in again. 'I found these,' she said. 'They'll be miles too big, but your clothes are wet. I put your boots by the fire to dry.'

She laughed. 'Hope they don't shrink. Come down when you're ready. Soup's done.'

Clare put on the pants and tee-shirt and jeans. They were indeed too large, but they were clean and smelled of flowers. She padded down the wide, carpeted staircase. She could see Rose in the huge kitchen dishing up soup.

'Come in. Sit down. Let me see your cut.' She examined Clare's hand which had a jagged gash at the base of her thumb. 'Mmm, looks cleaner now. Need to keep an eye on it though.' She fetched a first aid box from the drawer of a big wooden dresser and put a plaster over the cut. 'I learnt quite a lot of first aid from Grandma. There, let's eat.' She placed a steaming blue bowl in front of Clare. The soup smelled delicious, little pieces of vegetables floated on the top. Clare wondered if she would be able to eat it, but Rose was watching her, and she didn't want to appear ungrateful. She took a small sip, and felt it trickle, burning, right down to her stomach.

Rose sat down opposite her and started eating. 'Feeling better?'

Clare nodded. 'Thank you.'

'No problem. I just feel so bad about Sunday – not recognising you – I was distraught about my grandma.'

'It's all right.' Clare licked her dry lips. 'How is she?'

'Poorly, but better than she was.' Rose looked sad. Her face seemed thinner than it was last summer. But she didn't look so tired now. 'Anyway, tell me about you,' Rose said. 'What's happened since I last saw you? I vaguely remember dropping you outside the convent that wasn't there. Did you find your way to the new one?'

Clare nodded. 'It was still being built – I stayed in a bit of the old abbey – some of it was being demolished.'

'Really?' Rose pulled a face. 'Did the nuns look after you?'

Clare looked down at her bowl. 'Sort of.'

'Bit strict, were they?'

Clare nodded.

'Poor you.' Rose ate her soup in silence for a while. Clare tried to look as if she was eating too.

231

Rose glanced up. 'Do you mind me asking – did you have the baby? You don't have to tell me, if you don't want to,' she added hastily. 'I know the whole thing is traumatic. I had an abortion, just after I left you. That's where I was going, with Patrick.'

Clare felt shocked. Rose had been in the same condition, yet here she was, living at home, getting on with her life, accepted. 'Is that why you told me to come here, and said you could help me?'

'I wanted you to know there was a choice.'

'But it's different being Catholic. It's a mortal sin.'

'I know. I do understand that.' She reached across the table and squeezed Clare's hand. 'I've been working in Africa with women who have been through hell. But that's another story. We're all different. We just have to cope with it the best we can, don't we?'

Clare bit her nails for a while. 'I did have the baby – a boy,' she said, quietly.

Rose sighed. 'Did they let you see him?'

Clare nodded.

'I expect he's gone to a good home, don't you?' she said gently.

Clare looked at Rose's concerned face. She couldn't bear the undeserved sympathy she saw there. She covered her face with her hands and cried. She felt Rose beside her, rubbing her back and stroking her hair. She gave Clare a wad of tissues. When Clare had finished sobbing. Rose took her hands.

'Tell me, honestly, Clare. How old are you?'

Clare licked her lips. 'I'm er, fourteen,' she said. 'I was fourteen on the twenty-seventh of December – the day after the baby was born.'

'Jesus!' Rose cried, flinging her arms around Clare.

*   *   *

Fran watched Ted as she sat feeding Sam. He was restless, he'd been roaming around the house all day, looking for things to do. She knew he was hoping Sam's mother would appear to reclaim her baby. He was worried that all this would go badly for Fran.

Ted turned from the kitchen window to face her. 'Did it occur to you that Sam might not have been her baby? Maybe he was abducted.

His real mother could be heartbroken.' He glared at Fran. 'Women do crazy things.'

'It would have been in the news, wouldn't it?'

'Ah, I wondered why you'd started listening to the radio after all these years.' He put his coat and cap on. 'I'll take Cinders for a walk, see if there's anyone about.'

Fran noticed him pick up the car keys as he left. He didn't trust her, that was obvious. But there was no point in running away now. She got up and watched Ted, from the window. He went into the stable and came out again, then he walked around the back of it, which he'd already done several times. Eventually, he strode off through the courtyard with Cinders at his heels. Ten minutes later he was back. He came inside and stood frowning at Fran.

'Which direction did she go in?'

'I, er, didn't notice.'

'She handed you the baby, and you didn't watch her walk away?'

'I was a bit shocked.'

Ted took off his cap and threw it on the table. 'I don't believe you. You didn't see her at all, did you? There was no woman who knocked at the door and gave you her baby. That's a completely nonsensical story.' He pulled out a kitchen chair and sat down. 'Where did you get him, Fran? Did you steal him yourself?'

'Oh, God. No, Ted.' Fran put Sam over her shoulder to burp him. How could he think she would do such a thing? But why wouldn't he, after all the lies she'd told him? 'Someone did leave him here – in the stable. I found him the Saturday before last, late evening – Cinders heard him. I was going to go straight to the police, but the poor little thing was filthy and hungry—'

'And your nurturing instinct took over.' Ted slapped his hands on his thighs. 'That's more like it – now I believe you. Why the hell didn't you tell me straight out?'

Fran sat down at the table beside him, trying to keep her voice calm. 'Because I knew you would make me take him to the police. I did try – several times – just couldn't—'

'Don't know whether it makes things better or worse for you.' Ted seemed to be thinking aloud, his hands moving rapidly. 'But Fran,' his voice had lost its edge, 'you have no right to keep a baby, even one you find in your own stable – however neglected. You know that don't you?'

Fran was weeping. 'I just fell in love with him—'

'I can see that—'

'I was hoping – as time went by – that things would resolve themselves.'

'But how could they?'

Fran shrugged helplessly.

Ted came over to her and put his arms around her. 'You are an old pudden-head,' he said.

*   *   *

Rachel had given the kids a training session in the café. She'd dished up plates of lasagne and put bowls of green salad and crusty bread on the tables for their supper, but they wanted chips. She lowered the basket into the smoking oil. Ah, well, they deserved it; they were a nice bunch of youngsters. There wasn't much for them to do around here in February. And they'd been receptive to her lessons in customer relations and the art of waiting on tables.

She stood back, away from the heat. She could hear their banter going on. They were all trying to outdo each other, as usual. But they were so funny and quick-witted. Especially Aidan and Patrick, who could keep their repartee going for hours.

'What am I doing here?' Kate was saying. 'I could be sun-bathing on Bondi beach.'

'It's the lure of the British male,' Patrick said.

'What? White and puny?'

'Better than being bronzed and brainless,' Aidan said.

'That's racist,' Jules said.

'But possibly true,' Kate laughed.

Rachel shook the chip basket. She'd been trying to observe Clare, discreetly, all evening. She was sitting by Rose's side, not saying anything, unless she was asked. She was still looking dreadfully

234

pale. Rachel wondered how long it had been since she'd either had a termination, or given birth – and what sort of medical care she'd had. Maybe she was anaemic. But she looked better than she had on Saturday evening. Rose had obviously been looking after her. Her long red hair was shining and she was wearing a brightly coloured top that looked as if it were African. Aidan was backing off, she noticed, sitting at another table with Billy and Jules.

'You look nice, Clare,' Kate remarked.

'You certainly look better than you did when you turned up at Wraith Cove and fell into my arms,' Patrick smiled.

Rachel could see, through the glass shelves, Clare had flushed pink, but was smiling shyly, seeming not to mind the attention too much.

'I was in a bit of a state, wasn't I?' she said.

Good, thought Rachel, she's joining in.

'You were out of your head!' Billy said.

'She was ill,' Jules said. 'But you *were* very confused. First of all, you told us your name was Clare, and then you insisted it was Tess, and then Clare, again. You didn't know who you were. We had to call Medicine Woman to calm you down.'

'Medicine woman?' Clare asked

'Marguerite. That's what we've nicknamed her. She doesn't mind.'

'Clare is my middle name,' Clare said. 'But I prefer it to Tess.'

'Clare suits you better,' Aidan said.

'Chips!' Rachel called, tipping them into baskets and saving a few for herself. She came out of the kitchen and put the baskets on the tables. 'I'll leave you lot to enjoy yourselves. You can put your music on – not too loudly, if you don't mind. I'll be up above trying to get some peace.'

Upstairs in her flat, Rachel poured herself a glass of wine and sank into her favourite saggy armchair. Bit different from Jill's, but just as nice. She kicked off her shoes and put her feet up and tucked into her basket of chips. What a strange day. It had been such a relief when Jill had phoned to say that Rose had found Clare and was looking after her. Clare was going to stay at Cormorants for a while, so they could surreptitiously keep an eye on her.

Rachel closed her eyes. She could hear the murmur of voices, and the thud of music from downstairs. She realised how tired she was feeling. After Valentine's weekend was over she would be able to slow down for a while. There would be no point in opening the restaurant permanently this time of year. The season would start nearer Easter, and she could run her comfortable café during the day. She could do that blind-folded.

She felt her body relaxing. How nice it was to be without the permanent niggling tension that Sandro had brought into her life. She wondered where he was now. Back home in Italy, she hoped, grovelling in front of his bishop, or priest, for absolution from his sins. How could he believe all that? Surely we had to make some kind of internal shift for ourselves, and at least attempt to repair any damage we'd caused. How could a priest in another country make it all right for him to have committed adultery and participated in the conception of an unwanted child? He expected that kind of help, and yet he'd abandoned the girl he'd met who was in trouble. She could hardly bear to think about what he'd told her. And he'd had the nerve to ask Rachel to look out for the girl and tell her he was sorry – as if there were only half a dozen girls in Ventnor. What sort of a cop-out was that? Tess, he'd said . . .

'Tess!' Rachel sat up, sloshing her wine. She'd just heard that name spoken downstairs. Tess – who were they referring to? Did they know this girl? Hold on – it was Clare they were teasing, wasn't it? Rachel tried to think back over the scraps of conversation that she'd heard. Clare had simply said her other name was Tess, that's all it was. Just a coincidence. Tess was a popular name. Had Sandro said anything else? He'd met this girl in the Catholic church. She needed his help. Her name was Tess. What else? She was very young and had long red hair – *rossa,* he'd said!

There was too much here to keep writing it off as coincidence. She tried to think coherently, piecing it together. Clare was a young Irish Catholic girl, sent over to England to have her baby. She'd met Rose en route who'd felt sorry for her and given her an address here, if she needed help. Clare turns up several months later, ill and distressed. Rachel got up and paced up and down. And the unthinkable, shocking thing was: Sandro had told her this girl had left her baby in a shed to die. Maybe Clare had been ill, delirious. But why would she ask Sandro for help and tell him such a terrible thing? Was she seeking absolution like him, or was she trying to escape from something she'd just done, here on the island? She didn't know how long Clare had been here. Had she just arrived when she turned up at Wraith Cove? Rachel cast her mind back over the last few weeks. She couldn't remember hearing anything about a baby being found dead – in a shed. That certainly would have hit the headlines in *The County Press*.

She could hear the kids downstairs getting noisier. Should she go and ask Clare to come up for a chat? No, she couldn't possibly start asking the child those questions. It could terrify her – she might run away. It would be best to sleep on it and let things settle down in her tired mind. Tomorrow morning she would talk it through with Sophie.

*　　*　　*

Father Ryan was back at the ferry terminal at Pembroke, waiting for the passengers to disembark. He propped himself against a wall. He'd had rather a lot of whiskey this evening. But he'd so enjoyed himself at St David's, the cathedral had lived up to his expectations and he stayed for a recital of *Bach's Organ Mass*. The sound had carried him into a state of ecstasy. The combination of music and whiskey was miraculous.

The foot passengers were starting to appear – a never ending flow of jaded looking travellers. He struggled to keep alert, it was long after midnight, hard to focus . . . what with the whiskey and all. Maybe the musicians stayed on board the ferry to sleep, waiting for the return journey. Suddenly, he was jolted awake, there they were, walking past him, almost before he realised. He just happened to register that they were carrying instrument cases. He hurried after them. As he suspected, they went straight to an all-night bar and ordered drinks. Father Ryan sat nearby and bought himself a whiskey, trying to remember what he wanted to ask them. Oh, yes, about that girl, Rose. He sidled up to the men and introduced himself. They looked him up and down without recognition.

'I was wearing my black cassock – priest's robe. I remember some of your names – Carl, Jo, isn't it?'

The men smirked as if he were a lunatic.

'Drink a lot for a priest, don't you?'

237

'I'm on holiday. Would you let me buy you a drink?'

The men didn't refuse. They lit cigarettes and began joking and laughing about things he didn't understand.

'Can I ask you again,' he said, 'if you remember the girl, Rose, who played the fiddle with you? You remembered her before.'

'We'll let you buy us another drink first,' one of them said, pushing back his shaggy hair.

Father Ryan bought the drinks and waited, but the men continued their joking, much of which he suspected was at his expense. He felt in his pocket for the photo of Clare. 'Do you not remember? I showed you this photo of the girl I was looking for – she was with Rose – the one you did remember.'

'How many girls would it be that you're looking for?' one of them said, puffing smoke lazily out of the side of his mouth.

'Both.' Father Ryan was feeling angry and tired. Who did these insolent young men think they were talking to?

'Oh, will you stop winding the poor bloke up, Jo. Yes, I remember, Rose. Fancied the pants off her. Don't remember the other wee girl.'

'Do you remember, at all, where in Ireland, Rose came from?'

'She wasn't Irish. I never said she was Irish, did I? She was travelling back home.'

'Not Irish? Are you sure about that? Where was she from then?'

'England, wasn't it, Carl?'

'Where in England? It's a big place.' Father Ryan struggled to stay calm.

'Wish I knew. I'd pay her a visit myself.'

'You don't remember anything at all?'

'No! Sure, she never said anything for us to remember.'

Jo swigged his whiskey in one gulp and wiped his mouth with the back of his hand. 'Look, Father whatever your name is. She just joined in with our music for a couple of hours. She was very sexy and had a posh English accent. End of story. Now push off.'

Father Ryan looked around the bar – it was almost empty and he was feeling a little scared. 'Good night to you, then,' he muttered

238

and staggered outside. The cold air hit him, making his head reel. He should have found a hotel earlier, before he'd had so much to drink and forgotten. They'd be all booked up with travellers now. He tried to button his overcoat, but couldn't manage it and started to giggle. How silly everything was. He tripped on a paving stone and grabbed at a lamp-post. He slid down it and sat on the kerb.

'What a stupid fecking life this is,' he shouted.

CHAPTER
Twenty-Two

Rachel had been aware, all through her night of shallow sleep, that her mind was going over and over the facts about Clare. Now, in the concrete reality of another day, the story seemed improbable, but she couldn't dismiss it from her mind. If it were true, this would be infanticide she'd been presented with and, morally, she had to investigate further. She phoned Sophie, but Nick answered and said she'd gone back to bed for a while feeling a bit off colour.

'Make sure she's better for the weekend, Nick. Can't afford to lose another Italian chef.'

No Sophie to talk to. She couldn't risk telling Jill. She would probably grab Clare by her plait and demand to know what she'd been up to. Maybe she should just go and talk to Clare. But the girl seemed to shrink from too much adult attention. Perhaps if Rose was there – she was the one person that Clare seemed attached to.

After Aidan left for school, Rachel walked up the road to Cormorants. She hoped Jill and Ash would be at work, and the nanny doing whatever nannies did when their charges were at school. She knocked on the door. Rose answered, looking pleased to see her.

'Mum's at work, but please come in and have some coffee. Clare and I are being lazy – still eating breakfast.'

Rachel went into the warm kitchen that always smelled of spices. The veranda ran right along the outside of this room as well as the sitting room. Radio One was playing. Clare was sitting at the table, eating toast. Her hair was tied up on top with a green scarf and hung down her back in a pony tail. She glanced up at Rachel and smiled briefly. She and Rose looked like a couple of normal teenagers, hanging out. Rachel had no idea how she was going to approach this.

Rose started telling her about Stephanie's progress as she poured the coffee.

'Grandma's coming home in a couple of days. You will come and visit her, won't you? She loves to see people.'

'When she feels up to it, I'd like to,' Rachel said, wondering if Stephanie really wanted hoards of neighbours trooping in. 'What are you two planning today?'

'We're just messing about, really,' Rose said. 'We're going to drive to Wraith Cove later and collect Clare's stuff. She's going to stay here for a while. She shouldn't really be working down there in this cold weather – she's been ill.'

Rachel nodded. 'Good idea.' She sipped her coffee. 'Clare,' she began, not quite knowing the words, just letting them come. 'Was it you that put Sandro's wallet through my letterbox?'

Clare looked up, her face startled. 'Sandro . . . Angelo,' she whispered.

Rachel nodded. 'Sandro Angelo.'

'How did you know it was me?'

'He told me about you. How he'd met you in the church . . . '

Clare glanced at Rose, then bowed her head.

'He wanted me to thank you . . . and to tell you how sorry he was that he didn't help you.'

'But . . . I told him my name was Tess.'

'With long red hair. I heard you talking in my café last night, about sometimes calling yourself, Tess.'

Rose was looking from one to the other. 'What's going on?' she asked.

'Does Rose know?' Rachel said.

Clare nodded.

'Does she know everything?' Rachel asked gently.

Clare bit her lip and looked up at Rachel beseechingly.

'I do know everything,' Rose said. 'About the baby and the adoption.' She touched Clare's arm. 'It's all right,' she said. 'You haven't done anything wrong.'

Clare's white face suddenly flushed red. 'I have,' she burst out. 'And you'll hate me when you know.'

241

'I won't.' Rose looked surprised. 'I swear, I won't.'

Clare pushed her chair back and stood up, her whole body was shaking. 'I have to tell you.' Her green eyes were wide with fear. 'I left the baby in a stable to die.'

Rose was staring at Clare. She shook her head as if to clear her confusion. 'You did *what*?' She looked from Clare to Rachel and back again.

Rachel sat still. So it was true. And it hadn't taken much questioning for Clare to confess.

'Sit down,' Rose commanded. She took Clare's hands in hers. 'Where did this happen? In Ireland?'

'No. Here.'

'Here! On the island? Where exactly?'

'A farm, near the lighthouse.'

'Christ almighty,' Rose muttered. 'How long ago?'

'The night I arrived – two Saturdays ago.' Her voice was high and clear, as if now she had told the truth it was easier to speak. 'I didn't mean it, I was ill. I left the baby in the stable and went to the caravans for help.' Her eyes searched round the room as if she were remembering the night vividly. 'You weren't there, Rose. And then, I collapsed. I woke up – it was still dark. I went straight back to get him. He was on the ground, under the straw.' Her eyes widened again, with horror. 'I touched him, he was stiff and cold.'

Rose put a hand to her mouth. The room was silent. After a while she turned to Rachel. 'What shall we do?' she whispered.

Rachel was breathing deeply, trying to control the shivers running through her body. She needed to stay calm; she was the grown-up. The girls were looking to her to make a decision.

'It must be Rocken Edge Farm,' Rachel said.

'It was! I saw that name, on a sign,' Clare said.

Rachel got up. 'I'm going to go there,' she said firmly. 'I know Fran. I won't say anything directly. I'll just see if I can find out anything.' She looked at the two big-eyed girls who were now clinging together. 'Promise me that you'll stay here. Don't say anything to anyone. I'll be back as soon as I can.'

242

Rachel ran down the street to get her car. She drove as fast as she dared along Undercliff Drive and down St Catherine's Road towards the lighthouse. Her car bumped and shuddered down the rough lane to Rocken Edge Farm. She hadn't been here for ages; she usually spoke to Fran in The Buddle Inn. This was such an isolated place; beautiful, but really over the edge. She didn't think she'd like to live here alone, especially in the winter. Fran's Land Rover was in the cobbled courtyard. The place seemed quiet and closed up. She'd expected Fran to be pottering about, seeing to her animals, her dog at her heels. Rachel got out of her car, walked across to the kitchen door and knocked. To her surprise it was opened by Blackgang Ted.

'Rachel!' He didn't look pleased to see her. 'What are you doing out here?'

'Just called in to say, hello – and to see what you thought of the meal on Saturday.'

'Oh, er, we really enjoyed it. Thank you.' He held the door only partly open, and didn't appear to be about to ask her in.

'Cold wind,' Rachel hinted. 'Is Fran in?'

'She's, er, busy. Got visitors.'

'Of course.' Rachel smiled. 'I'd forgotten – her family from Australia. You brought the baby with . . .' Rachel froze mid-sentence. Oh, my God, it couldn't be, she thought.

Ted had such a worried look on his face, Rachel felt she ought to help him out. She took a deep breath and told herself to calm down – this could all be coincidence. 'That reminds me, Ted, talking about babies – I wanted to ask Fran if she'd seen anyone wandering around here with a young baby.'

Ted sighed, took his cap off, scratched his head and plonked his cap back on. Rachel waited. Ted glanced back over his shoulder into the kitchen. 'I think you'd better ask her yourself,' he said, opening the door.

Rachel went inside. Fran was sitting at the kitchen table holding a very small baby. She was giving him a bottle.

'Hello, Fran.' Fran didn't respond. Rachel walked over to her and looked down at the feeding baby. 'Gorgeous,' she said. 'Whose baby did you say this was? I couldn't remember.'

Fran still didn't answer. She started rocking the baby gently as she fed him. 'It's all right, Sam,' she cooed.

'Fran.' Ted spoke firmly. 'Rachel asked you a question.' Ted offered Rachel a chair.

'He's my baby,' Fran said gruffly. 'His mother didn't want him. She left him with me.'

Rachel glanced at Ted. He nodded.

'Fran. I know who his mother is,' she whispered.

Fran looked up at Rachel for the first time. Her face was crumpled with grief. 'Oh, no,' she whispered. 'Please don't take him away.'

'It's for the best,' Ted said.

'It isn't for *his* best,' Fran growled. 'How could she abandon him? He might easily have died. She doesn't care about him.'

'Fran.' Rachel leaned forward in her chair. 'She is a very young girl—'

'She must be cruel, wicked—'

'No. Traumatised, abused, but not wicked. And, she thinks the child is dead.'

'Then let her go on thinking that.' Fran's voice had turned into a wail. Rachel felt desperately sorry for her.

'That's not possible really, Fran, is it?'

'How do you know she's his mother? She might be making it up.'

'She has no reason to.' Rachel got up. 'I think it's best if I bring her here. I'm not going to tell her anything. You can ask her where she left him.'

Rachel went outside with Ted. 'Will you stay with Fran?' she asked.

'I've hardly left her since I found out,' Ted said, 'just to tend the animals.' He caught hold of Rachel's arm. 'She's been as loving to that boy as it's possible to be,' he said.

Rachel could see his eyes glistening with tears. 'I can see that,' she said. 'Don't say anything to anyone, Ted. Not before we have all the facts, and then we need to decide – all together – what's best to do.'

Rachel got into her car and pulled away.

'Thank God, thank God, thank God,' she kept saying, as she drove back to Ventnor. The child was alive – and thriving by the look of him.

244

And to think Fran had brought him to the restaurant on Saturday – with Clare in the kitchen, a few yards away. She grinned. It really would have been an evening to remember if that had all kicked off, as well as Rose's drama, and the Sandro saga. She wondered why Clare had thought the baby was dead – maybe she had been hallucinating in her distress. Or had there been someone else involved? Perhaps she'd been drugged, or coerced in some way. Rachel needed to get clear about this. She was a participant now, and she wanted to help without getting any of these people into trouble – if that was at all possible.

*   *   *

'She'll come back with the police, won't she?' Fran held Sam close and rocked him, back and forth, back and forth.

'I don't think she will.' Ted patted her shoulder. 'I *really* don't think she will. Rachel's too honest for that. She told us she'd bring the girl here, and that's what she'll do.'

Fran felt as if her age had suddenly caught up with her. Her back was aching and she felt so weak she wondered if she would be able to stand up. She wanted to wash her hands and face, and brush her hair, and make herself look like an efficient, capable woman. She wanted this irresponsible girl to see that she was a good and caring person.

'Quick,' she said to Ted. 'Tidy up the kitchen. I'll change Sam's clothes and smarten myself up.'

'Sam has just had his clothes changed, and you look fine.'

Fran looked at him imploringly. 'There must be something we can do,' she cried. 'Sweep the floor. Is it warm enough in here?'

'Look. This girl is going to be petrified. Rachel said she's been living with the idea that she left her child to die. She's going to be far more worried about what we think of her, and whether we will call the police. Do you think she's going to notice a bit of dust?'

Fran's heart was thumping so hard she wondered if Sam could feel it. He gazed at her, and smiled.

*   *   *

Clare and Rose were still sitting at the table when Rachel arrived back at Cormorants. Clare had tried to explain to Rose exactly what had

245

happened that night. But she was becoming confused – three times she'd gone to that stable, feeling ill and distraught, everything was becoming blurred.

'I'm not going to say anything,' Rachel said, firmly, 'and neither must you, Clare, because there must be no confusion. It will be best if you try to re-trace every step you took that night. The memories will come back to you more easily that way.'

Clare felt her legs shaking as she stood up. 'Can Rose come?' She would be able to cope if Rose was there.

'As long as she promises not to say anything. Do you understand, Rose? It's really important that we let Clare show us exactly what happened.'

'I understand,' Rose said.

They walked down the road and stood on the esplanade. Clare looked up and down.

'I came down here, from the bus station, thinking this was the way to the lighthouse,' she said. 'It was afternoon, cold, everything was deserted. I stopped outside your café, Rachel, but it was closed. I was freezing and hungry. I walked back up to the town and asked someone how to get to the lighthouse. I caught another bus. The driver dropped me off outside an inn.'

'Okay. Let's go,' Rachel said. 'My car's over there. Sit in the front with me, Clare.'

Rachel drove in silence. Clare remembered the bus ride and her exhaustion. Rachel stopped the car outside The Buddle Inn. She turned to Clare. 'Here?'

'Yes.' Clare pointed ahead. 'I walked down there, to the lighthouse. I could see the caravans among the trees. I was so glad. But the baby needed feeding; he was making noises, so I decided to find somewhere to sit down.'

'Okay.' Rachel drove as far as she could down the lane towards the lighthouse. 'We'll walk from here,' she said. They got out of the car and headed down the slope to the fields. Rose took hold of Clare's hand.

'You're doing fine,' she said.

Encouraged, Clare pointed ahead. 'I took that track.'

'Right. You lead, we'll follow,' Rachel said.

Clare walked slowly, hand in hand with Rose. Rachel followed, in silence. Clare found it hard to imagine that she'd done this alone, on a cold January evening, carrying the baby and her backpack when she felt so ill. She pointed again.

'I saw that big rock, and thought I could sit down there, out of the wind, and feed him. I walked down the track and then I noticed this.' They'd arrived at the gate of Rocken Edge Farm. 'I didn't think there could be anything right down there, but then I saw some buildings.' They walked through the leaning trees and came into the cobbled yard. Clare looked around. 'Those doves were flying about, but it seemed quiet, no dogs barked, there was no-one here. I thought the place was empty.'

Clare put a hand to her mouth. Rose made a move towards her, but Rachel shook her head. 'I went in that stable, there.' She didn't want to go inside again. Already she could feel her insides squirming.

'It's all right, Clare,' Rachel said gently. 'You're doing just fine. Just wait here a moment.'

Rachel went across to the farmhouse and opened the door. Clare could hear her talking to someone inside. Was it a policeman? Had Clare been led into a trap? She looked at Rose, but she shrugged, looking puzzled. A grey-haired woman emerged from the house. Maybe she was a plain clothes officer, or a social worker.

'Clare, this is Fran,' Rachel said. 'She lives here. Will you show us exactly where you left the baby?'

Clare moved slowly towards the stable and opened the door. Rachel and Fran entered behind her. Rose stood in the doorway.

'I sat down under that window to feed him,' Clare said, her voice shaking. 'I didn't feel well, so I put him on the bales.' She looked around. 'There's not so many now. There was an animal – a sheep, I think, over in that corner. I had to rush outside to get some air, I thought I was going to faint. I felt so ill. Somehow, I managed to get to the caravans. I was trying to find Rose. I must have fainted then, and I didn't wake up until early the next morning. I realised I'd left him. I found my way back here as fast as I could. But he was gone!' She put her hands up to her mouth. 'I searched everywhere. And then . . . I found him.' Clare remembered the horror as she stared at the place. Her lips started to tremble, her voice shook. 'He was under the straw – there.' She pointed. 'I felt him – cold and stiff. It was terrible, I ran away.' It was so awful, telling these people what she'd done. The nausea and giddiness of that night returned, she even felt a throb in her breasts, her knees buckled, and she sank down on the straw, sobbing. She looked up at the faces surrounding her.

The woman from the farmhouse was looking shocked. 'But that was—'

'Fran!' Rachel said. 'Let's go inside.' She helped Clare get up and put an arm around her. 'It's all right. Come on now, brave girl, nearly over.' She led Clare across the yard, into a warm, old-fashioned kitchen, and lowered her onto a chair. Rose was looking white and shocked. What must she be thinking? She wouldn't want Clare as a friend now.

'So, we've heard Clare's story,' Rachel said. 'What about you, Fran? Is that where you found the baby?'

'In the stable, yes. But not where *she* said.'

'But are you convinced that she's telling the truth, and she is the mother?'

Fran nodded.

'Then I think you'd better tell Clare your side of the story, don't you?'

Fran cleared her throat. She spoke to Rachel, turning her body away from Clare as if she didn't want to look at her. 'I did find the baby in the stable. Well, it was Cinders, my dog, really.'

Clare didn't want to hear this, but she had to know. 'Was it your dog . . . that got him?'

'Oh, yes. My Cinders saved his life.'

'What . . . what do you mean?'

'Can't believe anyone would be so stupid to mistake dead lambs for a baby.'

Clare stared at Fran, uncomprehending. 'But I felt him . . . wool . . . the shawl.' She remembered, vividly, the glinting eye.

'Lambs are covered in wool,' Fran commented.

'A lamb. I don't understand.' Clare glanced at Rose for help. But Rose looked puzzled too.

Rachel was leaving the kitchen. Where was she going? Clare could hear her voice, through the open door to a hallway. Had there been someone out there all the time, listening to her confession?

Rachel came back in followed by a man. He was carrying something in his arms. He came over to Clare.

'I think this boy belongs to you,' he said.

Clare leaped out of the chair. 'Are you all playing a joke on me?' she cried.

'Oh, my God,' Rose was saying. 'Clare, Clare. Don't you understand? It's your baby! He isn't dead. Oh, how amazing is that?'

Clare looked around at everyone. Rachel was smiling. Rose was jumping up and down. Fran was crying. The man looked as if he didn't know what to do.

'Do you want to hold him?' he asked.

'I, I, don't know,' Clare said.

'Let her get used to the idea,' Rachel said. 'This has been a huge shock.'

The man gave the baby to Fran. 'You'll know what to do,' he said gruffly.

Fran sat and rocked him. Clare watched from a distance, feeling a strange prickling in her breasts. The baby looked so different. How could he have changed so much in such a short time? She moved a bit nearer. His skin looked pink and smooth; his hair shone with a reddish glint. He was dressed in a nice blue suit with teddy bears embroidered on it.

She moved a little nearer. 'Are you sure . . . it's him?'

'I don't have a huge selection of babies left in my stable,' Fran snapped. 'This one was wearing pink knitted clothes, wrapped in a pink shawl. Ring any bells?'

Clare nodded. 'Mother knitted them,' she whispered.

'Your mother?' Fran said.

'No. Mother – in the convent.'

Fran looked puzzled. 'Didn't she have any blue wool?'

'She, er, wanted him to be a girl.'

'A girl! Was she mad?' Fran said. 'What did you call him?'

'Nothing. Mother had a name – a girl's name. But she wouldn't tell me.'

'Wouldn't tell you! A girl's name! God, help us. Well, we call him, Sam.'

Clare nodded, not knowing what to say. The woman seemed angry. Clare suddenly burst into tears. 'I wasn't meant to keep him,' she wailed. 'He was going to be adopted.'

'So, what *were* you doing with him? He was in such a state!' Fran yelled, her face red, her eyes blazing.

'Mother said I had to feed him. She said he would die if I didn't, and I would go to hell. I ran away . . . because . . . because Mother was going mad, and she kept a dead nun in another room, and—'

'Was it you that ransacked the stable on Monday, then? Why did you do that? Did you think he'd still be there, alive and well, waiting for his next feed?'

'No! I was looking for something . . . something to bury—'

'Oh, my God!' Rose cried. 'Leave her alone, everyone.' She wrapped her arms around Clare. 'I think we need to go home.'

Clare gazed at the shocked faces. What had she said? Did they not believe her?

'Good idea,' Rachel said. She took Clare's face in her hands. 'Look, Clare. I want you to trust me. Your baby is in the best place, for now. You can't look after him – you need some help to get through this. Is it all right with you if we leave him here with Fran?'

Clare wondered what this meant. There were too many questions coming at her. And she didn't know who she could trust. She looked from Rachel to Rose. She didn't think they would lie to her. But Fran – she was furious. 'Will she put him in a home?' she whispered.

'Absolutely not,' Rose said.

'This is his home,' Fran said. 'He won't be going anywhere.'

*   *   *

Father Ryan had spent the night in jail. He didn't quite understand why.

All he remembered was sitting on the kerb and calling out to passers-by that the world was in a terrible state. He was certain people did much worse things. If he'd been wearing his cassock, preaching from the pulpit, the congregation would have been quite impressed.

But still, it was degrading. He'd been sick on the floor of the cold cell, and no-one had been to clear it up. The police had looked incredulous when they asked for his details and he insisted he was a Catholic priest. They didn't believe him at first. *Oh, yeah. And I'm the pope,* one of them had said. But they didn't treat him with respect, even when they examined his papers and realised he was telling the truth. *We'll let you off with a warning this time,* the sergeant said. *If I was you, I'd get on that ferry to Ireland, ASAP – and stay there.*

They'd sent him out into the cold morning. Father Ryan made his way to where he left his car and found the wheel clamped. He had to find a phone box and pay a lot of money to get the car released. He decided to ration his whiskey intake for the rest of the day. He went to the terminal and booked himself on the next crossing. There was no point staying any longer. He hadn't found Clare. Even the Rose connection had come to a dead end.

At least he'd had some time to reflect overnight, in prison. Clare had told Sister Benedicta that she was going to find her friend Rose, and the musicians told him Rose was English and going home to England. The nun must have been confused about Ireland – most likely something to do with the fact she'd just bashed her brains out. Father Ryan smirked. So that was that. Once he was back on Irish ground, he could decide on his next step.

Anyway, he'd had enough of England – and Wales – inhospitable countries full of mad, rude people.

*   *   *

Rachel had driven Rose and Clare back to her flat and made them some cheese on toast. Rose seemed excited about the baby and was trying hard to cheer Clare up.

'It's, like, such a relief,' she kept saying. 'It must have been terrible for you thinking that he was dead. Oh, God . . . feeling the lambs . . . how horrible was that? And all the time, Fran had him safely down at Rocken Edge. Isn't that amazing?'

'Fran shouldn't have done it though,' Rachel reminded her, trying to uphold the grown-up view, whilst secretly agreeing. 'She had no right to keep him. She didn't know the circumstances in which he was left. His mother could have fallen off the cliff for all she knew. Or he could have been stolen.'

'I know, I know,' Rose said, with the easy dismissive gesture of the young. 'But the fact is, Rachel, it has worked out *so* well. The authorities won't need to be involved, will they?'

'Well, er—'

Clare looked up anxiously. 'Will they?' she echoed.

'Maybe not. But Clare, what about your relatives? Your parents? You're still a minor. We have to be responsible here.' She tapped Clare's arm, gently. 'Who actually knows where you are?'

'Nobody. I ran away.'

'From the convent? But won't they be trying to trace you?'

'Mother might. But I don't think so – she was going mad. And the other nuns that lived there never saw me. One of them was dead . . . '

Rachel didn't like the sound of this dead nun that kept cropping up. Was Clare imagining things? It sounded like she'd been through one hell of an ordeal. 'Clare, why don't you tell us everything, from the beginning. Who sent you to England, to this convent?'

'Father Ryan.'

'Your parish priest?'

'The nun was his cousin – a Poor Clare – my mam likes them. He said she was called Sister Bridget, but I must have got that wrong, she was Sister Benedicta. But she wanted me to call her Mother. She was going to arrange a foster home for me, until the baby was adopted. But when I got there – and I did go to the wrong place at first – she made me stay with her.'

Rachel was confused already. 'But where did you go to have the baby?'

Clare shrugged. 'Nowhere.'

252

'You stayed in the convent with the nun – Mother. Didn't you have a midwife or a doctor there?'

'No. Just Mother.'

'And the birth . . . was it okay?'

'It took ages, it hurt a lot.' Clare's eyes filled with tears. 'Mother was angry because it took so long. She kept telling me to push down. I didn't know what she meant. I kept pushing my stomach with my hands, and she said I was just being stupid. She kept slapping my face.'

Rachel felt a huge lump rising up in her throat. This poor, poor, child. What on earth had she been subjected to? She had to swallow hard in order to go on speaking.

'Were there any complications?'

'I don't think so. Except—'

'Except?'

'Mother wanted it to be a girl. She was very upset at first. She screamed and threw him onto me and ran away. She came back later and said the baby was a girl. I knew it wasn't, but I had to pretend.'

'Jesus!' Rose exclaimed. 'Mad old bat!'

'And it was just you and her, together – all that time?' Rachel said.

Clare nodded. 'I asked if I could see a priest, but she kept saying he would come when he could.'

'And you had no contact with your parents, your mother, your own priest?'

Clare shook her head.

'So, when did you last speak to your mother?'

'Mam? Not since I left Ireland. Father Ryan said it was for the best. He said he would tell her how I was getting on.'

'And did he come to see you?'

Clare averted her eyes and shook her head.

Rachel sat back in her chair. This didn't add up. It was like something out of a gothic novel from another century. Hard Times in Ireland.

Rose was scratching her head. 'Why were you treated so badly? It sounds like you were being punished.' She toyed with a teaspoon. 'Were you raped?'

Clare shook her head. She started biting her nails, voraciously.

'Was it your father?' Rose said.

Clare's head shot up. 'Father Ryan?'

'No, I meant—' Rose stared at Clare. '*Oh, my God!* Was it him? Your priest?'

Clare stopped biting her nails and hung her head. Rachel felt the hairs on her skin standing up with shock. Rose was asking outrageous questions. Rachel had wanted to stop her, but she'd gone straight to the heart of Clare's secret.

'Is this true, Clare?' Rachel asked.

'It was my fault,' Clare whispered.

'Oh, no it fucking well wasn't!' Rose shouted.

'You don't understand,' Clare wailed. 'I tempted him. I wanted him to love me.'

'I don't care if you stripped naked and lay on the altar and begged him. IT WAS NOT YOUR FAULT!' Rose yelled.

Clare stared at Rose, wide-eyed with astonishment.

Rachel found her voice. 'Rose is absolutely right. You were a thirteen year old child. He was the adult. You are not to blame.' She reached across the table, held Clare's arms, and shook her slightly, to make her look up. 'Your priest was someone you should have been able to trust. How old were you when all this started?'

'I don't remember. Just a wee girl. He measured my chest for the school choir. Mam said I should do what he said.'

'Jesus!' Rose bashed her fist on the table. 'Did he give you little presents and tell you secrets, and make you feel you were his *special* girl?'

'Rose,' Rachel held up a hand. 'Take it easy.'

Clare looked astonished. 'How did you know that? Do you know him?'

Rose took a deep breath. 'Sweetheart, it's what paedophiles do.'

Clare looked puzzled. '*No.* He wasn't one of those bad men. He was always kind to me – like a father. He knew about my daddy leaving—'

'I bet he did. Was he kind when he knew you were pregnant?'

Clare's eyes brimmed with tears. 'No, he was angry.'

'Did he make you feel it was your fault?' Rachel asked.

Clare nodded. 'It's in the bible.'

'So is a lot of other rubbish,' Rose said.

Clare's head was drooping forward. She looked completely spent.

'Sweetheart, I think you've had just about enough for one day,' Rachel said. 'Do you want to stay here with me, or go home with Rose?'

'I'm not letting her out of my sight.' Rose smiled ruefully, and put her hand on Clare's head. 'It's a hot soak in the bath and an early night for you my girl.'

Rachel watched from the window as they walked slowly along the esplanade and turned up the hill to Cormorants. They were arm in arm. Thank heavens for Rose, she thought. Rachel didn't know how she would have coped without her. What a mess. Something would have to be done. Something which involved the authorities, and accusations of child abuse, and court cases. And Clare's mother.

Rachel took a few deep breaths and looked at her watch. She felt as if she'd spent the whole day with adrenaline coursing through her veins, trying to remain clear and controlled. She still had so many things to organise for the weekend. Aidan would be home from school soon, needing food. And then Sophie and Kyp would be arriving for another cooking lesson. But compared to the revelations of the day, these things seemed of little importance.

She went downstairs and sat at a table in the quiet café. She thought about her own day of weeping last Sunday after Sandro left. Thank goodness she'd allowed herself to do that, and received so much insight into the nature of human suffering. It had enabled her to deal with this without being completely overwhelmed. Clare's white face and green eyes came into her mind. Poor little girl. It seemed she'd experienced every conceivable nightmare, without support from one single adult. Would she ever be able to trust anybody ever again?

At least something good had come out of the *Sandro Saga*. His remorse had been the catalyst for the connection – Tess with the hair *rossa*.

CHAPTER
Twenty-Three

Fran and Ted were taking an early morning stroll along the cliff path. The weather had turned milder after the brief flurry of snow and frost. The woodpeckers were already drumming, as if announcing an imminent spring. The clouds were heavy with the promise of rain, the dark sea throwing up peaks of white where the treacherous currents clashed and fought for the right of way. Ted was carrying Sam, strapped to his chest in the baby harness. It was his idea. *Give your back a rest,* he'd said to Fran. He'd grumbled while she fitted it on him. *Feel like some old girl in a flaming corset.* But Fran noticed he kept grinning proudly as they walked. They both had sticks and she was holding onto his arm. The grass was saturated and slippery. She breathed deeply. How glad she was that Ted had prevented her from leaving. Where would she be now? And what would have happened when Rachel came nosing? Ted confessed later that he'd been keeping an eye on Fran's movements, knowing she was flummoxed about something she wasn't telling him. *Like one of them private detectives, I was,* he said.

'Good idea of yours, this walk,' Fran said. 'I'm still feeling a bit shaken up after yesterday. Can't believe such things could happen, this day and age, to a fourteen-year-old.' Rachel had phoned last night to tell Fran some of Clare's terrible story.

'That's because you don't listen to the news. Appalling, what goes on.' Ted adjusted Sam's hat. 'Some blokes need castrating, that's for certain. I'd do it myself, if I could get my hands on him.'

'If I hadn't killed him first,' Fran said. 'And I tell you what, Ted. I could still give that girl a good hiding.'

'Her name's Clare.'

'Clare.' Fran said it reluctantly.

'She's no more than a child.'

'But she didn't seem pleased to see Sam. Not even when she realised it meant she hadn't killed him.'

'She was shocked. Anyway, why should she be pleased to see him? Motherhood was forced upon her in the worst possible way.'

'But still, you'd think, when she saw him . . . ' Fran leaned over to look at Sam. He was fast asleep, one pink cheek pressed against Ted's coat.

'Would you rather she'd grabbed him from you and refused to let him go? Is that what you're saying?'

'No! Just doesn't seem natural, that's all.'

'The whole thing isn't natural.' Ted waved a finger. 'And don't forget – this could work well for you. If you try and befriend the girl, she might be happy for you to carry on looking after him.'

'It's more likely she'll put him up for adoption.'

'If she sees you as a nasty old woman, then maybe she will.'

Nasty old woman? That hurt. She didn't want Ted to think of her like that. I'm not nasty, she thought, just scared out of my wits. But at least there were some things she didn't have to worry about any more. Being accused of child abduction for one thing. Maybe Ted was right; she should try and be friendly towards Clare. She had indeed looked like a frightened child. She wasn't one of those cheeky brash teenagers that would knock you off the pavement in Newport. Poor kid.

Back at the farmhouse, Fran prepared Sam's milk, while Ted fed Cinders and Sugar Plum.

'We're getting like a married couple,' he chuckled, as he went out to see to the animals. 'A couple of old grandparents.'

Fran walked up and down the kitchen a few times, eyeing the telephone. 'What shall we do, Sam?' she asked. Sam smiled. Now he had learned to do it, he seemed to want to practise as much as possible. With trembling hands she picked up the receiver and dialled Rachel's number.

'Tell Clare she'll be welcome to come and see the baby whenever she likes,' she said.

*　　*　　*

Clare and Rose were clearing up Rachel's kitchen after helping her

257

bake chocolate muffins. Clare liked the smells and clutter of all the warm kitchens she'd been in recently. Back home, Mam's kitchen was cold and smelled of disinfectant. Clare imagined showing her around these nice houses she'd been invited into – Rachel's Café, Cormorants, Wraith Cottage, Rocken Edge Farm. Poor Mam – was she lonely in the little brick house, all on her own?

'What do you think?' Rachel was saying

'I don't know,' Clare said. Rachel had asked if she'd like to go and see the baby this morning. She didn't feel ready for it yet. When she thought about him, a kind of sick feeling rose up in her, a mixture of body smells and throbbing pains and writhing fear. She sat down at the table and pulled her plait over her shoulder. She rubbed the end of it across her cheek. It was soft now, like it used to be before she left home and became scruffy and dirty.

'That's okay,' Rachel said. 'He's being well cared for. Fran told me to tell you he smiles a lot now. Oh, and she'd like to know his birth date – so she can work out how old he is.'

Smiling? Clare couldn't imagine him smiling. How had he learnt to do that? She thought back to the day he was born, and the few weeks of torture, trying to breastfeed him with cracked, bleeding nipples, Mother standing over her, threatening her with hell. She shuddered violently; Rose put a hand on her shoulder.

'Don't . . . don't think about it, if you don't want to,' she said.

Clare gulped some water and took a deep breath.

'He was born on Boxing Day. Mother was hoping he would arrive on Christmas Day – the same day the Blessed Virgin gave birth. She gave me some disgusting oily stuff to drink, but it didn't work. She seemed to think it was my fault because I kept sicking it up. She took me to the top of the kitchen stairs and threatened to push me down.'

'Oh, my God!' Rose said. 'It gets worse and worse! This woman has to be arrested for cruelty. She's a sadist. Where was this place?'

'Worcester, I think.' Clare felt so confused sometimes, she could barely remember back that far.

Rachel was looking at her calendar. 'That makes him about six

258

and a half weeks.' She put a mug of tea in front of Clare. 'Rose is right. This has to be investigated. I was wondering, Clare, if you'd like to see the local priest, here?'

Clare felt confronted, yet again. A priest? She hadn't expected Rachel to say that. Rachel and Rose kept insisting that she was blameless, so why did they think she needed to see a priest? They must know she wasn't blameless, that was why. And Clare knew the truth, deep within herself, that she *was* to blame. She could feel the ball of badness still squirming inside. She would have to confess – Rachel knew that. And wouldn't a priest agree?

'I'm not a Catholic – my husband was,' Rachel was saying. 'So I know Father Michael well. He doesn't even insist on being called Father, he's happy with just Michael. He's a good and caring man. Rose, or I, will stay with you. We have to start somewhere. It seems better than going straight to the police – which might end with Social Services taking you and Sam into care, immediately. Michael will be able to give you the spiritual things you need as well, to help you through this. And he'll know who to contact to bring these people to justice.'

'No! I can't do that. I don't want to get anyone into trouble.'

Rachel bit her lip. 'Look at it like this, Clare. That priest, Father Ryan – who should never have been a priest in the first place – and that insane nun, they will do this to other children. They won't stop because you've gone missing.'

'Won't they?' Clare hadn't thought of that. She suddenly remembered little Maria – whom she'd seen Father Ryan petting. Would she go through this?

'Christ, no!' Rose said. 'They're probably in league. I wonder how many other girls Father Ryan has sent to *Mother*.'

'Oh, none. I'm sure of that,' Clare said. 'It was just me. Because I tempted—'

'No! It was because he's a paedophile, Clare. You're going to have to grow up and face that fact. You weren't special. He used you purely for his own gratification.'

Am I stupid? Clare thought. Am I the only one who doesn't

259

know these things? Where did Rose learn all this? She's only nineteen.

'Not all priests are like that,' Rachel said quietly.

Rose made a snorting noise.

'No, listen,' Rachel said. 'I know Michael well. He's understanding and has a great sense of humour. There are many different shades of Catholicism, Clare. Some much more liberal than others. I really think it would be good for you to talk to him. He will know what to do.' She smiled. 'But only if you want to, of course.'

Clare sat biting her nails. It seemed like something she was going to have to do – not because she wanted to, but because she couldn't work out what to do next about the badness. She hadn't killed the baby, but what about all the other things? 'Will you both come with me?'

'How about if I ask him to come here – to my flat? We can sit round this table and eat those delicious muffins you've just baked, and have coffee together. Then you can see how you feel about him.'

Clare played with her plait. 'Will he send me home – to Ireland?'

'I shouldn't think so. But we will have to work out what's best for you. And, I promise we'll be with you every step of the way, won't we Rose?'

'You can count on it,' Rose said. 'You're among friends here. Nothing's going to happen to you that you don't want to happen.'

*　　*　　*

Rachel phoned Father Michael who agreed to call in at four o'clock.

'Right!' Rachel said to Clare and Rose. 'Be off with you. Go and do some girly things. Go into town and buy something pink and sparkly. Sophie and I have cooking to do.'

She saw Clare smile widely for the first time. Her poor little pale face was transformed into a delicate, almost translucent beauty. Rachel could see why Aidan had been attracted to her. 'Don't be late,' she called after them.

Sophie arrived soon after. She stood in the café kitchen, unpacking supplies while Rachel told her what had been happening.

'I'm just so glad she's ended up here,' Sophie said, winding her apron strings around her slender waist. 'If she'd carried this terrible burden with her for much longer, she would have ended up like the desperate people I used to work with in the clinic. Not that she'll ever be free of it – but the damage can be minimised. It would be good if she could see Marguerite too, eventually.'

'Do you think I did right suggesting the priest?'

'Michael isn't exactly your conventional Catholic priest is he? And it is her path – deeply entrenched. He could help her decide what she wants from it – or not. Maybe she can heal her relationship with her god, if someone like Michael can bring some truth and clarity into her life.' Sophie gathered her unruly curls back into a bunch and fastened it with an elastic band. 'As long as Rose doesn't dissuade her from the whole religious thing. And let's face it – Rose has become *The Saviour* in Clare's mind – her symbolic light in the darkness. Which is great – but Rose is human and will inevitably fall from grace. So, the input of other responsible, caring adults is essential.'

'Where did you learn such intelligent and reassuring things, Sophie? I could listen to you all day.'

'It's textbook stuff.' Sophie smiled. 'And my maternal instinct is blossoming.'

'Your maternal instinct? Are you trying to tell me something?'

Sophie nodded, her brown eyes liquid with tears of joy. 'I'm pregnant.'

Rachel hugged her. 'That is just the best news I've heard for weeks.'

*   *   *

Father Ryan had arrived back in Ireland. There seemed to him to be a different feel to the air. It was raining, of course, but maybe it was just the familiar accent of the voices around him. He was sitting in a wine bar in Cork. He didn't know why it was called a wine bar; he was drinking a small whiskey. How fortunate that he hadn't been in the car when he'd been picked up by the police and thrown into jail. Still, he deserved a bit of good fortune.

He observed the other people sitting at the tables, drinking. What were they all doing in here this time of day – it was the middle of the afternoon – didn't they have jobs? There was a group of young women, laughing and joking. They wore extremely short skirts and long leather boots, and although they were wearing jackets with fur collars, and big bright scarves wound round their necks, their midriffs were naked. Some of them looked quite disgusting, rolls of white flesh bulging over their belts. They must feel frozen when they went outside. What a strange way to dress. Frankly, the girls over here seemed not much better than the girls abroad. Clare was probably sitting in a bar like this, somewhere, showing off her body, trying to lure some other unsuspecting male into her trap.

He'd been sitting here trying to work out what he was going to tell Clare's mother. The truth, he thought. He'd tell Mrs Mulligan he'd made up the stories about receiving letters from Sister Bridget concerning Clare and the baby. He'd say he'd done it to spare her anguish, while he journeyed to England to try and find her. But all his efforts had proved fruitless. Clare had run away, and nobody knew what had become of her. He'd explored every possibility. There was nothing more he could do. They would just have to pray for her every day, and hope she would repent and return to them, eventually.

He thought this would satisfy the woman. He could see her becoming resigned to the fact that she'd produced a daughter as bad as her husband. She would probably go to join the Poor Clares, now she was free. That way she would be able to escape from the shame of it all.

He wondered how the choir was getting on without him. He hoped Maria had settled down and might be missing his little attentions. Surely she'd be glad to see him after having to put up with Father Christopher's loud and jocular manner. She would be more amenable, more pliable. And he'd bought some nice wee gifts for the children, from England and Wales. He'd spent a great deal of money – the whiskey was so expensive. He thought with pleasure of his new CDs, and the portable player. He was looking forward to showing it to Jeannie at the weekend, and telling her about his adventure. He'd bought her a big woollen stole – soft, scarlet – he'd always felt a little guilty about taking her shawl.

Life was going to be different from now on. No longer would he scuttle around like a frightened mouse. He would stand tall and confident, a man of experience. Maybe he would leave the Church – maybe he wouldn't. He would decide in his own time. He drained his glass and licked his lips. Just one more, it was pleasant sitting here – relaxing. He'd intended to head for home today, but Cork was a nice city – now he was getting used to it. Perhaps he could stay here for the night, explore a little, another concert. Tomorrow, rested, he'd complete his journey. He nodded his head, satisfied with his decisions. He'd done his best, and that was all a man could do. He got up to go to the bar

*   *   *

Father Michael was nothing like Clare had imagined. She realised she'd expected him to look like Father Ryan, and thought she might be unable to cope with this meeting. She'd feel like a little girl again, incapable of speaking. But he was an older man with a balding head and clear blue eyes. He was wearing brown trousers and a tweed jacket and a checked shirt with no dog collar. Was Rachel certain he was a real priest? He shook Clare's hand as if she were a grown-up, and asked her how she liked the Isle of Wight. He told her she could call him Michael, if she wanted to. He included Rose in the conversation and asked her lots of interesting questions about Africa. Rachel made tea and they sat around her table upstairs, and ate the chocolate muffins. Michael ate three.

'Now, Clare.' Michael put down his cup. 'Rachel has told me, briefly, what happened to you. I know she asked your permission first. Do you feel okay about that?'

Clare felt her tension returning. She nodded and put her fingers to her mouth, but she couldn't find any nails left to bite. She'd told them everything. Why couldn't that be enough? Why wouldn't they just let her get on with things now?

'There are some more questions that I need to ask you. Are you happy for Rachel and Rose to be present?'

'Please, don't send them away,' she begged. She didn't want to be alone with this unknown priest. Not yet, it was too soon.

'Of course I won't.' Michael smiled. He had a nice smile, but so did Father Ryan. 'Sometimes it's difficult to talk about certain things in front of others, that's all.'

263

'They know everything.'

'Well, that's good. It's important to have friends you can talk to.'

Yes, thought Clare, but Father Ryan was my friend.

'I need to know some very basic things first.' Michael took a notebook and pen from his pocket and passed it across the table to her. 'Would you kindly write down for me your full name and address, and the name of your priest, and your church? And then the name of the abbey, and the nuns who looked after you.'

Clare looked at the blank page. 'What will you do, then?'

'I will make contact with the people who are in charge.'

'Will they know it was me who told you?'

'No. And I *can* find out without you doing any of this. So, you don't have to. It just makes things quicker and easier this way.'

'Will Father Ryan get into trouble?'

'If he deserves to be in trouble – then yes, he will.'

'What will happen to him?'

'That's not for me to decide. But if what you've told us is the truth – and I see no reason to disbelieve you – then he'll go to a place where he will *never* be able to do this again.'

'I, I don't want to tell the police, or anything. I don't want to go back there.'

'Clare.' Michael spoke slowly, his eyes searching her face, as if he was trying to hold her gaze. 'I'm afraid this is out of your hands now, my dear. Nobody can make you go to court. But he can still be prosecuted. You see, you are underage – a minor. That means that responsible adults have to deal with this now. Even if he were to deny everything, you have a child – and it can be proved that he's the father.'

'What will happen to the baby?'

'He is being well cared for by a friend, isn't he? Someone you came here to find?'

'Well, er . . . ' Had Rachel not told him everything then? Or was he confusing Fran with Rose? Clare nodded; she suddenly really wanted him to stay in that nice big warm kitchen by the sea. Surely that would be better then putting him in a home.

264

'Well, I'd like to get acquainted with the young fellow. And then we could sort out his registration and deal with the official things – like medical care, and your financial support.'

'Will I . . . will I be forgiven?'

'My dear, it isn't you that needs forgiveness. You have been terribly wronged.'

'But . . . mortal sin . . . '

Michael looked at her and sighed deeply. 'What I would like you to do is to come to my church – your friends can come too. Perhaps it would be a good thing to tell me your story from the beginning. You can say everything you need to say, in the presence of God – not that God isn't present everywhere – but maybe you will sense it more there. You can bring the baby if you like, and we can talk about his baptism.'

'Can you baptise him soon?' Clare burst out. 'I thought he was lost in Limbo . . . It was the worst thing—'

'Of course.' Michael shook his head sorrowfully. 'Limbo is one of those Catholic vagaries that is being done away with.' He smiled. 'I have this picture in my head of thousands of tiny children all rushing for the open door and playing in the sunshine.'

Clare thought about the church in which she'd met Sandro Angelo. She remembered the stone bowl of holy water inside the door, the fourteen Stations of the Cross, the smell of incense and the candle that Sandro lit. She wondered what would have happened if she'd met Michael there, instead of Sandro, and been able to tell him her story. But Rachel said Sandro had begged her to find Tess, and tell her he was sorry. And then she'd recovered his wallet and taken it to Rachel. So they'd both helped each other in the end. That little church seemed important somehow.

Clare looked at the white paper in front of her and began to write.

CHAPTER
Twenty-Four

Fran was surprised when Rachel's car drew up outside Rocken Edge Farm on Friday morning. Although she'd said Clare could visit whenever she liked, she hadn't expected them to come so soon. Rose was with her. Fran suspected *she* had something to do with it. The girl had seemed so pleased to discover Sam – far more pleased than Clare had been. Cinders rushed around the visitors, yapping excitedly.

Rose went straight over to Sam's basket while Clare stroked Cinders.

'Oh, Clare, come and look,' Rose called. 'He's scrumptious. He's wearing a diddy little striped suit – and he's got a teddy.'

Fran felt a smile stretching her mouth. Good job she'd already got him bathed and dressed. Those clothes she'd bought from the Cowes woman were really smart – French labels in some of them.

Clare seemed reluctant to let go of Cinders. Eventually she wandered over and stood looking down at Sam, nibbling at her nails.

'He's smiling at you,' Rachel said encouragingly.

'Is he?' Clare lowered her hands and leaned a little closer over the basket.

'Smile back at him then,' Fran said gruffly. The girl didn't seem to have any idea what to do with a baby. How he'd survived she would never know. Fran was aware of Rachel frowning at her. I've got to make an effort, she thought, remembering Ted's lecture about her hostility. *Won't do you no good in the long run,* he'd warned.

Fran took a deep breath and squared her shoulders. 'Did you breast feed him?'

Clare nodded, pulling at her plait, looking embarrassed.

'Good girl,' Fran said, briskly. 'It's the best possible start for a baby.'

'Is it?' Clare looked encouraged, as if she might have got something right. 'He didn't always seem to like it . . . and it hurt.'

'Well, good for you for persevering,' Rachel said. 'It's not easy.'

'Pick him up, if you want to,' Fran said.

'I, er . . . ' Clare looked unsure.

Anyone would think she'd never held him before, Fran thought.

'Oh, can I?' Rose jumped up from the rug where she'd been playing with Sugar Plum.

'Wash your hands then,' Fran said. 'Can't be too careful – he's only just over six weeks old.'

Rose washed her hands and picked him up. 'Oh, he's so light.' She sat down in the armchair with him. 'Hello, gorgeous,' she said. Sam smiled at her. 'Did you see that?' Rose sounded excited. 'Look Clare, he smiled at me.'

Clare was watching Rose with a new expression on her face. Fran wondered if the older girl's enthusiasm might spark Clare's.

'He looks like you,' Rose continued. 'Oh, he's so soft and cute.'

'Does he? I thought he looked like . . . ' she glanced round at everyone, a pink flush creeping into her cheeks.

'He's going to have your colouring,' Rose said. 'See that reddish glint in his hair?'

Clare bent forward to look. 'It does look a bit red,' she agreed.

'And look at his tiny finger nails,' Rose said. 'He's amazing.' She looked up at Clare, her eyes shining. 'I wish he was mine.'

'You can have him, if you like,' Clare said. She turned away, walked across to the door and went outside.

'Ungrateful little—' Fran said.

'I'll go.' Rose got up and handed the baby to Fran. 'Please, Fran,' she said. 'Give her time. When she looks at him she's reminded of the most terrible things you can imagine happening to a little girl.'

Fran nodded. 'I know, dear. You're right. I just get so . . . protective of him.'

Rose laughed. 'Well, you're the proverbial mother hen clucking over her chicks aren't you? Thank God for people like you.' She poked

Cinders with her toe. 'Come on you. Come out and play.' She picked up her coat, and Clare's, and went outside.

Fran felt quite proud hearing her say that. She kissed Sam's head.

'She's a wise girl, that one,' Rachel said. 'If anyone is going to win Clare round, it will be her.'

'Trouble is, I don't know whether I want her won round,' Fran said, miserably. 'That will mean she'll take Sam.'

'Time will tell, I suppose. But Fran, think about this, if Clare stays here, she will have to go back to school. That will mean she'll need full time care for Sam. Aren't you in the best position to do that?'

'Hadn't thought of that,' Fran said. 'Hard to think of her as a school girl, isn't it?' She sat pondering. Clare would come home in the afternoons in her school uniform. Fran would cook tea. It would almost be like having two children in the house. She really did need to be friends with Clare. This wasn't her fault. And she hadn't intended to hurt Sam.

'Yes, we need to work at it gradually. Do you think it would be a good idea to try and get Clare to come for a while each day? I won't press her with anything. She can just play with the animals and be around Sam. And that's another thing – we need to check she feels okay about his name.'

Rachel smiled. 'Don't check too much. She might end up calling him Brad, or Leonardo.'

'Or Elvis,' Fran laughed. It was the only teenage idol she could think of. It felt nice to be laughing. But then her mind flashed to another worrying issue. She bent her head over Sam as if protecting him; what were they doing, talking like this – as if it were that easy?

'But what about Clare's mother? She is Sam's grandmother. Surely she will want to bring him up, if Clare can't – or won't.'

Rachel frowned, her smile disappearing. 'Father Michael is going to try and get in touch with her, to find out what she knows. We might hear something soon – and then we'll have a meeting. Do you want to come? He said he wants to see Sam.'

'I don't know. She could take Clare and Sam back to Ireland, couldn't she?' She hardly dared say the words, it felt like tempting fate.

Rachel nodded and patted Fran's hand. 'It's possible. I honestly don't know how all this will work out. It may be – because of the circumstances, and Clare's age – that the child protection people will insist that she's taken into care. You see, it's not as if you are the baby's grandmother, or even a close relation—'

'I can give him more care than any stranger,' Fran said, feeling panic rising inside her. She really didn't want to hear this.

'Or even a registered child minder, or foster mother,' Rachel continued.

'But they can come here and see for themselves . . . ' Fran gestured around the room. 'He's got everything—'

'Oh, Fran. I know that, and you know that, we all know it. But as far as the authorities go, Clare is a severely damaged, neglected, abused child. Their first priority will be to ensure that she – and Sam – are safe, and supervised. After all, they don't know you from Eve.'

'Why do the authorities have to know? Can't we work all this out between us? We know what's best to do.' Fran's voice was choked with sobs.

'Think about it, Fran. If nothing is done, that bastard will get away with this, and soon it will happen to another little girl. Could we live with that?'

Fran blew her nose and shook her head. It was hard for her to consider that. All she could think about was Sam's welfare, and what was best for him.

'Anyway,' Rachel said quietly. 'We don't have a choice, Father Michael knows and he's already onto it. There's no way he will cover this up.' She smiled, glumly. 'But Fran, he's a good, strong man. If anyone can get the right thing done – for everyone – he can.'

Fran grabbed Rachel's hand. 'I'll come to the meeting,' she said. 'I'll do anything, absolutely anything to keep Sam here.'

Rachel was gazing at her. 'As long as it's best for him?' she asked, quietly.

Fran couldn't hold her gaze, she looked away.

* * *

Father Ryan was making the most of his last few hours of freedom before he donned his clerical garb once more and returned to his priestly duties. But things were going to be different from now on, he told himself. He'd tasted the exhilaration of being his own person. Oh, yes; the Church didn't own him anymore, he could drop it just like that – he clicked his fingers – if he so chose.

'What time is it you'll be arriving?' Father Christopher demanded, on the other end of the phone.

'About tea time.'

'Would you be more specific?'

Father Ryan looked at the receiver. Why was Father Christopher sounding so cross? Ah! He didn't want him to come back at all; that would be it. He was already jealous of the travelling tales he might hear, and he'd have to stop his teasing. Father Ryan would have the upper hand at last, and he'd reclaim his position as choir master.

'I'll be home at eight o'clock,' he said. 'If there's a problem, I'll phone you on my mobile.' He put the phone down and grinned. He was so glad that Father Christopher wanted to be there to meet him. He planned to make a memorable arrival, in his casual clothes. He let himself out of the phone booth and walked back to his car. He needed to find a mobile phone shop.

*   *   *

Clare made her confession on Friday afternoon. She didn't do it in the confessional. Michael took her into a little side-room with armchairs and an electric fire. Rachel came with her, sitting quietly by the window. Rose sat in the church, reading. It took ages. Michael listened, without interrupting.

'Take your time,' he said softly, whenever she got upset.

She told him everything she could think of, about how much she missed her daddy, and now her mam too. She told him how bad she'd been, and all the things Father Ryan had said and done to her, and how she'd promised never to tell anyone about their secrets. She told him about her journey from Ireland, and Mother Benedicta, and her abandonment of Sam. It felt easier telling him like this, in the quiet church. It was the first time she'd talked without receiving any expression of disgust or horror or anger, or sympathy, from someone – just a freedom to talk, feeling as if

270

she were being listened to, without judgement. When she finally ran out of words, Michael spoke to her for a long time. His voice was quiet and firm. He said what Rose and Rachel had already said – that Clare wasn't to blame, she carried no guilt, no mortal sin, for what had been done to her by someone who had abused her trust.

But before she could believe this, there was one more thing Clare needed to tell him. It was hard to talk about; she felt as if everything might suddenly fall apart again. And Michael, and everyone, might know her for what she really was.

'I . . . I have worms inside me,' she blurted it out.

'Worms, Clare?'

'I can feel them, they squirm and squirm.' She pressed her hands beneath her ribs.

'And how long have the worms been there?'

'Ages and ages – since I was little. Father Ryan told me it was a vipers' nest – because of my badness.'

Michael was nodding his head. He was agreeing. Clare knew this would happen.

'Clare, sometimes, when bad things have been happening to someone for a long time, physical symptoms can be felt just as if they were real. I think your worms are a symptom of your anxiety.'

'No, they are real, I can feel them moving.'

'Okay. Now, tell me – have you been examined by a doctor, since you gave birth to Sam?'

Clare shook her head. Why would she need a check up when it was all over? She was back to normal; she'd even had a period.

'All mothers have a post natal check – at six weeks. I'd like you to see a doctor – there's a nice woman doctor here, a friend of mine. Rachel will go with you, I'm sure. Now, if there is anything physically wrong, she will be able to tell.'

'Are you saying there might not be any worms?' She couldn't really believe this.

'If there aren't any, and personally I don't think there are—'

'But I can't be imagining them . . . '

271

'Not consciously, no. The *feeling* of them, I'm sure, is real—'

'But how can I get rid of them, if they're not real?' This was terrible – she really was going to have them for ever.

'You will get rid of them, Clare. Believe me, you will. Not by taking medicine, but by healing all the pain and terror that you've been through. There are people that can help you with that.'

'What people, what will they do to me?'

'They will encourage you to talk, and let out all your feelings.'

'But I've done that. I've talked to you, and Rose, and Rachel.'

'I know you have, and it's a great start. But there will be other people who will want to question you about all this.'

'What people?'

'The police, and other people concerned with the welfare and protection of children. But they will be specially trained to help you. So, you see, Clare, you will need more counselling and support, my dear, maybe for quite a while.'

Clare bent her head, she'd thought her confession, and being told she wasn't to blame, would be enough.

'Marguerite!' Rachel said suddenly. Clare had almost forgotten Rachel was there, she had been so quiet. 'Marguerite will help you, Clare, she is a wonderful healer, so gentle.'

Clare remembered the night Marguerite came to her in the caravan. That dreadful night when she'd left the baby, and collapsed, and Rose had gone. Marguerite had placed her hands on Clare's chest and smiled so beautifully, and Clare had felt something relax inside and then fallen asleep.

'That's a good idea,' Michael said, 'but you must see the doctor as well. I'll write a letter. Do you want to go and see Rose while I do it?'

Tired and empty, Clare wandered around the church, lighting candles with Rose, and explaining the fourteen Stations of the Cross to her. Rose seemed quiet, thoughtful.

'It's a nice church,' she said. 'I can see why you like it.'

Michael came out of his room with Rachel and invited them to his small rectory, next door to the church. He made tea and toast, and they sat in front of his log fire while they talked about Sam's baptism.

'Are you happy for him to be called Sam? I understand that it was the name Fran gave him?' he said.

'I like it,' Clare said. 'Fran calls him Sam the lamb. And Samuel is from the bible. Can I give him a second name?'

'Of course.'

'Lachlan.'

'Lachlan?' Rose said.

'It was my daddy's name,' Clare said. 'He was Scottish.' She looked at them for approval. 'Do you think it's a nice name – Samuel Lachlan Mulligan?'

'Oh, fantastic!' Rose agreed.

'Strong and fearless,' Rachel said.

'A noble ancestry,' Michael nodded.

*   *   *

'Here's to you two – three,' Rachel said holding up her flute of champagne. 'I am absolutely delighted for you.' Sophie and Nick raised their glasses of sparkling grape juice. They looked ecstatic. How lovely it was to be sitting in front of the roaring fire in The Buddle Inn with these two special friends, sharing their joy. Rachel tucked into her glazed tuna steak.

'It has been rather a fraught couple of weeks,' Nick said, spearing mushrooms. 'Is the end in sight?'

'Nearly,' Rachel laughed. 'Ask me after the Valentine's weekend is over. If it all goes smoothly, then yes, *the end*.'

'I don't feel I've been much help,' Sophie said. 'I've been feeling sick in the mornings. But I eat feverishly in the evenings. This sea bass is good.'

'You've all helped in different ways.'

'Even Jill?' Sophie smiled.

'Even Jill. She's welcomed Clare into her home, and allowed Rose to get on with it, without interfering. Normally, she would have stormed off to Ireland and had that bastard, Father Ryan, eat his own balls for supper. And on top of everything else, Stephanie was discharged from hospital today.'

'Do Aidan and Patrick know – about Clare and the baby?' Sophie asked. 'I know Aidan was concerned – and attracted to her.'

'Yes. There's no way she can keep this a secret, if she's going to stay here. They don't know all the details, of course. But I think it made things easier for Aidan – he can understand now why she shied away from him. I think they feel desperately sorry for her – you know – *there but for the grace,* etc etc.'

'And Patrick and Rose – are they still together?' Nick asked.

'Not in the way they were. I'm not sure what happened between them. But I think they're still good friends.'

'They're very young. Rose seems like a different person since she returned,' Sophie said. 'She used to be the proverbial daddy's girl – some would say spoilt brat. But she seems to have really found something – in herself, I mean.'

'She's been amazing with Clare. I was treading carefully, trying not to frighten her away. Rose just asked blunt questions, and Clare answered.'

'The young can go where adults fear to tread, sometimes,' Sophie said.

'So much for trying to be a sensitive parent,' Rachel said. 'Who was it wrote that poem about, *your mum and dad – they fuck you up*?'

Nick laughed. 'Phillip Larkin, I think. But it's not just parents, is it? We can all fuck each other up—'

'Because we're all fucked up,' Sophie said. 'I sometimes wonder how we ever manage to help each other – the fucked up leading the fucked up.'

'Oh, I know,' Rachel said. 'But, don't you think, occasionally we move into a bigger space, as if we go beyond the crap? When we've had enough, bawled and ranted enough, something else fills us, and we feel better, healed, without doing anything at all.'

Sophie and Nick had both stopped eating and were looking at her.

'That's certainly been my experience,' Nick said.

'You put that brilliantly,' Sophie smiled. 'Is that something you went through – after the *Sandro Saga*?'

'I did, I wept until I nearly flooded the flat. I wept for myself and for just about every heart-rending situation that poured into my mind. I felt I came out of it feeling more at peace than I've done for a long time – and gained a greater understanding of human nature. The strange thing is, it all seemed to culminate in finding out about poor little Clare. So some good came out of Sandro.'

'Amazing,' Nick said. 'So, what happens next, about Clare?'

'Michael is still sorting things out. He said he'd phone me later this evening.'

Sophie was stealing chips from Nick's plate. 'And are we all set to pull off our triumphant evening tomorrow?'

'Oh, yes. Menus are printed. Kyp is happy. Staff lined up. Guests invited. Even the sign has been repainted. It came back today.'

'What did you have done to it?' Nick asked.

'I just asked them to substitute Sophie for Sandro.'

Sophie dropped her fork. 'So it now reads *Sophie's Italian Restaurant*?'

'Well, as Kyp says, you are half Italian and your cooking's not half bad. Why splash out on another chef?'

Sophie laughed. 'Oh, Rachel. That's such an honour. I hope I can live up to it.'

'You already have,' Rachel said.

*   *   *

Father Ryan turned into the small driveway to the presbytery. It was Friday evening, eight o' clock precisely. He'd had to stop for a while just outside Bantry, so that he could time his arrival perfectly. He wanted to show Father Christopher that he was returning home a calm and confident man. He'd had a few sips of whiskey to fortify himself, and then sucked a peppermint.

Father Ryan had to brake sharply. There was another car in his driveway – from the garda station. Had his house been burgled, or was it a welcoming party? He got out of his car. Father Christopher was in the porch, talking to the local garda. They stopped talking and watched him approach. Father Christopher didn't greet him, or say anything. In

275

fact he looked a bit embarrassed.

'Good evening,' Father Ryan said. This wasn't working out as he'd planned. He was even holding his new mobile phone in his hand – although he didn't yet know how it worked. Father Christopher was looking him up and down, frowning. Jealous, probably, of his new attire.

'Good evening to you, Father,' the garda said, unsmiling. 'I'm sorry about this, but I need you to come down to the station with me. Would you please move your car, so I can back out?'

'I beg your pardon.'

'I'd like you to move your car, sir.'

'Why do you want me to go to the garda station? What's happened – has there been an accident, a burglary?'

'We need to ask you some questions. I'll explain when we get there.'

Father Ryan looked at Father Christopher, expecting to see a grin or smirk on his fat face. But there was nothing, not even a flicker of recognition. Wasn't the man even going to offer an explanation?

Father Ryan got into his car and reversed out of the drive, thinking rapidly. He knew what this was about. That blasted policeman in Wales must have sent word about his drunken behaviour. Well, he could soon explain that. He locked his car and climbed into the other one, avoiding Father Christopher's eyes. He wasn't going to say anything in front of *him,* and have it spread all around the village.

'I can explain everything,' he said as they drove away.

'Uh, huh,' the garda said, as if he were American or something. 'If I were you, sir, I would wait until we get there.' Stupid fellow, playing silly games; Father Ryan had known him since he was a snotty-nosed schoolboy.

At the station, Father Ryan was shown into a small room and left on his own. How rude, to keep him waiting like this. He wished he was wearing his clerical garb; then they'd treat him with more courtesy. The door opened and a sergeant came in and sat at the table opposite him. A uniformed woman slipped in behind him and stood by the door. It all seemed very formal, not like the police station in England where he'd been offered tea and sympathy.

'I'm Sergeant Brennan,' the man said. 'Are you Father Ryan of—'

'If this is about what happened in Wales—'

'What happened in Wales?'

'Someone, in a bar, put something in my lemonade and I got drunk—'

'It's not about that, no. Maybe you can tell me that story later. We've had a complaint from a girl's parents – a member of the choir that you supervise. Before you say—'

'Clare! You really mustn't believe a word that girl says, and I'm certain her mother—'

The door opened and another garda came in. 'Can I have a word, sir?' he said. They went out together.

Father Ryan sat waiting. The woman at the door didn't speak, and why should he bother to make polite conversation with her? Was it a ploy to make him nervous? Well, Clare would not get away with this. He knew her mother wouldn't have made a complaint. So it must be her. What had she done – phoned the gardai, or written a letter? He wished he could have a drink of whiskey. He felt himself losing his composure. His hands were clammy, his heart starting to beat fast. The door opened and the sergeant came back in and sat down. He switched on a small machine and spoke into it as if he were introducing himself. Such self-importance.

'The girl the complaint concerns is called Maria,' the sergeant said.

'Maria?' Father Ryan's mind went blank.

'But you were telling me about Clare. Tell me some more.'

'Really, it was nothing. Sure, she's a trouble-maker, that's all.'

'That's all?'

'She's the type that would make accusations – just to get attention.'

'What sort of accusations?'

'Well.' Father Ryan attempted a casual laugh. 'You know what these young girls are like.'

'Do I?'

'Most men would agree that—'

'Father Ryan, do you have a solicitor?'

'I have no need—'

277

'You might like to think about that, before you say anything else. We have just this minute received a further accusation about another girl – Clare.'

*   *   *

Rachel had just arrived home from her evening with Sophie and Nick when the phone rang. Please! Not another emergency – she was hoping for an early night. She picked it up. It was Michael.

'Got him,' he said.

Rachel kissed the telephone. 'Yes!'

278

CHAPTER
Twenty-Five

Early on Saturday morning Clare was at the doctor's. Rachel was with her, holding her hand, while the doctor sat at her desk reading the letter Michael had written. Clare studied her expression. She looked quite young, would she be shocked at what she was reading? Eventually, she ran her hands through her short blonde hair and gave a great big sigh. Clare wondered if this was all a nuisance to her, but she looked up and smiled, kindly. She asked Clare lots of questions about her health and diet, and then finally about the birth. Just as Clare thought she'd finished, the doctor called a nurse into the room.

'We need to examine you, Clare,' the nurse said. 'It won't take long.'

'What for?' Clare grasped Rachel's hand. She didn't like to get undressed in front of people, didn't want them to touch her.

'I have to write a report. It will be all right, Clare, I promise,' the doctor said. 'Rachel will stay with you.'

The doctor weighed her and measured her height and asked her to undress. Clare felt tears welling in her eyes. She cried bitterly as the doctor examined her inside. She didn't want this – she didn't want anyone to touch her in those places ever again.

'You're a very brave girl,' the nurse kept saying.

But Clare didn't feel brave, at all. She was being a baby, crying like this when they were trying to help her.

The doctor examined Clare's breasts, and asked how long she'd fed the baby for. 'You've been a good mother,' she said. 'You're very young, it couldn't have been easy.'

That's what Rachel had said to her. If only they knew how she'd hated it all. She didn't deserve all this praise. The doctor seemed to want to examine every bit of her. She commented on her bruised leg and her cut hand, and asked her how she got these injuries. She listened to her chest, and pressed her stomach all over. Then she told her to get dressed and the nurse syringed blood out of her arm.

'Well, Clare,' the doctor said. 'You had quite a nasty tear, caused by the baby's birth. It should really have been stitched. But you're young and it's healing well. Otherwise everything is fine down there. You are underweight for your age, and somewhat malnourished. You may be anaemic too, which would account for your constant tiredness. We'll see when the blood results come back.' The doctor was rapidly writing things down as she spoke. 'I'll have to examine your baby as well – as soon as possible.' She looked at her watch. 'I'll call in at Rocken Edge on my way home, at lunch time.' She put down her pen and sat back in her chair. 'Now, about these worms,' she glanced at Rachel.

'It's all right, Rachel knows about them,' Clare murmured, holding tightly to her plait. The doctor's face was serious. What was she going to say? Would she need to operate?

'Okay. Clare, there aren't any worms. I've examined you thoroughly. Father Michael told you the truth. I know they are real to you, but they are a symptom of your anxiety, and they will disappear as you recover from all this.'

'Are you sure?' Clare said. 'Don't I need an X-ray or something?'

The doctor smiled. 'I'm absolutely sure. I'm going to prescribe you a course of vitamins and minerals.' She looked at Rachel. 'A case for Marguerite?'

Rachel walked with Clare back to Cormorants and left her with Rose. Clare was telling Rose everything the doctor had said when the phone rang. Rose answered it and then put her hand over the receiver.

'Oh, my God, Clare – it's your mother.'

Clare felt confused. 'Mother? Mother from the abbey?'

'No, your real mother – your mam. Just say *hello*,' Rose whispered, holding the phone out. 'If you can't cope, I'll take over and tell her you're not feeling well.'

Was it really her mam? Did her mam want to speak to her? She took the phone from Rose. 'Mam?'

'Is that you, Clare?'

It really was her. She was all those miles away, in Ireland,

and Clare could hear her voice clearly. Her mam! 'Yes, it's me,' she whispered, brushing away her tears.

'Are you all right?'

'Yes.' Clare struggled to get the word out, she wanted to cry and cry, she felt so glad to hear her mam's voice. There was a long pause, Clare wondered if she was still there.

'Sergeant Brennan came to see me . . . with Father Christopher, and the bishop . . . they said terrible things . . . they accused me . . . you should have told me what was going on . . . '

Clare didn't know who Sergeant Brennan was. Mam's voice sounded strange, as if she had a sore throat. 'I tried, Mammy, I did try. But you always said I had to do what Father Ryan asked.'

'Did you not think to use your common sense?'

Clare didn't know what to say – she thought common sense was doing what grown-ups said. 'I didn't realise—'

'Neither did I.'

'You should have protected me, Mam,' Clare said, remembering what Michael and the others had said.

'How could I, if I didn't know?'

Clare couldn't answer. She looked at Rose.

'Tell her about Sam,' Rose whispered.

'I had a baby boy,' Clare said.

'I know. He will have to be adopted – to a good home.'

'He already has a good home,' Clare said, fiercely. Mam wouldn't say that if she'd seen him, or met Fran.

'Are you saying he's already been adopted?'

'In a way, yes.'

'Oh.' She sounded surprised. 'Were you thinking of coming back home then? Only I'm wanting to go away – to stay with the Poor Clares.'

'*No!* No, Mam!' Clare felt she was losing control, her voice was breaking up. 'I want you to come here! I need you, Mammy. I need you to come and look after me. I want you to see the baby.'

There was a long silence. Clare held her breath to stop herself crying. She could hear little muffled noises coming from the phone.

Was Mam crying? Had Clare made her cry? Oh, poor Mam.

'I can't do that. I'd rather not see the child. And I can't travel all that way on my own.'

'But you let me!'

'I thought it was for the best. He, er, told me everything was properly arranged.'

'Did he?' Clare whispered.

'Maybe you could come and see me, when I'm settled. I can't stay in Bantry, after all that's happened. The shame—'

Clare felt the tears running down her face. Rose's hand was stroking her back. 'Don't be ashamed of me, Mammy. It wasn't my fault.' She could hear Mam blowing her nose.

'Perhaps we could write to each other. Would that be all right, now?'

'Mam, no, please. I want to see you.' The phone went dead. Clare put the receiver down and looked at Rose. 'We were cut off,' she said. She stood looking at the phone waiting for her mam to ring back. She waited and waited, until Rose gently took her by the arm and led her away.

*   *   *

Later that Saturday morning, Rachel held a meeting at her flat, trying not to think about all the preparations that still needed doing for the evening. Aidan had gone to Wraith Cove with Patrick. She was pleased; she didn't want him to be around with all this going on. Fran sat on the sofa giving Sam his bottle. Rose was sprawled on the floor, and Clare was curled in an armchair looking tired and pale after her visit to the doctor. Rachel felt concerned. Things were happening so fast, the poor girl was dealing with one stressful thing after another. She listened to Michael telling Clare about Father Ryan's arrest.

'Another girl's parents had already made an allegation,' he said.

'Maria?' Clare asked, her green eyes wide.

'I believe so, yes.'

'But she's only a little girl.'

'Indeed,' Michael sighed, heavily. 'I have something else to tell you, Clare. The convent you ended up in – Stillwater Abbey – it wasn't the place you were meant to go to. You were misdirected.'

282

'But Mother said she was expecting me. She said she knew Father Ryan.'

'She was deluded. She wasn't a well woman – as you came to realise. But you weren't to know.'

'How did you find out?'

'Father Ryan traced you there. He visited lots of institutions apparently.'

'He went there? From Ireland?'

'He did. His cousin – Sister Bridget – was worried when you didn't arrive. She had arranged a foster home for you, with a family in Hereford.'

'Had she? And Father Ryan came searching for me?'

Rachel briefly wondered what would have happened if Clare had made it to these foster parents. Clare was looking puzzled.

'But what happened to Mother – and the other nun – Sister Agnes, the dead one?'

'Well, unfortunately Mother, as you call her, has died.'

'Oh, no! Did she catch the same disease that Sister Agnes died from? It must have been something awful.'

'No, no. She fell down some stairs. Father Ryan was there when it happened. He called the ambulance and made a statement to the English police. When he was arrested in Ireland, he told the Irish police – the gardai – all the details about his *exciting* journey – searching for you.'

'Poor Mother. I expect he pushed her,' Clare said, matter-of-factly.

Michael made no comment, Rachel noticed, but he scribbled a note on his pad. 'I'm sorry, Clare, to keep telling you all these awful things. You see, when something like this happens, the authorities move in quickly and everything happens at once. I am aware how young you are; but it's best you know the truth.'

'I want to know,' Clare said, sitting up, her little face serious.

'Good girl. I have some other things to say to everybody,' Michael continued. 'I know we would all like to think that it's over now. Father Ryan is under arrest. Sam is safe and Fran caring for him. Clare is safe, and with people who will look after her. But I'm not sure the authorities will let it rest there. We certainly don't need to tell them the story about Sam being *lost and found*. And we can say that Clare came to the island specifically to stay with her friend, Rose. But there isn't a relative, not even an old family friend, that might be considered suitable to be Clare's – and Sam's – legal guardian.'

'Couldn't we say Fran was an old family friend, and Clare came to her for protection?' Rose said.

'They will check everything. No, the only chance we have of Clare and Sam staying here is if she moves in with Fran – and we get Clare's mother over here to stay there too. At least for as long as it takes to satisfy social services.'

Clare shook her head. 'I spoke to Mam this morning,' she said forlornly. 'She wants me to have Sam adopted, and she's going to stay with the Poor Clares. It's what she always wanted to do – if it hadn't been for me.'

Bugger the Poor Clares, Rachel thought. Why didn't the woman give some of her time and attention to her own *Poor Clare*? Didn't she have any feelings?

'Yes, I know you spoke to her.' Father Michael smiled. 'I also phoned her for a chat. I think it's fair to say that after she talked to you, she saw things differently. Apparently, she also spoke with the Mother Abbess at the Poor Clares' convent who asked her what she thought Our Lady would do in these circumstances. I think your mother has been overwhelmed by what she sees as shame, Clare. And now she is having to face up to her own responsibility, towards you and Sam.'

'It wasn't her fault,' Clare cried. 'My mam . . . if she'd known . . . '

Oh, the loyalty and trust that children show to their parents, Rachel thought. They cling to them voraciously, even after they've been beaten and tortured.

'Nevertheless, your mother needed to realise the consequences of turning her back on you and Sam,' Michael said, firmly.

'But I don't want to go back, I want to stay here,' Clare said. 'And she would never travel all this way.'

'Well, it may be possible. Father Christopher has offered to bring her. I know him from way back – good-hearted chap. And I think that's allayed her fears. She's thinking it over.' He turned to Fran who was patting Sam's back. 'Would you be willing to accommodate Clare and her mother, to see how things work out?'

'I'd be happy to have Clare . . .'

'Fran,' Rachel said. 'You said you would do absolutely anything. You have enough room. It would mean Sam would still be under your roof.'

'But how long for?' Fran said.

'How can we possibly know? We have no idea how this is going to work out. But it's a plan – the best we have at the moment,' Rachel said. 'Clare and her mother might decide to settle here, they might decide to return to Ireland . . . '

'Rachel's right. It is the best, and only, plan we have,' Michael said.

Sam let out an enormous burp and looked really surprised. Rose burst out laughing.

Rachel went downstairs with Michael to show him out. 'What happens next?' she asked.

'Father Ryan will be prosecuted, no doubt about that. The police and social services and various other bodies will want to question Clare. Whether Clare will consent to testify is another matter. It can be done by video-link these days; it isn't quite as terrifying for young victims as it used to be. We'll just have to take that one step at a time.'

Rachel went back upstairs. She was surprised to see Clare sitting on the sofa holding Sam while Fran packed his things. Clare was gazing at Sam, unsmiling. Rachel avoided making any comment, as if it were perfectly normal.

'We're going over to Fran's for lunch,' Rose said. 'And we'll take Cinders for a walk and help with the animals. Oh, and this evening we'll be working at the Valentine's dinner.'

'You won't be able to work tonight, young lady,' Rachel said to Clare. 'You're too young to be on the evening shift.' She smiled and patted Clare's crestfallen face. 'But you can be my special envoy. You can sit in the restaurant, eat until you burst, and spy on my posh guests, to hear what they really think of my cuisine.'

She picked up her apron. 'Kitchen, here I come,' she called.

*   *   *

That afternoon, Fran walked up to Niton village for the first time, pushing Sam in the buggy. Clare and Rose tagged behind with Cinders on a lead, chatting. People kept stopping Fran to peek in the pram.

'Is he your grandson, Fran?'

'No, I'm sort of temporary foster-mum to Clare, here. The baby's hers.' It felt good being able to say that. She'd another attack of anxiety earlier when a doctor had turned up unexpectedly at lunchtime to see Sam. But she'd been very friendly and complimentary about Fran's care of him. She'd examined him and talked about his feeding plan and the injections that he would need. Clare and Rose returned from walking Cinders while the doctor was still there and they'd chatted about Clare's future, going back to school, and the possibility of moving into Rocken Edge Farm.

Fran squeezed the buggy into the Post Office Tea Room. 'Let's have a cream tea,' Rose said. 'My treat.'

'I like it here,' Clare said, licking jam and cream off her fingers. 'It reminds me a bit of home – with the sea so close, and all. And I like the farm – and the animals.'

'Tomorrow, when you come over, you could look round the house and see what bedroom you like,' Fran said. 'It might need some clearing out, mind. Ted will help.'

'Oh, can I help too?' Rose said. 'I love going through old things. That's if my grandma doesn't need me – she's sleeping most of the time at the moment.'

'Course you can,' Fran said, wondering what she was letting herself in for. The old house was going to have a shock. But it was about time some of Phillip's junk was chucked out. He was never going to come back from Australia for it. 'We'd better have a think about your mother's room too, Clare – if she decides to come.'

There, she'd said it. Fran knew she was going to find this incredibly difficult. But she had to give it a try. If it didn't work out, then she would have done her best. And at least she'd have known the joy of Sam in her life for a while. Her eyes filled with tears. And she'd still have her animals, and her ballet, and Ted.

CHAPTER
Twenty-Six

Father Ryan's head ached. It seemed worse than before he'd discovered the cure. He wondered if his brain tumour had returned. Perhaps it would be a good thing and people would stop blaming him for things he wasn't to blame for. The lawyer the Church had provided made no sense. He rambled on about Father Ryan's rights, and obtaining bail, and where he might go if he were released, until he felt quite exhausted and told him to go away.

At least he didn't have to battle with a sermon for tomorrow. He got up from the uncomfortable chair and lay down on the bunk. He could hear men's voices, the clank of feet on stairs, distant music. It reminded him of the seminary. Where was he? What was he doing here? He didn't want to be amongst men; there would be no company, no-one to love. But why would he be needing someone to love? You couldn't trust other people with it. Take that girl, the one with the red hair, what was her name? He'd trusted her with his love, and she'd taken it and caused him harm. Never again would he give anyone his love. Not unless there was another sweet girl like Jeannie – she'd never do that to him.

The thought of her made his eyes fill with tears. Would she be worrying about him, wondering where he was? How long were they going to keep him here? He would have to ask someone to take Jeannie her new stole. He wouldn't be able to tell her the exciting story about his journey now – and he wouldn't be able to comfort her either. Not like he used to, when she crawled cold and frightened into his bed and they cuddled tightly together, trying to shut out the terrible noise of the fighting downstairs.

He smiled at the memory of Jeannie, and curled up on his hard bunk, drawing up his knees. He felt beneath the pillow where he'd hidden the red shawl. How he wished he could return to those days.

287

Fran lifted Sam out of the bath and wrapped him in a towel. She remembered the first night she bathed him, nervously unpeeling the sodden clothes from his poor little body. She felt so much more confident with him. She kissed his forehead.

. 'I know who you are now,' she said. 'But you're still my Sam.'

She thought about the pink clothes he'd arrived in, hidden upstairs in the drawer. She must remember to tell Clare that she'd kept them. But, maybe not, they probably held painful memories for her. Fran would keep them as her little secret. She could always look at those strange knitted baby clothes and recall the night Sam came to her. Not that she could ever forget. But if Clare and her mother should decide to take him away . . . she still couldn't bear to think about it.

She kissed him again. 'This foolish old woman loves you,' she said. Foolish she was; and she only had herself to blame. But her love was so strong – too strong. It had taken her over, and she'd shut out the painful thought of what the consequences might be.

She finished dressing him and put him in his basket while she prepared his bottle and fed Cinders and Sugar Plum. Then she lifted him and settled herself comfortably in the armchair to feed him.

'This is what we'll do,' she said, switching on the video. 'We never did watch the end of *The Nutcracker.'*

*   *   *

Rachel and Sophie had been photographed earlier by a journalist. They were standing outside the café before the official guests arrived. The blinds were open, light falling on the *Sophie's Italian Restaurant* sign, and the olive trees. Before they went back inside, they walked across the road to survey it from a distance.

'Looks good,' Sophie said. 'Was it worth the sweat and tears?'

'Ask me after the last course has been safely served. I'm hoping it will be an enjoyable, drama-free evening.' Rachel turned to look at the sea. 'It's astonishing, Sophie, when you think about it, just how many dramas have taken place along this stretch of coast.'

Sophie laughed. 'I should say – from Ventnor to Rocken Edge –

birth, death and every conceivable combination of events in between.'

'And that's only us.' Rachel grinned. 'Are we ready, partner?'

Later, Rachel paused in arranging heart-shaped amaretti biscuits on the desserts. She looked through the glass shelves at the restaurant.

It looked beautiful with the soft lights, the red roses, and the delicate gold hearts floating from the ceiling. The glass and cutlery sparkled. The waiters were looking smart in their black and white clothes. Aidan and Patrick were by far the most handsome young men on the planet. Even Billy's dreadlocks added a certain something. Clare looked like a young society girl with her classy dress and sophisticated hair. Rachel noticed her cheeks were pink, and was that a little smile on her face as she talked to Rose?

Sophie and Kyp were looking extremely Italian, tossing this and swirling that, allowing the customers an exclusive glimpse of themselves from time to time. Kyp even let forth an occasional musical yell. Sophie was too busy tasting everything in sight to speak. Every time Nick went into the kitchen he kissed her.

'Saint Valentine,' Rachel muttered. Who exactly was he? A lot of money was spent in his name that was for sure. Was she becoming cynical? Cynical about *love*? Maybe she was. Sometimes she wondered if it truly existed between humans. But then she only had to look at Sophie and Nick. And her boys. Of course love was real. But maybe she had learned something about being swept away by it. Perhaps love should come with a caution – like cigarette packets. *Love can seriously damage your sanity*. But nobody took much notice of such warnings it seemed. She'd just be a little more cautious next time, a little less blinkered . . .

Meanwhile – until the next time – there were keen appetites to satisfy out there. She ate a biscuit and took one for Sophie. She went into the kitchen where Kyp and Sophie were stirring and flipping, flourishing and sprinkling, in true Italian fashion. Kyp saw her coming and burst forth with a long warbling indecipherable line from a made up opera. Sophie laughed and Rachel popped the biscuit in her mouth.

'Mmm, delicious,' Sophie said. 'Feed me more.' She gazed at Rachel, her eyes shining. 'I think we've made it, don't you?'

'Well, I don't want to be spiteful,' Rachel said. 'But I just want to say—' she cupped her hands round her mouth, 'Sandro, eat your heart out!'

*　　　*　　　*

Clare and Rose sat at a table for two. Clare read the leather menu cover, *Sophie's Italian Restaurant.* She remembered the day she arrived in Ventnor, looking for the lighthouse. She'd stood outside this place – *Rachel's Café.* She wondered if it was Rachel that she'd seen sitting inside. Clare had felt so cold, so shut out and exhausted. And now here she was on the inside, feeling better, even a little bit happy. She could see tiny reflections of herself in the shiny cutlery and glasses. Her new crucifix glinted at her throat. She'd bought it in a charity shop – it only cost fifty pence – she really liked it. Rose said it was cool. She'd also found *The Girls' Book Of Ballet,* for Fran, and a blue bunny for Sam.

'You can stay with me at Cormorants until your mother arrives,' Rose was saying. 'I'd rather have you as a younger sister than my two demon-spawned siblings.'

'Would you?' Clare had seen Fleur and Tom each day when they came home from school, they always seemed to be screaming, and hitting each other.

'Oh, yes. I wouldn't have our nanny's job for the world. I do love the little darlings, but one of them is going to go down for murder, sooner or later. It just depends which of them is first to find where Mum hides the carving knife.'

Clare smiled, shaking her head. She wished she could stay with Rose – it was what she wanted most in the world. But she knew it wouldn't be fair now Rose's grandmother was home from hospital. She sensed Rose was torn between spending time with her and wanting to be with Stephanie.

'Michael thinks the best chance I have of staying here is if I move in with Fran and Sam. She really loves him, doesn't she? Then, if my mam comes, it will look good for us. But I don't want Mam to take him away from Fran. I don't know what will happen.'

'Well you will have a say in it. Do you think Fran and your mother will get on?'

Clare bit her lip and suddenly found herself laughing a little. She hadn't done that for such a long time – it felt strange. 'Mam can't bear

290

to see a speck of dust, let alone animal hairs, and baby sick.'

Rose laughed too. 'Oh, dear. Words like *chalk* and *cheese* come to mind.'

Clare didn't quite understand this, but it sounded funny.

'How do you feel about being alone with Fran – before your mother comes? She's a bit hostile towards you, isn't she?'

'Oh, Mam's like that too. She doesn't mean it. It's just their way, isn't it? They're quite alike really – apart from the cleaning.'

'Mmm,' Rose looked doubtful. 'I think you may need a few lessons in assertiveness.'

'Will I?' Clare wondered if this was something else to put on her mental list of things she had to learn. 'What's *your* mother like? She seems nice.' Clare had only spoken to Jill briefly, she seemed terribly smart and busy.

'*Nice*? Er, no. I would say, *insane*. She works as a psychologist – how mad is that? Mothers are strange beings, Clare, I mean, seriously odd. We have to look after them, sort them out. I'm always putting my mum straight, she hasn't got a clue.' Rose tore off a piece of bread and dipped it in olive oil. 'That's why I love my grandma so much – she just rolls up her sleeves and gets on with it. In Niger, when girls arrived, after having crawled for miles to her clinic, with dead babies hanging out of them, she didn't sit them down and ask them about their childhood.' She smacked her lips. 'This food is great. Anyway, just be thankful that my dear mother's been so busy these last few days. Otherwise she'd have had Father bloody Ryan, and your mother, strung up outside your village church, you'd be in a girls' boarding school, and Sam would be plonked in the arms of our nanny, with his name down for Eton. She's a bit snobby as well.'

Clare stared, trying to take all this in, Rose was grinning, so she guessed she was joking. She had the feeling that Rose really loved her mother. Rose seemed to love loads of people. Clare thought about the people she loved – her daddy – she'd loved him, and her mam. She'd had friends at school, and now there were lots of other people in her life. Did she love them? Did she love Sam and Fran and Rachel and Rose? She didn't know – she didn't know what it meant. She thought she had loved Father Ryan and that he'd loved her. But that was wrong. And what about Jesus and Mary and the Blessed Saints? What sort of love was right? When would she know? She looked at Rose, enjoying her food. These new people, they were being so kind to her. Perhaps she could watch them and learn, day by day, what was considered a normal amount of love to give – and to take. Then, maybe, she wouldn't be so foolish ever again.

'You never know,' Rose was saying. 'They might get on well – your mum can keep everything scrubbed, and Fran can look after all the babies – did you know Cinders is pregnant?' Rose smiled. 'And they can both be nasty to each other and leave you in peace.'

Clare was smiling now. This was fun, talking about the grown-ups as if they weren't so important after all. 'But I think I should help Fran, with looking after Sam.' She'd thought a lot about him in the last few days. She'd watched the way Fran did things with him – it seemed so much easier to feed him a bottle of milk, and put those nice nappies and clothes on him. And he did look sweet when he grinned. Sometimes her breasts still tingled a little when she looked at him, but the doctor said that would stop soon.

She thought about the little grave she'd dug to bury her gold crucifix and the baby's things. Maybe she should go back there and dig them up. But, she realized, she didn't want to. It was as if her past was buried in that hole – a grave for her old life – not for Sam.

'I'm going to be working down at Wraith Cove soon,' Rose said. 'Got to earn some pennies – and decide whether I'm going back to any sort of study – music or otherwise. So I'll be able to walk over to Rocken Edge to see you and Sam. I want to meet your mother when she arrives.'

'Do you?' Clare couldn't think why.

'Oh, yes. I want to make sure she realises how fortunate she is to have such a great daughter – and grandson.' She wiped her mouth on her napkin. 'That was truly fab. Got to go and do the honours for Rachel. Keep your ears peeled for gossip.'

Clare was already full. She sat nibbling at her salad, thinking about what Rose had said. She looked down at the long green dress that she was wearing. It had been such fun hunting through the charity shops with Rose. She patted her hair which was half piled up, half hanging down. She had looked in the mirror, when Rose had finished fiddling with it, and realised she looked quite pretty.

She sighed, feeling as if the little warm nub of comfort within her had grown. She noticed it more often, as if it were softening the ball of bad things. Tomorrow she was going to have a healing session with Marguerite. Clare had seen her at Cormorants, visiting Stephanie. Marguerite had smiled and brushed Clare's cheek tenderly with her cool hand. 'She's amazing,' Rose said. 'She's going to do me too – after she's seen you, and my grandma. You'll feel as relaxed as a sloth afterwards.'

Clare sat listening to the noise of the guests enjoying their dinner. And then she heard another sound. Rose came from behind the glass shelves playing her violin. Clare felt a shivery feeling creep over her skin. A vivid memory of Rose, on board the ferry from Ireland, playing with the band, came into her mind. It wasn't music like this – slow and romantic, but a lively Irish jig.

Two weeks, that's all it was, since she arrived here. Two weeks ago she was a scruffy, sick, bad girl, who wanted to die. But, like an ill-treated animal in a children's story, she'd been rescued by people who cared. Would they stop caring? There were heaps of things she hadn't worked out yet. But if she could learn so much in just two weeks, what might she learn in another two?

Rose smiled at her as she threaded her way slowly between the tables, playing such beautiful music. Clare wanted to know what the music was called. She wanted to know so many things.

ABOUT THE AUTHOR

Wendy K Harris was born in Surrey in an air raid shelter during a doodlebug attack. The youngest of four sisters, attending a girls' grammar school, she needed to write in order to get a word in edgeways. The writing of short stories and poetry was interwoven with working as a nurse, homoeopath, counsellor, interfaith minister and sharing the upbringing of five children.

A rattling old Herefordshire rectory and an aching back precipitated a change of life and she moved with her husband and a laptop into a caravan and trundled around Wales and England, finally becoming ensnared by The Undercliff of the Isle of Wight, entranced by its history of smuggling, shipwrecking and landslips. Here she was inspired by tumbling cliffs and precarious cottages to write *The Sorrow of Sisters* and *Blue Slipper Bay* which have been translated into German, Dutch and Norwegian. *Rocken Edge* is the third of The Undercliff Novels. She is now working on a fourth, *Trampling Snowdrops*.

www.wendykharris.com

ALSO BY WENDY K HARRIS

The Sorrow Of Sisters

Forty nine year old Jane sits in her comfortable, glass-walled designer home, tapping out lucrative novels. But the bequest of a cottage on the wild southern shore of the Isle of Wight by a woman unknown to her is about to shift the whole equilibrium of her life and relationships.

For a while, nothing is what it has seemed to be. Jane is brought up against shocking revelations of violence and deceit that cause her to question the assumptions she has grown up with about her past. Driven to pursue her own search for truth and identity, Jane uncovers a trail that leads her to reconnect with extraordinary relatives she never knew she had, and eventually to her own reconciliation and deep inspiration.

A compelling read, *The Sorrow of Sisters* tells the seemingly disparate stories of Jane and Lillian, and of how ultimately they weave into one.

REVIEWS FOR THE SORROW OF SISTERS

'A very rich and satisfying read.'
Phillip Norman. Biographer and novelist. Author of Babycham Night.

'This book has all the intensity of Brontes's work coupled with the gorgeous prose and deep humanism of Sarah Waters.'
Lisa Guidarini. Reviewer. Chicago, Illinois, USA

'The fifty chapters tell a story intensive, exciting. We wished this book had easily 100 chapters.'
Alex Dengler. Reviewer. Bild am Sonntag. (Translated from German.)

'A moving book, a fascinating picture language.'
New Week. (Germany)

'Rather soon I knew that the book was far too poetic and original to work as a serial in my magazine. But I couldn't stop reading. Everything around me just disappeared, and amazed I thought: This is the best book I've read for a very, very long time – Maybe one of the best books EVER. I read so many books in my profession it was magical to find this gem in the book flood.'
Sara Hemmel. Fiction Editor of Swedish weekly family magazine.

'Be warned: this is a page-turner and once started you won't want to put it down!'
Margaret Powling. Feature writer and reviewer.

'It was such a treat to have an unputdownable book in my hands again. Great characters, great story.'
Lynne Hackles.Writer.

'The author writes beautifully of the delicate ghost like quality of the island, together with acute observation of internal emotion. It's written with skill, change of pace and mood. The individual voices of her characters carry an exciting plot which makes for compulsive reading.'
Caroline Hunt. Theatre Director.

'The main characters are so well written that they stay with you long after you have finished the book. This is a wonderful first novel by Wendy Harris, and I hope she goes on to write many more.'
Jan Wright. Short Story Writer.

'This is an accomplished debut novel; plot and language are securely handled. *The Sorrow of Sisters* is the first of an *Undercliff* series and promises well for the further books.'
Carol Atkinson. Reviewer.

'This is a profoundly moving book. 373 pages of intriguing
and evocative prose.'
The Woman Writer

'A powerful and very moving story. A must read! I'll be passing this
copy onto another Bookcrosser as I wait impatiently for
Blue Slipper Bay to arrive.'
Bookcrosser Molyneaux. Oxfordshire.

First published in 2006 by Transita

*   *   *

Blue Slipper Bay

Sophie, bereft after the loss of her mother and her husband's betrayal,
walks out of her demanding profession and her home. She seeks refuge
with her friend, Jill, on the Isle of Wight, not suspecting she is about to
be drawn into another crisis.

Jill, a psychologist, is as obsessive and compulsive as the clients she
treats and has her own complex reasons for persuading Sophie to stay.

Over the cliffs at Blue Slipper Bay, Nick lives in a beach hut,
challenged by the sea. A seeker of truth, walled in by his own guilt and
grief, he finds solace in resurrecting the forgotten gardens of Wraith
Cove Hotel. Sophie, Jill and Nick all need to make peace with their past
before they can risk taking a second chance with the future.

REVIEWS FOR BLUE SLIPPER BAY

'Wendy's second novel, *Blue Slipper Bay*, is as lyrical and enchanting
as her first (*The Sorrow of Sisters*.) Again, it is set on the Isle of Wight
but whilst several of the characters from her first reappear, the main
characters are new... well, you will just have to read it to find out

what happens to them. Again, be warned: once you pick this up, you won't want to put it down! I'm really looking forward now to the third in Wendy's Undercliffe series, *Rocken Edge.*'
Margaret Powling. Feature writer and reviewer.

'Not only is this a book you will want to recommend to your friends, but I believe it will also boost the tourist industry on the Isle of Wight!'
Jan Wright. Short story writer.

'The second novel in Wendy K Harris's series set at *Blue Slipper Bay* was as pleasantly warm as her first, *The Sorrow of Sisters*, which I reviewed a few months ago. Having become acquainted with her style in the first book, I was very much looking forward to the publication of her second. And she most definitely doesn't disappoint. I look forward to the third in this wonderful series.'
Lisa Guidarini. Reviewer. Chicago, Illinois, USA.

'It's a cliché to say I couldn't put it down, but really, I was reading this late into the night. Wendy has the gift of conceiving fascinating, unusual characters and giving them truly engaging stories, so you just have to know what happens next. Can't wait for the next one now.'
Oxford Reader.

'*Blue Slipper Bay* is another page turner with a plot that will keep readers guessing and characters that are beautifully written. Harris's prose is lyrical and descriptive with images that burst off the page to dazzle and delight the reader. Her love of The Undercliff is obvious – in fact she is to the Isle of Wight what Daphne du Maurier was to Cornwall.'
Bristol Bookworm.

'*Blue Slipper Bay* is a deeply moving and highly compassionate tale by the UK's answer to Anita Shreve and Anne Tyler.'
Julie Bonello. Reviewer for SingleTitles.com

'This contemporary story was a worthy successor to the wonderful *Sorrow of Sisters*. One character in particular, a seeker of truth, is beautifully drawn and totally believable – I defy anyone who reads this book not to be half in love with him themselves by the end.'
Bookcrosser – Iyzzybee.

'No-one in the group had read anything by Wendy K Harris before, but it was a title we enjoyed. It was a gentle, rolling, restful read which engaged us all as readers – no mean feat we can assure you! Thoroughly enjoyed and now being recommended to others – in our opinion there can be no greater accolade for an author than for a reader to say they loved it.'
Chapters Book Club – reviewed for Bertrams.

First published in 2007 by Transita